THE
INCREMENT

**Center Point
Large Print**

**This Large Print Book carries the
Seal of Approval of N.A.V.H.**

THE
INCREMENT

David Ignatius

CENTER POINT PUBLISHING
THORNDIKE, MAINE

This Center Point Large Print edition
is published in the year 2009 by arrangement with
W. W. Norton & Co., Inc.

"The Demon-King Zahnak," from *Shanameh: The Persian Book of Kings* by Abolqasem Ferdowsi, foreword by Azar Nafisi, translated by Dick Davis, copyright © 1997, 2000, 2004 by Mage Publishers, Inc. Used by permission of Viking Penguin, a division of Penguin Group (USA) Inc.

Excerpt from "My Country I Will Build You Again" and "O Box Within Box" from *A Cup of Sin: Selected Poems by Simin Behbehani* edited and translated from the Persian by Farzeneh Milani and Kaveh Safa (Syracuse University Press, Syracuse, NY, 1999).

The text of this Large Print edition is unabridged. In other aspects, this book may vary from the original edition. Printed in the United States of America. Set in 16-point Times New Roman type.

ISBN: 978-1-60285-499-4

Library of Congress Cataloging-in-Publication Data

Ignatius, David, 1950-
  The increment / David Ignatius.
      p. cm.
  ISBN 978-1-60285-499-4 (library binding : alk. paper)
  1. Nuclear weapons--Iran--Fiction. 2. Nuclear physicists--Iran--Fiction.
    3. Intelligence officers--United States--Fiction.
    4. Intelligence officers--Great Britain--Fiction. 5. Tehran (Iran)--Fiction.
    6. Large type books. I. Title.

PS3559.G54I63 2009b
813'.54--dc22

2009010663

For Jonathan Schiller
and
Dr. Richard Waldhorn

I will rise, in slow increments.
I will make my face beautiful
like a mirror held to the rainbow.
I will scatter blue petals in the wind,
let my silk scarf flutter in abandon . . .
I will find myself suddenly in full bloom
and you doomed to rot.

—SIMIN BEHBAHANI,
"O Box Within Box," from
A Cup of Sin: Selected Poems

The Increment was (and is) a selected unit of SAS soldiers . . . allocated for use by SIS, the British equivalent of the CIA. MI6 undercover intelligence officers do not and never have had the fabled "license to kill" of James Bond mythology. But when such jobs are required, it is the Increment whose rules of engagement may permit the lethal use of firearms.

—THE CENTER FOR PUBLIC INTEGRITY

TEHRAN

Imagine a gaudy boulevard descending a hill, like a swath of icing dripping down the inside of a coarse earthen bowl. The broad street is lined with department stores and little shops; it pulses with neon signs shouting the brand names of cell phones and airlines and fast-food restaurants. But the commercial thoroughfare is grimly punctuated every few blocks with hand-painted banners commemorating the blood of the martyrs.

This is Vali Asr Avenue, the spine of North Tehran. The avenue rises in the burly districts of downtown, where rage against the unbelievers is nurtured and sustained every Friday at prayers, and it ascends mile by mile till it reaches the heights of Jamaran, where one might think, to look at the Parisian fashions and big German cars, that the unbelievers are everywhere. But that is wrong: atop these hills are the secrets of modern Iran, a nation whose very identity is in some ways a fabric of lies. Nothing along this avenue is quite what it appears to be. That is the warning, and the temptation. Even the name of the street is elusive: officially it is Vali Asr, but the smart set like to call it by its prerevolutionary name, Pahlavi Avenue.

Tehran plays tricks this way. It is the cockpit of the Islamic revolution and the capital of a nation that lives by reckless taunts, yet the police here insist that drivers wear their seat belts. The mullahs summon pilgrims to the holy city of Qom, but not too hastily; the highway patrol have radar guns to catch speeders. It is forbidden, of course, to watch the foreign television channels of the infidels. So everyone pays a small bribe to the local militiamen known as the *basiji* not to notice the satellite dish atop the roof. The spine of this noble city is pliable; like the nation, Tehran bends so that it will not break.

Our story begins along Vali Asr Avenue, with a young scientist who lived in an apartment down near the bottom of the street, in the neighborhood known as Yoosef Abad, but who was blessed to work up at the magisterial summit in Jamaran. He spent his days shuttling between these two worlds, a child of privilege and also of anger—not at the unbelievers, but at the people who presumed to rule over them. This is the story of his decision to abandon one idea of what is right and good in favor of another. Like all accounts of young men struggling to find their paths in the world, it is a story of fathers and sons. You could say that it is a story of betrayal, and also of fidelity.

On the morning the young Iranian scientist made his decision, he awoke to find the sheets wet under his body. He had sweated through the night once again in his anxiety, and he was ashamed as if he had pissed in his bed. That was the moment he knew he must act. He could not continue waking up with the feeling that he was a coward. It would be better to step across the boundary and embrace his fear than to tremble before it any longer. It was like any other decisive break—a divorce, or leaving home, or refusing to pray. You did it, really, because you had no choice. If there were another way, less painful, who would not take it?

The young man had been reading the night before from a book of poems by Simin Behbehani, an Iranian woman who was his nation's most beloved modern writer. His father claimed he had known her when he was a professor at Tehran University and she a student, and maybe it was true. Like his father, Behbehani had never left Iran for long, even in the worst days, but there was in her poems an anguish, and a yearning for escape. The young man had left the volume open beside his bed, to a poem called "My Country, I Will Build You Again," and now in the morning he read the words again:

My country, I will build you again,
if need be, with bricks made from my life.
I will build columns to support your roof,
if need be, with my bones.
I will inhale again the perfume of flowers
favored by your youth.
I will wash again the blood off your body
with torrents of my tears.

13

It should not only be the poets who tell the truth, the young man thought. The Islamic Republic of Iran was not his country. He had secretly become one of the *doshmand*, the enemy. He had wanted to disappear into the shadows of his work and enjoy his privileges, like any other hypocrite, but that had become impossible. That was what frightened him: he could not escape from himself. His father had told him that he must listen to his own voice, and not to those who impiously claimed to speak for God. He had said it the night before he died, and the scientist had answered, "Yes, Baba, I understand," which made it a promise. He didn't want to be a betrayer, but the promise was already inside him; it had taken root. It was crowding out the other voices, so that he heard only his own.

When he awoke that morning, he had the nub of a plan: he would drop a pebble into the pond. That was all. The pebble would be information, the smallest bit of the truth about what he was doing in his laboratory. And then he would let the water ripple where it would. No one would see him do it, or trace cause and effect. Something had come into his hand, and he would let it fall. That was what he thought was possible in the beginning.

The young scientist traveled that morning to a white office block in Jamaran. The windows were tinted, and there was no marking on the façade to suggest what work was done there. There were laboratories inside, with exotic equipment that had been acquired secretly from the West. But the real asset was the people, like the young scientist and his friends. At the side of the building was a door, halfway down an alleyway that curved like a crescent moon, and above this door was a surveillance camera that monitored every movement in or out. The building was part of a secret archipelago in this neighborhood and several others in the city, a string of addresses that couldn't be found on any map or in any public directory. You had to be part of the network to know that it existed. It was a condition of membership that you were always watched, and that you didn't know who the watchers were.

When his work was finished that afternoon, the young man opened the alley door and walked slowly toward the street. He was a handsome man in his early thirties, with a big Iranian nose and a shock of black hair that fell naturally in a thick wave. He wore a black suit of tropical wool and a starched white shirt with no collar; it was like the austere costumes worn by most of his colleagues, but a pair of gold cuff links peeked out beneath the sleeves of his jacket. They had been his father's, and he wore them in memory. There was a softness about his face, perhaps because he didn't wear a beard, and his eyes sparkled with a curiosity he did not try to hide. He walked with a looser gait than many Iranian men, his feet pointed out at a slight angle and his back arched, rather than pitched forward. That was a product of the several years he had spent as a graduate student in physics in Germany, where everyone could walk with that easy posture because they never had to look over their shoulder.

Today the young man was carrying a black valise under his left arm, held close against his side so that it was not visible to the camera as he turned into the alley.

It was early summer. The afternoon heat enfolded the city like a vaporous shawl, woven with the fumes of cars and scooters and gas generators. It was supposed to be cooler up here in the hills, but when the smog settled over the bowl of Tehran, it made the city democratic: everyone suffered in the heat together. A person who dreamed that he might escape was reminded on a day like this that it was impossible, except in the imagination.

From the hills of the Jamaran district, the city seemed to open itself to the world, cascading from the heights of the Alborz Mountains down toward the arid desert of Qom. It was a magnificent sight, this feast bowl of a city: close by were the skyscrapers and grand apartment blocks of North Tehran, mounting the hill so arrogantly. Then came the green spaces with their fountains and gardens—Mellat and Haqqani and Lavizan parks—where people went to escape the heat and dust. But it was the vast beyond that stretched your mind, the city tumbling mile after mile onto the plains, from the covered bazaar all the way south through the numberless alleyways of South Tehran to the martyrs' cemetery at Behesht-e-Zahra. Here it was—a city too big to take in with your two eyes, a city where nobody could know everything, a city so big that perhaps secrets could be hidden, and no one would see.

But that sense of open space was an illusion, especially in Jamaran. The whole of the district was under constant watch, from the men who sat all day in their cars observing the intersections to the cameras that were mounted on the rooftops of some of the taller buildings. When a taxi took a wrong turn and sped into the area, people made a note, and if the car lingered, they ran a check of the license plate. Even the phones here lacked a private status. If you called some of the numbers by accident, people called you back and asked who you were. The privileged residents of this black box of a neighborhood came and went in limousines with curtains drawn. Even they were not exempt from the watchers and listeners. If they made a mistake, they too were subject to what the authorities called *ershad*, which meant "guidance."

The young Iranian put on his dark glasses against the glint of the afternoon sun. After he had

17

walked a block, he stopped and put a piece of milk chocolate in his mouth. The taste reminded him of Germany. If he was looking at the men on the streets, observing their movements, it was not obvious. He paused again, farther down, outside a shop that sold cell phones, and looked at the storefront display of some of new models that had arrived in the last several weeks. Reflected in the window were the faces of dozens of passersby, but if the man was studying them through his sunglasses, it was impossible to see. He wasn't very good at this, but he wanted to do it right.

He put the buds of his iPod into his ears. A friend had bought the music player for him in Dubai a month ago as a present. He let it run on "shuffle." The first song was by a Persian rapper from Los Angeles who called himself MEC, for Middle East Connection. The music was very bad. He clicked forward to a song by Lou Reed. "Walk on the Wild Side." That was about right. Nobody could hear the music, and nobody cared what you listened to anyway, but halfway into the song, where Lou Reed was talking about how the colored girls go, do-do-do, the young man worried that he might look subversive, so he switched to a Bach piano recording he had learned to enjoy in Germany. The "Goldberg Variations." Then that made him nervous, too. People might think he was a Jew. He turned off the music altogether and folded the white cord back into his pocket.

The young man walked several more blocks down the hilly streets to a busy intersection, where he found a taxi. He asked the driver to take him to Haft-e-tir Square. The driver's wife was sitting next to him in the front seat of the Paykan, her head cloaked primly in a scarf. She had on thick glasses and sniffed the air like a mole. She looked at the well-dressed man and his gleaming cuff links and nodded deferentially, knowing instinctively that he was one of the *adam hesabi*, the good families.

They made their way down the Modarres Expressway in the slow ooze of rush-hour traffic. When the taxi reached the bustle of Haft-e-tir, decorated with neon signs for Nokia and Hyundai as well as the painted banners of the martyrs, the man got out and found a store that sold electronic products from the West. Here he bought a new memory board for a laptop computer, a thumb drive, and a set of software programs that had been copied in Armenia and trucked over the border. He put these items into his valise and then left the store. He walked two blocks east down Bahar Shiraz Street before catching another cab.

Outside was the street theater of the late afternoon. Women were testing the limits again this summer, flaunting their "bad *hijab*" with scarves that slipped back on their heads to reveal lustrous hair that sparkled in the sun. There was a new look that season, too, in the manteau: a tighter button at the waist that, with a push-up bra from Turkey, could give a woman a pleasing shape. The young men buzzed past on their motorbikes, in shades and cheap leather jackets, looking but not touching, dreaming of the women they could never have. Pedestrians skittered across the pavement like waterbugs, the onrushing cars missing them by centimeters.

"Would you like to hear some music?" asked the driver. He was looking in the rearview mirror with a solicitous eye toward his passenger. The young scientist did not answer. He did not want to speak; he was somewhere else. The driver's wife was clucking about the impossibility of finding good melons in the market at a reasonable price. The driver began muttering about the poor performance of his favorite soccer team, Esteghlal, hoping for a sympathetic audience from his passenger in the back. Yes, it was terrible, said the scientist. They could not play the game, these young men. They were dogs—no, worse than dogs; they played like women; they played like Arabs.

How long had the young man been thinking about what he was doing now? A year, at least; perhaps his whole adult life. No one could have suspected it from any outward sign, he was quite sure of that. Otherwise they would never have allowed him into the secret precincts of Jamaran, or given him an office in the white building that had no name.

That was their weakness. They suspected everyone, but they had to trust some people even so, and they could never be sure that this trust was well placed. They said they trusted in God, but that was not enough. So they created God's secret party, the conspiracy of God, and the young man was part of it. He had been loyal in every way except one, which was that he had allowed himself to think of the possibility of disloyalty. That idea had grown until it was a living thing. And then a moment had come when it was the only thing, and the boundary between loyalty and disloyalty had dissolved.

The taxi deposited the young man in Fereshteh Square, a half mile from the Ministry of the Interior. That was his joke. If you are going to defy them, do it in plain sight. He walked with his valise to a villa on Khosravi Street. On the first floor was the office of a small company owned by his uncle Jamshid, which fabricated aluminum siding for residential buildings. The young man helped out with the office paperwork sometimes, as a favor to his uncle. He had installed a computer a few months ago, and arranged for Internet access in his uncle's name. He came by sometimes in the late afternoons to work on the books and send messages to his uncle's suppliers here in Iran and in Dubai and Ankara. One of the Iranian companies had its own Internet server. It wasn't hard to hack into it, and to write code that could make it seem as if a message had originated there when it had really come from somewhere else. The young man was good with computers: he knew how to smooth out the sand, as it were, so that there was no sign that anyone had come or gone.

The young man had his own key and let himself in the door of Uncle Jamshid's office. A secretary was still there, an awkward girl from Isfahan who was a distant relative. She tidied up the wastebaskets and then said good night, leaving him alone. The young man had wanted to give her a few riyals for her trouble, but she left too quickly. Probably it was better this way; she might have remembered the tip. He powered up the computer and slipped a CD-ROM with his new software into the drive. It was cooler outside now. He turned on some music and let himself relax.

He was *posht-e-pardeh*. Behind the curtain. He had a secret. Or rather, he had a secret locked inside many other secrets. That was the Persian way. This was a land where it was bad manners to speak plainly; it was too forward, too disrespectful. If you asked a tradesman how much he wanted for his work, he would refuse payment and tell you it was for free. It wasn't that he didn't expect to be paid, but that he didn't want to name a price. And so it was with this special secret. It was a gift, but it wasn't for free. It told a truth, but not the one that you might at first have anticipated.

Why was he doing it? He couldn't really have answered that, even to himself. It was an emotion more than a word. It was the sting of an insult repeated, the way they were now insulting his cousin Hossein. His cousin had been their faithful servant. He was one of the boys, the *bach-e-ha*. But still they had destroyed him. That was part of it. And there were his father's words, always in his ear, and his example. His father had stood for something, and never wavered. Truly, the young man could not live as the person he had become. He was suffocating. He was losing respect for himself.

His bet was that the people he was contacting would not be stupid. Was that wise, with outsiders? It was like shaking hands; in Iran, the hand was limp and soft—deceptively submissive. But with these foreigners, they sometimes squeezed your hand so hard they might break the little bones— even though they meant it as a sign of friendliness. It had happened so often in Germany, that crushing greeting. It was barbaric, but forgivable. The culture of the West had so much to prove; it did not know how to hide. The young man began to type. If he was careful, and continued with what he had planned and no more, he would remain invisible. He would drop his pebble, and then he would wait.

Would they understand, the people at the other end of the pond who saw the motion in the water? He was frightened, but he tried to embrace this emotion. Fear can make you strong. His father had told him that, too, before he died. Fear is your master until the day you make a stand, and then it becomes your teacher and guardian. It guides you into the shadows; it instructs you in your lies. It is the cloak you wear as you prepare your revenge and your escape.

2

WASHINGTON

The Americans called him "Dr. Ali." He was, in the technical terminology of the Central Intelligence Agency, a "virtual walk-in." He arrived late at night, logging on to agency's public website, www.cia.gov, and then clicking on the little tab marked "Contact CIA," which took the visitor to a bland invitation to commit treason: "If you have information which you believe might be of interest to the CIA in pursuit of the CIA's foreign intelligence mission, you may use the form below. We will carefully protect all information you provide, including your identity." Below that, for additional reassurance, was a notice that the agency used a special "secure socket layer" encryption system. No explanation was offered of what this impressive-sounding system actually did. But this visitor didn't need help. He knew precisely what he was doing.

The electronic visitor uploaded his message in

plain text so bland and obvious that it was easy to miss. Then he disappeared back into the ether. He left no footprint, no clue as to his motivation, no hint of why he had risked everything to whisper his secrets across cyberspace. He didn't exist, really, except for these few bits of computer code.

It was a muggy night in late June. A rainstorm had swept the city, and a humid predawn mist was rising over the trees that surrounded Main Headquarters. The handful of clerical workers who monitored the agency's public website during the night shift were already packing up. They had spent the evening processing emails, most of them the equivalent of crank calls, looking for the one that might contain a scrap of real intelligence or a warning of a terrorist attack. The secret bureaucrats were tired; they wanted to find their cars out in the Brown Lot and Yellow Lot and get on home.

An African-American woman named Jana who had been working for the agency just three years was the first to notice the point of origin. The message had come from an Internet service provider in Iran. The first clerk who processed the message had missed it altogether. It was late, he was tired. He had already sifted a hundred messages. But Jana took a last scroll back through the incoming traffic as her shift was ending, and this one caught her eye.

Jana's colleagues were already heading for the

door, but she told them to go ahead; she would come along in a few more minutes. She was a single mother, going home to make breakfast for her daughter and send her off to high school in Fairfax. She was just a GS-9 and had traveled overseas just once, before the divorce, but she had that instinct, too. She knew that occasionally the strange people who sent anonymous messages to the CIA were for real. They knew secrets; they were angry at their government, or the security service, or maybe just at their boss down the hall. And they were Internet geeks who knew how to make contact from overseas without getting caught. Jana's shop had tracked several dozen of these electronic contacts from China since she joined the unit, and a half dozen from Russia, but never an Iranian. So she stayed.

The message didn't make much sense. It was just a list of dates and numbers. Maybe it was a technical document, maybe it was gibberish. Jana wasn't sure, but she knew it was coming from a place that mattered.

"Iranian VW?" That was the subject line of Jana's message forwarding the email. VW was the CIA's shorthand name for these virtual walk-ins. She sent the message to the Information Operations Center, which managed computer tactics for the clandestine service. For good measure she copied the Near East Division, the Iran "issues manager" at the Office of the Director of National

Intelligence, and the Iran Operations Division. That was too many addresses, it turned out, but how could she have known?

One of the cables went to Harry Pappas, the new chief of the Iran Operations Division. He didn't pay any attention to it the first day. He was so busy he couldn't see the water, let alone the ripples.

Harry was a big man in what had become a little institution. He had a face that was lived-in: a large, soft mouth, cheeks that were creased by sun and late nights, curly hair that had turned the dull gray of burnt charcoal. The most forbidding thing about him was his eyes, which conveyed a ferocity and also a weariness that all his strength could not dispel. He had come into the agency as a paramilitary officer during the 1980s after a stint in the army, and had gotten his start training the contras in Nicaragua. He spoke Spanish badly back then, with a Worcester, Massachusetts, accent, and he had since added bad Russian and now bad Farsi. Yet people always seemed to understand Harry Pappas, no matter what language he spoke.

"If people don't get what Harry is saying, he just talks louder." That was what his best friend Adrian Winkler liked to say about him. Adrian was British, and as with most SIS officers, he was a proficient linguist who did his business in lower decibels. But like Harry, he was a prankster. No matter how bleak things looked, Harry couldn't resist a wisecrack or an irreverent curse. That had helped him survive a career in the neverland of the clandestine service.

But Harry Pappas was wounded, and everyone knew it. He had lost his only son several years before, in Iraq. The mess over there was a stomachache for everyone at the agency, but for Harry it was something much worse. That was the reason he had taken the job running Persia House—to try to get through the pain.

Today it wasn't working. His desk was full of paper he didn't want to read. He had a request to brief the senior staff members of the Senate intelligence committee, whom he regarded as twerps and second-guessers. He had a summons, from the director no less, to brief a meeting of the NSC deputies committee. He wanted to say no to both but knew he couldn't.

They all wanted the same thing. The CIA director, the director of National Intelligence, the White House, the congressional intelligence committees—they were all howling for more production from Tehran. If there wasn't an item in the PDB each morning, the president would ask, "What about Iran?" The director had suggested that Harry to go to the White House once a week with the PDB briefer, to show the flag and make excuses, but Harry begged off. He didn't trust himself in their company.

What Harry really wanted to tell the president was, "Get your finger out of my eye." Go away, be patient, shut up. But that was the one thing he wasn't allowed to say, to anyone, especially when the comptrollers of the secret budget were throwing money at him. They wanted more of everything—more case officers, more platforms, more recruitments. They seemed to think that intelligence was a spigot they could turn wide open if they just spent enough cash. Harry kept saying no. He couldn't target the officers he had now, let alone a dozen more. The last thing he needed was more people bumping into each other, sending each other make-work cables. But they appropriated the money anyway. It made them feel they were doing something.

"Don't fight the problem." That was one of Harry's mottoes, which he had picked up years ago in a biography of General George C. Marshall. He had puzzled over what it meant until it occurred to him one day that all the great man was saying was, *Solve the problem.* Figure out what it is, and then get it done. And Harry could do that. He wasn't one of the smart guys who needed to show everyone how hard they were thinking. He was from Worcester. He had come up as a knuckle-dragger in paramilitary. He was happy if people took him for granted.

So Harry was patient: he knew the Iranian agents were out there. They were angry and greedy and lonely and needy. This one had been disrespected by the Revolutionary Guard. That one hadn't gotten the promotion he wanted. One man resented the corrupt officials who ran his program. Another man's wife had cancer that could only be treated in the West. This father wanted his children to succeed. That father has lost his only child and wanted to fill the emptiness. One was idealistic. Another was avaricious. This man had a mistress who wanted money. That man was a homosexual. Take your pick. They were out there. Harry knew it. He had lists of dozens of people his case officers would pitch, if they ever got close enough.

What Harry didn't realize was that his man had already arrived. His message was sitting in Harry's in-box, waiting to be read.

Harry's wife Andrea was out when he got home. She did volunteer work three evenings a week at a Greek Orthodox church in McLean. It was her form of penance. His daughter Louise was in the family room watching *Sex and the City* reruns. Harry sat with her for a while, drinking a beer, but he felt uncomfortable. The characters were talking about penises. He gave his daughter a good-night kiss and went up to bed. She was relieved to see him go, so she could watch television in peace.

Trying to get to sleep, Harry thought of his son, who had been killed in Iraq in 2004. The agency hadn't been tough enough for him, so he had joined the Marines. "Makeshift roadside bomb" was the caption under his picture in the "Faces of the Fallen" gallery that ran in the *Washington Post*, which made it sound like a sort of traffic accident. Back then, at least, his son had been able to think it all might lead to something good. He had been spared as a last thought: What a fucking mistake. But not Harry. He didn't sleep well that night, but he never did anymore.

3

WASHINGTON

Harry Pappas made his way to Persia House the next morning. He had a good parking spot near the front entrance now. They were all trying to be nice to him, as if he were a fragile instrument that might crack down the middle if it wasn't handled with care. Harry walked through the electronic gate with his head down, ignoring the guard and the colleagues arriving for work. It was six forty-five, and most of the other early risers made a point of looking perky, but not Harry. Persia House was down Corridor C in the Main Headquarters building, past a glass display case that housed an old gray spy submarine. There was a little ramp off to the right, and at the top of the ramp a cyber-locked door. And next to it, so small that it was barely visible, was a sign that said IRAN OPERATIONS DIVISION.

The first face Harry saw when he opened the door was that of the Imam Hussein. It was a brightly colored life-size poster Harry had purchased in the central market in Baghdad when he was station chief. The image startled visitors, which was why Harry put it there. We're not in Kansas anymore, boys and girls. He had mounted it just inside the front door of Persia House, next to the receptionist's desk, so that young officers who knew the streets of Tehran only from overhead reconnaissance could see it and understand, perhaps just a little, what a peculiar country Iran was.

It was a cheap, almost luridly sentimental poster, the sort of thing that would embarrass an educated Iranian, but it had the cartoon energy of folk religion: the martyr's sweet, dark-eyed gaze; his skin as fine as rice paper; his black hair as silky as a leopard's fur; his eyes moist with tears for the tragedy that lay ahead. When Iranians looked into those limpid eyes, they cried too, in shame and rage. The face spoke of the wound that never healed, of the martyr's blood that flowed like a perpetual fountain. The story was so cruel: the Prophet's descendant lured by the evil Yazid and murdered on the plain of Kerbala. Iranians marked the awful betrayal every year, whipping themselves into a collective hysteria. The abiding message was that history is a conspiracy against the believers. And if that were so, what counterconspiracies were not permissible?

Harry stopped to look at the poster each morning, to put himself in the mind of people for whom the events of A.D. 680 were as yesterday. The Iranians understood suffering. They knew that the decent young men were betrayed by the deceit and blunders of others. They knew that goodness is a secret and that happiness is an illusion. That was what Harry had in common with them.

Harry Pappas hadn't wanted to become head of the Iran Operations Division. After Baghdad, he had hoped to disappear into a senior staff job somewhere, jump to a safe lily pad, or perhaps just retire like most of his friends. Sign up for the "Horizons" course and be done with it. He was broken inside. Iraq had done that; not the big war that had destroyed everyone, but the private and desolate grief that comes from personal loss. The agency was broken, too, but that wasn't Harry's problem. Or at least, he didn't want to think it was.

But the director had made a special appeal, and several of his closest friends had told him it was his duty. The only way to avoid another Iraq was to have the right people do Iran. They told Harry he was the best; he was the teacher; he was the one who could say no and also yes. Harry might have walked away even from that, he was still hurting so much. But his wife Andrea told him that taking the job would help him get over Alex; that it was a way to keep faith with his dead son. That otherwise, he would die.

So Harry said yes, and he put the picture of the Imam Hussein up on the wall to remind himself that he was living in the country of betrayal and pain.

Harry's office was just inside the heavy door. There was a big oak desk for him, a fat leather couch for visitors, and against the back wall, a conference table and chairs for staff meetings. The room had no windows, and when the door was closed, it was an airless and colorless tomb of secrets. Harry hadn't bothered to decorate the office. He had cartons of memorabilia from his previous assignments—in Tegucigalpa, Moscow, Beirut; even a brief stint with an earlier Iranian "virtual station" known as "TehFran," located in Frankfurt, Germany. But he didn't have the heart to unpack all the old junk. It would only have depressed him to see the artifacts of his life up on the walls, so he left them in the boxes. As for the medals and testimonials from the agency, he had destroyed them, one by one, the night of Alex's funeral.

Harry's senior staff gathered in his spartan office for the morning meeting. They were kids, most of them. The agency was becoming like a university, with a few old professors and the rest young people who were called "officers" and perhaps had even had a tour or two overseas but were more like students. There was no middle; only a top and bottom. That was the good part for Harry, the fact that most of his young colleagues hadn't learned to game the system yet. Harry took his seat at the head of the conference table, his body too big for the chair.

"Sobh bekheir az laneh jasoosi," said Harry. It was the same Farsi phrase he used each morning. Good morning from the nest of spies.

"What do we have overnight?"

"Mostly we have a lot of nothing," rasped back Marcia Hill. She had a thin smile on her face, although Harry couldn't understand why.

Marcia Hill was Harry's deputy, a woman in her late fifties with a weathered face and a voice pleasantly ruined by whiskey and cigarettes; she had the tawdry appeal of a been-around movie actress. Marcia was Persia House's institutional memory—the last survivor from the Iran desk of 1979 when the embassy in Tehran had been seized and U.S.-Iranian relations had ground to a thirty-year halt. She had been a reports officer, in one of the shit jobs they gave women back then. But she had taught herself Farsi and made herself useful to the burnouts from NE Division who handled the "Iran target."

During the wasteland years, she became the repository of information about Iranian operations. She remembered names and family connections and botched leads—she was the only person, really, who knew just how badly the agency had done in its efforts to recruit spies in Iran. For her trouble, she was exiled to Support—where Harry found her, already halfway out the door to retirement. She felt sorry for Harry; that was the only reason she said yes.

Marcia ran through the string of operational messages they had received overnight from their listening posts in Dubai, Istanbul, Baku, and Baghdad, and from the several dozen other platforms that were woven together into the Persia House net. Her tally was a series of foul balls and strikeouts. A case officer in Istanbul had cold-pitched an Iranian on holiday in Turkey who was believed to be a member of the Revolutionary Guard. He had fled. A case officer under commercial cover in Dubai had met with an Iranian banker on the pretext of discussing an investment in Pakistan. The Iranian had said he would think about it, which meant that he wouldn't. A case officer in Germany had shadowed an Iranian scientist attending a conference. He had two minders from the Ministry of Intelligence with him whenever he left his room; the case officer couldn't get close. As Marcia said, it was a lot of nothing.

"What about the pitch list?" asked Harry. "Any new names?"

Persia House had a list of Iranian scientists it monitored and updated. They had been compiling it for years, adding every graduate student who passed through Europe, every Iranian who had his name on a scientific paper published in an academic journal, every traveler who came out with a purchasing team to buy laboratory gear or computer hardware. Anyone on this list who passed across an international frontier was a blinking light—a potential recruit. But the prize targets rarely traveled anymore, at least not alone. The Iranians weren't stupid. They knew what we wanted. When they let someone go overseas unescorted, it was usually a dangle.

Tony Reddo spoke up. He was a young officer on loan from WinPac, the unit that monitored nuclear weapons technology for the agency. He was so young Harry wondered if he had started shaving yet. He had gotten his doctorate in nuclear physics when he was twenty-four, and now he was all of twenty-six. The other kids in the office teased him because he was so smart.

"We're tracking three new papers," said Reddo. "On neutronics, hydrophonics, and wave dynamics. We're running traces on the names. No new delegations to report. No travelers."

"Anything new to work with from overseas? Anywhere?"

"Not yet," said Reddo. He glanced over to Marcia Hill, who gave him a wink, out of Harry's sight.

"Christ!" said Harry. He sighed and turned to Marcia. "Tomorrow is another day. Right, Scarlett?"

"Give me a break, Harry." She still had a trace of a smile on her face, despite all the bad news. She was holding something back.

Harry wanted to sound cheery for his kids, but it was a struggle. There was always tomorrow, until they ran out of time and there wasn't. That was how the business really worked: people making lists and waiting for the moment, which usually didn't come. It was like the old days in Moscow: you didn't make things happen; they happened to you. You waited for some crazy fucker to throw something over the wall, and then you tried to figure out how to keep him alive.

"Anything else?" Harry asked.

"Yeah, *one* thing," said Marcia with a sly nod. "You probably missed this. It came in yesterday from the website. They think it's a VW. I showed it to Tony. We think it's interesting. You ought to look at it."

"Can it wait?" said Harry. He wanted to focus on real cases, not chaff from the website.

"Sure, anything can wait. But I think you're going to want to see this. Tony can explain."

Reddo was brandishing some pieces of paper he had printed out. He was such a kid. He laid the papers down on the conference table like a puppy who has found a bone.

"What is this shit?" asked Harry, motioning to the papers.

"Assays," said Reddo.

"Come again?"

"Nuclear assays. Believe it or not, I think they are measurements of uranium enrichment."

"From Iran? Are you shitting me?"

"No, sir. There are notations about the composition of the sample, here, see? I don't really follow that. But look at the rows. I think they show the enrichment level after each pass through the cascade. They're just like IAEA documents. That was what got me thinking. I've seen stuff like this before, same patterns and categories. Now look at the columns. I think they are measuring what emerges—the enriched product and the depleted tails. See how the one goes up, with each pass, and the other goes down? And see numbers here at the bottom? There's one batch that's marked thirty-five percent, and another that's marked seven percent. And next to the second one there's a little note that says D_2O, with a question mark. See that?"

"Yeah, I see it. What does it mean?"

"Let me think." Reddo scratched his head. It was hard to explain complicated things simply.

"So it means the Iranians are enriching uranium, just like they always say. But the strange part is the two batches. One says seven percent. That's what you use to fuel a nuclear reactor. Okay. That's interesting. The other batch is thirty-five percent. Uh-oh. That's more than they need for a reactor. So you have to assume that's for a weapons program.

They'll keep enriching more and more, until they hit weapons grade, which is above ninety percent. That's bad news, but it's not really a surprise. We figured they were going in that direction. So they're halfway there. What's super weird is the 'D_2O question mark' notation."

Harry rolled his eyes. He had gotten a C in high school chemistry and he had never taken a physics course.

"Explain it for the dumb guy. What's D_2O?"

"It's the symbol scientists use for heavy water. Regular water—'light' water—is H_2O, two hydrogen atoms and one of oxygen. Heavy water has two deuterium atoms for each oxygen. And heavy water is what you use in the kind of reactor that can make plutonium. That's the creepy part. Maybe this notation means they're thinking of diverting the seven percent batch to a heavy-water reactor for a plutonium bomb program. In which case they wouldn't need to enrich it at all."

"The Iranians have plans for a heavy-water reactor at Arak, right?" said Harry. "But it isn't operational. Unless we've missed something."

"Uh, yeah," said Reddo. "That's the point, I guess."

"Shit." Harry shook his head. "And you think it's real? The document."

"Yeah. Maybe. Probably."

"Which means it came from someone inside the program?"

"Gotta be. Or someone with access."

"Well, fuck me," Harry said, shaking his head. "Where the hell did this come from?"

Reddo pointed to an email address at the bottom of the message. It said doktor.ali49@hotmail.com.

"What's that supposed to mean?"

"Um, I think *that's* the return address. That's how we contact the guy who sent this."

Harry closed his eyes. "Sweet Jesus," he said. "We're inside."

Harry asked Marcia Hill to stay behind when the meeting ended. He wanted to think out loud a moment before the Iranian message took on a life of its own. Marcia had a card-room smile. She lived for moments like this. She had put up with the shit for so long, she wanted to enjoy the rare good parts. But Harry needed to worry it, poke some holes in it before he let it out.

"This has to be bullshit," said Harry.

"No it doesn't. Sometimes good things happen. Even to us."

"Why would someone do it? Explain that. He's giving up big secrets. Why would someone send a message like this, on an open Internet line, out of the blue?"

"It's a calling card," said Hill. "He wants to talk. Or she."

"Is it a setup? Is it a dangle, to see how we react?"

41

"Maybe. But that's CI's problem, not yours."

"Is he crazy?"

"Possibly. But so what? If the information is for real, who cares?"

"Will he get caught? I mean, what's the chance of sending a message like this, and nobody seeing it? They have a good service. You know that better than anyone. You had to pick up the pieces after the postal fiasco."

"Hard to say. But you have to assume he knows what he's doing. He wouldn't have sent it if he didn't think he could do it without leaving fingerprints. Kids know how to do this stuff, Harry. Iran is full of hackers and computer nerds."

Harry was still shaking his head. He wanted to see in his mind the person who had sent the message.

"Help me out, Marcia. You understand Iranians. What kind of person would do this? Assuming that it isn't a setup, and that he isn't crazy."

Marcia pondered a moment. Why did anyone do anything? But Harry wanted an answer, so she thought back over the dozens of Iranian cases she had reviewed over too many years.

"He's smart," she began. "He's proud. He's unhappy. He's young. He has a need, for some reason, to share what he knows. He's not asking us for anything, he's telling us. But this message is a tease. An opening bid. Iranians never give you the whole slice. It's *taarof*."

"Remind me. What's *taarof*?"

"It's their way of doing business. The dignity thing. They don't want to name a price. That would be undignified. So they make a gift, and wait for you to respond. It's unmanly to ask. Unwomanly, too."

"He's trusting the agency, in other words," said Harry. "Not to fuck it up, I mean."

"What an idiot," muttered Marcia. "Doesn't he read the newspapers?"

It all moved slowly at first, before it hit the trip-wires.

It was Pappas's case, since, as the director liked to remind him, he owned every speck of dust blowing out of Iran. He filed the initial message under the designator BQDETERMINE, which was the agency's cryptonym for all Iranian collection operations, and gave "Dr. Ali" a provisional crypt of BQTANK.

But Harry knew he would have to share, right away, so he called Arthur Fox, the head of the Counter-Proliferation Division. He didn't like Fox, who was always trying to show everyone what a hard-ass he was, but he had no choice. He proposed a meeting that afternoon and asked Fox to bring one of his nuclear specialists.

"So what do you think, Arthur?" asked Pappas when they had gathered a few hours later in a secure conference room. "Is this for real?" His big body was hunched over the conference table, his shoulders stooped as if burdened by the new weight they were carrying.

"Looks real," said Fox. He held a copy of the Dr. Ali message up to his nose. "Smells real. So a logical inference would be that it *is* real." Fox was a fastidious man; when he sniffed his nose, you understood that he was accustomed to fine wines and gourmet sauces. There was money in his background somewhere. That was a funny thing about the new tough guys. They came from the better side of town. They talked hard, but they had soft hands.

Harry needed Fox's help, and he didn't mind acting dumb. He had done it to good effect his whole career.

"What does it tell you, Arthur, assuming it's real? Did we already know this?"

"It's showtime, that's what it tells me. We knew the Iranians were getting higher enrichment levels at Natanz, but we had not confirmed they were above seven percent. Suspected it, maybe; feared it, certainly. But the fact they're at thirty-five percent—assuming it's a fact—is news. Pretty serious news. Some people could argue—*some people*—that we should bomb the whole damn complex tomorrow, before it goes any further. Been saying that for years, in fact, but nobody has been listening."

"Hold the speech a minute. I thought they needed ninety percent before they had the goods. Maybe this message is telling us they're stuck. What about that?"

"Don't be ridiculous, Harry. You want to wait for them to explode a bomb before you decide they're serious? Bad idea."

Harry nodded. Fox was right, even if he was a jerk.

"What about the seven percent batch? My guy Reddo thinks that may be a big deal. He thinks the 'D_2O?' notation may mean they're thinking about sending enriched uranium to a heavy-water reactor, and then reprocessing it later to make plutonium. Does that make sense?"

"Any allegation about Iran makes sense, Harry. These people are *dangerous*. We didn't know about a plutonium program. But that doesn't mean they don't have one. If I had to bet, I would bet worst case."

"Why am I not surprised? Bomb, bomb, bomb. Let's bomb Iran."

"That's unworthy of you, Harry."

"Just joking, Arthur." Harry looked back at the text of the message from the mysterious Iranian correspondent.

"What about the other notations and formulas? Reddo wasn't sure what they meant. What do they tell you?"

Fox's nuclear expert spoke up. He was a young

man named Adam Schwartz. He had graduated from MIT a few years ago. Pappas wasn't sure why such a talented young man had joined a screwed-up government agency rather than making megabucks like the other smart kids.

"So I can't say whether our mystery informant is part of the Iranian nuclear program, but he certainly has access to what's going on," said Schwartz. He looked down at the paper in front of him, as if to double-check. "His hexafluoride formula has several unusual signatures that match some anomalies in the samples we have from the Iranian program. He must know that. I think that's why he sent the message. This is his statement of bona fides. So if I had to guess, I would say that, yes, he is a part of the program."

Schwartz looked at his boss, who was frowning. "But I don't know," the analyst added.

"Dr. Ali," said Harry quietly, half to himself.

"Say what?" queried Fox.

"Dr. Ali, you piss me off." Harry spoke the name louder, as if the Iranian himself were sitting with them in the secure conference room. "I mean, give me a break. We've been killing ourselves trying to recruit someone like you, and now you walk in the door. Except you don't even do that. You send a message to our website, like you're signing up for summer camp. Are you fucking with me, Dr. Ali?"

"Maybe he's real," said Fox. "Maybe not. But how would you know, eh? This is pretty technical stuff, Harry. Easy to get suckered." Fox was playing Pappas. His manner said that he wanted control of the case.

"Tell you what, Arthur. I know one problem with this case already, which is that too many people have copies of this message. A distribution list this wide and we'll be reading about it in the *New York Times*. And then we can kiss Dr. Ali goodbye, whoever he is. This is an RH case, starting now." RH was the agency's term for "restricted handling."

"Then close it down," said Fox brusquely.

Pappas just nodded. He had already done that, before the meeting even started. He had created a special-access program, an "SAP," many of whose members were sitting in the room.

"We need to create a legend for this guy," Pappas said.

"Meaning what?"

"Meaning that we've got to kill Dr. Ali off in cable traffic so nobody asks, 'Hey, whatever happened to that Iranian VW who sent the nuclear stuff?' We lay a trail that leads everyone off in the wrong direction, and then we handle the case in the SAP. Is everyone cool with that?"

"Who runs it?" asked Fox. The natural set of his eyes was a squint.

"We both do. IOD and Counter-Proliferation. It will be a joint case. We'll bring in the Info Ops Center for computer support, plus the director and the head of the clandestine service. That's it."

"Who briefs the NSC?" pressed Fox. Meaning, Who gets face time with the president?

Fox was still bargaining. He lived for turf battles like this. Pappas decided to give ground. He didn't like going to the White House. They got all wound up in the Situation Room, and then they did the wrong thing. The people who paid the price for their mistakes were kids like his son. Let Fox spin them if he wanted.

"You do it," he said. "It's about nuclear. Your people will do the briefings and the technical support. We'll run operations, like he's a real agent. And we'll work our asses off trying to find him and make actual contact, as opposed to this virtual bullshit. How's that?"

Fox smiled. What he wanted was to control access to the policymakers. This was potentially a very hot case. Pappas had given away the customers. He was a fool, in Fox's book.

"We'll see how it goes," Fox said. Everything was provisional with him, in case the wind changed. "What do we do next?"

Pappas shrugged his shoulders. It was an effort for him to tolerate Fox, who was one of those intelligence officers who had never run a big operation, never recruited an agent whose life was on the line. He didn't have the feel of the work on his fingertips; the sticky-sweet touch of espionage. Nobody did anymore. That's why they were reduced to waiting for the VWs.

"We fucking well answer Dr. Ali's message, that's what we do next. But we do it very carefully. And then we start generating the traffic to tell everyone he was a phony."

Fox's eyes narrowed tighter, like a cat that hasn't made up its mind whether to eat the food or bolt.

"Just one more question," said Fox. "How are we going to use this guy, once we get started?"

"Very carefully. So we don't get him killed."

"Don't overdo the tradecraft stuff, Harry. We need information. This is a big one. We need to exploit it now, for all it's worth. Assuming it's for real."

Harry shook his head. Wrong. Fox's bravado was the kind of talk that got agents killed.

"Here's what we're going to do," Harry said. "We're going to be smart. And we're going to be patient. And we're going to remember that there is a human being on the other end of that email address. And we're going to make sure that whatever we tell the White House is true. How's that?"

Fox shrugged. Pappas didn't get it. The message had changed the stakes. This wasn't about what the CIA wanted. This was going to ring the bells downtown. But he did as Pappas suggested. The White House was briefed, but cautiously. The tearsheet version was that a new Iranian source said the Iranians had passed the enrichment level needed for civilian nuclear use and were moving toward weapons-grade level. The new source also indicated the possibility of an Iranian heavy-water reactor program. The report was unconfirmed. The source was of untested reliability. His identity and bona fides were unknown. The agency was working to confirm and evaluate the reports.

What they put in writing, in official channels, was all true. But Pappas suspected that Fox was already talking behind his back, spinning the information with his friends downtown nearly as fast as the rotors on those Iranian centrifuges. That was what Fox did. He lived to make trouble other people would have to fix.

4

TEHRAN

The setting summer sun glittered in the western windows of the young scientist's apartment in Yoosef Abad. He put his feet up on the coffee table and tried to relax. The stereo was playing a CD by a folk group from the Persian Gulf called Jahleh, which had won a prize at the Tehran Independent Music Festival. They were hip, but also safe. That was his protection—to be ordinary. Deceit was a habit; you put it on and took it off like a suit of clothes. That was his ritual each morning when he rose and prepared for work, and each night when he came home to this apartment. But what was normal? Was it to be afraid or unafraid? Was it to remember things or forget them? He took off his coat. His father's gold cuff links shone with the same faint light as the disappearing sun.

He was restless. He rose from the leather couch and walked to the small study where he kept his computer. It was a Mac PowerBook, only six months old. It had cost him over four thousand dollars at Paytakht, a Tehran store that managed to import, with a hefty markup, most of what you could get in Dubai. When he bought it, he had imagined that it was an escape hatch that would allow him to leave the velvet prison of his "special" job and flee to other worlds. The computer was so fast, and with his new satellite connection, he could land on any virtual space he liked. In the beginning, it had been exhilarating. But now he was frightened of the computer. The Ministry of Intelligence and the Revolutionary Guard had its IP address, just as they had the coordinates of anything else that was officially connected to him. He had to live outside his body now, in the shells of other creatures.

The young man walked to the bookcase and took down one of his parents' photo albums. They had been shutterbugs, his mother and father. They seemed to buy a new camera every other year, and miles of Kodak film—always Kodak, his father didn't trust the Japanese. Some of their devout Muslim friends said it was a profanation, to make these images, but his father just laughed. These were the *jahiliya*, the ignorant ones. They thought they could dam up the sunlight, and make day into night.

He turned the pages of the album. There were pictures of his mother and father at their little beach house at Ramsar on the Caspian Sea. His mother looked like a 1960s movie star in the early pictures, dressed in her bathing suit and wearing her hair in a lacquered wave. As the years passed, the bathing suit was shrouded by a cover-up and the hair disappeared behind a scarf, and then his mother disappeared altogether, dead of cancer before she was fifty years old. He had been just eleven when she died; he could remember her smell, and her gentle touch, but she survived for him mainly in these albums. In addition to pasting in his father's photographs, she liked to add pictures she had clipped from glossy magazines, of Iranian writers and movie stars. There were shots of the handsome Fardin and the lovely Azar Shiva, the stars of the romantic film *Sultan of My Heart*. They were ghosts of a lost world.

The album fell open to a photograph he had never examined closely before. It showed Jacqueline Kennedy Onassis on a visit to Shiraz in the early 1970s. His mother had written a caption with all the details. He studied the picture. Jackie was dressed in white slacks low on the hip and a royal blue shirt, so slim and elegant. The camera had caught her in motion, pushing her long black hair away from her beautiful face as she looked to her left toward something that had caught her eye. She was walking down a grand array of stone steps, leaving the covered portico of some sort of monument. There were bodyguards on either side of her, dressed in black suits and skinny black ties. He looked at her more closely: so much wondrous hair, uncovered, and the pants so finely cut you could see the shape of her hips and thighs. Could this now be the same country to which the Queen of the World, Jackie Kennedy, had once paid a visit? If she were to come back now, would they cover her in a sack like a dead animal? Yes, of course they would. Jackie was an offense against their idea of Islam.

His father must have taken the picture. But what was he doing in Shiraz when Jackie Kennedy visited? Perhaps he had been asked to give lecture on Persian literature. Or maybe he had just been a tourist.

The shah was a pimp, his father had told him once, when he was a boy. His father had hated the shah, and the Pahlavi regime in turn had hated him. The young man had to remind himself of that now. His father had been an intellectual and a free-thinker, and probably in his youth, a communist, too. No one had ever talked about that, but it must have been so.

Whatever it was that his father had believed, he had suffered for it. He had been arrested twice, the second time just after his son was born—just before the revolution. The shah's men must have thought he was still dangerous—this broken-down professor living in a dream world of memories of his dead wife and Kodak pictures. That was how stupid the Savak had been, that they imagined this harmless man was a threat.

When the revolution had come, his father had rejoiced: you could see that in his face in the pictures taken at the great demonstration at the Shahyar monument that marked the beginning of the end. The look in his father's eyes was one of revenge. The son had never asked him what the shah's men had done to him in prison, but he could imagine. When he was a boy, after the revolution, the simple *basiji* treated him like a hero's son, a martyr's son. By then, his father had seen the truth, and though he never said it out loud, he had come to despise the revolution.

They are liars, his father had said. They have made a refuse dump and called it a green park. He told his son to go away, to study in Germany and never come back. But the son hadn't listened. He liked the power that knowledge brought him. He liked knowing secrets. He thought he could be smarter than his father, and make a hiding place for himself where the *jahiliya*, the ignorant ones, couldn't find him. But after several years in the white offices of Jamaran, he knew this was impossible.

He closed the album. He wasn't hungry, but he thought he should eat. He went to the kitchen and found some rice and chicken the maid had left. This was his life, living inside the exoskeletons of other people. He was warming the chicken in his new microwave oven when the phone rang. He didn't like to answer it anymore at home, for fear of who it might be. But when the recording of the answering machine clicked on, he recognized the voice and picked up the receiver.

It was his cousin Hossein. The bitter one. He had served with the Revolutionary Guard for so many years; he had done everything they asked of him, and now they had thrown him away. You could hear it in his voice. They had taken his balls away. His wife was visiting her sister, Hossein said. He wanted to go out and have some fun. Go to a restaurant, maybe meet some girls. There was a little slur in his voice, as if he had already started drinking, or maybe smoking opium or taking pills—it didn't make any difference once they took your balls away. The young man said he was tired; he'd had a long day at the *daneshgah*, the "university," which was his euphemism for where he worked. But Hossein wouldn't hear of it. He was urging, almost pleading for company. He said that he would pick up his cousin outside the apartment in Yoosef Abad in fifteen minutes. The young man agreed; anything to get Hossein off the phone before he said something really stupid that someone might overhear.

Hossein had a jar of home brew in his car. It had the sharp, acidic taste of raw alcohol, masked with some orange juice. The young man said no at first, but then he took a swig. He wanted obliteration and escape tonight, as much as Hossein did. He looked at his cousin; he still had the hard, pitted face of a Revolutionary Guard, but the eyes had gone soft. He was rotting from the inside out. Now there was nothing for him to do but drink and be angry; eventually he would make a mistake, and they would destroy him for good. Hossein did not know how to live inside a lie; that was his problem. He had actually believed in the revolution, and now that it had expelled him, he didn't know what to do.

They cruised the streets for a while in Hossein's green Peugeot, crawling up Vali Asr Avenue in the slow traffic that allowed them to look at the pretty girls in the streets. They knew how to be sexy, even in their scarves and cloaks. They were wearing spike heels, the daring ones, so that their legs were long and tight and their asses swayed from side to side. The girls could watch Fashion TV on the pirate satellite stations, so they knew how to move like models. The boys could watch it too, and jerk off when they showed lingerie and swimsuits.

56

"I want a woman," said Hossein. He was drunk. They had finished the first bottle of home brew and started a second.

"Do you want a disease, too?" asked the young man. "Because they go together."

"You are too careful. What's the matter with you? Have you been visiting Qazvin?" That was an insult. Iranians liked to joke that the men of the city of Qazvin, northwest of Tehran, were all homosexuals.

"Fuck you, my dear cousin," said the young man. "We'll go wherever you want."

Hossein drove to a little coffeehouse called Le Gentil on Gandhi Street, a few blocks over from Vali Asr. He said there would be pretty girls there—foreign ones, which meant girls who maybe would fool around. But when they arrived the tables were filled with couples, and the few single women drew back from them. Hossein still looked too much like a Revolutionary Guard. That was his problem. He wanted to be a rebel now, but he still looked like a soldier of Allah. Hossein went out to his car to smoke some opium. When he came back he was talking too fast.

"They screwed me, you know that!" Hossein growled. "They can shit on their beards, for all I care."

"Shhh!" said the young scientist. "Of course I know that, but keep your voice down. You never know who's listening, even in a *gherti* place like this."

"They screwed me," Hossein repeated. "I did everything they asked me to. I did more than they asked me to. Nobody understood the imam's line better than me. Nobody felt the blood of the martyrs like me. But then they screwed me."

"Hayf," said the young man. A shame. "It was wrong what they did. Everyone knows that. You must get over it. Move on, cousin."

"Agh! Do you know why I lost my position? Because I caught them stealing. That's the reason. Otherwise I would still be a colonel and tell them what to do. They are dogs! *Pedar-sag.* The sons of dogs. No, they are the *shit* of the dogs on the bottom of my shoes!"

"Kesafat!" muttered a woman at a nearby table. Filth. She was embarrassed by this loud, sloppy *pasdaran*, sitting in what was supposed to be a cosmopolitan café.

"Shhh!!" said the young man again. His cousin was making him nervous. Even in a noisy café, the police had informants.

"Yes, I did. I caught them stealing. Our company was very, you know, quiet-quiet. It did business abroad. I don't have to tell you . . . you know what. So they thought they could take money and no one would see. But I saw. And I tried to stop them. And now . . ."

Hossein stopped as the misery of his current circumstances enveloped him.

"And now you should go home," said the young

man. But Hossein ignored him. He leaned over and whispered hoarsely in his cousin's ear. His breath reeked of alcohol.

"Do you think I could get a job in America? Or in Germany, I don't care."

"Sure. If you can get there."

"But that is what I mean, cousin. Can you help me? My stick is broken, you know. Nobody will help me except you."

This was what the young man feared most. That his cousin, in his misery, would try to use him to escape. This was truly dangerous, to be dragged down by a ruined ex-*pasdaran* with too many enemies.

"I don't think I can help, my dear."

"But you have power, cousin. You have connections. You have everything. We all know what you do. We know you are part of the network."

"Be quiet!" said the young man sharply. "That's enough. Let's go."

Hossein wagged his finger at his cousin. *"Khak tu saret."* Dirt on your head. It was almost a curse.

"Quiet," repeated the scientist.

"You are ungrateful. You are one of them, the privileged ones, so you think you can shit on your cousin when he is in need. How can you say this? For the memory of your father, my dear uncle, you should help me. You must help me. Otherwise I don't know what I will do. I don't know. It is so hard, to keep a face on . . ."

There were tears trickling down Hossein's cheeks. The young man put his arm around his cousin's shoulder. People were watching, but he didn't care anymore.

"I will try to help you, Hossein. I will do what I can. But you must be very careful now. We all live on the edge of a knife. You know that. If you slip, it will cut you."

The young man paid the bill and helped Hossein out of the café and back onto the street toward the car. Hossein was in no condition to drive, so the young man took them back to Hossein's apartment off Mirdamad Avenue. He had passed out in the car, so they both slept there in the Peugeot for a few hours, until it was dawn, and then the young man went to look for a taxi to take him back to his apartment in Yoosef Abad.

He had a headache from the booze. His eyes were bloodshot. To rouse himself, he thought of his work. They had scheduled more tests of the equipment this week. Probably more failures. They would go to the special laboratory where they kept the most sensitive instruments. Probably he would have to stay overnight, perhaps for the whole week.

The stupid *pasdaran* who ran the program would ask him to take the measurements and calculate the pulses to milliseconds. They had all the power, but not enough knowledge. They wouldn't explain to him how his piece fit with the other parts of the puzzle, but he knew. They all knew. Every time an experiment failed, it made the young man happy. He would pretend to be angry like the others, but inside he was happy. He did not want the program to succeed. That was one of the seeds of betrayal, the fact that he was devoting all his brainpower to a project he hoped would fail. That had told him something.

He made himself concentrate. His brain felt tight against his skull. It must be the dehydration, caused by the alcohol. He looked for a taxi. He would go home and shower, and then be in the office early. He would be the dedicated one. That was his mask. He was a scientist. He would be diligent. He would try to make his experiments work, and hope that they continued to fail.

The police in their bottle green uniforms were out early. They were suspicious, when they saw a young man on the streets at this hour. He must have been drinking, or whoring, or spying, or some other bad thing. The young man searched in his pocket for a chocolate, to hide the smell on his breath, but the candies were all gone. He slowed his step as a policeman walked toward him and asked for his identification. The policeman had a sneer on his face, thinking he would make an arrest, or at least take a good bribe, until he studied the young man's papers. They identified him as a special government employee, with special permissions.

Now it was the policeman who was frightened. He made a slight bow and apologized, and then he apologized again. But there was a glint in his eye, as if he suspected that something must be wrong with this special servant of the revolution that he was walking the streets in wrinkled clothes just after dawn on a midsummer morning.

5

WASHINGTON

Harry Pappas watched the wind rustle the trees outside the old headquarters building. The summer sky was darkening out west, up the Potomac River. The rain would begin soon. He closed his eyes. On summer days like this, he used to take his son Alex out sailing. Harry would leave work early and pick up Alex at home, and they would drive to a marina south of the airport. In July, the thunderstorms would arrive almost every evening. The slack Potomac would begin to churn; the cypress trees by the river would billow and bend. Alex loved it. Even when the bolts of lightning began to spark in the far distance, he would want to continue.

They would race out of the marina on a strong breeze. When the tide was out, the river was so shallow near the shore that they would have to pull up the centerboard to clear the bottom, so that they could barely tack. But in the deeper water of mid-river, with the board down, a strong puff would make the boat heel over so far they would bury the lee rail, with water spilling into the cockpit. Alex would head the boat off the wind even farther, deeper into the puff, hiking out to keep the small boat from flipping over. Harry would hold on tight to the gunwales, inwardly pleased that he had a daredevil for a son.

They would watch the rain move downriver toward them, an advancing sheet of liquid darkness. The air would chill a bit just before it came, and the first bolts of lightning would crack. They would race for the cover of shore and scramble up the riverbank while the rain pelted down and the lightning sliced a jagged line to the water. Sometimes Alex would scream, an animal howl of pure pleasure to be out there with his father amid this raw energy of nature. He was a risk taker, always. But he trusted his father to make sure it wasn't too crazy a risk—to pull him out of the river before the lightning actually hit. That was the worst of it for Pappas. His son had trusted him.

Pappas opened his eyes. It was a mistake to remember. The only way out was forward. Otherwise he would just give up.

Pappas moved quickly to create the new compartment in which Dr. Ali would live. The first step was to send an answer to the Hotmail account. The

Iranian was waiting. He knew how to hide in the entrails of the Internet—how to send a message from a computer and an ISP that bore none of his fingerprints. He knew all of these things, assuming that he existed at all.

Pappas prepared the response message. It was one of several the agency had designed to contact virtual walk-ins. The text was a simple email in the recipient's native language, in this case Farsi. It said: "We received your message. We wish you a happy and peaceful summer." If anyone was monitoring the line with a packet sniffer, that's all they would see. But once the Hotmail account was opened with the proper password, it would display another message, with a set of instructions that told the recipient how to establish encrypted communications through what amounted to a hidden virtual private network.

The agency usually asked its new recruits to wait sixty days before contacting the CIA again, to make sure there was no electronic or physical surveillance. But in this case, the need for communication was too urgent. The Iranian nuclear program was "an imminent threat to global peace and security," according to the White House. The Iranians supposedly had halted their actual weaponization project a few years before, but nobody was really sure if that was true. There were people in the administration who wanted to go to war, now, to stop the Iranians from making any more progress.

Pappas assumed that Fox was a member of this party of war, but he had never asked him, not wanting to hear the response. Policy was for downtown, and for ambitious men like Arthur Fox.

Where and when will we hold our next meeting? That was always the first question for an agent, virtual or physical. You asked it first because you never knew if contact might suddenly be disrupted. So in his encrypted response message, Pappas asked the basics: Can you travel? Can we contact you in your home country? Where do we reach you? He told Dr. Ali to wait fifteen days before responding to the secure web address using the agency's encryption system. Fifteen days was too quick. Good tradecraft would have dictated a longer delay, to sanitize contact. But there wasn't time.

Pappas summoned Marcia Hill again. He wanted to talk, but not with Arthur Fox or the director or anyone else who could come back and bite him if he said something wrong. Marcia was good that way. She had stopped believing in the institution a long time ago, and now her loyalty was to people only. He wanted one of the kids around, too, so he asked Martin Vitter, Marcia's operations chief, who had just come back from Iraq and who reminded him, in his deadly seriousness about destroying "bad guys," of his son Alex.

They gathered in Pappas's windowless office.

The admin officer had brought some coffee and cookies from the cafeteria to make it seem like a proper meeting. Pappas was edgy. He wasn't comfortable with good news.

"How are we going to run this guy?" he began. "We're going to need him five years from now as much as we do today, but how do we keep him alive? How do we find him, meet him, and train him? Otherwise he's going to end up a dead man."

"Duh! Let's start with *finding* him?" said Marcia. "Right now we don't have an agent, we have an email address."

"Okay, so let's assume Dr. Ali wants to play. He answers my message and tells us how to initiate contact. Let's think about that. What do we do then? Do we try to meet him in-country?"

"Negative, sir," cut in Martin Vitter. "They'll make us, then they'll make him. Then he's dead. Meet him outside. Get him to Dubai or Turkey, where we have some operational control."

"But suppose he can't travel," said Pappas.

"Everyone travels at Nowruz, right?" Nowruz was the Persian New Year.

"Wrong," said Marcia. "The nuclear people are on a no-travel list now. Even at Nowruz. And besides, that's nine months off. They don't give these guys pilgrimage visas, even. I think we have to meet him in Iran."

Pappas thought about it for a moment. The right answer was outside, but outside was impossible.

"I agree with Marcia. If he's really part of the nuclear program, they won't let him out. We have to poke him at home. So how do we do that?"

He wasn't asking them, really. He answered the question himself.

"First we get him a cov-comm device in Tehran. Right? We don't try to meet face-to-face at all. We leave it for him at a drop. In a park somewhere. We get someone who's totally clean to lay it down. A traveler who has no record with us. Someone with a Turkish passport, maybe Kuwaiti. Someone with balls who will just go into the park, drop the toy, and get the fuck out of there. And then Dr. Ali picks it up, and bingo, we have communication. And then we go from there."

"What kind of toy?" asked Marcia. "What does it look like?"

"I don't know. A rock. A clod of dirt. A soda pop can. Whatever the tech people say will blend with the drop site."

"Sounds kind of dry," said Marcia. "Iranians like a kiss. Something to tell them you love them."

"Okay. As soon as we know who he is, we reach out and touch him. We send something to him, unmarked, that could only come from us. Perfume for his wife. Medicine for his kids. Something that says 'America loves you.' Something that says 'Even right here in the center of fucking Tehran, in the goon capital of the world, we can put something on your doorstep.'"

Vitter's eyes were wide as saucers. This was how he wanted the CIA to be. All-powerful, able to navigate every alleyway on the planet.

Marcia Hill brought them back to reality.

"We don't have an address, remember? We don't know where the guy lives or works. We don't know if he's young or old. We don't know if he has a wife or kids, let alone whether they like perfume or need drugs. As a matter of fact, dear boys, we do not know whether Dr. Ali is a man or a woman. What if *she* is reading *Lolita* in Tehran this summer and thinks it's a turn-on to send messages to the CIA? Consider that."

"You're a pain, Marcia. You know that?" Pappas smiled. "Let's start again. This time, let's assume that our boy doesn't want to make contact at all. No meet. No address. No cov-comm device. No nothing. He's too scared. What do we do then?"

"We let him write the rules," said Marcia. "He's going to do that anyway."

"No way!" said Harry. "Without a handle on him, we can't evaluate what he says. He may be playing us. How would we know? We have to find him."

"*How,* Harry?" Her voice was respectful but insistent.

"I don't know," admitted Pappas. "I'm thinking about it."

Pappas still had to kill Dr. Ali in the cable traffic. He had to cover the tracks so that people wouldn't ask questions about the Iranian VW or pass along corridor gossip. And Harry was a good liar: as a young officer, he had felt uncomfortable with that part of the job, until he realized that *was* the job.

The CIA had burned too many Iranian agents already. Like the postal screwup, in which the same translator had written the SW letters to the whole string of Iranian agents, all addressed in the same neat script. They spent hundreds of hours finding accommodation addresses all over Germany to receive the "secret writing" correspondence, but somehow nobody thought to wonder if the Iranians would notice so many messages in identical handwriting. And a dozen years later came the dead-drop screwup—in which an agent was told to collect a message from a site in a Tehran park that was so blindingly obvious that officers from MOI—the country's intelligence service—staked it out and waited for the poor fool to show up. The Iran task force had made so many mistakes over the past twenty-five years, it was astounding that any Iranian still thought of sharing secrets with the CIA. That was the kicker with Dr. Ali: Was he stupid, or reckless? Or was he the most dubious case of all—a spy who just wanted to do the right thing?

Pappas's first phony message was to Fox in Counter-Proliferation, with copies to the rest of the distribution list, asking if they could advise about the mysterious message from Iran. In the special channel of the new SAP, he sent Fox a prepared response. It said that the CP Division had examined the document and concluded it had been used in a set of Pakistani centrifuge specifications that were widely available on the Internet. That was sent to the full distribution list as well. The implicit message was that the Dr. Ali case, BQTANK, looked like a bust—a promising initial contact that turned out to be a hoax.

Pappas waited a few days and then had the head of the Information Operations Center send out another message, again to the full distribution list. The computer center had done some technical work inside the Hotmail servers, the message said. The "doktor.ali" account had been opened by a computer in Tehran that had been purchased by the Ministry of the Interior. That was a lie, too. The IOC had tried to establish the precise origination of the message, but they couldn't. Dr. Ali was too clever.

That nailed it, in terms of the legend. So far as anyone outside the SAP compartment would know, Dr. Ali was a hoax—worse, even. He was probably an Iranian provocation, created by the MOI. Pappas made it official by sending out a "burn notice" that all agency personnel should avoid any contact, electronic or otherwise, with the Iranian. Any attempts by "Dr. Ali" to resume communication should be reported to Pappas personally. That was it. The Iranian VW was dead and gone, as far as the agency's official traces would show.

Harry brought one other intelligence service into the loop, but only at the highest level. By secure encrypted cable, he informed his friend Adrian Winkler, the chief of staff of the British Secret Intelligence Service, that the agency had a new lead that had come in via the website. The new source appeared to have access to the Iranian nuclear program, but the agency was still struggling to confirm his information and discover, if it could, his identity. Harry gave the few other details they had, and asked if they rang any bells in London.

He sent the cable for two reasons: he wanted to make sure that the British were not running the same agent; and he had a glimmer in the far horizon of his mind that he might need their help at some point in the future.

Harry took his wife Andrea to the movies that Friday night. It was a "summer blockbuster," one of those movies that had gotten its start with a character from a comic book, and then had been stretched through so many remakes there wasn't much left. They sat through the first half, but when yet another tedious special-effects sequence was cranking up, Andrea nudged her husband.

"I hate this movie," she said.

"So do I," whispered Harry.

"Then let's go."

They walked out, pissing off all the people who had to miss a second or two of computer-generated nonsense as they stepped past knees and ankles along the row of seats.

They had dinner at Legal Sea Foods in Tysons Corner. It was the first place Harry thought of, because his agency friends often came there for lunch. Andrea ordered a piña colada, which she usually did only on vacation. Harry had a whiskey, and then another. The two were getting pleasantly plastered. It felt like the first time they had relaxed together in several years.

Andrea asked Harry a question she wondered about sometimes, especially during the hard times, but would only have asked him when she was a little tipsy. Remind her why had he joined the CIA in the first place? He had seemed happy as an army officer when she first met him in Worcester. Why had he traded that for such a complicated life?

"My father wanted me to do it," said Harry, looking at his glass and taking another gulp. "He loved the CIA."

"Why?" she pressed. "What had it ever done for him?"

"Matter of honor," said Harry. "He thought we owed them. He was a Greek, to a fault. So if he made a friend, that was it, friend for life. Before I

72

was born, when he was still living in Greece, he got involved in the fighting. They had a civil war in the late 1940s. People forget that. My dad was on the side fighting the communists. The Americans helped him. It wasn't the CIA back then. They called it something else. But they were American spies, basically. They gave him weapons and money, and when he got wounded they helped him come to America. They saved his life. That was what he always told me."

"So he wanted you to join up?"

"The army, yes. And then when I got pitched by the agency, I asked him what he thought. I wasn't supposed to, but I couldn't help it. We were Greeks. We didn't have secrets from each other. I had never seen him so happy. He kissed me. Tears were streaming down his face."

"So it's a chain," said Andrea. "Father to son, father to son."

She didn't say it bitterly or angrily. It was just the truth.

6

TEHRAN

The young Iranian was in his office in Jamaran, reading back articles from the *American Journal of Physics*, when they came for him. He didn't hear the knock because he was listening to his iPod while he read, so they had to push the door open.

The young man rose with a start, pulling the buds from his ears. Two burly men entered the room. They wore dark green suits the color of a fir tree. Behind them stood Dr. Bazargan, the laboratory director. He was trying to maintain his dignity, but without much success.

"Sobh bekheyr, Doktor," said one of the men in plain clothes, bidding the scientist good morning. He took out an official card and proffered it toward the young man. It identified him as an officer of the Etelaat-e Sepah, the Revolutionary Guard's intelligence service, which had responsibility for the security of the nuclear program.

"Salamat baush," continued the officer. Good health to you. He observed the rituals of Muslim greeting, even when he barged in the door.

"Alhamdollah," returned the young Iranian. Thanks God. He felt a moistness glistening on his forehead. He wanted to flee, but that was impossible. Be calm, he told himself. They have come like this before. It is probably nothing.

"We would like to ask you some questions, Doctor."

"Yes, certainly. Please sit down." He felt naked. He wished he had a beard to hide behind, instead of showing all this skin.

"I am afraid your office would not be convenient. I think some other place. We have apologized to Dr. Bazargan." He nodded toward the director, still standing anxiously just outside the door.

74

"My work is important," said the young scientist. That was his only card of authority.

"Yes, Doctor. Of course. Thanks God."

The officer did not say that it was all routine, that it would be over quickly, that he would be back at work soon. The young man reached in his pocket for his handkerchief and patted his forehead before it got wetter. The handkerchief felt cool on the skin and the sweat stopped as suddenly as it had begun. Perhaps this would be easy. They couldn't know. He had been careful.

The scientist reached for his valise, but the officer told him not to bring anything except his passport. The two security men followed him out the door, one on either side, a few steps behind. As they entered the main corridor, faces peered out from the other offices to see who the authorities had summoned. The office in Jamaran was morbid that way. They never talked about security, but every six months or so someone disappeared and never came back. Usually the person resurfaced on some other island of the scientific archipelago—thinner, quieter, more cautious. Nobody ever spoke about what happened. That was part of the price of working on sensitive projects. You never knew when the floor under you might give way, or how far you might fall.

The young man could hear his own footsteps echoing in the corridor. He walked past several of his friends. One winked and gave a faint wave, but the others looked away.

The officers led the young doctor to a new black Samand sedan and put him in the backseat. They asked if he wanted the air-conditioning on, and when he said yes, they turned it up full blast. There was a police radio in the front seat, and the driver had a fat pistol in a shoulder holster. On the dashboard was a red light and a siren, but they didn't turn it on. The young man waited for the blindfold. It was whispered that when the security men took people away to interrogation, they blindfolded them. But not today.

Outside it was high summer in Tehran. People with money had gone to their villas on the Caspian Sea or, if they had real money, to the Cap d'Antibes or the Costa del Sol. The city was a mélange of sounds and smells: ripe melons in the market stalls; kebabs grilling on outdoor charcoals in the parks; the birdsong of the car horns. In the heat, people didn't try so hard to look pious.

As they drove past one of the offices of the Ministry of Intelligence, the lead officer muttered a curse that sounded like, *"Gooz be reeshet,"* which meant, roughly, "Fart on your beard." The young scientist laughed, despite his predicament. It was well known that the Revolutionary Guard hated the Ministry of Intelligence. It was a common joke around town—a rivalry like between Persepolis and Esteghlal in soccer.

A silence settled around the car. It was a bubble, floating among other bubbles. The young man waited for the fear to come back, but it didn't. Instead he felt an odd sense of power. He was in control. They were guessing; he knew.

They took the scientist to a building he had never seen before. It was off the Resalat Highway, north of the airport. It was late morning, so the traffic was light. Nobody talked on the way over— not the driver, not the headman in the green suit, not his thickset assistant who sat alongside in the backseat and who probably had a gun, too, under his ill-fitting jacket.

The young man tried to lose himself in the ordinary sights of Tehran out the window. The teenage boy talking on his cell phone on the sidewalk; the girls primping in the backseat of the car next to them, perhaps off to have their toenails polished or their legs waxed. The space needle in Nasr Park, so tall and ugly; which people imagined was really a big listening tower for the secret police. The noisy knot of young men outside the *filmi* shop in Sadegiyeh Square that rented the latest pirated DVDs. The *kebabis* beckoning people for a mid-morning snack.

The headman told the driver to turn right near the Azadi Monument on the edge of the airport. *Azadi.* Freedom. What a joke. Its four massive pillars had been built by the shah in 1971 to last for all the generations of Pahlavi rulers to come. That dynasty survived just eight more years. The young man's father had come here to protest the shah, in the crazy days of the revolution. *Ostad*, the young bearded men had called his father. Honored teacher. The scientist was only a baby at the time, but he had heard the stories retold so often. He knew this was why the Revolutionary Guard and the MOI and all the other guardians of the new regime had trusted him, even though he was from the old elite. They reasoned that he was a child of the revolution. He would feed off revenge. And they were right in that, although not in the way they imagined.

The car turned into a side street, and then another, and soon they were at a walled compound. There were guards at the front gate; and then, at a second gate, there was a more elaborate checkpoint. They searched the young man thoroughly, emptying every item from his pocket: his pens, his wallet, his eyeglasses. They patted him down and then, not satisfied, they took him into a room and a guard asked him to drop his trousers. That was unusual. Even in the most secret parts of the archipelago, they did not shame people in that way. As he pulled his pants back on a few moments later, he gathered what he imagined as an invisible cloak around him, the cloak his father had described as his solace and protection, which was woven of fear.

The office was modern, like a doctor's conference room. The interrogator sat behind a teak desk. He had the latest issue of *The Economist* in front of him, and a copy of the *International Herald Tribune* that was just a day old. He must be very powerful. As the young scientist entered the office, the interrogator was looking at a flat-screen monitor. He tapped in a few commands and then studied what appeared on the screen and smiled. A formula for interrogation, perhaps.

The interrogator turned toward the scientist. He wore a goatee that was trimmed neatly, like a jazz musician's, and there was an unlikely twinkle in his eye.

"Hello, Esteemed Doctor," said the interrogator. He said that his name was Mehdi Esfahani, and he showed the young man his identification card from his service, the Etelaat-e Sepah, as if that made it all proper. He looked very merry, almost as if he were trying to suppress a chuckle. He stared back at the screen and then laughed aloud.

"I am sorry, Doctor. Do you like jokes? The American kind. From the Internet, you know. Jokes about blond women who are stupid. Jokes about priests, rabbis, and ministers. Jokes about people called 'rednecks.' I collect them, you see. People send them to me from all over. Even from America. Can you imagine that? Do you like them, these Internet jokes?"

The scientist didn't know how to respond. The question was so odd. What was the right answer?

"A little, I guess. I don't see them very often. My work—"

"Yes, yes, I know. Your work. But you use the Internet of course."

"Yes, for my work." What was he getting at? Did he know something? The scientist couldn't tell, the man's manner was so peculiar.

"My favorite are the redneck jokes. Do you know this word? The Americans use it to describe someone who is not too smart. You know you're a redneck when your wife has to move the transmission to take a bath. That is one." He laughed aloud. "That is very funny, don't you think? You know you're a redneck when your house gets a parking ticket. Isn't that amusing? They live in mobile homes, apparently, these rednecks."

Mehdi Esfahani was waiting for the young scientist to laugh, but there was silence.

"You do not understand these jokes?"

"I guess not, Brother Inspector. I am sorry." The young man was confused, in addition to being frightened.

"Well, pity, I had hoped you had more of a sense of humor. We have enough serious ones, I think. But you, a bright boy, good background. Studied abroad. Access to foreign literature. You should have a sense of humor. Be funny. Tell jokes. But you look so serious. You must be frightened. Is that it?"

"Yes, I guess so. I mean, I do have a sense of humor, Brother Inspector. But not so much now."

"Because you are afraid?"

"Yes."

"What are you afraid of?"

"Of you, Brother Inspector. You confuse me."

"Don't be a donkey, Doctor. Do know why you are here?"

"No," said the young man.

"Yes you do," said the interrogator. "Everyone who comes here knows why."

"And why is that, sir?"

"Because you did something wrong. Otherwise, why would we have brought you? The service never makes mistakes. You *do* know what the reason is, and it is *my* job to help you find it." He stroked the whiskers of his goatee. In another situation, he would have seemed entirely ridiculous, like an Iranian Inspector Clouseau. But in this case, the eccentricity only made him more menacing.

"Tell me about your time at the University of Heidelberg," said the interrogator.

"I've already told the Etelaat everything I can remember, Brother Inspector. Many times. They questioned me once a week, for nearly a year, when I came home."

"Yes, yes. I know. But that was routine questioning. This is special."

"Why special, sir?"

"Because you are special, my dear. You have knowledge that is a prize—one so valuable that all the gold in Tehran could not buy it. So please, tell me about Germany. Who was your best friend there?"

"I told the others before. I had no friends. The German boys did not like me."

"Yes, I know. I have read the file. But there was a girl, wasn't there? A German girl."

"Trudi."

"Yes, Trudi. Why don't you tell me about her?"

"There is nothing to tell, Brother Inspector. I have explained before. She was very pretty. I thought perhaps she would, you know . . ."

"Have sex with you."

"Yes. That was very wrong, I'm sure. She was not a Muslim. But she would talk to me, when no one else would. She would sit with me in the café sometimes. She would ask me about Iran. She would listen to my stories. I was very lonely."

"Did she have large breasts?"

The young scientist sat back in his chair with a start. Was this his crime, that he had let himself imagine having sex with a German physics student?

"I don't know. I think so. I never touched them. She wanted me to, perhaps. But I wouldn't. I was too frightened. Then I stopped seeing her. She tried, Brother Inspector. But I was not impure. I knew that it would be *haram* to have her, even as a temporary wife. So I stayed away."

"Yes, that's in the file. All that." Mehdi the interrogator paused and fingered his goatee again. He leaned toward the young scientist. His eyes were flashing suddenly.

"Did you know that she was an Israeli? This Trudi? Did you know that?"

The color went out of the young man's cheeks. The beads of perspiration formed immediately on his forehead.

"No she wasn't," the young man answered. "She was a German. I met her father. He was a businessman."

"He was an Israeli, too. Two passports. An agent of their famous Mossad."

"How do you know this? It is a lie. If it is true, why didn't anyone ask me about it when I first came home?"

"We didn't know it then. We know it now. We have our friends in the German security service, you see. We can recruit them, just as they try to recruit us. We can pretend to be Americans, just as they do. Israelis, even. Oh yes. We are everywhere."

"What did they tell you? My God! What do you know?"

"Trudi was studying physics at the Max Planck Institute, just like you. But her job was to look for young Iranian students. Who were lonely. Who wanted to have sex with a German girl. Who might be useful later. The German service was watching. They listened to her phone calls. They monitored her mail. They watched her. It took us many years to get this file, but now we have it. There are several Iranian names, I am sorry to say. And yours, my dear Doctor, is one."

The young man was trying to find his balance. He knew that if this was his "crime," he was safe. He had said nothing to Trudi, let alone her father. He had broken off contact. He had done just what a servant of the revolution was supposed to do, which was nothing. The interrogator was still waiting for an answer.

"I have told you everything, Brother Inspector. I denied nothing, because there is nothing to hide. My father warned me about the foreign spies and their tricks. We talked about it before I left Tehran. Your people warned me. Before, during, after. That is why I was careful. That is why avoided the German girls."

"Who is Hans?"

The young man shifted awkwardly in his chair. The sweat started again.

"Who is Hans?" repeated the interrogator. "We know that Trudi received messages from him. But we think there was no Hans. We think this was a code name."

The young Iranian felt a rattle inside, a tremor that wanted to come out. It was like a suppressed sneeze that left you quivering. They knew. It was useless to lie. If this was his crime, he would survive.

"I was Hans," he said.

"Why did you use a code name? If this relationship was so innocent and you had nothing to hide, why did you make up a false name?"

How could he explain? The truth was so pathetic. "Hans" was his imaginary name for himself. He had begun calling himself that in his mind when he first arrived as a student in Heidelberg. It began as a defense. He was embarrassed about his big nose, and his thick black hair that always looked greasy, even when he had just washed it. He wanted to have cold blue eyes and frozen blood in his veins, like the German boys, and not to have emotions that were always about to boil over like the water in a teakettle. He wanted a hairless body like the German boys, instead of his matted torso from the monkey world of the East. He wanted one of the big-breasted German girls who made him hard when he was sitting at his desk in the library, trying to read his physics text books. He was embarrassed about who he was, so in his mind, he imagined another person who was living inside this Iranian body, and that person's name was "Hans."

"I was ashamed," said the young man. "I was embarrassed to be an Iranian, so I made up this German name for myself. Trudi thought it was funny. So when I sent her an email or I called her, I would say, 'This is Hans.'"

The interrogator shook his head. "That story is completely absurd, Doctor. But that does not mean it is true."

• • •

Mehdi Esfahani continued with his questions for another two hours. He asked about details of the meetings with Trudi, and about what she had asked him. He asked the young man to repeat several times the story of how he had broken off his contact with Trudi, after she propositioned him, and he got him to admit that one reason he had done so was that he was afraid she was a spy. His father had warned him about spies, and yes, he was afraid that she might be one. She had tried to contact him again, several times, but he had not responded. That was the truth. That was what made it easy.

The questions continued, but the interrogator already seemed to know the answers, and it became increasingly obvious that the real point of this interview had been to see if the young man lied. Their agent in the German security service, whoever he was, had told them that Trudi's contacts with the Iranian boy at the Max Planck Institute had come to nothing. But they wanted to see for themselves.

There was a pause, at the end of one more string of questions about Trudi's efforts to reestablish contact, after he had broken it off.

"How do you know when you're a redneck?" asked Esfahani.

"I am very sorry, sir. I am sure that I do not know."

"You know you're a redneck when you light a

match in the bathroom and it blows your house off its wheels."

The young man stared at the interrogator. Finally he understood. He tried to laugh, feebly.

"Really, you are pathetic. No sense of humor. That is the only thing that is suspicious about you. A normal man has a life. He is married by now. He is not so careful. But you, I do not understand. What are you so afraid of? Why don't you start living?"

The young man felt light-headed that afternoon when he returned to his apartment in Yoosef Abad. He had a peculiar feeling of invulnerability, like a man who has been shot at close range and survived. It was not the time for him to be caught. He was a fatalist in that way. If it had been time, he would have panicked in the interrogation room and confessed to his real sin. If it had been time, he would have told a lie they could easily have discovered. If it had been time, he would be spending this night in prison.

But it was not time. It was not God's will that he should be caught, so it must be God's will that he should not be caught. They were looking for him, but they did not see. He was invisible. If he could drop a pebble into the water, he could drop a stone.

Late that afternoon, Mehdi Esfahani received a visit from a man he knew only by his Arabic pseudonyms. He was sometimes called *Al-Sadiq*, "the Friend," but more often he was referred to as *Al-Majnoun*, "the Crazy One," by the few Iranians who knew of his existence. That was the name Mehdi knew him by. His real name was Badr, or Sadr, or something else entirely, nobody seemed to be sure. Mehdi Esfahani was a powerful man in the intelligence service, and he was frightened of few people. But he was frightened by Al-Majnoun.

Al-Majnoun was a Lebanese Shiite who had come to Tehran in the mid-1980s. It was said by the few people who claimed to know anything about him that he had been involved in the kidnapping and torture of the CIA station chief in Beirut in 1984, and that he had needed to escape to Iran to cool down. He had taken up a kind of permanent shadow residence in Tehran, under the patronage of a wing of the Revolutionary Guard's intelligence service. He operated independently of the normal bureaucracies—both at the Guard and the intelligence ministry. He was a lone wolf, an enforcer. It was said that he was sent on special projects, at home and abroad, and that he had unusually wide latitude. When people in the regular services tried to question his missions, or even to probe for details, they usually regretted it. In two cases, it was said that his rivals had ended up dead—in cases that were never explained even to officials at the highest level.

That was why people in the bureaucracies were

afraid of "the Crazy One." It was clear that he had the most powerful patronage—some even whispered that he reported ultimately to the Supreme Leader himself and was his personal intelligence adviser. There were stories that the two men liked to visit together, and lie on the tufted cushions of the leader's palace reading each other couplets of ancient Persian and Arabic poetry. But nobody knew. That was the problem. And so when Al-Majnoun knocked on Mehdi's door late that afternoon, the interrogator worried that he had done something very wrong.

"Allah y'atik al afia," said the Crazy One, in Lebanese Arabic dialect. He had learned to speak passable Farsi, but he often lapsed into his own language.

The Lebanese was not an imposing man, physically. He was gaunt and walked with a bit of a stoop and shuffle, as if he were an older man. He usually wore sunglasses, even indoors, which was partly to mask his appearance and partly to hide the scars from his surgeries. It was this plastic surgery that made Al-Majnoun such a singular person, and gave him a transient, elusive appearance. It was said that he had been operated on at least twice to disguise his appearance after he fled Beirut. The surgeries had left traces of two different faces. There was one above the mouth—the soft eyes, rounded nose, and prominent cheekbones of a

European—and one below. That second face had a cruel Eastern set to the mouth and chin. It was a face that was going in two directions at once, it seemed, and there were the odd little lumps of tissue that remained from the several surgeries. It was more a mask, really, than a face.

Mehdi wished his visitor good health and bid him take a seat. He inquired what had brought such a senior figure to this humble outpost of the far-flung realms of intelligence.

"I have a new assignment," said Al-Majnoun. He took off his sunglasses as he spoke, revealing the eyes. The surgeon had botched his work around the edges, leaving little lines where the skin had been cut and drawn and the stitches sewed.

"What is that assignment, General? I am sure that I am at your service." The interrogator didn't know how to address his guest, so he chose a high military rank.

"I have been asked to look at penetration of the program." Al-Majnoun did not have to say the nuclear weapons program. That much was understood.

"Why, General? Is there reason to be concerned?"

Al-Majnoun stroked his lower lip. It was tight, like the rest of his face. It was impossible to be sure whether these creased lips had been chapped from the wind and sun, or cut by the surgeon's knife. He spoke in a voice that was thin and reedy, from high in the throat rather than deep down.

"Information is like the dust in the wind, Brother Inspector. We do not know where it is blowing. What we have is more like a feeling. Sometimes we know that a door is open, even if we do not see it or feel it. We sense a rustle of wind. Or there is a little flutter at a curtain. Or we hear a creak in the floor that should not be sounding. We sense it before we know it. Perhaps this is the same."

"But is there a leak?"

Mehdi nervously fingered the hairs of his goatee between his thumb and forefinger. He feared that he was going to be blamed for something.

Al-Majnoun laughed. It sounded more like a cough, heavy with phlegm. "Not a leak, my friend. More like an opening through which a leak might pass."

Mehdi nodded, but he didn't understand. He wanted to show that he was doing his job, so that he wouldn't be blamed later if something went wrong.

"We are always vigilant, General. I had a boy in here today, from the research center in Jamaran. Very sensitive work. I took him through his paces. We do that every day, sir. Every day, I assure you. A tight, serious boy, this one was. Studied in Germany."

"Yes, I know," said Al-Majnoun, nodding.

Mehdi continued on, thinking that Al-Majnoun was praising his work in general.

"This one gave the right answers. He did not lie.

That is the best test. I think. One lie, and there will be others. But this one told me the truth."

"Yes, I know," repeated the Lebanese. This time Mehdi realized that he was referring specifically to the young physicist who had visited that afternoon. "I want to make sure that the boy's case is handled . . . properly."

"I keep the file open, General. I wait for the lie. But I am also opening another file, and another. That is the way for us, isn't it? We must suspect everyone. But we must watch and wait for the case to play itself out, or else we have nothing. Isn't that right?"

Al-Majnoun didn't answer Mehdi Esfahani's question. He put his sunglasses back on the bridge of his man-made nose, rose from his chair, and walked out of the room.

7

WASHINGTON

Harry Pappas got a call in early August from the chief of the Information Operations Center. He supervised the agency's public website, and he was cleared for the Dr. Ali special-access program. Pappas was at Bethany Beach with his wife and daughter, taking a few days of vacation and trying to forget how screwed up everything was. When he went walking along the beach at night, he heard his son's voice in the waves—a hollow imaginary echo like the sound of the sea in a seashell. But he was glad of it. He worried sometimes now that he might forget what Alex had sounded like.

"I think your Iranian friend is back," said the chief of the Information Operations Center.

"How's that?" Pappas held his breath for a moment.

"We just got another message over the transom from Iran," continued the IOC chief. "We ran traces. It's from a sheet-metal factory in Shiraz, routed via a server in Turkey, but that's chaff. The size of this message is larger, but the tags look similar. This guy is good."

"Sweet," said Pappas. "God is Great."

He had been worried that Dr. Ali was dead. He hadn't resumed communication after fifteen days as Pappas had requested, and he remained silent for the next thirty days. Pappas had been like an uptight parent waiting for a child to return home. What had gone wrong? They had spooked him. They had made a mistake without realizing it. The return message had scared him off. Or worse, he had been discovered. But now he was back.

"What do you want me to do?"

"Get it out of the system, right now. Give it a scrub. I'll be back in Washington tonight."

"What's the rush? I thought you were on vacation."

"We won't get another chance like this. If it's our man, we need to reel him in quick."

Pappas drove the Jeep Cherokee back to Washington that afternoon. He apologized to his wife, but she was almost relieved. Harry was lost when they were alone. He had been away for a full year, in 2004, when he was in Baghdad. Now he was away even when he was at home. She had her own life. She taught at an elementary school in Fairfax. She spent her days around children, which helped take her mind off her dead son. She was going to yoga classes, and she had joined a book group where they drank wine and the divorced women talked about their sex lives. And she had her daughter Louise—"Lulu"—though the girl had become withdrawn since her brother died, as if she blamed the parents.

Harry said he would be back that weekend to pick Andrea up. She said that would be wonderful, but she knew she would be getting a ride home with friends.

Harry went straight to the office. He blew into the main entrance, past the guards and the electronic entry gates. There was a warning sign in C Corridor, FOREIGN LIAISON IN AREA, and he saw a group of visitors he guessed were Malaysian or Indonesian, tidy little men in black suits. He bowled past them, up the ramp way into Persia House. His secretary had already left for the day, but the luminous, cherubic face of Hussein watched over the entry room. He went into his office, closed the door, and logged on to his secure computer.

When the new message came up, Pappas drank it down like a shot of whiskey. The message was in English, written in a kind of business code, as if the sender were discussing a commercial transaction. It began with an apology.

We are sorry. We received your message about sheet-metal orders, but we could not respond as you requested. Also, we do not like Hotmail anymore. We worry that our business competitors may be curious. We will use our own system. We will share an email account. The address is iranmetalworks@gmail.com. The password is "ebaga4X9." Do not send messages to or from this account. Write messages, and save them, and we will look in the "saved messages" space. We are sorry that we cannot meet with you. It is not good business. You do not know this market, but we know. Do not contact us in any other way. We will arrange the business, not you. We cannot travel to other markets. We are very sorry, but it is not wise.

The message continued with some sentences in Persian. Pappas showed the text to an Iranian-American woman who had been cleared for the SAP. She said after an hour's study that they were lines from Ferdowsi, perhaps the most famous poet in Iranian history. The translation read as follows:

He said, "Is it good or ill these signs portend?
When will my earthly life come to an end?
Who will come after me? Say who will own
This royal diadem, and belt, and throne.
Reveal this mystery, and do not lie—
Tell me this secret or prepare to die."

The email also contained a technical document. That was the prize. That was what changed everything.

Pappas waited for Tony Reddo and Adam Schwartz to analyze the details. They were seated at the little conference table in his airless office, studying the paper and trading quick technical comments that Harry didn't understand. He tried to read the cable traffic from Dubai, but he couldn't concentrate. Finally Schwartz spoke up.

"This is a big deal," he said. "In fact, if it's what we think it is, it's a *really* big deal."

"So what is it, goddammit? Don't play with me, boys."

"Do you know what a neutron generator is?" asked Reddo.

"It's something that generates neutrons," said Harry in exasperation. "That means no, I don't know what it means."

"A neutron generator is one of the ways you trigger a nuclear weapon."

"Well, holy shit! That's what this is about?"

Schwartz and Reddo both nodded.

"This is a lab report," said Schwartz, the MIT whiz kid who worked for Arthur Fox. "It describes a test in which the researchers tried to make a neutron generator perform at the level needed to produce fission in the core of a nuclear bomb. But it malfunctioned."

"Malfunctioned?"

"Yes. It didn't work. This neutron generator is sort of like a fancy spark plug. They used to call its predecessor a 'zipper,' back in the Manhattan Project. Don't ask me why. It's sort of complicated: It starts with explosives, which create energy that heats up a wafer of deuterium. Ionizes it, to be precise. The explosion accelerates this ionized deuterium so it bombards a target of tritium, and it produces a whole lot of neutrons. And the neutrons create a runaway chain reaction in the plutonium core of the bomb. And then, boom! If you follow me."

"I don't have any fucking idea what you're talking about, but so what? I take it this thing—whatever it is—would produce a nuclear explosion. If it worked."

"Correct," said Reddo. "This is one of the technical puzzles in building an actual nuclear weapon. In the test this message described, the neutron pulse fizzled. It would not have been able to start a proper chain reaction. But that isn't the point: this document says the Iranians are building a triggering device. An initial test failed, but presumably more are planned."

"Are they close?"

"I don't know. From this document, there's no way to know how serious the technical problems are, so we can't really evaluate the message that's being sent. If they keep trying it this way, they'll keep failing. But they won't, presumably."

"It's pretty fucking scary, isn't it?"

"Yes, sir." Reddo and Schwartz spoke the words in unison.

Pappas closed his eyes and tried to take in what he had just heard. This was the red flag—no, more than that, it was the wailing siren. If the message was true, the Iranians had restarted their covert weapons program. They had done some basic work on these problems through 2003, but then stopped. Or at least, that was what the agency had believed until about thirty seconds ago. Dr. Ali's message described a failure. But if they solved the trigger problem and assembled enough fissionable material, they could test a nuclear weapon. And if they did *that,* then the whole world would be turned upside down.

Pappas summoned the members of his special-access program. He gathered them with a sense of foreboding. It wasn't that he wanted to keep the intelligence to himself. He just knew that this was a piece of information that would carve its own course, like a flash flood, once it was let loose.

The Dr. Ali SAP group met the next day. Fox had returned the previous night from his vacation house on Nantucket. He was tanned and relaxed. His face didn't have Harry's perpetual look of sleeplessness; he was innocent, in that way. He didn't know the worst that life could do to someone. That was what made him talk like a tough guy; he had never really had to be very strong himself.

"We should go to the White House." Those were Fox's first words when they were seated in the conference room.

"For sure," said Harry. "But not yet. We just got the damned message."

"Don't be absurd," said Fox. "This is an Iranian declaration of war."

"No it's not. It's a document we have barely had time to analyze. To the extent we understand the message, it's telling us that they fucked something up. The White House doesn't even know about Dr. Ali. Let's not pull people's chains downtown until we're sure what we have here."

"You don't seem to understand, Harry. This is the breakout. They are back in the weaponization business. They're working on the trigger for a bomb. They're almost ready to test. That's the message. Nothing else matters. We need to take this to the

White House, *today.* If you won't, I will. And the director will back me up. He wants it briefed to the national security adviser this afternoon."

"How do you know?"

"Because I already asked him. Not to go behind your back. But I thought the admiral should be informed." The director was a navy four-star, still serving in uniform. He liked to do things by the book, but in his job at the CIA, he wasn't sure what the book was.

"You're right," said Harry. As much as he disliked Fox, he knew that he was correct. This wasn't something to sit on. But he was worried just the same. Once something went downtown, you couldn't control it anymore. It took on a life of its own.

"Excuse me?"

"I said, 'You're right.' Let's go up to the seventh floor and see the director. And we'll go downtown this afternoon, just like you wanted."

Fox didn't look happy in triumph. He was peeved that Harry would be coming along to the White House.

8

WASHINGTON

The White House, curiously, was one of those places that reminded a visitor what Washington used to be, before the layers of institutional deception had hardened and the staffs had expanded like replicating zombies in *Night of the Living Dead*. The West Wing was so small it didn't fit many people, for one thing. The president and his top aides were all jammed together in adjacent offices, so that they couldn't escape each other's company. And you realized, once inside the Secret Service cordon, that the president of the United States was just a *politician,* surrounded by courtiers and glad-handers and people seeking favors. He was as prone to making stupid decisions as any other politician, maybe more so. The real secret about the White House was that it was so ordinary—mediocrity on steroids.

The West Wing lobby was like the sitting room outside a governor's office—and not a very big state, either. A secretary manned a desk to the right of the door; sofas and easy chairs were arrayed at the three other corners of the room. Primping on the upholstery were cabinet secretaries, presidential chums from back home, conniving lobbyists, and shopworn members of Congress—all waiting to see the president and his top aides. The walls were decorated with old paintings—cowboys and Indians and landscapes of a frontier nation; Washington crossing the Delaware, that founding myth of American determination. If you added a spittoon and the smell of stale cigars, you would be back in Lincoln's White House.

Intelligence briefers didn't enter through the main lobby, though. They usually took the side door on the ground floor, which opened onto the little street between the West Wing and the Old Executive Office Building. They would arrive by car from Langley, or on foot from the intelligence community's hush-hush office on F Street. Often they would descend to the Situation Room and other hidden bunkers crammed with electronics. The CIA emissaries in this respect were part of a different White House, one that had no connection with spittoons and cigars but was a product of the imperial superstate that had emerged after 1945. They were the side-door boys, unaccountable to the politicians and petitioners camped out in the West Wing lobby.

They arrived just before 7:00 p.m. The director was wearing his summer dress navy uniform. Starched white, accented by the gold of his admirals' stars and the multicolored battle ribbons. He always looked more comfortable in his uniform, like an actor in his proper costume. Fox and Pappas followed along behind in their business suits, the former sleek and well tailored, the latter creased and baggy.

The president was hosting a cocktail reception that evening in the Yellow Parlor upstairs for a few members of Congress and their spouses. He hated that sort of socializing, it was said, but they were desperate for votes. The plan was for the agency team to brief the national security adviser, Stewart Appleman, and then, if he decided it was appropriate, to summon the president.

The director climbed the stairs from the ground-floor entrance, followed by Fox and then Pappas; upstairs they took a left down the narrow corridor toward Appleman's office. The NSC intelligence liaison was waiting there, and the visitors could barely fit in the anteroom. Eventually the door opened and the adviser peered out of his corner office. He was an uncannily youthful man, for all the secrets he had digested over a thirty-year career as a national security bureaucrat. He dressed in the tidy, timeless look of a Brooks Brothers lifer, still wearing the same style of penny loafers and button-down shirts that he had in prep school.

"Can we do this here?" asked Appleman, motioning to his inner office. The last sunlight of the late summer afternoon was filtering through his windows. The room was the bland color of eggshells, decorated with nautical paintings and the inevitable tableaux of the Old West. Appleman stood at his door deferentially, waiting for them to enter. He was so polite, even the president tended to treat him dismissively, barking out his last name as if he were a house servant.

"Perhaps downstairs," said the director. "This is a little sensitive."

So they went down to the Situation Room. Through the big door at the bottom of the stairs, past the guard post that was staffed twenty-four hours a day, just in case. They made a peculiar parade, descending the stairwell and assembling around the conference table. The national security adviser took off his suit jacket, even though the room was chilly as a wine cellar, and everyone else did the same.

"The Iranians have restarted the weapons program," said the director. "They're working on a trigger." He wasn't one to beat around the bush.

"Holy Toledo!" said Appleman. He did not like to use curse words. "Are you sure?"

"We have an agent inside. Or so it seems."

"At last!" said Appleman. He ventured a thin smile, but it was hard to read: at last they had an Iranian agent, or at last they were telling him about it? Fox had probably briefed him weeks ago.

"The president had almost given up on you fellows. But what's this 'so it seems'? Either you have an agent or you don't, right? Or am I missing something?"

The director's navy cap was sitting on the table, all gold braid. He was out of his element. He turned to Pappas. "Harry can explain."

"He's what we call a virtual walk-in," said Pappas. "He came in through the website. He's like the Soviet defectors who walked into our embassies in the old days, but the computer-era version. We call him 'Dr. Ali,' but we don't really know who he is. We can make some educated guesses based on the information he has sent us, but we've never laid eyes on the guy. He first pinged the website in June. We messaged back and got nothing, so we were suspicious. But a few days ago we got some good stuff. Very good. So I'm thinking he's the real thing."

"Tell me more about this 'good stuff,' please." The national security adviser was leaning across the table toward the agency visitors.

"Stewart, if I might," broke in Fox. "Let's not make this too complicated. Our asset in Tehran has sent proof that the Iranians are making a bomb. Not thinking about it, not preparing the fuel, but doing it. They are working on the neutron generator. Bingo. This is what we've been looking for. The smoking gun. Next thing, they will be conducting an actual nuclear weapons test."

The air seemed to go out of the room suddenly, suspending everyone in a vacuum. Fox was trying to look grim, but there was a smile of satisfaction on his lips, just a trace. It escaped no one's attention that Fox had used the national security adviser's first name. They were social friends, it was rumored at the agency. Political friends, too.

"How can you be sure, Arthur?" said the national security adviser, breaking the silence. He nodded in Harry's direction. "I mean, if you don't even know who he is."

Appleman was a believer, but he didn't want to get burned if the intelligence was wrong. He had watched that movie play out with Iraq.

"We don't *have* to know his identity, Stewart," replied Fox.

"Why not?"

"Because his information is his bona fides. He has sent us documents that could only come from inside the nuclear program. The first message was a summary of their enrichment of uranium. It told us two things: that they were moving toward weapons grade on their highly enriched uranium track, and that they might—might—have a second track to produce plutonium. We briefed it to you, but we didn't have any collateral. Now he sends this new document. It describes Iranian experiments with a neutron generator. This fits with either a uranium or a plutonium track, but that's not the point. The fact is that they are assembling the pieces of a bomb, Stewart. They are nearing a breakout. They're having trouble getting the hardware to work, but they'll figure it out. We're running out of time. *That's* the point."

The national security adviser asked the director if he agreed with Fox's technical assessment. The director nodded. "If Arthur and his team at CPD say it's the real thing, I'm ready to weigh anchor."

Harry winced inwardly as he listened to the simple formulation offered by Fox and endorsed by the admiral. They were making it sound too easy. Open and shut. He looked toward the screens and monitors that lined the walls. This room had been designed as a command post for the president to wage war. Those were the stakes.

Harry cleared his throat to speak. Fox pulled back uneasily, but Appleman was attentive.

"Can I say something?" asked Harry.

"Of course," said the national security adviser.

"We need to be careful, sir. I'm sorry to sound like a pussy, but I have to tell you that. This case is murky. We don't really know the source, or where he's coming from. To the extent we understand this document, it says they're having trouble making things work, not that they're about to break out. You policy folks have to make the big decisions, but as an intelligence officer, I wish I had better information for you. That's all, just a blinking yellow light from an old case officer who has been burned too many times."

Appleman removed his tortoiseshell glasses and polished them against the silk of his striped orange-and-black tie. He was a Princeton man. He shared that distinction with Fox. Pappas had gone to Boston College, hustled his way into ROTC, and felt lucky to graduate. Appleman put his glasses back on and raised his hand, palm outward, as if he were stopping traffic.

"Caution noted. Registered. Appreciated. But, ah, before we go any further, the president needs to hear this. Right away, I think." He paused, thinking something over, and then continued. "The president doesn't like crowds, so I want just two of you to join me." He turned toward the director. "Whoever you like."

The director nodded to Fox. He was the designated briefer on this case, anyway. "Arthur?"

"Whatever you say, sir." He relaxed his squint for a moment.

The president was contacted in the family quarters. He would be down in fifteen minutes, as soon as he finished making his apologies to the congressmen. Pappas went upstairs and waited in the anteroom outside the national security adviser's office. He had been there nearly an hour when his stomach began to growl. He thought about going over to the snack bar in the Old EOB and getting something to eat, but he wanted to be there when the director returned. That was his ride. It was also the only way he would know what had been discussed outside his hearing.

When the director and Fox finally trundled back upstairs, it was nearly 9:00 p.m. Fox looked disappointed that Pappas was still there, but the director seemed pleased. He wasn't stupid. Fox apologized that he would be going back to the agency separately. He had a dinner meeting downtown, he said, and he would summon a car from Langley when he was done. Pappas rolled his eyes. Fox was so obvious. He was going to have dinner with Stewart Appleman. Why didn't he fucking say so?

"Let's go home," said the director.

He didn't say another word until they were in the limousine, heading toward the George Washington

Parkway that would take them back to Langley. The silence was oppressive in the big car.

"So?" said Pappas when they had gone a few blocks.

"So . . . what?" answered the director.

"So what did the president say, for chrissakes?"

"He said 'holy shit,' or words to that effect. He said we need to prepare military options if the Iranians are moving toward a nuclear test. He also said we need to know more. About the neutron gizmo, and the plutonium track, and the whole damn thing. I told him he was right. The truth is, we don't really know very much."

Pappas smiled. He was relieved. He was never sure the director really understood how imperfect a picture was drawn by intelligence information. And he had no sense at all of how the president made decisions. But this had turned out about right.

"Arthur must be disappointed," said Pappas. "It sounded like he wanted to launch the cruise missiles tonight, from the way he was talking to Appleman."

"He gave the president a hard-edged briefing. As you would expect. But he didn't go beyond what we have, if that's what you're worrying about. He was . . . appropriate."

The director looked tired. Weighed down by all the secrets he was carrying around. Even his uniform didn't look quite as starchy as usual. Pappas put his hand on the boss's shoulder. They weren't friends, really, but he looked like a man who needed one.

"This is dangerous," said Pappas.

"No shit."

"What do you want me to do?"

"I want you to find out more about Dr. Ali. Who is he? What does he really know? What else can he tell us about the program? How can we run him effectively? That's just for starters. They're going to want to squeeze him hard, and rattle the cage some. After tonight, we can't make any mistakes with this case. None."

"Not so easy, Admiral. We have nothing on the guy, and we don't have good ways of finding out more. We don't have a station in Tehran. And I don't want to send in a non-official cover. If a NOC got caught, he wouldn't have diplomatic immunity. A few days in Evin Prison and even the toughest son-of-a-bitch would give it up. Dr. Ali would be dead and we'd have no information."

They were humming along the George Washington Parkway now. There was a full moon out and the river was bathed in pale light, the few boats upriver outlined in half shadow. Harry looked down at the broad estuary. A new species of fish known as snakeheads had invaded these waters in recent years. They had come originally from Asia, nobody quite knew how, and now they were eating the local fish. Someone in NE

Division had suggested that perhaps the thing to do was to get an even bigger and meaner fish from somewhere else, and let them eat the snakeheads. That was what it was coming to.

"What's the alternative?" asked the director. "If it's too dangerous to send in a NOC, what do we do?"

Harry thought a moment. He had been pondering this question himself for several weeks, even before the receipt of this latest message. How could they identify a frightened Iranian computer geek who insisted on remaining in hiding? How could they reach into the miasma of Tehran, a city of nearly 12 million people, and pluck out the one person they needed? You couldn't do it from Dubai. You couldn't do it from Istanbul. You certainly couldn't do it from Langley. You had to be there. That was the puzzle Harry had been trying to solve, and he knew he needed help.

"The Brits," he said after a long pause. "SIS had two people in their Tehran embassy the last I knew. Maybe they could help us find him. Maybe they could get enough collateral that we could ask better questions of Dr. Ali, assuming we ever have two-way with him."

"Can they keep it quiet?"

"Sure. The Brits are the best liars in the world. Plus I know Adrian Winkler, the new SIS chief of staff. He'll do anything I ask him. We were together in Moscow and Baghdad. I could go over, brief him and his boss, work up an ops plan. Keep it tight."

The director didn't respond until they were almost to the gates of the headquarters complex. He had too much on his mind now. He had been a happy man when he left the military to come to the agency. At first he had treated CIA like a big navy base. He went to the cafeteria with his wife, played softball at "Family Day," gave out the medals and the supergrade promotions himself. But the easy part was over, and now he had a big dysfunctional organization to worry about. Pappas sensed that he didn't really like this work, or the people who did it. He liked driving boats. The CIA was another tribe.

"Do it," said the director. "Go to London as soon as you can make arrangements."

Pappas promised he would be on his way in twenty-four hours. The limousine had parked in the garage now. The director was about to take his private elevator to the seventh floor. There was one more question.

"Are you going to tell Fox?" asked Pappas.

The director didn't answer, which Pappas understood to mean no.

9

LONDON

Adrian Winkler might have posed for an SIS recruiting poster, if that most secret of secret services had wanted to advertise. He was dark-haired and intense, with a furtive twinkle in his eyes. He knew how to shoot a gun, jump from an airplane, speak an exotic language, tell a wry joke. He operated with a panache that reminded you that intelligence work was really an extension of life in a British public school—the hazing and deception shaped by cunning intellect. When he completed a particularly good operation, Winkler would confide as if to a fellow schoolboy, "That was a good wheeze!" Most Americans were intimidated by him, put off by his sardonic wit and his refusal to tolerate incompetence. But Harry Pappas was so far from Winkler on the social landscape that he didn't feel threatened. He liked Winkler because he was good at his job and seemed to enjoy it.

Pappas had met him in another lifetime, when they were both young officers in Moscow. The CIA at the time was in one of its recurring panics about Soviet penetration of the agency, and life at the old U.S. Embassy compound was grim in midwinter. The station chief had told his restless cadre of case officers to stand down on new operations until the situation was clearer, which meant that

Pappas didn't have anything to do. To pass the time, his colleagues drank heavily, flirted with other people's spouses, and tried to avoid saying anything that might get them in trouble. Pappas was so bored he would take rides on the Moscow subway, back and forth, Kurskaya to Kievskaya, just to confuse the KGB surveillance teams.

Then along came Adrian and Susan Winkler. They arrived in Moscow by car from Finland, a more harrowing trip in winter than it sounds, bearing their two young daughters. The roads were icy and treacherous, the children were wailing, the Soviet police were menacing. They drove day and night to get to Moscow before a blizzard that was moving east. Exhausted by too many hours of driving, Adrian had searched for a spot he could pull off the road and get a little sleep. He finally found a little hideaway just off the main highway, tucked behind the fir trees. It was so dense and dark back there, you could almost disappear. He closed his eyes and fell into a deep slumber, until he was awakened by the cries of one of his girls.

But Winkler had remembered the spot: that was the point of the story, when he recounted it for Pappas late one night. He had remembered the little rest area, filed it away in a compartment of his mind where it lay . . . until one day a few months after his arrival when he needed a covert rendezvous point, urgently. The SIS had ordered a crash operation to exfiltrate a Soviet KGB agent they were running. The agent was supposed to go out via Finland, but they needed someplace where he could disappear along the way. Winkler recalled the rest area in the woods—located it on the highway almost down to the precise kilometer. And that was the ops plan: the Russian agent drove in from one side; a British NOC from the other. One car emerged, with the agent in disguise. The exfiltration scheme became a legend within SIS. Winkler was just twenty-nine at the time.

Winkler shouldn't have told Pappas the story. It was still a secret. The Brits wanted the Soviets to think the agent was dead. But he and Harry were out of Russia at the time, in a safe house in Stockholm drinking vodka, and as Winkler said, "You have to trust someone."

"Did he thank you?" Pappas had asked.

Winkler had shaken his head ruefully.

"Who? Pavel? Are you joking? He was a right bastard. He thought he did it all himself." Winkler had paused.

"That's the thing about this business, isn't it? We work with the worst people in the world. If there wasn't something wrong with them, why would they be talking to us in the first place? And you know what? Some of it is going to *rub off.*"

From the moment Adrian Winkler arrived in Moscow, he and Pappas had made common cause. They both had young families. Pappas's son Alex was just four then—a little roustabout who never seemed to get cold no matter what the temperature was. They weren't supposed to socialize, but they lived near each other, and Winkler was sending his girls to the American School because he had decided that the British School was run by a sadist. And their wives liked each other. So they became friends. Winkler loved to hear Harry's stories about training the contras in Honduras; he wanted to hear about guns and bombs and the other toys that paramilitary officers played with. Harry wanted to understand espionage, so they taught each other.

They started a film club, to animate the bitterly cold Moscow nights. They watched old Cary Grant movies, and classic French films by Jean Renoir and François Truffaut, and when they could get them, tapes of Monty Python and Rocky and Bullwinkle. It was an education for Harry. His taste in movies growing up in Worcester had been *Butch Cassidy and the Sundance Kid*.

Winkler was the star; everyone in Moscow station seemed to know that he had pulled off a coup, even if they didn't know what it was. But people were jealous, too, especially Winkler's colleagues. Nobody likes someone to be too successful, especially at a young age. And Harry was something of a star, too. The director himself had taken a shine to Harry after meeting him in Honduras. He liked people with mud on their boots, and he personally arranged Harry's assignment to Moscow to make him a real case officer so that he wouldn't have to take shit from the Career Trainee prima donnas anymore.

Harry did what the old man wanted. He shook up Moscow station and got it back in the operations business. He developed new tradecraft for doing the simple things—shaking KGB surveillance, checking radio propagation, finding good drop sites. He and Adrian even worked together servicing an agent the Brits and Americans had recruited jointly in Germany. For a man who'd just left a shooting war in the jungles of Nicaragua, the risks of running agents in Moscow seemed small indeed.

The two young officers watched each other's backs. They weren't supposed to do that, either. But CIA and SIS were "cousins," and it all flowed together back at headquarters, so they figured, What the hell? When Pappas had to travel on operations, Winkler would look in on Andrea and Alex; Pappas would do the same for Susan and the girls.

Winkler didn't have a son of his own, so he sort of adopted Alex. When it was finally time to leave Moscow, Alex was referring to the British man as "Uncle Adrian." Winkler sent him gifts every year at Christmas. They were always books—adventure stories like *Captains Courageous* and *Horatio Hornblower* at first, and then later, real war stories about real wars. That was all that ever interested Alex, other than sports.

When Alex died, Pappas and Winkler were both in Iraq, as chiefs of their respective stations. They had that in common, too; they had watched a catastrophic mistake unfolding, tried fitfully to stop it, and failed. But on the day Alex died, it stopped being a policy problem. When Pappas heard the news, he went to Winkler's liaison office in a half-destroyed building near the palace that served as the CIA station, closed the door, and started to cry. He couldn't stop. He kept saying, "It's my fault." Winkler sat with him. This was a house of grief he couldn't enter. Eventually he drove Pappas to BIAP and put him on a plane back home to Andrea. A sadder man he had never seen. Winkler flew to Washington several days later, to be with his friend when the body arrived at Dover, and to help put Alex in the ground. Nothing was the same after that, for either of them.

Pappas met Winkler at the antiseptic SIS headquarters known as "Vauxhall Cross," on the Albert Embankment along the south side of the Thames. Winkler was a certified big shot now. He was chief of staff, which was perhaps a stepping-stone to becoming head of the service. Pappas took the elevator up to the top floor where Winkler had his office, just down the hall from Sir David Plumb, the knight of the realm who was the current custodian of the famous initial "C." In the corridor were sharp-eyed young men in gaudily striped shirts who noted the presence of the visiting American.

Winkler beckoned Pappas into his office and closed the door. The room was decorated with African masks and spears, which seemed odd if you didn't know that Winkler had grown up in Uganda. He'd lived on a farm in the bush, until his father was killed. Relatives had arranged for him to go to school at Rugby, and then he had won a scholarship to Corpus Christi. What brought him to the attention of the dons, who in those days still acted as spotters for SIS, was that Winkler spoke the Niger-Congo dialects of Uganda with uncommon fluency. In addition to the facility with languages, they noted that he was a young man who needed a father. He might as well have had SIS stamped on his forehead.

Winkler's office had a view across the Thames toward Victoria Station and Pimlico and in the distance downstream, Westminster Abbey and the Houses of Parliament. He motioned for Pappas to sit down on the couch and pulled up a chair for himself. The bulky gray corridor of Whitehall, the SIS version of "downtown," was concealed behind the riverfront buildings a mile away.

"You look like you got hit by a truck," said Winkler. It was true. Pappas had deep ruts under his eyes and an unhealthy pallor to his skin.

"Up all night on the plane," said Pappas. "I thought I could drink myself to sleep, but it didn't work."

119

Pappas was too tired for small talk. And he didn't want to leave an empty space in the conversation, into which memories of Alex might fall.

"I need a favor, Adrian. I figured you'd take me more seriously if I came in person."

"I always take you seriously, Harry. It's one of my life rules. What's it about?"

"Iran."

"Very nice. Flavor of the week. Iran and what, perchance?"

Harry cocked his head, as if appraising his old friend one more time, and then gave him a wink.

"This is for you only. You and Plumb, I mean. Nobody else gets briefed, unless we give the okay. Is that acceptable?"

"No. But I don't have any choice, do I?"

"Nope. And if this gets out, I personally will make sure that you never get another secret from Uncle Sugar until the day you die."

"Gosh! Very intimidating. So Iran, then. How can we be helpful?"

"How many people do you have in your embassy in Tehran?"

"One."

"I thought it was two."

"We just had to pull one back. His wife had an ectopic pregnancy. I think that's what it was. She almost died. He got soggy, asked to come home. Not long for the service, I'm afraid. Pity. Very good at languages."

"Any NOCs?"

"A few travelers in and out, same as you, but not many."

"Can your man in Tehran operate? The one who's still there."

"Well now, that depends on what he's asked to do." Winkler looked at his friend slyly. "You've got someone on the hook, haven't you? Someone good. You lucky bugger. And you need our help servicing him. Is that it?"

"Something like that. More complicated, really." He paused again.

"God, Harry! Really! You're less communicative than my daughters."

"Okay. It's what I told you in the cable a few weeks ago. We have an Iranian walk-in. Except he didn't exactly walk, he telecommunicated, through our website. We still don't know who he is. But he has access to some very good material. Or should I say, 'seems to have access.' We call him Dr. Ali, but we have no idea what his real name is."

"Where does he work?"

"We're not sure, but we know the general area, from what he has sent us. You can guess what that is, given that I flew over here on twenty-four hours' notice."

"The weapons side of the nuclear program. They've started up again."

"Roger that."

"Those little bastards. Well, we knew they would, didn't we? Knew they'd never actually stopped. You lads were the gullible ones, frankly."

Winkler sat back slowly in his chair, as if taking it in. There was an even brighter twinkle in his eyes than usual.

"And now you've got a Joe. Well done! And he's legitimate?"

"I think so. At least his material is. Or so Arthur Fox keeps telling me."

Winkler made a face as if he had just eaten a bad oyster. "I don't like that man, Harry. He's a show horse."

"Tell me about it. But he has the president's ear, literally. He's the one briefing the White House on our new guy. He's got people so cranked up some of them are ready to drop a bomb on Natanz tomorrow morning."

"Are they that crazy?"

"Not yet. That's why I'm here. The director wants me to run our guy like a real agent and extract what he knows. But first I have to find him. We don't have the assets on the ground. That's why I'm here. As I said when we started this conversation, I need help. From you."

"How endearing," said Winkler. "We always like you Americans when you are needy and vulnerable. It brings out your feminine side."

"Fuck you, Adrian. But I will assume that means yes."

They got a map of Tehran and spread it out on Winkler's desk. Neither of them had ever served there before, but they had both looked at so much overhead imagery of the city that they felt as if they knew it. Winkler put his finger on a spot in the middle of the map, just below a big intersection marked Ferdowsi Square.

"Here's our embassy, on Jomhuri-ye Islami Avenue. From here, we can get a fix on radio propagation. Does your guy have any commo gear?"

"No. I told you, we've never laid eyes on him. He's just an email address. But from the messages, I have the feeling that he's in one of the nuclear labs. Maybe the big one in North Tehran, maybe one of the satellite shops under commercial cover."

Winkler moved his finger up to the top of the map, to a small spot on the edge of the Alborz Mountains, near an old tuberculosis sanatorium that was now one of the city's main treatment centers for AIDS patients.

"Right here," said Winkler. "Ground zero for Fox and friends. If they had their way, they would just bomb this place—and take your lad with them."

"Have you got anyone inside?"

"No. We tell you that every time you ask."

"I know, but now I'm asking you again. And this time I really need to know. Have you got anyone?"

Winkler smiled, and gave his friend a little wink. You had to trust someone.

"One person," he said. "A scientist, who goes in and out. He's sort of a consultant, in physics. He doesn't have badge access, so he has to be cleared each time. But he can carry radiation monitors and some other gear."

"Has he ever left anything behind? Any close-in?"

"You mean like needle mikes in the sofa? No. He's too scared. We're trying to bring him along slowly."

"How did you recruit him?"

"We pitched him five years ago, when he was finishing his doctorate at Utrecht University. He was game in Holland, all right, but they gave him such a grilling when he got home, he broke off contact. They do that to all the students coming back. We warned him about it, but he got spooked anyway. The way it worked out was probably good for us, actually. What's more secure than having no communications, eh? We kept an eye on him through some Iranians who know his family, and when we heard he was doing hush-hush work nobody would talk about, we thought, Bingo! We pitched him again on the street, in the middle of fucking Tehran—and now we had a handle on him, and he knew it."

"Good case. No wonder you didn't tell us."

"He was studying physics, X-ray transport in plasmas, which interested us. Because that's the key to making a hydrogen bomb work."

"Oh shit. Are they working on that, too?"

124

"We don't know. They're sniffing around it, if our lad is reliable. He's not Rev Guards so they don't really trust him. But this is a long game, isn't it? We're working him slowly, so we don't freak him out or blow his cover. We tried to get him to Dubai six months ago to pick up a new communications device and get some training, but he said no-go. His next out is skedded for Qatar, but he's worried they'll put him on the restricted travel list, which maybe is a good sign."

"What's his name?" asked Pappas.

"Fuck off! I love you, Harry, but not that much."

"We need a marked card," proposed Adrian. "Something you give to your Ali, which our Ali can see. You follow me?"

They had been talking for more than an hour, trying to cobble together the pieces of an operational plan. Harry had gone back over the material he had shared with Adrian when the VW first surfaced, and filled him in on what had happened since. Winkler had been listening, but not all that closely, and there was a restless look in his eye, as if he wanted to get on to the action part. That was when he mentioned the marked card.

"What kind of marked card?" asked Harry.

"Something that requires your guy to leave tracks, which my guy can follow. Let's say you task him to look for something that my guy knows about, in the area where he's doing his consulting."

"Which would be physics, you said. X-ray transport."

"Just so. And then my guy will hear about it. We'll tell him to report any particular queries in his area, so he'll find out who was asking the question. That sound right?"

"Will your Ali suspect anything? I mean, let's be honest. Your guy could be bent already. I don't want to risk blowing my guy out of the water."

"He's not bent. He's straight as the Archbishop of Canterbury. Straighter! He's just a scared kid. But I promise we'll be careful. We'll put in a couple of other special requests, so he won't think this isn't cricket. Don't worry, Harry."

"I like to worry. It's recreational."

Harry stared out the window again. The London Eye was turning almost imperceptibly several miles downstream. Harry wished the world would move that slowly.

"How quickly can you get to your guy?" asked Harry.

"In person?"

"Yeah. I don't think this is something you would want to drop into his in-box."

"A month or two to arrange a meet outside Iran, if we're lucky. He can still travel, maybe, but he has to be careful not to dirty his knickers."

"That's too long. We need to move now."

"We could do a crash meet in Tehran, I guess. We've got safe houses the station thinks are clean.

But I hate to do that. If we expose our guy, then we've got nothing at all."

"Do it, brother. If this works, we're inside the tent."

"Does it have to be face-to-face?"

Harry nodded. "The only lie detector that really works is looking someone in the eye. We need it. I wouldn't ask otherwise."

"I'll need to ask the chief," Adrian said solemnly.

"He'll do whatever you tell him."

"Get your hand off my pud, Harry. I don't need any extra strokes."

"Does that mean yes?"

Adrian nodded. "It's a long shot, but I reckon it's the best you've got. If you don't find out who your Ali is, he's useless. And if the Iranians are really building the Big One, you need to know who he is *now*—yesterday, actually. So what do we task my man to find out—that your man will hear about?"

"I'll have to ask Fox. Let me work out the details with him."

"I told you, I don't like Arthur Fox."

"Get over it, Adrian."

"I'll try. I'm going to have to tell the chief, you know."

"Of course. I already told you that was okay."

"And I will have to tell our one-man station in Tehran, so he can tell our Joe what to look out for. Good lad. A kid, but smart."

"Understood. So long as you don't tell him why you're asking the question."

"And then what do we do, when your lad surfaces? Do we meet him? Do we get him out of the country?"

"I don't know yet. But I note that you are using the word 'we' in reference to this operation."

"Fucking hell! Of course I am. In for a riyal, in for a toman, old boy. Joined at the hip, you and me. Am I right?"

The door to Winkler's office opened without a knock just before noon, and in strode Sir David Plumb, Winkler's boss and the head of the service. He was a sturdy-looking man in his early sixties, with thinning gray hair and traces of red on his nose and cheeks that testified to a career of late-night meetings poached in claret, port, and anything else that was handy. He might have been a senior civil servant in any of the Whitehall ministries, except for the playful look in his eyes. Plumb observed the map of Tehran on the desk and nodded approvingly.

"I heard you were coming, Harry," said Plumb. "I thought I might join you two for lunch. Talk things over. Where do you like?"

"Anywhere but the Travelers Club," said Harry. The club was notable for its high quotient of SIS members and its poor food.

"I've sworn off the Travelers. Everyone there

seems to be working for the *Daily Telegraph* these days. Even the porter. Tell you what. Let's go to the Ritz."

Harry smiled. The Ritz was known to be Sir David Plumb's favorite spot for lunch. It was fabulously expensive, with prices that would make even a Saudi prince check his wallet.

Sir David went back to his office to collect his umbrella and summon his driver. Harry had something more he needed to say to Winkler, in these last few moments they were alone.

"This may sound strange," said Harry, "but I have a funny feeling about this case. I don't like where it's going."

Winkler's brow tightened. "What do you mean? Seems to me like a jolly good case. Don't you trust us?"

"No, no. It isn't that. Of course I trust you." Harry lowered his voice. "The stakes are too high. We are tasking an agent to find out the details of Iranian plans to build a bomb. Suppose they provide the details. What do we do then? The linkages are too tight. How are we going to stop that without going to war?"

Winkler ventured a cocky smile. It was a look Harry remembered from Moscow, back when his friend was the golden boy, the rising star of the service.

"There are ways and ways and ways, Harry. Don't let them rush you. One thing at a time. And don't let the worriers push you to make bad decisions. That has become the American disease. Don't succumb, old boy. You're the last sane American I know."

They walked together toward the elevator. Plumb was coming out of his office, fifteen yards away.

"There's one more thing, Harry, before we go," whispered Winkler.

"Tell me."

"Mahmoud Azadi."

"Who's that?"

"That's the name of our agent in Tehran."

10

LONDON

The maître d'hôtel at the Ritz had prepared Sir David's favorite table, in a far corner of the dining room by the windows overlooking Green Park. It was hardly a secure spot for a confidential discussion, but that didn't seem to bother Plumb. He operated as if he were in his own security bubble, trusting those he deemed suitable and ignoring everyone else. The SIS in that respect hadn't changed much from the old days, when the fact that you had known someone at school, or had dated his sister at Oxford, was deemed sufficient proof of your reliability.

Even in late summer, the trees and lawns of

Green Park had a rich, languid color worthy of the name. The foliage blocked a view of Buckingham Palace a half mile away, but the vista remained much as it had been in Victorian times. The British Empire had come and gone—and then come back once again in an unexpected way, as the "little people" of bygone days, Indians, Saudis, Kuwaitis, Chinese, had returned to Britain to spend their newfound wealth with abandon. The gray, gritty days were past. London was as flush and verdant that season as its parks. The Brits were better at post-imperial life than the Americans, but then, they were better at most things.

The luncheon party was merry, good food and wine and especially delicious gossip about their respective services, but it was obvious that Plumb had a more serious reason for asking a visiting American to join him for lunch.

"We are worried about you," said Sir David. He had just finished his Dover sole and his second glass of Puligny-Montrachet, and was waiting for his cheese.

"Not about you personally, of course," he continued, "and not even about the agency, although we do wonder sometimes whether perhaps you are losing a step. No, we are worried about the administration. They are becoming, shall we say, accident-prone. They remind me of a gyroscope that has been knocked off-balance and begins to wobble, more and more. September 11, well, bad luck. Pick yourself up, get on with it. Iraq, terrible mess. God-awful mess, actually. But such is the nature of life. Make mistakes. Try to fix them. Suck it up. Get on with it. But this natural process of regeneration does not seem to be happening in your fair land at present. Not only was the previous administration a disappointment, but the new one seems likely to be equally so, and perhaps the next after that. This worries us. It worries the prime minister. He isn't sure what to do."

Harry was silent, staring at the lamb chop bones on his plate.

Sir David looked over the top of his glasses, into Harry's eyes. "Am I overdramatizing?"

"No," said Harry. "Things are bad. I can't really blame them on Iraq. We all made mistakes. We should have seen it coming. We shouldn't have gone in . . ." His voice trailed off.

There was an awkward silence. Harry was looking away from the table, trying to keep his composure.

"Harry lost his son in Iraq," said Winkler.

"Yes. I'd heard that. I am terribly sorry, Harry. For you this is not a discussion in the abstract. Forgive me. We'll talk about something less unpleasant."

Harry shook his head. "We are in a hell of a mess, David. It's true. We do need to talk about it. I need to talk about it, more than most people. I just don't know what the answers are."

"You and Adrian were discussing Iran, I gather."

"We have started a joint operation. Adrian can give you the details, perhaps in a place that is less ... noisy."

"Well, I'm jolly glad that we can be of help. That is our role in life. We are the pilot fish, who live to nibble the bacteria off the great shark. And perhaps to perform other services from time to time."

"Give me a break, David. You have a station in Tehran and we don't. And from what Adrian tells me, you're actually using it."

"Perhaps so. But you see, it's Iran that worries me most of all, Harry. That's a place where your mistakes might become truly consequential. Iraq's a mess, true enough, but that's their problem, isn't it? Bloody difficult. But from our perspective, well, Saddam is gone and the Iraqi military is destroyed. So you might say, what's all the fuss about, really? Not the ideal outcome, certainly. A bit untidy, to be sure. But we'll all survive."

Plumb paused, took a sip of his wine, and continued to speak in a lower voice.

"Whereas Iran, you see, is a different matter altogether. You start a war with Iran, Harry, and it will take us all thirty years to dig out from the rubble. Number 10 is nervous. Terrified, actually. You're not going to start a war with Iran, are you?"

Harry wasn't sure how to answer the question. "I don't know," he said after a moment. "I hope not. But I don't know. This White House, as you say, is

133

wobbly. You can't be sure which way it's going to spin."

The cheese trolley arrived. Sir David asked for four different kinds, arrayed on his plate in ascending order of sharpness of flavor. A ripe Camembert, then a chèvre dusted with pepper, then a sharp Irish cheddar, finally a fat wedge of Stilton. A look of contentment momentarily softened his face as he contemplated his cheese, but then the frown returned.

"You see, Harry, we really can't afford another American mistake. It's too damned costly for us. We travel along in your wake like the faithful little brother, helping you pick up the debris after your misadventures. But I'm not sure how much longer we would be prepared to do that. The 'special relationship' is not good for our health, you see."

Plumb paused and sampled the Camembert, which was oozing onto the plate. He went on to the chèvre, and then the cheddar, while Harry pondered what to say.

"They're building a bomb," Harry said eventually. "We have it out of Iran. They're working on a trigger. That's what Adrian and I were discussing. That's why I'm here."

"Yes, yes," said Sir David. "I've heard about that. The director phoned me last night. But even if it's true, let me pose the impolite question: So what? Everyone wants a bomb these days, but we haven't gone to war to stop them. Chinese, Indians, Pakis,

North Koreans, for goodness' sake. They all have their bombs, and *mirabile dictu*, none of them seems at all inclined to use them. But in this case, people in the White House seem to think that military action may be necessary. Or so we have been led to believe by our, forgive the term, 'spies.' But you're a man whose judgment I trust. Seasoned, tempered by life. So I put it to you: Is America going to war again? It's rather important to us."

Harry shook his head. He felt mildly disloyal, even having this conversation. The Brits did their best to make you forget that they were a foreign nation, feeding you lamb chops and fine wines and a little pudding, and would you mind please telling your innermost secrets to your dear, innocent cousins.

"I can't answer," said Harry, "because I don't know. There's a group around the president that wants a confrontation with Iran. There's another group that doesn't. There's the Congress, which is sick of war but listens to the Israelis. And the Israelis keep saying we have to strike Iran before it's too late. And there's the president, who is so battered you wonder how he can stand up straight. You tell me how all those pieces fit together, and I'll tell you whether we're going to war with Iran."

Sir David had finished his cheese by now, and was polishing off the last of the Gevrey-Chambertin he had ordered for Harry and Adrian to go with their lamb chops. The dining room was beginning to empty out. He wasn't in a rush. He looked out to the green of the park and then back toward Harry, his eyes twinkling with that mischievous look that had marked him as an operator from the days he was a schoolboy. He was getting to the point, in his own eccentric way.

"Time," he said. "That's really the issue, isn't it?"

"I don't follow you," said Harry.

"I had an economics professor at Cambridge. He was an Italian. Piero something. Ancient man, when I encountered him. He had devoted his life—wasted it, most people thought—to proving that Ricardo's Labor Theory of Value was correct. What a folly! An economist who has been dead for nearly two hundred years, whose theories are held in disrepute by all right-thinking people, but never mind. That was this fellow Piero's life's work, which he distilled in a little monograph called *The Production of Commodities by Means of Commodities*. Fancy that. What he did was to build a model in which 'capital' was actually labor—'dated labor,' he called it. And that was his point. It was *time* that added value to the products of human labor. Pick a bunch of grapes off a vine, even in Pomerol, and they're practically worthless. But press them and ferment the juice and put it in bottles and lay them down for a few years . . . by God, now you have an investment. See what I mean? Capital is time."

Harry was wondering whether the SIS chief had

perhaps had a bit too much to drink when Plumb wheeled on him suddenly and clasped his hand.

"Do not make the mistake of thinking that this is a short clock, Harry. You are not running out of time. The Iranians are not about to detonate a bomb. They have not built a heavy-water reactor. They do not have plutonium. They don't have a working trigger. Oh yes, I know all about the new panic, but it is misplaced, my boy. We have more time than your skittish friends in the White House seem to think. Perhaps even more than you think. The essence of wisdom here is to avoid acting rashly, in the belief that you are running out of time. You are not. I assure you."

Harry was taken aback by the intensity of what Plumb had said, and the oddity of it.

"You're telling this to the wrong person, Sir David. I am a career intelligence officer who is running a CIA division. I don't make policy. I don't have much influence with the people who do make policy. If you want to influence whether America goes to war against Iran, you're talking to the wrong guy."

Plumb took his napkin from his lap, folded it carefully, and placed it atop the table. He pulled his chair back from the table, preparing to leave. Adrian Winkler did the same.

"I'm not at all sure of that, Harry," said Plumb. "Actually, I rather think you are the 'right' guy. You just don't know it yet."

11

DAMASCUS/TEHRAN

The Crazy One traveled to Damascus for the weekend. Nobody dared to ask him why, and he wouldn't have given an answer, even if they had. But the truth was that he was bored. He had requested a private jet from the president's office, and flown alone from Mehrabad to Al-Mazzah military airport outside Damascus. He arrived as a shadow person, without a passport or any other trail.

A black sedan brought him to the new Four Seasons Hotel, where a suite had been booked for a Mr. Nawaz. The hotel was told that he was a Pakistani businessman working in Iran on sensitive business. The security man who had accompanied him spoke a few hushed words to the desk clerk, and a suite on the top floor, the presidential floor, had been cleared for him, and the usual check-in arrangements were waived.

And now Al-Majnoun was sitting on his balcony, smoking a hubbly-bubbly pipe laced with opium. He looked toward the old tombs across the way; they were being restored as part of the manic refurbishment of Damascus, cranes over the centuries-old stone crypts and passages, scaffolding surrounding the sacred burial ground. He puffed hard on the pipe and looked again, and he could see the *jinns* hovering anxiously over the tombs, their rest disturbed. They were alight, ghosts in the air, jittering to and fro. Could he hear them crying? No, he was not that stoned, but he would put another gummy wad of opium in the pipe until he could hear them talk.

It was a pleasure to be in this Arab city. That was all the Crazy One really knew. He was not a Persian. His adopted country's nuances and rituals were not his own. Even its religion embarrassed him. Iranian Shiism was so noisy and overdramatic—pilgrims weeping sentimentally at the mere mention of Hussein, and clanging their chains so histrionically on Ashura day. This was more like the professional wrestling matches he watched on satellite television than real religion. Where was the austerity, the purity of the desert? These Persians were city people with gloves on their hands. How could they touch God? Their culture was so ingrown, it was as if everyone had grown up listening to the same bedtime stories and could finish them all by memory. Whereas for Al-Majnoun, the Crazy One, everything was invented and everything was new.

"Mr. Nawaz" had **meetings** in Damascus. Important people came to see him, and brought him letters from other important people. He sent emissaries and sometimes, under armed guard in cars with blackened windows that didn't open even to the Syrian moukhabarat, he went to visit others.

He had to be very careful where he went. The Israelis would want to kill him, of course, if they knew he was alive and traveling about, and so would the Americans. Some of the Syrian intelligence barons might want to kill him, along with the Fatah Palestinians and the Nejdi Saudis and the Dubai Emiratis. He had killed their people, or so it was said, and so they would want to kill him in revenge. His protection was that he was a nonperson. The world officially thought that he was dead, killed twenty-five years ago by the Israelis, and the Israelis were never wrong. Rumors persisted, but that was always the case in this conspiratorial world. So the man survived, year by year, and the longer he lived the more the myth of invulnerability grew up around him, among the handful of people who knew the truth.

Power was not what you did, but what people believed you did. That was the essence of Al-Majnoun's authority. People who worked with him in Tehran truly believed he was the Crazy One. They thought that if he looked at them cross-eyed, they might end up dead. When he walked into a room in one of the security ministries, people pulled back and opened a path to give him a wide berth. When he took off his sunglasses, they didn't look at his eyes. They were afraid.

And so they did what he wanted, or what they thought he wanted. They called him "General," or "Emir," and tried to please him because they were frightened of him. A few Iranian intelligence officers who had seen the movie *Pulp Fiction* called him "Mr. Wolfe" because they imagined that he was in some way like the mysterious character played by Harvey Keitel who cleans up after other people have made a mess. But outside the circle closest to the Leader, people knew little about him, except that it was prudent to do what he asked. And inside that circle, more like a black box really, it was impossible to know what anyone actually did or thought. And so Al-Majnoun was carried forward, and powerfully, by the motion of his own reputation.

He spent only a long weekend in Damascus. He had run out of opium, for one thing. And he'd had his booster shot of Arabism. Someone sent a woman up to him at the Four Seasons, a beautiful blond girl from Minsk who couldn't have been more than twenty. She looked like a model. He made her take off all her clothes and then gave her a deck of cards and told her to play solitaire on the bed, while he watched. She thought she was supposed to do something erotic, so she touched herself and moaned. But he just wanted to watch her play cards. The next morning he flew back to Tehran on his private jet.

Al-Majnoun visited Mehdi Esfahani when he returned to Iran. He didn't want to see him at his office again. Indeed, he rarely visited the same building twice, even in the secure environs of Tehran. It was a mistake to be predictable, in what you said or where you went. He was thinking about another round of plastic surgery for that reason—not that he needed it, or even could tolerate another reassembly of his tissue. There was so little original skin left to work with. But still, it would upset people like this ridiculous Mehdi with his goatee if he couldn't be sure if he was looking at the same man, or someone pretending to be him, or someone altogether different.

The Crazy One summoned Mehdi to the Revolutionary Guard compound in the northeast sector of the city. He had an office there, which he had used years ago and then left empty, padlocked against intruders. He had hideaways like that across the city, his own network of safe houses.

Mehdi knocked on the door. A muffled voice inside commanded him to enter. The room was so dark it was impossible at first to see Al-Majnoun, hunched over his desk at the far end. The interrogator stepped forward, walking toward the play of shadows he thought must be the form of the man who had summoned him. As he got closer, Al-Majnoun lit a match, illuminating his head in a flickering half-light. His sunglasses were off, and the low light seemed to catch every scar on the Lebanese man's face. Al-Majnoun touched the glowing match to the top of his pipe and sucked down on it hard. The smoke disappeared into his lungs.

"You have a problem," said Al-Majnoun, his voice rough from the smoke.

"What is it, General? I am sure that it is nothing I have done." He was so frightened, the poor man. He didn't know why he had been called to this remote location in a part of the Pasdaran headquarters he had never seen before.

"Of course it is not your fault," rasped Al-Majnoun. "Don't be a fool."

"What is the problem then, General? Tell me so that I can help you solve it. I am at your service, always."

"A document from the program has gone missing," said the Lebanese. "It concerns some of the tests that have been done at Tohid Electric Company. That is one the companies you are supposed to watch. That is bad."

"Bad." Mehdi coughed. They would blame him. Tohid was indeed one of several covert installations that came under his review. It was his fault.

"Very bad."

"Was the document taken from the files of Tohid?"

"We do not know. Perhaps so, perhaps not. Do not make any assumptions in such a sensitive case."

"Of course not, my general. What was the document about? If you can tell me."

"Of course I can tell you. That is why I have summoned you. It describes test results for the triggering device for the unit. In the project. Tohid has been having problems with these tests. We do not know why."

"Do we have the . . . document?" Mehdi was confused.

"No. We only know that someone was looking for it. And may have found it. All I can tell you is the general area of experimentation. That is enough for you to begin."

Al-Majnoun handed Mehdi Esfahani a black folder. The Iranian intelligence officer touched it warily.

"I want you to be like a cat, Mr. Mehdi, a fat cat with your whiskers and your little beard," said Al-Majnoun. "Move carefully and quietly. Do not imagine that you have friends, or that you know what is true. This case may be nothing, or something. We do not want to frighten people, if that is unnecessary. The revolution never makes mistakes. The Leader's authority depends on that. So if there has been a mistake, it must be handled with great care. Do you understand? Ask questions, but carefully."

"Yes, General. Of course."

"As you make your inquiries, keep me informed. But nothing in writing, *min fadluk*. And I want no one else to be briefed on the investigation. That is an order, from the very highest level. The authority of the revolution rests on our ability to see our way through this darkness. Am I clear, Brother Inspector?"

Mehdi bowed his head. How had this catastrophe befallen him?

"Nothing in writing," he repeated. "I will brief you alone."

"I am always watching, you know. Do not make the mistake of others, who thought they knew, but did not."

"I understand, General. I do not knock on doors that are closed."

With a wave of his hand, Al-Majnoun sent the intelligence officer away.

As Mehdi Esfahani retreated from the mottled form in the corner, the Lebanese man seemed to disappear into the darkness itself, a cape of black. Even when Mehdi opened the door, letting in the light of the hallway, it was impossible to distinguish clearly the form of the man in the shadows.

12

WASHINGTON

Harry Pappas returned to Washington feeling that he was living in someone else's body. No matter how he positioned himself in the airplane seat, he couldn't get comfortable. He couldn't sleep and he couldn't read, either, so he just sat there hour after hour, fidgeting, until the plane touched down at Dulles. He would have liked to stay overnight in London and dine comfortably with Adrian Winkler, but he had promised his daughter Louise that he would attend a play at her summer camp. He was bone-tired, and the last thing he wanted to see was a bunch of fifteen-year-olds in *Plaza Suite*. But she had been complaining that he was never around, and although he told her that it wasn't so—that love wasn't measured in hours and days—he still felt guilty. So he returned.

The play was depressing. It told the stories of three dysfunctional couples; none of them were getting what they wanted out of life, and most didn't even seem to know what it was they wanted. Lulu played a middle-aged suburban mom from New Jersey who is bored with her husband and wants to have an affair with her old boyfriend, but can't quite summon the courage. Harry was surprised by how well she acted the part: she had great timing, and she hit all the laugh lines just right. How did she know so much about adult angst?

"How did you like it?" she asked when Harry met her backstage after the show. He had forgotten to buy her flowers, but Andrea had remembered.

"You were great," said Harry, giving her a big hug.

"But how did you like the play?" She wanted a review.

"It was funny," said Harry. "A lot of funny lines. But the people were so screwed up. Real people aren't like that."

"Yes they are. That's the point, Daddy. Life is empty. That's what the play is about." He gave her a pat on the back but she turned away. She was peeved, wanting to pick a fight with her jet-lagged father.

Harry looked to Andrea. "Come on, sweetie. Mommy and I aren't like that." But that was the wrong thing to say.

"You don't understand," groaned Lulu. "I don't want to talk about it." She was slipping away from him. In another few years—hell, in another few minutes—she would be gone.

Harry drove her home. Andrea went separately in her own car, so they were alone. He tried to talk about London, her acting, and how it was almost September and time for the start of a new school year. She answered as little as she could. She leaned away from him, toward the passenger door, as if just being in the same car was painful.

"Why don't you polish the door handle while you're over there," Harry said.

Lulu didn't laugh. There was a little sound of air being exhaled, like a sigh but without even that energy.

"Why are you so angry with me?" Harry asked finally, as they were nearing the house in Reston.

"I'm not! I just don't want to talk about it."

Harry felt an empty chill, as if a cold wind were blowing through his body. This was what despair felt like. He was near tears, suddenly. He tried to fight it off.

"It's not my fault, darling."

"What are you *talking* about, Daddy?" She said it furiously, her voice brimming with hurt. She knew exactly what he was talking about.

"Alex."

"No!" It came out as a wail, puncturing the membrane of her grief.

"It's not my fault. I didn't want him to go. If you knew . . ."

She was sobbing now. Not little sniffles, but convulsive sobs as if she had just discovered her brother's body. When they reached the house, she ran to the door. Harry stayed in the car. He couldn't move. After a few minutes, Andrea came out and brought him inside.

Harry saw his boss alone the next morning. The director was wearing his navy uniform again. It made him seem like a visitor, a liaison officer from another department. Harry told him about the meeting in London, most of it, at least. He explained that SIS had someone in Tehran, an Iranian agent in place, who might be able to flush out their mystery correspondent, Dr. Ali. The director listened to the operational plan, but he seemed distracted. What Harry was explaining wasn't on point, it seemed. The train had moved on.

"The White House is all fired up," the director explained when Harry had finished. "You need to understand that. They met yesterday. They don't regard this as a fishing expedition. More like a turkey shoot."

"What does that mean?"

"It means you've got to push your man. Get as much as you can, as fast as you can. They want to move. Rattle the cage. Your finesse play with SIS is nice, but it's going to take too long."

"Sorry, but the SIS contact is all I've got. Do you have a better idea?"

"No. But Arthur does."

Harry shook his head. This was what happened when the merry-go-round started up. Things started to spin, and everyone got dizzy. He wanted to tell the director, "Get another guy. I quit," but that would be unprofessional, and also stupid. So he just said, "I'll talk to Arthur."

Harry had a lunch meeting that day with the head of French intelligence, who was visiting Washington. He proposed a French restaurant, of course, a little place called Chez Girard near the White House. He was a neat, well-spoken man who had tried to rescue his service from some of the swashbucklers and fixers who had given it such a bad reputation. He was Cartesian; he talked about big strategic ideas in a way that Harry, the operator who had come up through the paramilitary branch, could only admire.

Harry had gotten to know him during his brief stint in Beirut, after the CIA station chief had been kidnapped and killed. The Frenchman had been chief of his service's station, no easy task in a country where French and Lebanese dirty money were so thoroughly mixed. Harry liked him, and the two men had stayed friends in the years since. Harry visited him occasionally at his creamy white offices on the Boulevard Mortier, near the municipal swimming pool that gave the French service its nickname, "La Piscine," and the Frenchman reciprocated when he was in town. He always addressed Harry by his full name, heavily accented, *Har-ry Pap-pas.*

It was a pleasant enough lunch; more gossip than real business. But toward the end of the meal, the Frenchman had said something that troubled Harry. We are worried about you, he had confided. We are concerned that the CIA is losing a step. We would like to help, but we don't know how. Harry didn't have a good answer for him.

Fox was sitting regally in his office when Harry paid a call that afternoon. He was wearing a bow tie, even on this hot day in late August, when most people had their ties at half-mast or had dispensed with them altogether.

"We missed you at the White House yesterday,"

said Fox reproachfully. "There was a principals meeting."

Fox didn't seem to know that Harry had been in London. That was good. At least the director had kept his word about that.

"Sorry. I had promised to take my daughter on a trip. She's been missing me. I couldn't break the date." A double lie.

"We have some ideas," said Fox. "We talked them over in the Sit Room yesterday." By "we," he seemed to mean himself and the president.

"I'm all ears."

"We need proof from this Dr. Ali of what was in his email, in a hurry. That's the drill: We get him to confirm the neutron generator tests. We find out where the equipment is from. We ask what's up with the plutonium program. If he can't help give us answers, so be it. *Dommage.* Move on. And then, unless people lose their nerve, we bust their balls."

Harry winced. Fox was especially unconvincing when he tried to talk like a street tough. "Meaning what?"

"The president likes the idea of a naval embargo in the Gulf, once we have the goods. Go to the UN with the evidence that they are building a weapon. Say it's unacceptable, and that under the Non-Proliferation Treaty we will stop ships at sea to make sure they aren't carrying material that could be used to make a bomb."

"No disrespect to you and the president, Arthur, but that's a mistake. If you go public, you'll blow our source. Get him killed before we know what the Iranians are really doing. You might get your rocks off, but what next? They'll keep going, and we won't know shit."

Fox had set his jaw, but there was a little smile, too, almost a smirk.

"They won't keep going if we bomb their facilities."

"Jesus, Arthur! We don't know enough to be advising the president that he should go to war. We don't know anything. Get real, man."

"I'm not asking you, Harry. I'm telling you. This is what the president wants to do. Our job is not to make policy, but to carry it out."

"Our job, Arthur, is to do our job. Which is to provide reliable intelligence. I thought people might have learned that, after the past few years."

Harry surveyed Fox's office. The pictures in the silver frames on his desk told the story. Fox sitting with the president at Camp David. Fox standing with Stewart Appleman on the deck of a boat somewhere, Nantucket probably. That was where his authority originated. It was dressed in Top-Siders and sipping a gin and tonic. There was absolutely no point in challenging Arthur Fox head-on, none at all. Harry took a deep breath.

"Let's go back to basics. Leave the bombs for later. How's that?"

"Fine, Harry."

"The first thing we need to do is communicate with our agent—or the person we hope will become our agent. What is it that we are going to tell him? Have you and the president discussed that?"

"I made a list." Fox took a sheet of paper out of a red-clad folder. "We ask him where and when the neutron emitter was tested. We ask him where the parts came from. We ask him what other components of the trigger have been tested, and where, and when. We ask him—"

"You can stop there," cut in Harry. "By that point, he's already dead."

"Goddammit, Harry. You don't seem to understand. The Iranians are building a nuclear weapon. We are running out of time to stop it. We don't have the luxury of waiting to do all your nice tradecraft exercises. We need answers. To this list of questions. Now."

Fox stopped. He realized that he had been shouting, which was unbecoming and unnecessary. He began again, more slowly.

"You realize that I speak for the director in this."

"Afraid so. I saw him before I came down here."

"Don't be selfish, Harry. Be a team player, for once."

Harry took a step back from Fox's desk. The hairs on the back of his neck prickled like tiny electrified wires. Team player. What a prick. It was people like Arthur Fox who had gotten his son killed.

"Tell you what, Arthur. I'll write up a message for the 'iranmetalworks' Gmail account he wants us to use, tasking him on the items you mention."

"Unnecessary. Already done."

"Have you put it in the 'saved' file?"

"Not yet. Waiting for you. Director's orders. I would have done it yesterday. You were gone. But he said no."

Harry went to Fox's computer and read the message. It was a set of instructions, written like a message to a maid. Harry shook his head.

"May I?" he asked. "Just a little editing."

"Sure, if it makes you feel better."

Harry sat down at the computer and began massaging the text. He added a few phrases. Grace notes, personal admonitions, the kinds of things he would say to an agent if they were sitting together in a safe house. He took out some of the specifics, the words that could get Dr. Ali killed if the message was intercepted and filtered along the way. He did the things Fox would have done if he had ever actually handled an agent in his life. When he was done, he pulled his chair back so Fox could read.

Dear Friend:

We thank you for contacting us again. We are interested in a continuing business relationship. We have questions about the last message you sent. It described testing of a certain

154

device. For business purposes, it would be helpful to know when and where these tests took place. We wish to know also where the pieces of this device were obtained. We also wonder if there is another technique to make the final product, using a different material. We cannot find a working site in any of our business directories. Can you advise? A final question: We would like to make an investment in X-ray transport technology that might be useful in new designs. Can you query any of your business associates on this topic?

Please know that your messages have been read by the chairman of our company. He is very grateful for your help, and wishes to show his gratitude. Would it be possible for one of his business associates to meet with you, at home or somewhere nearby? We can make arrangements better outside, if that is possible for you. Time is very urgent, as you know. You will make millions with your inventions, dear friend, if that is what you desire.

Harry added a last phrase, in Persian. *"Yek donya mamnoon."* A world of thanks.

Fox studied the message carefully. "You can't be more specific with him?"

"Not yet. If we can get him out to Dubai or Istanbul, we can do a lot more. I'm working on ways to contact him in Tehran, too."

"We don't have time for all this, Harry. Time is running out. And what's this crap about X-ray transport technology? We don't care about that."

"I do. It's a tell."

"What kind of 'tell'? We're not playing poker."

"If he asks the X-ray question, maybe someone's going to hear about it. And maybe that someone is going to tell us. And then maybe we'll know who we're dealing with."

"Oh," said Fox. He pondered the situation for a moment and realized this was the best he was going to get.

"Save it," he said.

Harry saved the message on the "iranmetalworks" account. And it was gone, though they couldn't be sure where.

13

TEHRAN

Mahmoud Azadi squirmed nervously in the backseat of a Paykan taxi in Tehran, heading north in the afternoon traffic. The cars were moving along the Kordestan Expressway, big and breezy like Los Angeles, the city that Tehran secretly mimicked in its dreams. When the cab reached Vali Asr Avenue, the traffic slowed to a crawl. The driver asked his passenger what kind of music he wanted to hear, Persian or Turkish, but Azadi said he didn't care. The taxi stopped for another passenger, a single woman. Azadi moved to the front seat, as the rules required, so that he wouldn't have to sit next to her.

His mind was somewhere else. He hated meeting the British in Tehran. They weren't supposed to do this. They were supposed to wait and talk in Qatar or Dubai. They were supposed to use the mysterious communications device they had left in the bushes in Lavizan Park many months ago. Something bad was happening, it could only be that. When Azadi received the message the day before summoning him to the apartment, he had been sick to his stomach. He had been afraid even of his own vomit, that it was a telltale sign of his secret work.

The September smog had settled over the city like a noxious cloud. Azadi couldn't even see the Alborz ridge through the haze, and it was only a few miles away. He had grown up in this neighborhood, born in the last gaudy days of the shah. He was lucky that his father had been a religious man with the right friends in the bazaar. Otherwise the family would have been destroyed, and he might be driving a cab instead of riding in one.

The traffic edged up Vali Asr. At each corner, cars entering from the right pushed their way in, defying the oncoming traffic. People drove here by inches. They were ready to die for a car's length of space. It hadn't been that way in the Netherlands, when Azadi was a student at Utrecht. "Sun of justice, shine upon us." That was the university motto. There were rules. People stood in lines. They stopped at traffic lights. A man's dignity wasn't at risk every time he entered an intersection.

Azadi got out on the corner of Vali Asr and Satari Boulevard. The driver said he didn't want any money for such a short ride, but of course he didn't mean it. Azadi gave him five tomans. Too much, but he was nervous. The apartment was two blocks north, on Foroozan Street. He walked slowly, looking in the store windows the way the Englishman had told him to do. There was someone behind him, a man in sunglasses, walking as slowly as Azadi. Why was that? He had that queasy feeling again, as last night, that he wanted to be sick. The man in the sunglasses continued past him, but then he stopped at the corner of Foroozan Street and began reading a newspaper. Nobody did that. Azadi was panicking now. He wanted to run, all the way back to Holland if he could. The foreigners were devils, and they had made him a devil, too.

He hailed an empty taxi coming up Vali Asr. From the driver's open window came the buoyant sound of an American country singer. He recognized the voice: it was Sheryl Crow; Azadi had a bootleg copy of one of her CDs. The young taxi driver asked Azadi if he minded the music, and when he didn't answer, he let it play. The driver was a brave man, or maybe just a careless one.

Azadi was reassured, either way. Why should he be so afraid? Perhaps he had just imagined the surveillance.

He told the driver he wanted to go to the Nigerian embassy, on Naseri Street. They inched their way two blocks north, so close to the other cars that the metal skins seemed to be touching. They turned right off the main drag and moved slowly down the side street. Azadi looked up at the rooftops of the buildings. You could see satellite dishes on most of them, sucking down the sweet signals of pirate television from Los Angeles and Toronto and Dubai. They were illegal, officially, but that didn't matter most of the time. When the authorities decided to crack down, there would be a little story in the paper, and people would move the dishes back from the edge of the roof so they couldn't be seen from the street. A few dishes would be confiscated, and then sold on the black market by the police. And then after a few weeks everything would go back to normal. The authorities didn't lose face; the people didn't lose face; the rituals were preserved.

Azadi was feeling almost relaxed now. The taxi crossed Afriqa Boulevard, and a few moments later they were at the Nigerian embassy. Azadi knew it because he had worked there as a translator, before he went to Holland. He had been reporting for the Ministry of Intelligence, of course, not that the Nigerians had any real secrets to steal. But it was enough to get Azadi his permission to travel abroad. He gave the driver a few tomans and began walking south, back toward Foroozan Street, approaching the apartment from the other direction. He wasn't so scared now. They weren't here. They knew nothing about him. The British were powerful. They were devious and vile, as every Iranian knew, but they were the clever ones. How could someone be in danger if he was in the hands of the Little Satan?

Azadi entered a modern apartment building, next to another new one that was still under construction. Everything was being rebuilt in this part of town. Iranians living abroad were sending money home to buy apartments for their parents or their cousins, or just to sit empty. The English must have played that game to get their safe house. They had found an Iranian businessman in Geneva or Frankfurt and had him fill out the paperwork, and wire money to the right bank accounts in Dubai. It was just another "hot" apartment, bought quasi-legally as an investment. The exiles were convinced the mullahs could not last much longer, so they speculated in real estate. They didn't care about politics, these rich exiles. That was the problem. They would never pry power loose from the street urchins of South Tehran who filled the ranks of the Basij and the Pasdaran. The good people were always too soft.

Azadi rang the bell of an apartment on the third floor and waited.

The Englishman opened the door a crack. He called himself Simon Hughes, but Azadi knew that must be a false name. Why did they bother? He could call himself "John Bull," and that would be fine. He had red hair and a big belly, and big glasses that shielded his eyes. It must be a disguise. That was what these spies did. They changed costumes like they were in a Hollywood movie. "Simon Hughes" didn't say a word until they were in the salon and he had turned up the radio. He began by repeating the time of the next scheduled meeting, in Doha in three months. Why hadn't they stuck to that plan? Something must be wrong.

"We are looking for someone," said the Englishman. He sounded so serious, but he wasn't very old. He was in his early thirties, probably no older than Azadi himself. He spoke good Persian. The British did that right. Were they all spies, all the people who graduated from the schools of Oriental studies at Oxford and London? Was that their secret?

"Who are you looking for?" asked Azadi. "Can you give me a name?"

"No," said the Englishman. "But the person we want may be looking for you. That's how you will know him. Or her, possibly."

Azadi was confused, and also worried. "Why

will he be looking for me? Please? Does he know who I am?" There was a tremor in his voice.

"No, he doesn't know who you are. Not at all. But he will be expressing an interest in your scientific specialty. He will be asking about nuclear physics, X-ray physics. That is how you will know who he is. It is possible that he works at the Tehran Nuclear Research Center, or she. It is likely that he is a scientist, like you. If you learn of such a request, I want you to make note of the name and send it to me as soon as possible. And then I want you to forget it."

Azadi nodded. He was really frightened now. He was putting his head into the mouth of the lion if this person worked at the TNRC. That was the place of "no one knows."

The Englishman had some other requests. Had there been visits from foreign scientists to the lab at Tehran University where Azadi worked? Any new shipments of materials from the West, or new requests for suppliers of scientific equipment? They were always asking about that. You would have thought these British were selling laboratory equipment, from all their commercial requests. The Iranians had a saying: "The British have a hand in everything." That was why people feared them, and loved them secretly, too. They were the puppet masters. They had their hands on the strings. How could the puppet not love the puppet master?

The Englishman went over the communications protocol one last time. Then he said goodbye and Azadi walked out the door and down into the sheltering chaos of the streets.

A week passed. The rains came, and they broke through the shell of smog covering Tehran. Azadi tried to concentrate in his lab, but he was nervous. He left work early the day the rain stopped, and went up to Darband, to walk in the hills north of the city. He took something with him, a copy of an official message he had received on the Internet. He didn't want to look at it in the lab, where others might see him—or simply see his face after he had read it.

The drive to Darband was slow, up the steep streets near the shah's old palace. The taxi dropped him near the top, where the trails began. It took an hour of hiking to escape the juice peddlers and knots of tourists and feel free of the city and its tightness. Up here, the women began to let their scarves fall loose, showing their hair. If they were young and daring, they found a hideaway off the main path and took their bras off, too, so that their boyfriends could touch their breasts under the cloak of their manteau. That was the orb of freedom, the soft whiteness of a woman's bosom, to be touched and kissed. Azadi had brought his girlfriends up here, the adventurous ones. He had been a spy of love then, risking everything for a touch of flesh. Was it a version of that same excitement that he felt when he went to his meeting with Simon Hughes? Was that why he did it? There were easier ways to find a secret life.

Azadi climbed another steep trail until he was certain that he was alone. He turned back and looked down the hillside. Building after building, mile after mile; dreams and lies behind every door. How was he any different? Lies were the fuel on which this city ran; everyone had something to hide. He was in a crowd of liars, millions of them. That was his protection. Why would they look for him, when everyone had a secret?

Azadi took out the email message he had printed from his computer. He unfolded the piece of paper carefully. He read it twice. It was a research request, addressed to his department, seeking information about recent literature in the field of X-ray physics. It was sent by a scientist named Dr. Karim Molavi at the Tohid Electrical Company. Azadi thought he had heard of that company. It was owned by the Pasdaran. Did he remember that? Who was Dr. Karim Molavi? The sickness was beginning to rise in his stomach again.

He knew what to do. His anxiety made him smart. He had brought with him the communications device the Englishman had given him after their first meeting, and now he typed the details of the message. The name, the email address, the workplace at Tohid Electrical Company. He pushed a button and it was gone. It had never existed. He tore up the printed copy of the Internet message and was going to throw it away, but he thought, No, they will find the pieces. He would take it home and burn the paper with a lighter, and throw the ashes down the toilet. He wished he could escape in the same way, flush himself back to the Netherlands, or London, or maybe just to Doha.

Now he would quit. If Azadi was looking for somebody, that somebody was also looking for him. He would skip the next meeting with the British in Qatar, and refuse to answer any more of their communications. And never, ever meet them again inside Iran. He would disappear back into the anonymity of his laboratory at Tehran University. He would go to Friday prayers and bow so low he would make a callus on his forehead.

Azadi began walking back down the trail. His steps were heavy. It was one thing to be above the city of lies, here at Darband, but it was another to descend back toward its belly.

Azadi tried to calm himself that night by reading one of his favorite books. It was an Iranian novel called *My Uncle Napoleon* that had been written in the mid-1970s, around the time he was born. It was about an irascible old man who was convinced that the British controlled every aspect of Iranian life.

The lead character, "Dear Uncle Napoleon," took that name because he identified so passionately with the French emperor's hatred of the British. The only real British person Dear Uncle actually encountered in the novel was the bossy wife of an Indian businessman, but never mind. Like most Iranians of the time, Dear Uncle assumed that the British and their agents were everywhere. The Americans were not yet the Great Satan when the book was written. They were wicked, but in a phantasmagorical way. Dear Uncle's friend Asadollah was always admonishing his chums about the importance of "going to San Francisco," which was his euphemism for having sex. If you couldn't make it to San Francisco, Asadollah would say, you should at least try for Los Angeles.

Dear Uncle Napoleon was crazy, or maybe not. He said the things people believed, but were too polite to say out loud. The British were wicked; they were the cause of every bad thing; their agents were omnipresent. Every Iranian believed that. The book became a wildly popular Iranian television series during the 1970s. The ayatollahs had tried to ban it—it satirized the mullahs of Iran, in addition to obsessing about the British—but they gave up. It was like trying to ban laughter.

Azadi liked to read *My Uncle Napoleon* because it covered his trail. It showed that he despised the British and their spies, like every other Iranian. He carried the book with him to the laboratory sometimes and read it during lunch, laughing aloud at the funny parts. But it wasn't just that. Though it was a farcical comic novel, it reinforced his sense that there really was a foreign hand that steered Iran's destiny—and that by assisting it in secret, he was making the only rational choice. He fell asleep that night with the book open on his bed.

14

WASHINGTON/LONDON

Harry Pappas got the news from Tehran in a back-channel message from Adrian Winkler. The cable was tentative, cautious, almost stinting. "We may have a useful lead in Tehran," Winkler wrote. "Can you perhaps pay us another visit soon, so that we can make some plans?" *May, perhaps, some.* These were words for a diplomatic reception. Harry suspected that Winkler had delayed a day or two before sending the message so that he could think about what to do and make a few inquiries of his own. Harry couldn't really be angry. He would have done the same thing.

Harry cabled back that he would be in London in forty-eight hours. Things were moving quickly in Washington. "Dr. Ali" had responded to the tasking message left in the "iranmetalworks" Gmail drop box. He didn't have any information about an alternative plutonium program, or the heavy-water reactor. Those projects must be in a different compartment, if they existed at all. But he had provided the date of the test of the neutron generator, three months before. And he had specified the location, a research complex at Parchin, twenty miles southeast of Tehran.

The confirmation of the test site was enough for Arthur Fox and the planners in the Situation Room. Now they had coordinates to feed into the topographical mapping system for a cruise missile strike. Centcom was informed; the ships of the Fifth Fleet on patrol in the Persian Gulf added Parchin to their target set.

"Dr. Ali" had added a final note to his response. "Please be careful. The risk for your business now is very small, but for my business, it is very great."

Harry tried to talk to Fox about what that might mean. *"The risk for your business now is very small."* Was that part of his message? The Iranians were trying to make a bomb, but they weren't doing very well at it. They were having technical difficulties. Perhaps the counter-proliferation analysts at the CPD and the policy planners on the NSC staff were missing the point. The Iranians weren't on the verge of anything, except more failure.

Fox was dismissive of Harry's speculation. "You're looking for a way to avoid confrontation," he said.

"What's wrong with avoiding confrontation?"

Fox rolled his eyes, as if the aging case officer

just didn't get it, which made Harry angry. Usually he let conversations like this go; they were pointless. But not this time.

"Hey, Arthur, if you hadn't noticed, we don't have enough troops to fight the wars we've already got in that part of the world. But that's not your department, is it? You start them; let other people finish up."

Fox just snorted. He had the cards he needed. Harry could wring his hands all he liked, but it wouldn't make any difference. Power flowed to the people who were prepared to be decisive, not to the worriers and nitpickers. Even Harry knew that he lacked the information to challenge Fox. He couldn't be sure what "Dr. Ali" meant—and the real meaning of his information about the Iranian nuclear program—without knowing who he was. And on that front, so far as Fox could tell, Harry had made no progress whatsoever.

Harry went to see the director and get his approval for another trip to London. It was an awkward meeting. The director remained a military man at heart. He had filled his seventh-floor office with navy bric-a-brac from his previous commands. Little models of subs and cruisers, awards and decorations, even his diploma from the Naval Academy. Perhaps he kept them around to ward off the bad vibes of the agency. Harry felt sorry for him, beached here at Langley like a four-star whale. As a military officer, the director appreciated an orderly chain of command. He didn't like conflict among his subordinates. And as much as he valued the help of MI6, he wasn't eager to share his most precious secrets with another intelligence service. But Harry wouldn't let go.

"I think London has a positive ID on our man," Harry explained. "We shouldn't do anything big until we chase this down. Right now we're making policy based on bits of intelligence, and we aren't even sure what those bits mean or where they come from."

The director nodded wearily. It wasn't as if he didn't understand the dangers. "What's your alternative, Harry?" he asked. "The White House wants to move."

"Find our source. Debrief him, outside the country if we can. Do the normal things. Polygraph him, train him, give him covert communications. This could be the agency's best asset since Penkovsky. But first we have to find him. SIS has a lead. That gives us a chance."

"But we don't have time."

"Of course we have time. Unless I'm missing something, Dr. Ali is telling us we have lots of time. His boys are messing up. That's what these messages say, if you turn them upside down and shake them. We are rushing into this for no good reason. We should work this case, instead of acting on impulse."

"Arthur Fox and his friends have another idea about what to do with your boy," said the director.

"Great," Harry muttered. "What is it?" Fox hadn't told him about another plan, but then, he wouldn't.

"Task him to look for more things we can make public, when we go to the United Nations."

"When we attack Iran, you mean? Or announce an embargo? That's crazy, based on what we have."

The director shrugged. That was what Appleman and the president were talking about. They wanted to build enough of a case that they could get at least a fig leaf of international support if they decided to strike.

Harry had a sense of vertigo. He had been here before, sitting in this office with a previous CIA director who had wanted to play ball with the White House. People assumed that the United States had the goods when it made a presentation at the United Nations. Even after everything that had happened, that was still true. Young men and women pledged to risk their lives when their leaders said they had proof the nation was threatened.

We have to stop them now, Dad, before they get the big one. His own son Alex had said that, before he deployed to Kuwait at the start of OIF. That was what Alex had always called it, the official name, "Operation Iraqi Freedom." Harry had known in his gut that it was a lie. He was playing along, like everyone else in NE Division, because they all understood that nothing could stop the march to war. But Harry knew it was bullshit. He would be an old man in a wheelchair before the Iraqis got close to building a nuclear weapon. He hadn't said that to his son at the time. And he couldn't say it now.

"Give me a little more time, Admiral," said Harry. "I'll be back from London by this weekend." It wasn't a request, but a statement. "Please don't tell Arthur about the trip. And don't let him send any more messages to Tehran until I get back. Please protect me. You're all I've got."

"As long as I can, Harry. But there is a clock ticking downtown. It's going to take a lot of juice to turn the damn thing off. And don't play any games with your British friends. They may speak the same language, but they don't salute the same flag. Don't forget that, or you'll get in a kind of trouble I can't help you with."

Harry went into his daughter's room that night to say goodbye. He would be on the plane for London the next evening when she got home from school, and he had always made a habit of giving his children a farewell kiss before going anywhere on assignment. He was superstitious that way, never sure which trip might be the last one. He expected that his daughter would be clipped and sullen with him, the way she usually was these days, but tonight was different. Lulu's face was illuminated in the glow of her laptop computer when he opened her door, listening to her music and visiting the Facebook sites of her friends, probably, but she closed the lid and put the computer aside when he came into the room.

"Hi, Daddy," she said brightly.

"I have to go away for a few days," said Harry. "I wanted to give you a goodbye kiss."

She reached out her arms. She never asked where he was going. Neither did Andrea. That was part of the family bargain.

Harry kissed her cheek and held her, longer than he had intended. Her head felt small in his arms, the way it had when she was a baby.

"You seem sad, Daddy," she said.

Harry pulled back. He hadn't meant to seem like anything.

"I guess I am." He paused. "I miss my family when I go away." Something made him want to keep talking. "Sometimes I miss my family when I'm home, too. There's never enough time. It's hard to say the words."

"We know how hard you work, Daddy. We know it's important."

"It's not more important than you, Louise."

She smiled up at him. It was almost a look of compassion, like what he used to see in Andrea's face back when she didn't turn away when their eyes met.

"Don't be sad, Daddy," said Lulu. "We love you."

Harry got into London very early on the United flight, and he had some time to kill before his meeting with Adrian. He took a taxi into the city, and walked along the Thames for an hour. London was just coming awake. The delivery trucks were out, but otherwise the streets were empty. He strolled down Victoria Embankment, just below Whitehall, and then crossed the Waterloo Bridge toward the railway station and Royal Festival Hall. Britain had still been in a post-imperial daze when these graceless concrete buildings were constructed. Maggie Thatcher was just getting started with her wrecking ball.

Harry walked along the south bank until he came to Century House, the old headquarters of SIS before it moved upstream to Vauxhall Cross. How many times had he visited this building over the years? Dozens, maybe scores. The British were junior partners in the firm, but courtesy calls were part of doing business. Harry always came away from these meetings with a sense that his British colleagues were better suited for the game than Americans were. They weren't any better at keeping secrets, but they were better at telling lies.

Winkler was waiting for him when he arrived at Vauxhall Cross. He had set up a secure video conference link with the embassy in Tehran so that Harry could talk directly with the station commander there. The SIS officer's face was on the screen, staring into the video camera, his blond hair neatly combed and his tie knotted up to the top of the collar. He looked very young, but that was the way the British did it, in and out early. Winkler said his real name was Robin Austen-Smith, but not to use that during the conversation.

"Hello, Tehran," said Adrian.

"Hello, London. Sorry I can't see you on this hookup, but I hear you fine."

"We won't keep you long. Tell our American friend a bit about what we've learned on the Bullfinch matter," said Adrian. Apparently that was the code they were using for the operation they had mounted over the past month.

"We believe the target works at an establishment called Tohid Electrical Company. It's part of the Iranian nuclear establishment. We think it took over some of the functions of the Shahid Electric Company, when the Iranians closed down its covert activities in 2003. Tohid is probably owned by the Revolutionary Guard, and we think the personnel there are on a restricted, no-travel basis. But we don't know that. We've never gotten inside."

Harry was taking notes. In a whisper, he asked Adrian whether he could ask questions. His host nodded yes.

"We know a little about Tohid," said Harry. "Your description fits what we have. Why do you think the target works there?"

"Because someone working there contacted our source, Ajax 1, with the programmed query. Probably better to leave the details offline. Mr. Winkler can explain them to you. We have a name for the target, too. We've done some checking on our end, based on some collateral we gathered, and we think it's real. Mr. Winkler can give you that as well. But we haven't taken any further action, pending word from London."

"Good job," said Harry. He turned toward Adrian and tipped an imaginary cap.

"Yes, well done, Tehran. An extra watercress sandwich for you at teatime."

"Thank you, sir."

Winkler flipped a switch and the video screen went fuzzy, and then dark.

"Fuck me," **said Harry.** "You did it."

"Not quite, old boy. But we started it. The question is, what do you want to do next?"

"I don't know yet. Let's start with the basics. What's the name you've got?"

"Dr. Karim Siamak Molavi. He's a scientist, attached to a covert department of Revolutionary Guards intelligence. His father was a dissident intellectual, anti-shah. The son studied in Germany, at the University of Heidelberg. His name surfaced on some scientific papers in the late 1990s, then disappeared."

"Why's he contacting us?"

"We don't know. Maybe it's a provocation. But probably he's pissed off."

"Why?"

"Because his cousin Hossein Shamshiri got cashiered six months ago from a senior position in the Rev Guard. He was a colonel. We picked up word of that after it happened. We did traces and found the family link to Shamshiri. That's what Austen-Smith meant about 'collateral.' "

"What did cousin Hossein do to get himself canned?"

"He picked a fight with the wrong guy. A Pasdaran general who was taking more than the normal cut from an enterprise Shamshiri was supervising. He complained to higher-ups about this un-Islamic behavior, but the general had friends. Someone at the top decided that cousin Hossein was a troublemaker and forced him out."

"So Molavi has a motive?"

"Precisely. That's what makes us think he's legitimate."

"Shit. You know a lot. You've been holding out on me, Adrian."

"Not at all, mate. And don't overstate the importance of a few stray facts we may happen to know. We remain a very poor relation, with our noses pressed up against the windows of our betters. Still, we do have a few crumbs of intelligence that we can bring to the high table."

"Give it a rest. I can take everything but the false

modesty. So what are we going to do, now that we have a name and a motive?"

"Ring his bell, don't you suppose?"

"But how? Your man Austen-Boston, or whatever his ridiculous name is, he obviously can't do it. They'll make him in a minute if he gets near a guy with this kind of security clearance. And you don't have another officer in the station. What about your access agent Mahmoun?"

"Mahmoud Azadi is the name of that worthy gentleman. But he isn't answering the phone at present, I'm afraid. I suspect he got a bit spooked after the last mission that brought us to Mr. Molavi."

"Shiiiit." Harry drew the word out, so it was multisyllabic. "So what's left? Do you have any other assets in country to handle this? Because we don't."

"Not yet," said Adrian. He seemed to be debating something in his mind, and then resolved it in the affirmative. "Not yet, but we might be able to get something in place."

"And what's that, if I might ask."

"We have a certain operational capability we don't like to talk about. Even with each other."

"But you're going to tell me."

Adrian nodded. But still he didn't say anything.

"Come on, boy. Cat got your tongue? What is it?"

"We call it 'the Increment.' It doesn't exist, legally. But there you are. The Increment."

Harry cocked his head. He had heard the term once, a few years before, from another British officer. But when he had pressed, the man hadn't responded.

"What the hell is the Increment? Some kind of secret unit?"

"It's looser than that. More ad hoc. We use soldiers from the Special Air Services, mostly. Black ops people, highly trained. Many of them are from the—forgive the term—former colonies. Indians, Paks, West Indians, Arabs. They all speak the languages fluently, like natives. They can operate anywhere, and more or less invisibly. Or so we like to think. They are seconded to SIS for certain missions where we have to get into a denied area, do something unpleasant, and get out. They have the mythical 007 'license to kill,' as a matter of fact. I like to think of them as James Bond Meets *My Beautiful Launderette*. They give us certain capabilities that we would not have, even under our own rather expansive rules. You don't know about the Increment because, strictly speaking, there is no such organization."

"And you would be willing to lend these versatile individuals to the United States government?"

"No. But we might be willing to lend them to you, Harry."

15

LONDON

Adrian proposed that Harry stay over and have dinner. He wanted to talk some more, you could see that in his eyes. Harry suggested that Susan join them for a festive meal at a Russian restaurant, where they could drink shots of vodka and remember the old days in Moscow. But Adrian said no, they should go out just the two of them, and he proposed that they dine at Mirabelle's, the grand dame of French restaurants in the West End. He sounded wary at the mention of Susan, and Harry wondered why.

They drank a lot of whiskey before the meal, and Adrian eventually blurted it out.

"Susan and I have separated," he said.

"I'm sorry," said Harry. He didn't know if that was the right thing to say, but it was what he felt.

"Don't be. It was going to happen eventually. Would have happened earlier, if Susan hadn't thought she could make it all work. But I finally busted the connection."

"How? I mean, Susan always knew that you had other women. She talked to Andrea about it. I always suspected she had a lover or two of her own along the way. That's why you two were such a fun couple."

"She told the truth about her affairs. I lied. That's

the difference. The lies got bigger. I have another child, by another woman. Bet you didn't know that. Susan didn't either. And that's not even the woman I'm with now. Life is complicated, Harry."

"Does the service know?"

"Of course. You think I'm daft? They know everything. That's the problem, isn't it, Harry? Other than inside the firm, it's all a big fucking lie. And finally that's all that's left, is the lie."

"You're drunk," said Harry.

"Maybe so, maybe so. But I'm right, too. The problem with our business is that we're *supposed* to lie. We're required to, for fuck's sake. When someone asks what we do, we tell a lie. Every time we get on a plane, we have a different passport. We stay at one hotel under one identity and another when we're using a different identity, and we just hope the desk clerk doesn't remember a face. We get people to do bad things, the very worst things, and we say to ourselves, 'higher calling,' or 'can't be helped.' That's if we still have a tinge of guilt left. But pretty soon that goes away. I wouldn't know how to talk to a woman if I was using my true name, Harry. I couldn't get a hard-on."

"Go back to Susan. She knows who you are."

But Adrian wasn't listening. He was going to explain to Harry, his one and only friend, what he wouldn't say to anyone else, even in the House of Lies that was his service. He took another deep drink of his whiskey and lowered his voice to a whisper.

"It's not that simple. I'm corrupt, old boy. I needed money to support my 'lifestyle,' if you will. So I took money. First time was in the Middle East, as a matter of fact, after we left Moscow. I went to meet a Syrian agent in Cyprus, to give him his cash. It was two hundred and fifty thousand pounds. He was a greedy fucker, too, we paid him a lot, and I had always wondered why.

"So, so, so . . ." He took another gulp of whiskey. "The case had just been handed off to me, and I didn't know much about him, you see. When I got to the safe house, he motioned for me to turn off the sound system, with little hand signals, pantomime, you know? He knew the drill. So when the sound was off, I opened up the briefcase to show him the cash, and he said, 'Take your cut.' Just like that. His previous case officer had been skimming, and he just assumed I would too. So I asked what the deal was with my predecessor, and he said twenty percent. And I thought, Blimey! That's fifty thousand quid. That could put a down payment on a nice flat in London back then. So I took it."

"Everybody does little shit," said Harry. "It's a cost of doing business."

"This wasn't little shit, Harry. Over the years, it's a lot of money. It paid for women, and apartments, and abortions, and school fees for my girls, and a boob job for Susan when she still thought she could pull me back."

"And nobody in the service knows?"

"Of course they know. Not the details. But we're all in this together. We hand off the agents, officer to officer. We know we're all skimming at the casino, but it's SIS *omertà*. That's why we're a band of brothers, dear boy. Because each of us has the next guy by the balls, and it's in no one's interest to do anything except to keep the skim going. I'll be next chief of the service, after Sir David. That's the corridor talk. And you know why?"

"Because you're a good intelligence officer."

"Bullshit, Harry. It's because I'm one of them. I won't upset the applecart, because I've got a big fucking handful of apples myself. They'll like me even better when I'm divorced, because they won't have to worry that Susan will straighten me out. I'm bent, Harry. You're just too straight to see it. That's why I love you and nobody else does. How can anyone trust an honest man?"

Adrian called Harry the next morning at his hotel as he was getting ready to leave for the airport. He voice was businesslike, as if he were trying to make up for the indiscretions of the night before. He must have a killer hangover, but it didn't show. That was another British skill, the ability to drink like a fish and come up all dry and fluffy the next morning.

"How about you stay in London another day, old boy?" said Adrian. "There's someone I'd like you to meet. One of our chaps, though he would never describe himself that way."

"I really don't have time for socializing, Adrian. I'm already a day late. People back home are ready to pop."

"I know, I know. But this isn't socializing. Trust me. I wouldn't ask if I didn't think this was worth the time. For you, I mean. The gentleman in question is a Lebanese businessman. Rich as god, he is. Worked for the Libyans in the 1970s, marketing consignments of oil and anything else he could get his hands on. Now he's businessman. So to speak. Very discreet, very quiet. Flies so far below the radar he's almost touching the ground, but he never gets dirty, never a stitch out of place. Useful chap to know."

"Sounds like a heck of a guy, Adrian, but I should get back."

Harry paused. "Unless this involves the matter that we were discussing yesterday. What's his business, if I might ask?"

"Ah yes. Well, that's just the point, isn't it? He's in the business of selling certain very-hard-to-obtain items of scientific equipment. Things that would be quite difficult to acquire from any other source, if you follow me."

"Yes," said Harry, smiling to himself. "I think I follow you. Where do we meet the gentleman in question?"

"We're having lunch with him, actually. I took the liberty. At his place in Mayfair. He doesn't like to go out. And we rather encourage that sense of . . . entertaining at home. I told him we would be there at half one. Hope you don't mind."

"Does he have a name, your friend?"

"Kamal Atwan."

Harry pulled the phone away from his lips for a moment. He knew many prominent Arab businessmen in London, but this name was unfamiliar to him. Evidently he really did fly below the radar.

"Pick me up at the hotel. And when we're done, have a car take me to the airport so I can catch the late flight. I still have to get back tonight."

"Of course. The workaholic thing. Protestant ethic. We understand. But there's one more thing about this little luncheon party, if you don't mind."

"What's that?"

"Well, he's our asset, you see. Mine, to be precise. Very close hold, too. The kind we don't share even with our American cousins. So when we meet him, you'll have to go as one of us. That's what we're telling him. That you're on our team. We own the information. It stays in our circle. Doesn't enter yours. Otherwise he would never agree to see you."

"That's an odd arrangement, even for you, Adrian. What's his problem with Americans?"

"I know this will come as a shock, Harry, but he doesn't trust you. He thinks the CIA is incompetent. He thinks America doesn't protect its friends. I can't imagine where he got such an idea, but there you are. So let's just make you an honorary British agent for the day, shall we? No harm in that."

"I guess not," said Harry. He didn't even think about it, really.

16

LONDON

Kamal Atwan lived in a Regency townhouse on Mount Street, just behind Berkeley Square. To another wealthy Arab, it would have been a convenient spot to bring guests after a night carousing at Annabelle's, around the corner. But Atwan was an altogether more serious man. A burly servant opened the door—by the looks of him, he was more bodyguard than butler. He nodded to Adrian, whom he seemed to know, and invited the two into an elegant parlor. The first thing that caught Harry's eye was the dazzling color of the painting hanging on the far wall. It appeared to be one of the *Water Lilies* series by Monet, but that couldn't be right.

"Is that what I think it is?" whispered Harry, nodding toward the painting.

"Uh-huh," answered Adrian. He pointed across

the room to a bright canvas of a dewy-lipped young woman. "And yes, that's a Renoir."

Atwan was waiting for them upstairs in his library. It was lined with bookshelves on three sides, with a ladder to reach the upper shelves. The books appeared to be organized and catalogued, much like a small college library. The fourth wall of the room was glass, looking out on an indoor pool.

Atwan rose to greet them. He was a tidy man, slim and carefully dressed. His hair was a burnished silver-gray, the color of pewter. He was wearing velvet slippers monogrammed with his initials, and a cashmere sweater under a tweed jacket. On the table next to his chair he had placed the book he had been reading when he was interrupted. It was a collection of essays by Isaiah Berlin. Harry noted the book. In his experience Arabs didn't read much—certainly not books by Jewish philosophers. Beside the Berlin book was a well-thumbed copy of the latest survey published by the International Institute of Strategic Studies.

Adrian Winker approached the host and kissed him on the cheeks, three times, Lebanese-style. He introduced Harry, not by his real name, but as "William Fellows." He hadn't told Harry he was going to give him a work name.

Harry extended his hand to Atwan, who shook it limply.

"Mr. Fellows is American, but you can trust him," said Adrian. "He's one of us. Reliable."

"I am certain of it, my dear," said Atwan, smiling up at Harry. He took notice of the American's size and demeanor. "You might almost be Lebanese, if you were not so big."

"I'm Greek," said Harry.

"Fellows is not a Greek name, I think."

"The name was changed. At Ellis Island."

Atwan motioned them to sit in a sumptuous leather couch and chairs by the far wall. A bottle of white wine was sitting in a silver cooler. A servant arrived to open it and pour them each a glass. It was a 1996 Bâtard-Montrachet; next to it was an open bottle of 1990 La Tâche, breathing a bit before the main course. The two bottles of Burgundy would have cost Harry a month's salary.

"Perhaps Mr. Winkler has told you about my business?" said Atwan.

"Not at all," said Harry. "I know only what I can see with my own eyes. Which is that business seems to be pretty good, whatever it is."

"Good boy, Adrian," said the Lebanese, patting Winkler on the hand. It was a gesture of such familiarity, almost as if Adrian were a member of the family. Harry pondered the nature of the relationship between Adrian and Atwan, and then put the thought out of his mind.

Atwan tasted the white wine and pronounced it adequate, and glasses were poured for the two guests. The host, it turned out, didn't drink himself—except to make sure that what he was serving was of the required quality. A servant brought him a Diet Coke. Adrian took a sip of his wine, wet his whistle, so to speak.

"I thought perhaps you might tell my friend Mr. Fellows about some of your recent dealings with Iran," said Adrian. "He is working with us, as I mentioned to you, and I think it's important that he learn a bit about some of the transactions that are under way."

Atwan arched his eyebrows. "How much detail would you like me to share with Mr. Fellows?"

"Some. Not all. Enough."

"I see." Atwan smiled. "I should take Mr. Fellows into the library. But not into the bedroom."

"You might say that. Into the bedroom, even, but not under the covers."

"Well then, how to begin? I suppose you could say that I am in the import-export business. I obtain products that are scarce in world markets. And then I sell them to people who want to buy them. Not under my own name, of course. I have many companies. They operate so effectively that I can, as you might say, hide in plain sight. What could be simpler? Except that it is not so simple."

"Why not?" asked Harry. He wasn't sure where the conversation was going, or why Winkler had brought him here.

"Because I deal in products that are somewhat unusual, my dear. They are not the sort of things you find at Marks and Spencer."

"Such as?"

Atwan looked to Adrian for guidance. The British spy nodded.

"Go ahead, Kamal. I told you: he's one of us."

"Very well. The sorts of products I might be looking to buy and resell at present would include, let me think . . . fast rise-time oscillographs, to measure very short electrical pulses. That would be one item. And something known as a flash X-ray, which can take a picture of an imploding core. That's a useful device. And, let me think . . . hydrodynamic measurement tools that chart the movement of shock waves through materials. And very fast computers that can take data from these measurement instruments and use them to simulate a complex process. I'm quite interested in those, with the proper software tools."

"Do you perhaps see a pattern here, Mr. Fellows?" asked Adrian with a wink. "Care to hazard a guess as to how one might use this equipment?"

"They're tools for developing a nuclear weapon," said Harry.

"You cheated," said Adrian. He looked over at Atwan, who was sipping his Diet Coke.

"Since we're playing twenty questions, let me ask the next one," said Harry. "What about heavy-water reactors? The kind whose spent fuel can be reprocessed into plutonium. Any orders to get one of those up and running?"

Atwan laughed. There was a lightness about him,

a Fred Astaire quality, despite the deadly seriousness of his business.

"You have a feel for the market, my dear. I can
see that. We have no orders yet to complete that
reactor. But I tell you frankly, I would not be surprised to get such a request soon. It is in the
pipeline, shall we say."

"And who are your customers? If I may ask."

"I am afraid I never discuss that. Except with
Adrian. A matter of business confidentiality, sir.
Not something to talk about."

"Go ahead," said Winkler. "Tell him who you've
been dealing with recently, Kamal. It's all in the
family."

Atwan cocked his head suspiciously, but Winkler
nodded for him to go ahead.

"Well then, my dear Mr. Fellows. My most
recent customer for this scientific equipment has
been an Iranian company. It operates through inter-
mediaries, of course. Several layers. But the end
purchaser is a company called Tohid Electrical
Company. Not very well known to the world. But
known to my friend Mr. Winkler."

Harry didn't move a muscle. Of course he knew
the name. Tohid Electrical Company was the business address of an Iranian gentleman named Karim
Molavi. Also known as "Dr. Ali."

"Sorry," said Harry. "Never heard of it." He
looked over to Winkler and saw him nod his chin
ever so slightly, in homage to Harry's discretion.

They ate a splendid lunch. A waiter brought stuffed grape leaves and kibbeh and a dozen other Lebanese appetizers, then a fish course of fresh lobster tails, and then rare lamp chops adorned with paper bibs so they looked like little choir boys dressed for chapel; and then a groaning board of cheese with a dozen different varieties. Atwan barely ate himself, just nibbling at the food, but Winkler went at it like a trencherman.

Harry matched him until the waiter brought out a dessert of hot fudge sundaes, which he waved off, but Adrian kept on eating—enjoying every mouthful. It seemed clear that he had sampled Atwan's cuisine on other occasions and was eating as if he were the man's own son—or perhaps business partner.

Atwan talked about his library. That seemed to be his dearest possession, more even than the Impressionist paintings that decorated the walls downstairs. He had first editions of all the great English novelists, he explained. Austen, Eliot, Dickens, Thackeray, Trollope. The British Library wanted to buy his collection but he had refused. The books were his most intimate friends, Atwan said. He had given up on people, but his library never disappointed him. He revisited the books, year to year, always finding in them things he had missed the last time around. He was presently rereading Trollope's *The Way We Live Now*, he explained, which was written in the 1870s as new wealth was flooding into London, creating the hedge funds and private-equity billionaires of their day.

"Haram," he said, using the Arabic word that connotes wrongdoing. "This new money. I do not trust it. It gives people too much freedom. These businessmen think they are gods, come down from heaven. They forget their obligations. That is something I never do. I am loyal to my friends."

He took the British man's hand in his, in that same intimate way as when they had first arrived, and held it for a long while.

"And so is Adrian. Loyal to his friends. And so, I trust, are you, Mr. Fellows."

"How did you like Kamal Atwan?" said Adrian as they exited the townhouse. "I told you that he would be 'worth a detour,' as they say in the Michelin Guide."

"Quite a man. Never met an Arab quite like him. You two seemed mighty friendly. Do I sense that you have, perhaps, a business relationship? Outside the intelligence business, I mean."

"Don't ask, don't tell, old boy. Especially not now."

"I practically fell over when he mentioned Tohid. We need to talk about that."

"Quite right." Winkler looked around. A car was waiting, but he didn't trust it. "Let's take a walk," he said. "Where nobody can listen, eh?"

Adrian marched off on long strides, with Harry keeping pace. They walked along Mount Street and ducked into the narrow lane of Hay's Mews. Adrian didn't speak until they were invisible from the larger streets.

"You get the trick, don't you?" he asked Harry. "I mean, you see what this is about?"

"Your man is selling stuff to the Iranians. So you know what they're buying for their nuclear program."

"Well of course, old boy. I mean, fuck yes, we're monitoring the shipments. But it's the value-added that matters. That's what this game is about."

"What's that supposed to mean?"

"Well now, Harry, all that technical gear that Kamal was mentioning. Oscilloscopes and flash X-rays and computer simulations. All very precise and calibrated, wouldn't you think? I mean, these are the tools that you're using to measure how your nuclear material moves toward the core, for the big bang, right? You follow me?"

"Beginning to." A smile was forming on Harry's face. "Tell me more."

"So think about it, Harry. Since we know who's buying it, we can go into the warehouse where this cargo is sitting, in Dubai or Islamabad, and make a few, shall we say, adjustments. Nothing that would make a difference at first—or even for a year. Just a little tiny wobble. But over time, that wobble would continue, you see? And those very precise measurements would be just slightly off. And then, relying on them, you would be off a little bit more. It's like a compass that doesn't point true north, but you can't tell that. So you start off thinking you're going to Birmingham. But blimey, you end up in Penzance. You with me, Harry?"

The London air was moist. A shower cloud was forming to the west. Harry put his hands in his pockets, looked at the ground, and then turned his head up toward Winkler. He was smiling.

"You're damn right a picture is forming."

"And what might that picture be, old chum?"

"Our mystery correspondent at Tohid Electrical Company is giving us a readout on the errors. The point isn't that these tests are working, but that they're not working. That's the game."

"Precisely right, old boy. He is telling us that the sabotage and deception are succeeding. He probably doesn't realize it, but that's the gist of his message."

"Which is the opposite of what Washington thinks."

"'Fraid so."

"What the hell am I going to do?"

"Tell you what you're not going to do, mate. You're not going to breathe one bloody word of what you've heard here today. Remember, you have joined our family. We own this information. We gave it to Harry Pappas, but not to another soul."

"You're muscling me, Adrian. I don't like that."

"No, we are doing the opposite. We are trying to help stop your government from doing something quite catastrophic. We are helping the 'special relationship' stay special. And the only way to do that is by bringing you offside, and whispering in your ear. You have to figure out what to do next. We're not smart enough for that. Not even your old pal Adrian. This is your show now, Harry. But if you tell a soul what you learned today, I promise that you will bring the house down. On yourself and everyone else. Promise, old chum. Bank on it."

They walked back to Mount Street, where the car was still waiting. Harry was late arriving at Heathrow, but such was the power of Adrian and his colleagues that the plane had mysteriously been delayed an hour because of a security review by the British Airports Authority. Harry tried to sleep on the long flight home, but he couldn't.

17

TEHRAN

Karim Molavi's door was open just a crack inside the white building that housed Tohid Electrical Company. Dr. Molavi had left it that way on purpose—neither open nor closed. He worked on secrets, but he was not secretive. That was the message his door told. They had given him less work the past few weeks, and that made him wonder: Did they trust him less? Had they put his name on a watch list? But those were questions you couldn't think about for very long. They made you weak.

The young scientist repeated to himself the passage from the Koran that the regime took to be its guiding precept. *Amr be marouf, va nahi az monker.* Promote virtue and contain vice. That was what he did every day. He had just turned the idea inside out, supplanting the liars' definitions with his own. He had to be smarter than they were, every day and every minute. That had always been his protection, that he could see things before the others and process them more quickly in his mind.

Molavi was dressed in his usual white collarless shirt, but without his father's gold cuff links. He had put them in a box and hidden them in his apartment a few weeks earlier. He wasn't sure why. The jacket of his black suit was neatly placed on a wooden hanger on the back of the door. He had cut his hair so it wasn't as thick and lustrous; he had looked too elegant before, he feared. People would notice. And he had let his beard grow. Good grooming for men had become dangerous in recent months. The police were visiting the barber's shops now, warning not to trim men's eyebrows or the hairs in their nose. It was against God's will. When Molavi thought of that, it made the idea of betrayal seem easier. Who could not betray such lunacy—the idea that God commands us to have bushy eyebrows?

On his desk were several articles he had printed out from journals in the West. He was underlining them; yellow ink for information that would be useful for the university institute where he lectured once a week as part of his cover; red ink for information that would be useful for his secret work at Tohid. He walked to the window and pulled back the dark curtain. It was so bright outside; it was another world. The push of the traffic, the babies in prams, taken by their grandmas and nannies for a morning walk. The rich men who lived in Jamaran and the poor men who served them—whose biggest secret, nearly all of them, was the dream of what lay between a woman's legs.

"Karim?" There was a rap at the half-open door and then a push, and his boss, Dr. Bazargan, entered the room. Dr. Bazargan wore a white coat, as if he were a medical doctor or a laboratory technician. He was stupider than the people who worked under him. That was why they had given him the job.

"May God grant you good health, Director," said Molavi.

"And to you. Thanks God." Bazargan hovered awkwardly, unsure whether to stand or sit.

Molavi rose and offered him a chair, but the visitor declined. It wasn't that sort of courtesy call, evidently.

"People have been asking more questions about you, Karim. I thought I should tell you."

The young scientist blinked, his eyelashes falling like a curtain.

"What are they asking?" said Karim as confidently as he could manage. "Do they wonder how I do my work? Do they read my papers and wish to discuss them?"

"No, Karim. It is not that. I do not think these people are scientists."

Molavi remained standing. There was a roar in his ears.

"Who are they, then?"

"They are with the Etelaat, I think. Like the men who came before."

Molavi understood. The Etelaat-e Sepah. The intelligence service of the Revolutionary Guard.

"And they asked more questions?"

"Yes. They wanted to know things I could not answer. I did not know. I told them they would have to talk with you."

"They are welcome. My only wish is to serve the revolution and be faithful to the teachings of the Imam. They are most welcome."

"They will come soon to see you, I think."

"How soon?"

"Well, Karim, they are here now, actually. They told me to come get you. I am sorry."

How like Dr. Bazargan this charade was. He could not say the thing itself; he tiptoed up to it. He was almost trembling now. Indeed, he looked more frightened than Karim Molavi, as if something terrible was about to upset his world of privilege here in the Jamaran district. He was not a good liar. He had not embraced his fear and learned to hide in it.

"They are most welcome," repeated Molavi. He took his coat from the hanger on the door, put it on carefully, and followed Dr. Bazargan out the door.

They put on the blindfold this time, more to scare Karim than to hide where he was going. When they took it off, he seemed to be in the same walled compound off the Resalat Highway. But this time they deposited him not in the modern wing that looked like an Ikea showroom, but in another building. It was older and darker. Even the light inside seemed to have been pressed and shuttered. The walls of the room were decorated with stern posters of the revolutionary martyrs, and with warnings against the treachery of the *monafequin*, the hypocrites.

Mehdi Esfahani was waiting for Molavi, tugging at his goatee. He shook Karim's hand when he arrived, but there was a cold menace in his eyes.

"We meet again," said the interrogator. "What a pity that is, for you. No jokes this time. No laughs at all. I am sorry, but you have disappointed me."

"I have done nothing wrong, Brother Inspector. You are mistaken, whatever you think."

"Do you know why we have summoned you?" asked the interrogator.

"No," said Molavi. He shuddered slightly at the word "summoned." It sounded almost like "arrested." He wanted to protest that it was an outrage, bringing him from his office for no reason. But he held his tongue. Any sort of embellishment would only make him look more guilty.

"Of course you know," said the interrogator.

Karim kept his silence. He had heard this invitation to self-incrimination before.

"Something is not working in your laboratory, and we want to know why. Some of your colleagues think you are the cause."

"It is not my fault, Brother Inspector. Truly. We may have problems, it is true. The instruments do not always work. But I cannot tell you why, because I do not know."

"I do not believe you, Doctor. I have an intuition that you are lying to me, and I am very rarely wrong. But we shall see."

The interrogator had papers, from the Tohid laboratories and from other places. The questions were very technical. He wanted Karim to explain the calculations performed by some of the instruments Tohid used. He showed him a list of numbers from the measurements of an oscilloscope operated by Tohid, and then asked him to compare those measurements to ones taken with an identical oscilloscope operated by a university in Britain.

"Do you see any difference, Dr. Molavi?" asked the interrogator.

"Yes, of course. They are measuring different things, so the numbers are different."

"That is not what I meant, Dr. Molavi. Do you see any difference in the sequence and accuracy of the readings? That is what I want to know."

Karim looked more closely at the documents. He was breathing a little easier now. His worst fear had not been realized. He had thought that someone would confront him with copies of messages to a foreign website, and that he would be in the torture room before nightfall. But that hadn't happened.

"There are small discontinuities in measurement," Karim said eventually. "But I cannot tell whether they are due to what is being measured, or to imperfections in the measuring equipment. I am sorry."

The interrogator started again with another set of documents. This second set also involved aspects of measurement and testing in Tohid's work. So much of their work involved computer simulation that it was difficult to establish real effects and the simulation of those effects. Karim tried to explain. The interrogator listened, and then asked more questions. They went on that way for several hours. The interrogator seemed intent on trying to identify something. He gave a hint of what he was after just once, as they were reviewing data provided by a simulation of the triggering mechanism of the secret, monstrous object Tohid was helping to design.

"Is it better than it looks from the measurements, or worse?"

"What do you mean, Brother Inspector?"

"The measurement says that our device will not work. That we are not able to make the trigger work. But do we trust these measurements? Or are they a lie, to make us doubt our success? Which is the way out of this puzzle, I am wondering . . ."

Esfahani's voice trailed off, and when Karim asked him again what he meant, he wouldn't answer.

Molavi requested lunch, but the man behind the desk said no. Did they think he would be more cooperative on an empty stomach, sitting in an uncomfortable chair behind a locked door? Esfahani continued the interrogation until late afternoon.

"Can I ask you a question, Brother Inspector?" said Molavi finally. He was nearing the point of exhaustion. "What is it that you are looking for?"

"We are looking for lies," said the interrogator.

"Which lies?" asked Molavi.

"The ones we cannot see. The ones in the machines, which will deceive us without even a whisper. The ones from the scientists who are hiding things. We are at a crossroads, Dr. Molavi. The signs point us in different directions. Esfahan is two hundred and eighty kilometers south of Tehran. Kermanshah is four hundred kilometers west of Tehran. But we do not know if the signs are accurate. Do they point us toward the right places? Do they give us an accurate measurement of distance? Or do they lie?"

"And why do you ask me about this, Brother Inspector?"

"Because I do not trust you."

"And why is that?"

"That I cannot tell you, my dear Doctor. It is enough for you to know that you are under suspicion."

Molavi felt a shiver. He shook his head to say that the interrogator was mistaken, then looked into his eyes.

"I have done nothing wrong." He said it with utter sincerity. But the interrogator just shook his head.

"Khar kose!" he muttered. Your sister's cunt. It was a crude remark, out of place even for an interrogator, and it startled Molavi.

"We will have more questions for you another day. Harder questions, I think. Perhaps with harder men asking them. I am sorry. But we must know where the lies are. *Alhamdollah.* It is God's will."

The interrogator asked Molavi if he had his passport. Yes, of course, said the young man. He carried it with him always, as most Iranians did. Just in case. The interrogator asked him to surrender it, for safekeeping. "It will be easier that way," he said. Molavi asked when his passport might be returned to him, but the interrogator did not answer.

When Mehdi Esfahani was finished with his interrogation, he left his office in the complex near the Resalat Highway and traveled west toward Karaj. He was driving his own car, and trying to follow the directions he had been given to a villa in one of the new suburbs near Bahonar, where the Quds Force had a training camp. He got lost once, and was late arriving. The shutters of the villa were closed, and there was no answer when he first knocked at the door, so that he thought he had come to the wrong place. But eventually the door opened a crack, and in the shadows Esfahani could see the shards of a ruined face.

The interior of the villa was dark and dusty. The only light filtered in through slats in the shutters that were not quite tight. The dank light, illuminated by these few, tiny beams, made the room feel as if it were underwater, with motes of dust floating in the murky space like plankton. The room had the smell of a stale box.

Al-Majnoun sat down on a worn couch and bid his visitor do the same. He was smoking from something that glowed in the dark with each puff; it was the bowl of a hookah pipe. He offered Esfahani a pipe stem attached to a serpentine cord, but the visitor refused. The sound of the bubbles as he sucked down each breath was like the noise of a deep-sea diver. Al-Majnoun didn't speak for a minute or so, while he drained whatever was in the pipe, and then he put aside his mouthpiece. His voice had a higher pitch than usual.

"What did he say?" demanded Al-Majnoun. The voice was almost squeaky, as if he had been breathing in nitrous oxide from the pipe instead of smoke.

"Too much, and too little, General," answered Esfahani.

"Do not tell me riddles, Brother Inspector. Does he know anything? Does he understand why these tests are failing?" The voice was deeper now, as the effect of whatever Al-Majnoun had been smoking began to dissipate.

"I do not think so. If he does, he is a very good liar."

Al-Majnoun roared an oath and kicked at the pipe in front of him. There was the sound of breaking glass as the bubble chamber shattered.

"Of course he is a good liar, you fool. He is an Iranian. But does he know anything?"

Mehdi Esfahani didn't know what the right

answer was. Was he supposed to suspect this young man of treasonous activities, or was he supposed to clear him? Al-Majnoun gave no clues as to where the truth lay in this most secret investigation, and Esfahani could only guess.

"I think he is guilty of something," said Esfahani. "I see it in his eyes. They are too proud. They know a secret. Otherwise, if he had done nothing, he would be more afraid. That is all I can report. You will have the transcript of my interrogation tomorrow, and you will see. He knows that the tests are failing; I think he is not unhappy that the tests are failing. But I do not think he knows why."

Esfahani could see Al-Majnoun's head nodding in the viscous light. He was calculating sums on a mental tablet.

"And what next, Brother Interrogator?" asked Al-Majnoun eventually.

"We could use harsher techniques, of course. I have been waiting for your order. I am quite sure they would get us more information, but I cannot say that it would be reliable."

"Not yet," rasped Al-Majnoun. "There may be a time for that, but not now. Watch him, follow him, listen to what he says on the phone, in the dark, in his sleep. Look at his dreams. Play the music in his head."

"Yes, General."

Mehdi Esfahani had no idea what Al-Majnoun

was saying. He waited patiently for more, but after five minutes it was evident that the Lebanese man had fallen asleep, or perhaps just stopped talking. Mehdi rose from his chair, bowed silently, and let himself out the door of the villa and into the light.

A driver from the Etelaat-e Sepah brought Karim Molavi back to the white building in Jamaran. Dr. Bazargan and most of his colleagues were still there, but they shunned him when he returned. They knew he was under a shadow now. Karim was happy, if that is possible for a man who has spent the day being interrogated by the secret police. Whatever they were looking for, it was not the thing he was trying to hide. He went to the office of his friend Abbas, who had also taken his doctorate in physics.

"Shab bekheyr," said Karim, sticking his head in the door, trying to smile as he wished his friend a good evening. He asked if Abbas would like to join him for dinner. They could go get sushi at the Seryna restaurant in Vanak Square. Karim knew that his friend liked sushi, and the place was trendy. But Abbas said no, he was sorry. He had too much work to do. Okay, fine, no problem. But there was a look in his eye, as if Karim were carrying a disease.

Molavi went back to his own office and returned to the scientific papers he had been reading when Dr. Bazargan came by that morning. He would keep to his routine. That would be his protection. The picture of innocence. If they really had something solid on him, he would be in Evin Prison now, or someplace worse.

He closed his eyes and tried to think. He could hear people walking along the corridors outside his office, going home at last. One of the secretaries called out a singsong *"Khoda hafez!"* to wish one of her mates good night. They were still in the cocoon of ignorance, but he was not.

Their game was so obvious: They would watch him for a while, restricting his access to information day by day. They would wait for him to bolt. To contact someone, or make an unwise move. What did they have on him? How much did they know? That was the clever part. They didn't tell you that. Perhaps the whole of the establishment—the employees of Tohid Electrical and the several dozen other companies in the secret network—came under periodic suspicion like this. Maybe that was the game, to shine a harsh light on everyone and see who flinched.

Molavi took a taxi to the Vali Asr district. He wanted to be with other people. He went to the movies at the Farhang Theater and then stopped by a little coffee shop around the corner on Shariati Avenue and ordered a *Faludeh*, with extra rosewater and syrup. He wondered if they were following him. He struck up a conversation with a young man in an expensive leather jacket who was cradling a Nintendo Game Boy. All this young privileged man cared about were video games, it turned out. At home he had an Xbox and a PlayStation. He rattled off all the bootleg games he had managed to obtain, as if they were trophies of a better world. Karim tried to sound interested, just to have the company, but he wasn't, and he eventually apologized that he was sleepy and paid his bill.

He went home to his flat in Yoosef Abad and tried to sleep, but when he closed his eyes, all he saw was light. He took his father's yellowed volume of Ferdowsi's epic poem, thinking the heavy words would lull him to sleep. The opening chapters told of Kayumars, the first king of the Persians.

You will not find another who has known
The might of Kayumars and his great throne
The world was his while he remained alive,
He showed men how to prosper and to thrive:
But all this world is like a tale we hear—
Men's evil, and their glory, disappear.

Karim read the metered lines, wishing to be embraced by the timeless epic, but always his heart was racing. He was in mortal danger. If he stood still, they would eventually catch him. If he tried to escape, they would also catch him. If he spoke or was silent, either way, they would detect his crimes. Was there any path that was not an illusion? What would torture feel like? What would it be to . . . die? As dawn was breaking, in the half-dreaming state after a white night, he had a thought: He would communicate without communicating. He would send a message that was not a message. It would contain its own cover. He thought it would work. But was that the sleeplessness talking, the dream of escape?

18

WASHINGTON

Harry Pappas didn't believe in disloyalty of any kind. He couldn't abide it in others and he had never, so far as he could remember, been guilty of it himself. But he returned from his latest trip to London with a feeling not so much of a breach as of having traded one loyalty for another. He couldn't quite explain it to himself. He was a man who had never experienced ambivalence about things that mattered—not toward his wife, nor the agency; certainly not to his country. But he had that sense now. A part of him felt he was doing something wrong, but a much stronger voice said that his actions were correct and necessary. He was going to tell Andrea about it, but she was tired when he got home and he didn't know how to begin. So he poured himself a deep glass of whiskey.

The first morning he was back he met with Marcia Hill and his young staff. The operational routine continued, with its reassuring checklist of tasks attempted and completed. A case officer in Yerevan had cold pitched an Iranian businessman who was living in Nekichevan; the man hadn't said no, and the case officer thought he would say yes if they sweetened the deal by fifty thousand dollars. An Iranian scientist attending an IAEA meeting in Vienna had left his laptop computer in his room when he went to dinner. The hard drive had been copied, and the take from the computer was now being analyzed. The staff went through the rest of the in-box, and it all sounded serious—operations approved, agents vetted, source reports approved for dissemination. But who could say how much of it was real?

When the meeting broke up, Marcia Hill lingered in Harry's office. She knew him in a way that none of the others did. She had covered for him when he ran off on his trip, but he hadn't told even Marcia where he was going. For all she knew, he had been playing craps in Las Vegas, or banging a hooker in Boca Raton.

"So how are you?" she asked. It was a woman's question. If a man had asked it, Harry would have barked that he was fine and that would be the end of it.

"Okay, I guess," said Harry. "Why? Do I look tired?"

"Yes, but you always look tired. It's more that you look distracted. Want to talk about it?"

She was smart, Marcia Hill. She had that instinct. That was what had made her a great spotter, in the old days. She could sense vulnerability in a man and home in on it.

"No," said Harry. "Not now, maybe later. There's a lot going on."

"No shit, Harry. Those fuckers downtown are getting ready to bomb Tehran." She took a woman's special pleasure in swearing.

Harry shook his head. "They don't get it. They don't have a clue."

She looked up at him, her boozy old eyes twinkling with the animation that age and hard living couldn't destroy.

"Do *you* get it, Harry? We're running out of time."

"Yeah. I'm beginning to, a little. I'll tell you about it when I can."

Harry had been home three days, trying without success to schedule an appointment with the director, when a new message from Iran arrived. This wasn't left in the Gmail drop box, but in another direct message to the CIA's overt website, sent via a server in Tabriz. At first the IOC didn't realize it was Dr. Ali, but Harry knew as soon as he saw the message. Dr. Ali had gone back to his original mode of contact. That was the only communication he really trusted—the onetime code pad, using a computer he knew was secure. The new message was brief, and disturbing:

It is cold in Tehran this fall. I think we must leave for a vacation. Perhaps you can help me get the tickets. Leave a message for me in my box. The problem you are worried about will be okay.

The Iranian included with his message a jpeg digital picture. It showed a young woman in a head scarf cradling a smiling girl of perhaps three or four. The woman was an Iranian beauty, dark eyebrows over enormous eyes, and soft face sculpted in a perfect balance of light and dark, but there was a wary look in her eyes, as if she were imploring the photographer to stop what he was doing and get away. In the background were the wooded slopes of what the analysts decided must be Mellat Park, in North Tehran.

The first assumption was that the people in the picture must be his wife and daughter. Molavi must have come to the park with his family on a Friday afternoon, to eat sweets and walk in the gardens. That was what Harry imagined. The Iranian scientist didn't want his family to know that anything was wrong, but he was showing his handlers what he had at stake, the beautiful woman and helpless child. He had taken them for a picnic in an anonymous park in the midst of Tehran—hiding for a day in a city where every street had a dark corner, where everyone was afraid, always—and he had taken a digital picture. And then he had sent the picture to underscore the message. *It is cold in Tehran this fall. I think we must leave for a vacation.*

Something had happened. The Iranian was scared. Pappas knew it. He could feel the sweat on Molavi's hand, as if he were greeting him at a safe house.

The Iranian had seen something at work, noticed surveillance on his way home, found a hidden program on his computer. Pappas had handled so many agents over the last twenty-five years that he could smell their fear, even in an email. They walked down the path of betrayal so confidently, thinking they knew what they were doing, and then one day they heard footsteps nearby, and they saw menacing shadows, and they knew. That's where Dr. Ali was now: his hands were trembling, and his knees were buckling under him. He wanted out.

Pappas could see it in agonizing clarity, except for one thing. He still had no real idea who Karim Molavi was, beyond the name and address the British had obtained. He had decided he would keep those details to himself, for now. He knew too little, and thanks to Adrian, he knew too much.

Pappas gathered the members of the SAP group later that day. Fox sent his deputy. He was already on to a different page.

"Our man is spooked," Pappas told his colleagues. "I think he wants out." People around the table groaned and shook their heads. They knew how valuable the Iranian was, even if Fox didn't, and that it was critical that he remain in place. Now he was sending a cryptic message asking to defect? Nobody wanted to hear that now, when the clock was ticking and the president himself talked in the Situation Room about "our man in Tehran."

"What are you going to do?" asked Fox's deputy. He was worried that Harry would do something rash that might derail the policy train.

"Nothing," said Harry. "Just tell him that we received his message and that we'll get back to him soon."

People around the table were relieved. At the modern-day CIA, doing nothing was usually the desirable course of action. If you did something, it was bound to make someone angry, and then they would start asking questions and demanding answers. But Harry meant something a little different. He would do nothing through CIA channels. He had entered a separate space. That was what Adrian had achieved. He had drawn Harry into another compartment.

Harry wanted to understand the photograph. It was a clue, but what did it mean? He sent a copy of the jpeg to the Iranian-American analyst in Persia House who had recognized the fragment of

Ferdowsi's poetry many weeks ago. Could she identify the woman using any of their databases? Could she find out more about when and where the photograph was taken?

The analyst was suspicious. She thought the photograph was too perfect, and wondered if she had seen it before. She did some research, and after twenty-four hours, she found an identical picture—of an Iranian movie actress and a child. It was a still photo from a new Iranian film, which had appeared in *Kayhan* newspaper a few months before. A little more research revealed that the woman in question was married to an Iranian movie director—so she could not be the wife of their Dr. Ali. It was a haunting photograph, in its way. But why had he chosen to send this false documentation?

Pappas asked the analyst for more information. What was in the background of the photograph? Was there any Farsi writing that might be a clue? Who was the movie director? What films had he made? The analysts sent Harry a list of the films made by the director. The most famous of them was called *Paper Airplanes*. It was about illusions, the analysts said. Was that part of Dr. Ali's message? Did that explain his comment that "the problem you are worried about will be okay"? Was it part of his plea for help in escaping?

And then it occurred to Harry that there was a simpler explanation. Dr. Ali had sent a false picture because a true one would have given him away. He had sent a picture of someone famous, whom the Iranians could identify if they tracked the message. They would ask all their questions about the director and his wife. When they realized that the movie director was blameless, they would assume that the sender of the message must have a wife and child, too—that this was part of the communication. But it was a veil, over a mask, over a lie.

"I say we leave him in," said Fox. "A few more months, while all this plays out. He can still do us some good, if he's in. Once he's out, he's worthless." He looked toward Harry and stuck his chin out, as if to show that he was in command of the situation.

They were sitting in the director's office, on the couch by the window. The director was fiddling with a set of pearl-inlaid dice he had received on a recent trip to Oman, from the chief of the intelligence service there. He kept shaking them in his hand, but he didn't let them roll. The rattle and click of the dice was the only sound in the room.

"What do you think, Harry?" asked the director, setting down the dice. They showed double sixes. Boxcars.

"He's our agent," said Pappas. "He's frightened, and he's asking for help. He trusts us. If we screw him and he gets caught, it may be years before anyone else takes the plunge. Plus, we need to talk with him. We can't understand what his intel means without a real debrief."

"Could we get him out, assuming that we decided we want to?"

"Maybe," answered Harry. "We have an exfiltration plan for Tehran, same as for everywhere. But it's complicated because we don't have a station there." He debated whether to tell the director and Fox about what Winkler had said about the special British capability. "The Increment." But that wasn't his secret to share, so he fudged it.

"We might be able to get some people in on the ground, with help from other services. They could help us get our man out, or at least to somewhere we can debrief him. It would take a little time to organize, but I think it's the best bet. The worst would be to go public with the information our source has provided so far. That's sure to get him killed."

"Don't be sentimental," said Fox. "I think we should stop worrying and leave him in place. More to the point, so does the White House. I asked, when the message first came in. That's what they think. I quote: 'We can't sacrifice U.S. national security for the sake of one person.' Sorry. That's what they think. Direct from Appleman."

Harry looked at Fox, smugly asserting his White House connections, and then at the director, who was fumbling with the dice again. Harry didn't want to take a suicide dive. But he knew that if he didn't speak up now, it would be too late.

"Stewart Appleman isn't running this case, Arthur. I am. And as long as it's mine, I am going to protect my asset in every way I can. We don't know anything new about the Iranian bomb program except what he has told you. You wouldn't know that they had tested a neutron generator unless this man had risked his life to tell you. You don't know if they can get it to work, or whether they're five months away from a test, or five years, or never. You won't know *anything* until we have more information."

Harry turned to the director. "That's what I think. If you disagree, you better find someone else to run the Iran Operations Division."

"Are you threatening me?" sneered Fox. "That's outrageous."

The director didn't like conflict. He wanted to make everyone happy. He was nervous about Fox and his political patrons, but he was also wary of Harry and the permanent bureaucracy of the clandestine service, where Harry was a beloved senior officer.

"Take a deep breath, everyone, for God's sake," said the director. "We don't need this. Let's remember who the enemy is."

He looked at Pappas. He wished he was back in the navy, where he could just give an order and know that everyone would salute.

"I don't want you to quit, Harry. God knows. But I can tell you that Arthur is accurate in describing the mood at the White House. They are ready to roll, even if we are not. So here's what we're going to do. We're going to give Harry a little more time, to see what he can do about his man in Tehran. But not so much time that the president will think we are stalling. Because we're not."

Harry looked at his boss. This was the best he was going to get.

"Okay," he said.

"Suck it up, Harry," said Fox. "Instead of pulling your boy out of the hot seat, why don't you figure out a way to squeeze him? If this guy is as wonderful a source as you say, then why can't you find him? And why can't you figure out a way to use him? Why can't you get more information that would actually help us understand what's going on? Otherwise you're wasting everybody's time."

"Fuck you," Harry muttered under his breath. He wanted to say a great deal more, but he checked himself. He needed to be careful now. He had to start covering his tracks, and create space where he could operate. These people weren't listening to him. He had been down this road once before and he knew where it ended up.

Harry opened the "iranmetalworks" Gmail account late that afternoon. He wrote a message and saved it. The message said:

We are working on vacation plans. We will bring the tickets to you. Be careful about that cold. Stay away from germs and wash your hands regularly.

19

WASHINGTON

Harry Pappas tossed and turned so much in bed that Andrea finally asked him groggily what was wrong. "My back hurts," he lied, telling her to go back to sleep. He lay in bed for another hour and then went into Alex's old bedroom. It had the musty, empty smell of a room that was never visited. Andrea had wanted to clean it out after the funeral, and put their son's things into boxes and take them down to the basement. That was her way of saying goodbye, but Harry had said no. He wanted to leave the room the way it had been.

The bric-a-brac Alex had accumulated since childhood filled the room: a Redskins banner from one of their Super Bowl seasons, along with a foam rubber pig nose to celebrate the team's offense line, known as "the Hogs"; athletic trophies and ribbons Alex had won through school; a model sailboat he and Harry had built one winter from a balsa wood kit; a pennant from Princeton, which Alex had attended for the academic year that began in September 2001, before he dropped out to enlist in the Corps. A picture of him in his marine uniform, taken on the day he completed basic training.

The colors in the picture had faded since it was taken: a softer blue, a duller red, less shine to the brass. Alex looked fierce and determined in the picture, a fighting machine rather than a fragile young man, but Harry knew what was in those eyes: Are you proud of me, Dad? Is this enough?

Harry lay down on the bed and closed his eyes. He told himself that he could lie there until dawn and not bother Andrea anymore. Next to the bed was a picture of him with his arm around Alex, after his son had quarterbacked his high school team to a Northern Virginia divisional championship. Alex was as tall as Harry, but leaner and more fair-skinned. Did God ever create a more handsome boy? Harry turned the photograph over, and then took it back and studied it. There was a glow on Alex's face, a smile of achievement that made Harry smile as he remembered the game. Then Harry felt the tears welling in his eyes.

Alex had been stationed in Ramadi, the capital of Anbar Province. The insurgency was in full swing then and Americans couldn't move without risking their lives, but Washington was in denial and so, by God, were the Marines. Harry had become station chief in Baghdad a few months earlier. A friend at the Pentagon said they could arrange for Alex to go somewhere else, where

Harry wouldn't have to worry about him, but he wouldn't hear of it. Alex would be furious if he was taken out of his unit. He was a corporal now, trained as a "recon" commando to do the toughest and most dangerous work the Marines encountered. The Corps had wanted him to apply for OCS, figuring that he was a natural officer, but he had refused that, too.

Harry looked for any excuse to visit Ramadi that summer of 2004. It was hotter than hell itself in the Euphrates Valley. He would pay a call at the CIA base, spend a few hours, and then scoot over to the Marine encampment where Alex was stationed. Sometimes he would call ahead and sometimes he wouldn't. Alex was always glad to see his father— never embarrassed. He didn't have anything to prove now. Harry would stride over, big as life, dressed in his light khakis with his sidearm in a holster strapped to his thigh. His personal protection detail would disappear for a while, and Harry would embrace his boy, usually covered in sweat and sand from a day out on patrol.

"How's it going out here?" Harry would ask, and his son would always give a version of the same Marine Corps answer.

"It's fucking great, Dad. We are kicking ass."

Harry would nod, and they would take a walk for a while, sit in the shade, and drink a Coke until it was time for Alex to go back out, or for Harry to return to the Green Zone. He didn't need to ask his son for details of what he was doing. The reports came over his desk every morning. He studied them, looking for the name of Alex's unit, just the way he studied the raw casualty reports as soon as they moved. He knew too much about what Alex was doing; that was part of the problem.

Several times, the Marine base was mortared while Harry was visiting, and he dove for cover with his son, behind one of the big cast-concrete shelters that had been arrayed every fifty yards. That was strangely exhilarating, to be huddled together with your boy as the shells came in, tight smiles on both their faces. That was the part he could never have explained to Andrea: the fun of it.

When it was time for Harry to go, his son would give him another hug, and some more upbeat talk.

"We are taking these fuckers down, Dad. You tell them that back at the Republican Palace."

Harry would nod and pump his fist in the air, or say, "Go get 'em, boy," or "Right on!" Words like that. That was what upset him the most, when he thought back on those last months of his son's life: he had never told him the truth.

It wasn't going "fucking great" out in Anbar. That's what Harry knew but didn't say. The insurgency was gaining strength, day by day. The CIA's requests to be allowed to work with Sunni tribal leaders were being rejected by civilians in the

Pentagon and the viceroys of the Coalition Provisional Administration, who thought they knew better. Harry was sending Washington increasingly stark warnings by mid-2004: the insurgency is recruiting new members more quickly than we are killing them; control of Iraqi cities and towns is falling into the hands of criminal gangs that make deals with Al-Qaeda and the insurgency; the Iranians are pumping millions of dollars across the border each week to finance the Shiite militias. These were the real powers in Iraq, not the straw men in the Green Zone. Harry said it all in his cables, so much that when a particularly gloomy one reached the White House, the president was supposed to have demanded to know whether the station chief was some kind of defeatist. Or a Democrat. Harry told the White House that the Iraq mission was unraveling. But he didn't tell Alex.

Back in the spring of 2002, Harry had tried to talk his son out of quitting Princeton, but not very hard. September 11 had just happened, and in his heart he agreed with his son that any able-bodied young man who didn't help his country now didn't deserve to be an American. It was sentimental crap, but back then everyone believed it, Harry as much as anyone else, and he was proud of his son. He had always wondered what it must have been like for people who stayed in college in 1944 and 1945 and didn't serve in World War II. Did they ever get over the shame?

But by late 2002, when Alex was starting his "recon" advanced training and it was obvious that America was going to invade Iraq, Harry wondered if he had been wrong to allow his boy to follow along behind the marching band. Harry knew the Middle East. He had served an emergency tour in Beirut after the station chief was kidnapped, tortured, and killed, and he knew that the Arab world was at bottom a chaotic mess. The idea that Iraq was going to become an American-style democracy was preposterous to him. But he didn't speak out within the agency. Almost no one did back then, except for a few analysts in the Directorate of Intelligence. What was the point? The decision had already been made. We were going to invade.

Harry knew, too, that the White House was lying when it suggested, with winks and nudges, that Saddam Hussein had been linked in some way with September 11. They never quite came out and said it, but the pitch was obvious to Harry the first time he had visited the Green Zone. On the wall of the main dining room in the Republican Palace, where the soldiers came to eat after a day out in the shit, there was a big mural that showed the Twin Towers, surrounded by the crests of the military services alongside those of the New York Police Department and the New York Fire Department. It might as well have been in neon lights: This is what it's about, boys, going after the guys who took down the Trade Center.

It was the same thing in the gym, over by the transplanted Pizza Hut. When Harry went to work out, he could see the images on the wall behind the reception desk. There was one of Muhammad Ali, standing over the fallen body of Sonny Liston and brandishing his fist like a cocked pistol. Okay, fine. And there was a big blowup of the cover of *Time* magazine's 2003 Person of the Year—"The American Soldier." Amen to that. But the biggest image of all—the one that told the grunts what they were there for—was a giant image of the World Trade Center, with the inescapable message: Those Iraqi motherfuckers did this. It's payback time.

Harry knew that it was a lie. He had studied the intelligence about Saddam's contacts with Al-Qaeda. Thanks to Adrian, he had even read the reports from an agent the British had inside the Iraqi moukhabarat in 2000, when Osama bin Laden had proposed working with the Iraqis, and Saddam himself had said no.

It was a lie, a fabric of lies. But Harry hadn't told that to Alex, who was out in Ramadi living with the consequences. And it had begun to eat away at Harry, as the weeks and months passed. He never said a word to Alex. How could he? As long as the boy was here, he needed to maintain his confidence and belief in the mission. So Harry poured his anger into his cables back home, using language that was so blunt his colleagues back at

Langley wondered if he was committing career suicide. He was raging at the men in suits, the policymakers, the White House—but really, he was raging at himself for not having spoken out sooner, in time to have kept his own son from carrying the weight of the criminal mistake that Harry, by his silence, had tolerated.

On the day Alex was killed, the Marine commander tried to keep the news from getting to Harry. He wanted to chopper into the Green Zone and deliver it himself, in person. But Harry was too sharp-eyed. He read the dispatch as it moved over the secure communications net. Corporal Alexander Pappas had been killed by an IED while conducting a raid near Ramadi. He read it once, twice, and then he let out a cry of anguish that could be heard across the cavernous building that housed the CIA station. He fell to the floor and put his head in his hands. People tried to comfort him, but he needed to be alone with a friend he trusted, who was outside this American circle of deceit and death.

Harry went to the office of Adrian Winkler, the British SIS station commander, and when he arrived, he closed the door and began to sob. What he kept saying, over and over, was: "This was my fault."

Harry dozed off for a few minutes, just before dawn. He was awakened by Andrea, who was calling his name. She had gone looking for him in the bathroom, and in the kitchen downstairs, and even in the recreation room in the basement, never thinking that he had gone into Alex's room. He opened the door, rubbing his eyes.

"What are you doing in there?" she asked.

"I couldn't sleep," he said. "I didn't want to bother you."

"What's wrong?" she asked.

"Everything," he answered, shaking his head. "They're doing it again."

"Who's doing what again?"

He looked away. His voice trailed off. "I can't talk about it."

She took his hand for a moment, and then let it go. She spoke to him now with a wife's deep emotion.

"You have to do something, Harry. This is eating you up, whatever it is. You have to do something."

"I know," he said. "I will."

Harry needed to talk to someone he trusted. He went through a mental list. His closest friend from the old days was the former NE Division chief—a little firecracker of a man, rough and profane, who had mentored him when he first joined the agency. He hated people like Arthur Fox even more than Harry did, and he had advised Harry to quit the agency after he came back from Iraq. But he lived in Williamsburg now, and when he came to Washington he liked to have breakfast at his club and gossip about the new crowd and how they were screwing everything up. Harry liked him, but he wasn't sure he would keep his mouth shut.

A better bet was Harry's ex-boss, Jack Hoffman, the former deputy director for operations. He was an agency lifer, from a family that had sent a string of brothers, cousins, and uncles to the CIA. Jack had survived them all, but nobody lasts forever at the Fudge Factory. He eventually had been thrown overboard by the White House as one of the designated fall guys for Iraq, and by and large he had kept his mouth shut. He had protected Harry during all the months the White House was badmouthing him, and he had tried to give Harry a medal after Baghdad, when he was getting ready to retire himself. But Harry had refused to take it. The idea that he would be honored for Iraq only deepened his sense of shame about Alex.

Harry always called him "Mr. Hoffman." Never by his first name. He had the manner of a retired Mafia don. He was tough, and talked even tougher, but he kept the secrets. If they told him to go down with the ship, down he went. That was the deal. Harry called him that morning at his home in McLean. He was gardening, he said. Sure, he would be happy to see Harry. He suggested that they meet at a coffeehouse in Tyson's Corner, near a string of fancy women's clothing stores. They could talk there with reasonable confidence that nobody would be listening.

• • •

Jack Hoffman was waiting for Harry. He had come early to size up the place. Good tradecraft, as ever. He was seated in a corner, with a view of the door and the Louis Vuitton salon next door. He had an unlit cigar in his hand. Harry took a seat next to his former boss. The chairs were small, designed for ladies who shop, and Harry's large body spilled over the frame.

Hoffman motioned to the waiter and ordered two coffees and a donut. The waiter said they didn't carry donuts, but that they did have *viennoiseries.* Hoffman said he'd take one of those.

"And there's no smoking," said the waiter, pointing to the cigar.

"I'm not smoking. I'm remembering. Now, go away." He made a little shooing motion with his hand, as if he were flicking away a bug.

The waiter was going to protest, but something in Hoffman's manner deterred him. Two ladies who were seated several tables away were looking at the cigar. They whispered to each other and moved to another table across the café. Hoffman turned to Harry.

"What's up, Harry? You don't look so good."

"I'm worried about Iran."

"You got me out of my garden to tell me that?"

Harry started to apologize, but Hoffman punched him gently on the shoulder.

"Just joking with you, Harry boy. Lighten up.

232

Tell me what's bothering you. You look like shit."

"I'm getting squeezed. The White House wants to hit Tehran. They don't know how yet, but they're looking at options. They think the Iranians are about to break out. They're preparing a dossier, just like Iraq. But the intel doesn't show that. It's crap. They think we've got hard facts, but we don't. The truth is, I'm not sure what we have. I'm trying to find out, but it takes time, and this crowd is impatient."

"You think?" said Hoffman sardonically. He had his own scars to show on that account. He put the cigar in his mouth and bit down on it.

"So I don't know what to do. I'm trying to unravel this ball of string, you know. I'm talking to the Brits, who have a station there. But it makes me nervous. I worry that I'm going to do something wrong. You understand? I worry that I am being disloyal to the White House if I don't do what they want. But I'm being disloyal to myself if I do. See what I mean?"

"Honestly, Harry, I have no fucking idea what you're talking about. You better start at the beginning."

"Okay, okay." The waiter brought the coffees and a sad-looking little bun with a crown of spun sugar.

Harry took a breath. Normally he wasn't nervous, but he found Hoffman intimidating. He started again, lowering his voice.

"Here's what it's about, Mr. Hoffman. We have an agent inside the nuclear program. He came in as a VW, and we haven't met him face-to-face yet. But he has sent us a couple of documents, and they look totally legit to me. The question is figuring out what they mean. The first was a readout on their enrichment program; it says they're at thirty-five percent, which is close to a bomb, but not there yet. We don't know how long it will take to get the rest of the way."

"You need to debrief the agent."

"Exactly. But that will take some time, and some help from London. And the White House says we don't have time."

"Well, tell them to piss off." Hoffman winked. He knew as well as Harry that defiance was not an option. If you couldn't do what they told you to do, you were supposed to quit.

"It gets more complicated," continued Harry. "The Iranian sent us another document. This one was about a triggering mechanism for an actual bomb."

"No shit! The Holy Grail."

"Looks like it. The weapons program is back on, for sure. But this second document is hard to read, like the other one. It's scary stuff when you first look at it, but it's describing something that hasn't worked. Maybe that's the real message our Iranian friend is sending us. Maybe he's saying, 'Watch out! We're trying to build a bomb.' Or maybe he's saying, 'Relax. We're trying to build a bomb but it isn't working.'"

"That's why you need to talk to him."

Harry nodded.

"Do you know who he is? This Iranian scientist?"

"It took a while, but we finally got a real name and workplace. With help from SIS. The director authorized it, sort of. The White House doesn't know they're helping. I think they would shit if they did."

"Good for the admiral," said Hoffman. "I wasn't sure he had the stones. So what are you and your British friends planning to do? Can you run him in place?"

"Well, that's the question. There's one more data point. We just got a new message. He says he's scared. Not in so many words, but it's obvious that he thinks they're on to him, and he wants to get out."

Harry thought of the picture of the Iranian actress, and the brief plaintive message.

"But the White House says no?"

"Correct," said Harry. "Arthur Fox is telling them this is it. They already have the smoking gun. They don't need any more intelligence."

"I hate Fox. I should have fired the prick when I had the chance. So what about your agent? The guy who wants out."

"They want to leave him in place, but use his

information in a public dossier about the Iranian nuclear program."

"That will get him killed."

"Yes, sir. But that's not the real problem." Harry moved awkwardly in his little chair. He wanted to make sure Hoffman understood him. He wasn't sentimental about losing an Iranian he'd never met. That wasn't the point.

"I'm ready to sacrifice an agent if we have to. But in this case, we don't even understand what he's trying to tell us. Maybe he's telling us that the equipment is malfunctioning, but that nobody realizes it. Maybe he's saying that a sabotage program is working."

Hoffman looked uncomfortable. He put his cigar down on the table and backed his chair away from Harry.

"What would you know about a sabotage program, Harry?"

"Nothing." Harry thought of his meeting in London with Kamal Atwan, and his promise to Adrian Winkler that whatever he learned there would belong not to him, but to the British.

Harry noticed the discomfort of his former boss. Hoffman was rarely ill at ease about anything, so he was curious.

"So you don't know about a sabotage program, Mr. Hoffman?"

Hoffman looked around. The coffee shop was nearly empty. Even so, he lowered his voice.

"I didn't say that," he answered quietly. "I said that *you* don't know anything about such a program. You're not cleared for it."

Hoffman had drawn a red line, but Harry decided to step over it.

"Help me out. What would I understand, if I had been cleared?"

Hoffman shook his head. "This subject is out of bounds, my friend. On beyond zebra. I'm deaf and dumb."

"Don't play games with me, Mr. Hoffman. My ass is on the line here. These people in the White House want to take the country to war again, and I need to know what the hell is going on. I need a friend right now."

"Hum, hum, hum." Hoffman balanced his coffee spoon on his finger, playing for time while he tried to decide what to say. He leaned toward Harry and began to speak again, barely above a whisper.

"We did have a program of the sort you describe. We were running it through Dubai. The folks at Los Alamos put together all kinds of fancy shit. Computers that dropped a stitch. Centrifuge parts that worked for a year but then began to malfunction."

"What happened?"

"They rumbled us, that's what happened. They realized that the trader who was supplying all this tainted shit was bad. They tortured him. Very bad scene. He gave up the whole goddamn network."

"How come I don't know about this? It's not in the files."

"Our biggest successes rarely are, Harry boy. Neither are our biggest fuckups. This one was a combination of both. End of story, unfortunately."

Harry knew that this was not, in fact, the end of the sabotage story. But he didn't say that to Jack Hoffman. That information existed in a different space, under a different flag. In his silence, he crossed another line.

The waiter came back with the check, obviously hoping that this set of customers was leaving. Hoffman ordered more coffee and, once again, a donut. He hadn't touched the bun in front of him. The waiter shuddered. Hoffman put his cigar back in his mouth and the waiter retreated.

"What should I do?" asked Harry. "That's what I wanted to ask you. The White House is trying to roll us. I don't trust anyone at the agency enough to tell them what I just told you. But I am stumped. I don't know what's right."

Hoffman looked out the window to the parking lot. BMWs, Mercedes, Lexuses. Maseratis. There wasn't an American car in the lot.

"Don't let them do it," he said. "Don't let them take the country to war again without real evidence."

"But I can't disobey orders. Can I?"

"No. I suppose not. Not technically. But drag

your feet. Work with your British friends. Find some way to debrief this Iranian. Make sure you understand what the intelligence means before you let them make it public."

"Should I tell the director?"

"Would he make you stop?"

"Probably, if I was honest with him."

"Then don't tell him. Just do it."

Harry nodded. He knew that there were situations that didn't fit the usual categories, but he was uncomfortable with what his former boss was telling him. It amounted to insubordination. Something worse than that, perhaps.

"Do what's right, my friend," said Hoffman. "You're the one who has to decide what that is." He opened his wallet and dropped a twenty-dollar bill on the table, and then, in what he seemed to regard as a gesture of contempt for the waiter, another ten. He turned back toward Harry.

"This conversation never happened. If anyone ever asks me about it, I'll tell them I don't know what the fuck they are talking about."

"That means I'm on my own," said Harry.

"Yeah. Pretty much. But that was true anyway." Hoffman put his cigar in his mouth, walked out the door, and when he reached the open air, lit it and took a deep breath of the pleasing, noxious smoke.

20

WASHINGTON

Harry asked his wife Andrea to have dinner with him Friday night at the Inn at Little Washington, a fancy restaurant about an hour south of their home in Reston. She thought something must be wrong. They used to come there on anniversaries and other special occasions, before Alex died and their easy pleasures ended. She suggested someplace cheaper and nearer to home but he said no, he really needed to talk, and he wanted to be somewhere private and far away. That made her more nervous. What was it that had kept him up all night, that had taken him out of their big old bed?

Andrea went to the beauty parlor and had her hair done, and then went to the little Vietnamese place on Route 7 and had a pedicure. She wanted to look good for him, whatever was coming.

Andrea had been Harry's dream girl, a lightning bolt, as the French say, from the moment they met in the 1970s. She was tough and smart, but she was also feminine in a way that most women had given up trying to be back then. At teachers college in Waltham, she was pursued by law students and medical students, and even the interns at Mass General. They were all multimillionaires now, those boys who had looked longingly at her short skirts and tight blouses, and it wasn't that she had disliked the idea of being a lawyer's or doctor's wife. But then she met Harry.

Their parents knew each other; that was how they were introduced. Harry was already in the army, graduated from Ranger school and about to make captain. He had been off on missions overseas that he couldn't talk about, so there was a mystery about him. And he was intelligent—not book-smart like the medical students, but smarter. He knew what ordinary people knew, and he didn't seem to realize that he was quite extraordinary himself. That lack of pretense was part of what attracted Andrea. He was big and reassuring; when she was in Harry's arms at the end of their second date, she didn't want to be anywhere else. And he was a funny man, ready with a wisecrack that punctured the self-importance of the Massachusetts people with whom they had both grown up. He made her laugh, back in those days when things still seemed funny, and they didn't know what loss was.

Harry ordered cocktails, and then a bottle of wine. He was so deliberate about it, knocking back big sips of his whiskey and staring at the empty glass until they poured the wine. He acted as if he wanted to get drunk. But he was tongue-tied, for some reason. What was going on? Andrea wondered. She was frightened.

And then her face fell, because it was obvious: he was going to ask her for a divorce. He had been so far away from her the past few months, taking trips he didn't even bother to explain, why hadn't she seen it coming? He didn't know how to be unfaithful, he was so bad at it. But she had let him slip away to wherever he was now, pounding down the drinks in this too-expensive restaurant until he could find the right words. Andrea wondered what she would say, whether she would cry, what she would do if he left her. Men still flirted with her; she could find another husband if it came to that. She didn't want to stay married to this man if he didn't love her anymore. She was as proud as he was.

Harry sat across from her, staring at his glass. He was fumbling for words, trying to frame the question he wanted to resolve. He took her hand in his, but she pulled it back.

"I don't know how to say this, Andrea. It will probably sound crazy. But I'm trying to understand what loyalty means. I need to talk to you about it."

"So talk, Harry," she answered. "But don't play games. Loyalty is simple. It's about being true to the people you care about."

Harry took another swig of wine. Her mood was sharper than he expected, but he couldn't blame her. This was so hard to talk about.

"But what if your loyalty gets tangled up? You get involved with people you're not supposed to?"

Her hands were trembling, and she put them under the table so that he wouldn't see.

"You have to be true to yourself, Harry. And to your values. That's all. If you can't, well . . ." She didn't finish the sentence.

"That's what I think. But I'm trying to decide what it means."

A tear was rolling down her cheek. She brushed it away. She really didn't want to cry.

"Oh God, Harry. What's wrong? Just tell me."

"I can't," he said. He was looking at his wineglass again. He was so absorbed in his own dilemma that he didn't understand how she was hearing his words, until he looked up and saw the trembling lip and the eyes brimming with tears.

He laughed. He didn't mean to, but he couldn't help it. Her eyes flashed, and then softened.

"Oh Jesus, Andrea! This isn't about you and me." He took her hand again.

"It's not?" She wiped the tears from her cheeks with her napkin.

"God, no. It's about work. Christ, I'm sorry. I must have scared the hell out of you."

"I thought you wanted a divorce."

"From you? You're all I have left."

She took a deep breath. She looked at her nails. They were a fiery red. "Pour me another drink, Harry. And then let's talk about your problem at work."

And so he did. At least as much as he could explain, without telling her things he should not say. He took off his jacket and loosened his tie. As he drank more, he got a glow on his cheeks, talking with animation in the way he used to when they were dating.

"I'm a loyal person," Harry said. "I've loved the agency every day I worked there. I loved it even when it didn't love me."

"I know that, Harry."

"I did what they asked, even when I knew it was wrong. That year in Baghdad, I saw things that were crazy. I sent cables. When they didn't listen, I sent more cables. But I did what they asked me to do, always. That was what I signed up for." He paused and looked away. "But then something broke."

Her hand reached for his, the red nails folded around his clenched fist.

"When Alex died, I couldn't be a good soldier anymore. It wasn't just our son, you know, it was all those other kids. We *knew* it wouldn't work. We fucking knew it. All of us. But we let it happen. People at the agency cut me slack. They gave me the Iran job, made me a division chief. They thought I was still the good soldier deep down. But I'm not. And I'm not going to do it again."

"What are you talking about, sweetheart?"

He looked into her eyes. He wasn't debating it anymore. He had made a decision, and it was suddenly obvious to him that he had to protect her from it.

"I think you know what it is," he said.

She nodded. "Iran," she said. She understood him better than he realized.

"There are people who want another war. They want me to help. But I'm not going to do it again."

She looked toward the other tables. Nobody was listening.

"What are you going to do, then," she whispered, "if you can't be a good soldier? Are you going to quit?"

"No. I don't think so. That would make things worse."

"Well, what, then?"

"I don't know."

A shadow fell over her face. She was putting the pieces together. "You can't go against them. They'll destroy you."

He nodded. This was not something to discuss further, even with her, especially with her. Someday people might ask her questions, if things went bad.

"I won't do anything that's wrong, or too stupid. Trust me."

She rolled her eyes.

They got a room in the hotel and made love that night, something they hadn't done in many months. The next afternoon, Harry left again for London. He did not tell his colleagues at the agency.

21

GREATER LONDON

Adrian Winkler was waiting at Heathrow on Sunday morning. Harry had sent him a jabberwocky message from his personal email account. "Let's get incremental," adding his arrival time in London. Harry slept soundly on the long flight, the first good night's sleep he'd had in a while. In the Arrivals Hall at Terminal 3, Adrian was holding a sign that said "Mr. Fellows." That made Harry laugh when he first saw it, but he realized it wasn't a joke. That was his work name now. He was Adrian's agent.

Adrian had a car waiting; a late-model Rover, nothing too fancy. He was dressed simply, in jeans and an old sweater. The Sunday morning traffic was light on the M-4 into London. Adrian asked if Harry wanted to sleep after his flight, but Harry said no, he needed to be back in Washington in forty-eight hours; they should use every minute they had. They stopped at a simple hotel in West London near the Hammersmith flyover; Adrian waited in the car park while Harry checked in and changed into jeans and a black leather jacket. The two men looked like punters out to do a bit of business; not quite shady, but not entirely respectable, either.

The Rover chugged to a suburb called Neasden,

almost to the North Circular Road. There wasn't a more anonymous neighborhood in London. The housing estates and council flats had been built for the working classes of several generations ago, but now it was a neighborhood for immigrants—Pakistanis and Indians, mostly. Adrian drove through the market streets of Neasden until he reached the Dollis Hill Housing Estate, and then pulled up outside a garage. A Pakistani man was inside, working on a motorcycle—a muscle bike, big and bright with chromed exhausts. Bhangra music was playing on a boom box inside the garage.

Adrian parked the car and got out. "Hey, mate," he called out.

The Pakistani emerged from the shadows of the garage and waved. He turned down the music, but you could still hear a faint exotic beat. The man's skin was a dusky brown, the color of tobacco. He was wearing coveralls, but you could see from the way he walked that he was a muscular man. His neck was thick, his shoulders broad.

Adrian extended his hand. The two men shook hands, palms and then fists together.

"What up, my man?" said the Pakistani.

"Hakim, I want you to meet a mate of mine," said Adrian, motioning to Harry. "His name is Bill Fellows. He's working with me on that little project we discussed."

"My brother." The Pakistani bowed.

Harry looked at the tough little man. He was taller than the Pakistani by almost a head, but he doubted he could take him in a fight.

"How's your bike?" asked Adrian.

"Pretty fucking good, man," said Hakim. "I had it up to one-forty the other day."

"Not on the road, I hope."

"Nope. Out at Credenhill. Putting on a show for the lads in Hereford."

"Hakim used to race motorcycles," said Adrian. "He used to do a lot of things. That's part of his cover, eh?" He punched Hakim on one of his thick biceps and the Pakistani ducked into a fighting crouch, bobbing and weaving.

"You used to box, too?" asked Harry.

"Still do," said Hakim. "Amateur only, man. Not a *professional*." He laughed. The Pakistani was a professional killer, that's what he was. Adrian took the Pakistani by the arm and pulled him close.

"So here it is, lad. We meet tomorrow with Mr. Fellows and the team. Same meeting place you and I used last time, down in Brixton. You remember?"

"How could I forget? Sorry how that one went down."

"Not our fault," said Adrian. "Unlucky."

Hakim winked at the SIS man.

"Are we cool, then?" said Adrian.

"Most chillful, sir. But you ain't seen me bike show yet. Want to see your boy burn a little rubber, then?"

"Sure, mate. Just put it in your pants afterwards."

Hakim went back into the garage, wheeled out the big bike, and started it up. The roar made Harry jump. The Pakistani put on a helmet decorated with a red crescent and the words "Allah's Warriors," and jumped into the saddle of the big bike.

"Impress me," said Adrian.

Hakim smiled. He rolled the bike to the center of the road, waited for a car to pass in the other direction, and then took off. He hit sixty miles an hour a few seconds later, and a hundred miles an hour a few seconds after that. People in the neighborhood looked out the window and thought, What a crazy fucker this Hakim is.

The Pakistani turned around at the top of the road, near where it met the A406, and then drove back slowly to where Adrian and Harry were standing.

"Don't you dare me, man," Hakim said. "Because, you know, I will always do it. I am a dangerous boy, you know."

"Yes," said Adrian. "I am quite aware of that. See you tomorrow in Brixton."

The next stop was in Barking, in the far East End, north of the sewage works. This was another dreary working-class neighborhood. Adrian made his way to a sports ground off Longbridge Road. Another muscular young man was waiting for them. This one appeared to be an Arab—his skin the light tan color of a paper bag. It being a Sunday, this gentleman was also getting some exercise in the old neighborhood with some of his mates. He had been lifting weights on an ancient bench whose padding was worn down to the nub. He excused himself from the lads when Adrian and Harry arrived. The young men stood back as he parted, black and brown faces, hooded eyes. You could tell that they worshipped the Arab. He was the neighborhood hero.

"Greetings, Marwan," said Adrian. They shook hands, with the same routine he had used with the Pakistani. "Meet Bill Fellows. A friend from work."

"Allah y'atik al affi," said the Arab. Harry knew the words. May God grant you good health. The young man's grip was tight as a vise.

"What are you bench-pressing these days?" asked Adrian.

"Two-fifty," said Marwan. "Three hundred on a good day."

"Well stop pumping, now. You're too . . . noticeable. Where you're going, you want to look like a coffee boy."

"Got it," said Marwan. "I have my baggy shirts. Nobody is going to make me. Not bloody likely."

Adrian explained the drill. The group would meet the next morning in Brixton. After that, they were rolling. Settle up any outstanding matters, and be ready to move. Marwan was smiling from ear to ear. He still didn't know where he was going, but it didn't matter to him. It was action.

"He's Yemeni," explained Adrian as they were walking back to the car. "But he can mimic almost any Arabic dialect. Iraqi, Lebanese, even Moroccan, although that's a stretch, I have to say. Incredible gift for languages. Pretty strong, too. A good man to have in a tight spot, I'll tell you. One of the best."

"The best what?" asked Harry.

"You'll find out. All in good time."

Adrian was showing off. He was demonstrating for Harry what the action arm of British secret intelligence looked like today. It wasn't James Bond in a tuxedo drinking a martini, or some upper-class twit driving an Aston Martin and saying "Sorry, old boy" as he shot his adversary with a bespoke pistol. Instead it was these righteous Pakis and Arabs, ready to kick ass for Queen and country—blowing people away while they listened to Bob Marley on the iPod. "M" and "Q" and Miss Moneypenny and the rest of the doting, end-of-empire gang were gone. The Increment was Sex Pistols, Prince Nassim, and Hanif Kureishi all rolled into one. It was New Britain, with a vengeance.

There was an urgent message on Harry's BlackBerry from Marcia Hill, his deputy back in

Washington. She asked him to call in as soon as he could. He decided to ignore it. He didn't want any electronic record of where he had been that weekend. Whatever it was, it could wait.

They had one last stop that Sunday afternoon. The third member of Adrian's team was waiting in the very center of London, on the dirt pathway that surrounds Hyde Park. Adrian parked the Rover on the Knightsbridge side, just past the barracks of the House Guards, and led Harry into the park through Rutland Gate. The midday sun was high in the sky, its rays sparkling against the inky water of the Serpentine. They stopped at the bridle path that skirted the grass. Harry looked up and down the trail. All he could see was a handsome woman atop a sleek brown horse. She looked like an equestrienne socialite with a fancy flat in Sloane Square. Harry looked in the other direction, down the park toward the Albert Memorial, searching for the final member of Adrian's team.

"If you please, Jackie," called out Adrian to the woman on the brown stallion. "Get off your high horse and say hello."

The woman dismounted and took off her black riding hat. The blond hair cascaded down her shoulders. Clad in her tight jodhpurs and high leather boots, crop in one hand and horse's reins in the other, she wasn't simply handsome, but quite strikingly beautiful. She stuck the crop in the

252

waistband of her trousers and extended her hand toward Harry.

"William Fellows," said Harry. The horse started for a moment, rearing as Harry walked toward the rider. She jerked the animal back with a sharp pull on the reins.

"Delighted," she said.

Harry couldn't take his eyes off the young woman.

"Jackie's a looker, isn't she?" said Adrian, drawing close to the other two. Rather than being offended, the woman smiled. "That's her cover, you see, the fact that she's so bloody attractive."

"How so?" asked Harry. The woman was flicking the crop against her lower thigh. "Jackie seems pretty conspicuous to me."

"Precisely."

Adrian surveyed the area to make sure no one was in listening distance.

"That's the whole point, my friend. Beautiful Western woman in Tehran. Traveling on a German passport. There to see her Iranian lover. A businessman who visits her hotel at odd hours. The woman goes to restaurants, parties in North Tehran. Gets up late and eats breakfast in bed. Maybe even goes riding at the Jockey Club with some posh Iranians. What could be more clear and obvious than that, eh? She fits every prejudice and stereotype held by your average Ministry of Intelligence wanker."

"And the MOI wanker's fear," said Jackie. "Don't forget that. Except they won't know to be afraid, if I do this right. I should move around the city more or less at will. Because they will think they know precisely who and what I am. But men are so easily manipulated. Really."

"Tomorrow at ten. Brixton," said Adrian. "The lads will be there. We will go over the whole ops plan."

Jackie gathered her hair and put the helmet back on. The horse had turned away from them and was munching some of the stubbly grass. She put her left foot in the stirrup and swung her body over the horse's flanks. Her bottom was smooth and tight under the elastic fabric of her riding pants. She nestled snug in the saddle and trotted off.

"Wow," said Harry.

"Yeah." Adrian sighed. "She's a peach. Brave as a lion, too. Tough sending her off on this one. It's dangerous. She'll be in charge. If anything goes wrong, she'll be the vulnerable one. Not easy for me."

Adrian shook his head and looked down at the ground. He seemed upset.

A thought occurred to Harry. He put it out of his mind, but it came right back.

"You're not . . ." began Harry.

"Not what?"

"You're not . . . involved with her."

"You mean am I fucking her, Harry? Is that what you mean?"

"Well, yes. I guess that is what I mean."

"Here's all I will say about that, Harry boy. As I told you at dinner the other week, life is complicated. Shit happens, isn't that your American expression? And when it happens, it happens. This isn't America, Harry. We aren't infected with all your politically correct cultural reeducation crap, my friend. We don't have the same rules about not sticking your pen in the company inkwell. Here in Britain, it's 'don't ask, don't tell' for heterosexuals, too. Follow my drift?"

"Yeah, sure," said Harry. "Whatever. I just don't want it to complicate our operation, that's all."

"My operation," said Adrian. "And it won't."

Harry didn't talk at first when they were back in the car. He wanted to let the balance return between him and his old friend, after the disruption of this beautiful woman and the complicated "other" life she evidently was part of. It wasn't his business, except in the sense that the life of Adrian was dear to him, and he knew that for all his professional skill, the British officer was wandering. He thought of Susan, Adrian's wife, a woman he had always thought of as a perfect match. Bright, witty, caustic when necessary. A life companion, he would have thought. But some lives require complication. They can't live with too much happiness. They seek out danger. A lover who is borderline crazy, who will draw you into a spider's

255

web and suck you dry of whatever impulse made you want to risk your happiness in the first place. Adrian wasn't a lover so much as a thrill seeker.

The tension between them ebbed away, and soon enough they were talking about the operation. Harry stopped the car at an off-license and brought some beers out to the Rover. It was the safest place to talk about secrets. They ran through what Harry would need to contact his Iranian agent, and what Adrian and his team could deliver. Harry made notes for himself, but then wondered if he should even bring them back to the United States. They were incriminating. In that sense, maybe he was a thrill seeker, too. He had gotten tired of his life partnership with the Culinary Institute of America and wanted something a bit spicier.

"Tell me to fuck off," said Harry, "but who are these people of yours? I mean, who owns them? Is the Increment a real organization? Or is it just a cute name?"

"They're all special-ops people, by training. Members of the Special Air Services, our esteemed SAS, and a few navy chaps from the Special Boat Services. They are seconded to us for one-off missions. They do what we ask, on our rules, extralegal. Whatever it takes. And then they go back. The thing is, for the right sort of person, you really don't want to go back, do you? You want to play James Bond forever. So is the Increment real? I would have to say, 'Yes and no.'"

"Deniable."

"But of course. Isn't that sweet, Harry? I mean, this is a world that doesn't have enough mystery left. And here, to excite the blood, we have a bunch of stone-cold killers who can get in and get out, and get the job done, and nobody is the wiser. And if anyone ever asks a question, we just say, 'Sorry, mate. That's a state secret. Can't really help you with that one.' Never-Never Land. That's the Increment."

22

BRIXTON

The five conspirators met Monday morning in a warehouse off Brixton Road, in the heart of the West Indian ghetto of South London. The sign on the door said it was an import-export company, GENTLE WINDS, and that was surely true. Adrian gathered them in a conference room in the back, past a mailing room that was all boxes and twine. He sat "Mr. Fellows" down in an overstuffed leather chair, as guest of honor. The SIS chief of staff was dressed in an old corduroy jacket with worn leather patches at the elbow, and a blue denim shirt open at the collar. He had an easy command of the group, a manner that was relaxed but also focused on the mission. It was evident that he had worked with the members of this team before, and that they trusted him.

The three operatives were dressed in the clothes they would wear in Iran. Hakim, the Pakistani from North London, wore a simple cotton shirt and a pair of trousers of the kind you might see on South Asian migrants throughout the Middle East. The daredevil on the motorcycle of the day before had vanished; now there was a faint submissive wobble to his head and a deferential smile. Marwan, the Yemeni from Barking, wore a cheap brown suit and a gray and blue polyester tie; he looked every inch the Arab businessman trying to hustle a buck. He too had managed to disguise the athletic vigor of the previous day. His suit was baggy; it made him seem bulky, rather than muscular.

Jackie was the most transformed. In place of the striking riding habit of Sunday afternoon, she wore a loose-fitting gray gabardine jacket that covered her down to her knees, and a black scarf that almost hid her blond tresses. Sunglasses shielded her eyes; but her lips were colored and glossy. When they sat down in the back room, Jackie unbuttoned her manteau. Underneath she was wearing a low-cut silk blouse in a vivid print that resembled the spots of a leopard.

"Work clothes are great, you lot," said Adrian. "Just right." He turned to the Pakistani, who was sitting humbly on the arm of a chair, not permitting himself to slump down the way the others had.

"Hakim, your papers will have you on a temporary visa working a construction project in Shiraz that's supposed to be completed in six months. You're in Tehran to purchase supplies; it's all backstopped with the Pakistani construction company in Lahore. They have your name and passport number at the site manager's office in Shiraz, if anyone needs it. But they won't."

"Tight," said Hakim. "What languages do I speak?"

"Urdu, English, and a little Farsi and Arabic. You worked in Dubai before this. That's backstopped too, if anybody gives a shit. Try to eat a little less over the next week, lad. You look too healthy."

"South Asian starvation diet has commenced, sahib," said Hakim with a little wobble of his head.

"Marwan, you look sleazy as hell, man. Just the kind of low-life Arab who would be in Tehran trying to rub two tomans together. Where did you get that appalling tie? You will be using a Yemeni passport—not your real one but the one with the Saleh identity that you used the last time in Iraq. Okay?"

"Yes, boss. For sure. You want to make business with me? I give you very good price. What you like? I buy carpet, pistachio, used car, as you like. Best price."

"Down, boy. You're giving me a headache. You have any more bad suits like that one?"

"Yes, boss. Three. All dirty."

"Perfect. Your identity is backstopped, too. You

have a letter of credit on a Yemeni bank that will allow you to draw up to one hundred thousand dollars, in the unlikely event that you should need to do any actual business. You have a multiple-entry commercial visa. You work for a trading company in Sanaa with a branch office in Muscat, and the managers in both offices will vouch for you. That work?"

"You are too kind, *habibi*."

"You're right. I am. So Jacqueline will be running the show. She'll have the command post at an apartment hotel in Vali Asr. We'll have the main communications module there, hidden in a makeup kit. There's a rooftop restaurant with some flower pots where she can put a little relay antenna, so the transmission quality should be good. You've all got your gear?"

"Not yet," said Marwan.

"Tomorrow," said Hakim.

"Well, once you get it, do some dry runs with Jackie. Different parts of London, different propagation characteristics. If there are any problems, Jackie will get onto us."

"What passport am I using?" asked Jackie.

"Same German identity as last time. Working girl, femme fatale, lady with a past. All backstopped. As if you needed a legend. Only joking, love."

"Ha-ha," said Jackie.

"How's your German, then?"

260

"It's pretty fucking good, actually. How's yours?"

"Nonexistent."

The boys laughed. They liked Jackie taking the piss out of the boss.

"How do we get in-country?" asked Jackie. "Nobody had decided that last week. Waiting for you to decide, they said."

"Each of you different, to fit your cover. I was thinking of bringing you all in together across the Turkish border, and then having you find your ways separately to Tehran. But I don't like it. Our Turkish friends have gotten so squirrelly lately. What is their problem anyway? I don't trust their intelligence boys, and I don't even trust the army anymore. So better to come in separately. Right?"

Everyone nodded.

"So, Hakim, you will come in overland from Pakistan, crossing the border at Mirjaveh. Then take Iranian buses to Shiraz. Sorry, mate. Not exactly business-class, but it can't be helped."

"Don't worry about me, boss. I like traveling rough."

"Famous last words." He looked down at a notebook he had brought, which listed the logistical details. "You'll be staying at the Hotel Shams, right in the bazaar in South Tehran. Lots of Pakis. No showers, I am afraid."

Hakim sniffed his armpits and laughed.

Adrian turned to the Arab.

"Marwan, I want you to fly in from Qatar. There's a daily flight to the new airport. Imam Khomeini International. Doesn't sound quite right, does it? So you'll fly from Sanaa to Doha, then Doha to Tehran. Back of the plane. Discounted economy, bought from a bucket shop in Saana." He looked at his paper again. "We've got you staying at the New Naderi Hotel, off Jomhuri-ye Islami Street. Business hotel, big with the commercial-traveler set from Dubai. Road warriors, Tehran-style. Some of the desk clerks speak Arabic, apparently.

"And now you, madam base commander. You will be staying top-of-the-line, *naturellement*. At the Aziz Apartment Hotel in Vali Asr. Big suite. Lots of room. Wide-screen TV. Swimming pool that actually has water in it. Health club, Jacuzzi. You're never going to want to come home. You will fly in on the Lufthansa flight from Frankfurt. Very nice. And you actually are flying business-class. Drink your fill on the plane, lassie, because when you land, there ain't no more."

"What's the jumping-off point?" asked Jackie.

"RAF Mildenhall to Ramstein. When you get off the plane in Germany, you assume your new identities. New passports, the whole lot. We'll have you all stamped into Germany in pseudonym. Then off you go—Hakim to Pakistan, Marwan to Yemen, Jackie lives it up in Frankfurt for a few days. Are we set on the basics, then?"

"Sure," said Jackie. "But what's the mission?"

Adrian turned to his American friend. Harry had been taking notes as his SIS colleague talked, wanting to get the details set in his mind. But now the preliminaries were done and it was time to get to the heart of the matter.

"I am going to let Mr. Fellows explain that," said Adrian. "This is his baby, really. We are mother's little helpers."

Harry looked at the three SAS warriors in mufti. It was impossible not to like them, or to have confidence that they would do their jobs. It was a feeling he didn't have often enough at the CIA. That was what had brought him here, really. The British could execute a daring mission, decisively and deniably, and his own service couldn't, or wouldn't. That bothered him, but it wasn't a problem he could fix.

"This is an exfiltration," Harry began. "We have an agent in Tehran, Adrian and I do. He's frightened, and he wants out. He's in a very sensitive position in a program run by the Revolutionary Guard, so he can't travel. But we need to talk with him, face-to-face, and then decide what to do next—whether to pull him or send him back in. We can't decide that until we talk to him. And we can't do that without an exfil. So that's why we're here. But there's a problem."

"We like problems," said Jackie.

"Yeah? Well, that's good. Because we are asking

you to exfiltrate someone we have never met, never contacted directly, never trained. We know where he works, but we have never seen him. We're trying to pluck a fish out of a moving stream, but we aren't sure where he is in the water."

"That *is* interesting," said Jackie. "And how do you propose to move this little fishy toward our net?"

"We message him that we're coming. We don't tell him any more than that, in case he has already been flipped. Then you guys find him. We'll have a work address, probably a home address, too, by the time you get there. We'll do whatever surveillance we can to give you a picture of him. You'll have to stake him out, shadow him, and contact him. I'll figure out some kind of recognition code."

"And then?" Jackie was smiling. There was a taut look of expectation on her face. She liked this. Harry looked toward Adrian, who had that same flush of operational excitement, and then turned back to the team.

"You'll do it in three steps. Step one: brush pass him a message saying where you will leave the commo gear. It will be one of the parks. Adrian can work with his Tehran station to figure out a toy that will blend in. Step two: when he picks up the toy, you talk and arrange details of the exfil. Step three: you move him to where we can talk to him. And then, maybe, you get him back in."

"Will we have support in-country?"

Harry looked to Adrian. The agency certainly wouldn't be providing any.

"A little, if we're in extremis," answered Adrian. "Our Tehran station commander has a few agents and safe houses. But I want to keep your team away from that lot. It may be contaminated. Better to have you three in as singletons."

"Will the target be under surveillance?"

"We don't know," said Harry. "He's spooked. He sent us a message saying he wants out. So we have to assume the Iranian service is watching him."

"How good are they?" asked Jackie. She was doing the talking, but the other two were listening carefully. Adrian was watching Jackie with a hungry look in his eye. This was part of how they got off.

"We'll find out, won't we?" said Harry. "But everything I know about the MOI says they are quite competent, especially on their own turf. So you will just have to be smarter."

"I like it," said Jackie. "A test of wits. You give us the Tehran locations, office and home, and we'll work it out. Where do we exfil him, once we've found him?"

"Not sure yet. Azeri border, Iraqi border, Turkmen border. Take your pick. Adrian and I will decide which works best for us."

"What do you mean, 'us.' Are you lot coming along?"

"Most definitely. We need to meet him. Face-to-face. Talk to him, see how scared he is. Decide on an ops plan. The only way is to eyeball him. You're the delivery service. If he insists on defecting, then we have to arrange something that makes it look like he's dead. If we send him back in, then you'll have to get him back."

"Does he have a wife and kids?" asked Jackie.

"Don't know. My gut says no. But honestly, I don't even know what this guy looks like, let alone his marital status."

There was a pause while they all digested the risk and uncertainty of the operation. Jackie broke the silence.

"What happens if we get caught?"

"You're fucked," said Adrian. "No black passports on this one. You shoot your way out, I would say, if you're near a border. If they grab you inside Tehran, there isn't a lot you can do, except pucker up. We'll get you a good Iranian lawyer. Promise. And we'll send a fruitcake to Evin Prison every Christmas."

The three laughed, politely. They didn't want to think about the risks. Part of being a successful operator was assuming you would never get caught. In your mind's eye, you had to believe you were invisible.

"So what do you think? Come on, Adrian and I want to know."

All three smiled. It was no bullshit. They were excited.

"Are you joking? This is what we *live* for." Jackie was looking at Adrian as she spoke.

Harry wanted to fly back home that afternoon so that he would miss only one day at the office. He had sent Marcia Hill a message at 6:30 a.m. Washington time saying that he had a stomach flu and wouldn't be coming in that Monday. She messaged back that she needed to talk with him, urgently. The boys "downtown" were in a sweat, but it could wait another day if he was sick. Harry knew that if his "flu" stretched two days, Marcia and other colleagues would be calling him at home to make sure he was okay.

Adrian drove Harry back to Heathrow in the same Rover sedan. The SIS officer seemed preoccupied, perhaps thinking about Jackie—worrying about her, or wishing he was bonking her, or probably both. But that wasn't it.

"Should we talk about arrangements?" said Adrian as they passed Chiswick and neared the airport. "For you, I mean."

"What are you talking about?"

"What we're doing is out of the normal lanes, old boy. Unauthorized. Illegal, even."

"That's my problem."

"Quite right. Don't mean to intrude. But what if you should get caught? Then it's our problem. Loyal ally. Hands in the other fellow's cookie jar. Naughty, naughty. The P.M. got a tad . . . concerned. We had to tell him. He *hates* upsetting Washington, you see. Thinks we shouldn't be suborning the services of a CIA division chief. There's a name for that, I think."

"Treason," said Harry. "I think that's the technical term."

"Yes indeed. So the question is, what would we do for each other, in the highly unlikely event that anyone tumbled to what we've been doing."

"Deny it," said Harry.

"And then what? I mean, supposing someone had, forgive the term, 'proof' that you had been a naughty boy? What then?"

"I take it you've talked this over with Sir David?"

"Well, yes. I really thought I should. Flap potential. Blowback, and all that. So here's what we think, Harry. In the highly unlikely event that any of this should ever become known, we would have to disavow it. Say you were operating on your own. Rogue cell, that sort of thing. They might have to throw me overboard. That's up to Sir David. But the point is, we would take care of you. And Andrea, of course."

"Meaning what?"

"An annuity, tuition payments for your daughter. Resettlement when the unpleasantness was over."

"You mean when I got out of prison?"

"Well, yes, I suppose. Sorry even to raise it, but Sir David said I must. Better safe than sorry."

"Okay, here's my answer. You tell Sir David to fuck off. I'm not a British agent. I wouldn't take your money, or your tuition, or a free bottle of Scotch. The very idea is ridiculous. I am using my authority as a CIA division chief, working with a liaison service on a case we are running jointly. As per the oral instructions of my boss, the director."

"Not written."

"Of course not. But I am acting under his authority, and that's what I am going to tell anyone who asks. But nobody will. And what are you going to tell Sir David?"

"To fuck off."

"Good. Then I guess that takes care of everything. And while we're at it, you want a little gratuitous advice from me?"

"No."

"Stop fucking Jackie. She may be the greatest lay in the world. But it's unprofessional. And it's stupid. If you're tired of Susan, screw one of the secretaries. But romancing a paramilitary from the SAS is sick. Even as a midlife crisis, it makes you look silly."

"She is a great lay, Harry. And let's be honest. What you're doing is a hell of a lot stupider than what I'm doing. The difference is that you have a guilty conscience, and I don't. So let's be good mates and get each other through this, eh? I won't judge you and you won't judge me. Are we cool?"

Adrian took his hand off the shift knob and gave

Harry a friendly pat on the back. The big American stared ahead for a moment, and shifted uncomfortably in his seat. He turned back to Adrian.

"We're cool," said Harry. "So long as you tell Sir David that I'm working with you. Not for you."

23

TEHRAN

Dr. Karim Molavi went to visit his uncle Darab one Friday evening in early October in the western suburb known as Sadeghiyeh. He wanted to check the Internet to see if his call for help had received a reply, but he was afraid to touch any computer he had used in the past. *It is cold in Tehran this fall. I think we must leave for a vacation.* He hadn't asked for an answer, but he was sure that one had been sent. If he could read it, he would feel less alone.

He didn't like putting his uncle Darab and aunt Nasrin in danger, but he couldn't think of any other safe way to check his email accounts. The man had a shipping business successful enough that he had bought a new villa near Pardisan Park. And he had a new computer at home for his kids. Molavi had helped install it when they brought the big crate back from Istanbul last Nowruz.

Karim didn't call ahead to his uncle. He was afraid of that, too. And he didn't go to the house directly. He walked from his flat in Yoosef Abad through Argentin Square to the subway stop at Mosalla. It wasn't so busy on Fridays. He took the line 1 train south. A woman's voice named the stops. *The Martyr Behesti. The Martyr Mofateh.* He stared out the window of the train, trying to will himself into stillness. He stood up at several stations and went to the door to see if anyone moved to follow, but no one did. When they reached Imam Khomeini station, he transferred to line 2 and went two stops to Baharestan. He exited the subway and took a stroll around the Parliament building. He couldn't see anyone following him, but if they were good, he wouldn't know.

He walked a few blocks south to the Melat station. Outside he bought some expensive Belgian chocolates for Nasrin and a book for Darab, *The Future of Freedom*, by Fareed Zakaria, translated into Farsi. That would make his uncle nervous, but it would impress him, too. A knockoff Baskin-Robbins was open, so he bought some ice cream for the kids.

Karim texted his uncle and said that he was in the neighborhood and would like to stop by. A minute later, Darab texted back and invited him for dinner. Of course he did. As far as he knew, his nephew Karim was a successful young man, doing important work that nobody ever talked about. Karim suspected that his uncle was even a bit afraid of him.

Karim walked toward the entrance to the station.

There was more of a crowd now, as families returned home from their Friday trips to the park. Before he reached the concourse, he took out a cap and pulled it low, so that it half covered his face. They must have fixed surveillance in these stations, television cameras that monitored everyone in and out. He wouldn't make it easy for them. Karim traveled west for ten stations, listening to the rumble of the train and clutching his bag of gifts. He hoped the ice cream wouldn't melt. When he got to the western terminus at Sadeghiyeh Square, he exited and walked the few blocks to his uncle's villa. He stopped several times, and took one deliberate detour down a dead-end alley. He didn't think anyone was following him.

His aunt and uncle welcomed him at the door with many kisses. Darab was overweight, with a thin mustache and a sneaky look in his eye. Nasrin was a beautiful woman who had let herself go. She belonged to the caliphate of food. They sat him down in the new sitting room. Plastic seat covers were still on the couches and chairs. They hadn't seen nephew Karim in months. Where had he been? He looked too thin. Was he eating? He needed a wife.

Karim was embarrassed. His uncle's family bored him. They were *bee-farhang*, "uncultured"—the worst thing a decent Iranian could say about someone—a crass bourgeois household becoming prosperous off the tidbits of the regime.

One of Uncle Darab's silent partners in the shipping business was a clerical family from Qom. Karim doubted that Darab prayed once a year, let alone five times a day, but he was playing along like everyone else. Just as Karim himself had played along, until a few months ago. Who was he to judge?

Uncle Darab said he liked the American book. "They trust you," he said with a wink. Yes, answered Karim. They trust me. He hoped Darab wouldn't get in too much trouble later, if things went bad. His uncle was an ass, but he didn't deserve to suffer more than anyone else because of Karim's inner compulsion to connect and live.

"It is terrible about Hossein," said Uncle Darab when Nasrin had gone into the kitchen. "Why did they make him leave? He loved the Pasdaran. It was wrong."

"Yes, uncle. *Hayf.* I was very sorry for Hossein. They had no reason to treat him that way."

"What did he do?" whispered Darab. "Was it something very bad?"

"No," answered Karim. "He had the wrong friends. A new team came into his section, and poof. That was it. They made up something about him, to get him out of the way. But I do not think it was true."

"Did you try to help him, Karim? You have influence. I know that."

"I did what I could," he said. Karim looked down

at his shoes. He was embarrassed. In truth, he had done nothing to help his cousin. He had been too afraid.

"Well, I can tell you, it has been hard for me. Hossein was a help. He knew the people who mattered. When I had a problem, he could help me solve it. And now, I have to find other ways." He looked at Karim expectantly.

So that was it. Uncle Darab's sorrow for cousin Hossein was a business matter. What really upset him was that he had lost a fixer high up in the Revolutionary Guard.

"I wish I could help," said Karim. "But you know, my work is scientific. I don't meet these politicians."

"I would never ask, my dear. Never. But it's not easy for a businessman. There are so many hands out. Still, we do all right. I am opening a new office in Bandar Abbas. Did you know that? What would your father say about that, if he were alive? His kid brother Darab, with three offices and a new house. He would say I am a success. He would be proud of me, rest his soul."

"I am sure Father would be very happy," said Karim. He thought, in truth, of the contempt his father had felt to the day he died for the vulgar cheerleaders of the new Iran, people like dear Uncle Darab.

Nasrin served up a mountain of food. Somehow in the few dozen minutes between Karim's text message and his arrival, she had managed to cook minced lamb *chelo kebab* over a heaping tray of rice, a roast chicken covered with a *fesenjun* sauce of pomegranate juice, walnuts and cardamom, and a *dolme bademjun* of eggplant stuffed with meat and raisins. It was the best meal Karim had eaten in weeks, and he went back for seconds, which made Nasrin very happy. She brought out home-made sweets, and in deference to her guest a selection of the Baskin-Robbins ice cream, but Karim had no more appetite left for dessert.

After coffee, Karim offered to go and play with the kids on the computer. There was Ali, now twelve, and little Azadeh, who was six. Uncle Darab had a fairly fast connection with one of the satellite ISP providers. Karim knew that because he had helped him set up the Internet link. He and Ali and Azadeh played for a while on some Persian websites for kids, but soon enough they got tired and lay down on the floor of the playroom. Nasrin was doing the dishes, and Darab was in the parlor talking on the phone.

Karim didn't have long. His aunt and uncle would come eventually to take the children up to bed. He thought about checking the "Dr. Ali" account at Hotmail and decided that would be too dangerous. It had been his opening card. They had moved to another system. He found the URL for Gmail, and when the interface came up he typed in

275

the username and password of the "iranmetal-works" account he had created many weeks ago.

His heart was racing. Fear is your friend, he reminded himself. Live inside it. Climb it like a wall. The Gmail account had to be clean. Why should it be otherwise? Millions of Iranians had free Internet accounts with Yahoo and Gmail and MSN. The authorities couldn't monitor them all, and so far as Karim knew, they didn't try. But still, he paused a moment before he hit the "enter" key that would take him into the world of secrets. There was a delay as the request moved out along the wires and satellite links and fiber-optic nerves. The system was slow on a Friday night. People were at home checking their mail, playing Internet games with their kids, downloading music, and surfing porn. The wait seemed to go on for more than a minute, and sweat began to form on Karim's brow. But finally the interface showed bright on the screen. Karim went to the space that held drafts of unsent messages, and there it was:

We are working on vacation plans. We will bring the tickets to you. Be careful about that cold. Stay away from germs and wash your hands regularly.

He read it twice, then closed the file. He felt a sense of elation. It was like a current of electricity entering his body from a distant power source. He exited Gmail and went to a popular website run by the conservative newspaper *Kayhan* to cover his tracks. He was reading an article about Mahdism when Nasrin came in a few minutes later, singing a Persian lullaby. He powered down the computer and helped his aunt carry the children up to bed.

Uncle Darab offered to drive Karim back to Yoosef Abad, and he was mildly offended when his nephew declined. Karim apologized that he needed some exercise after eating two dinners. Nasrin liked that, so she gave him more kisses and sent him on his way.

Dr. Karim Molavi walked away from the villa in Sadeghiyeh as if in a daze. There was a benign and mysterious force out there, at the other end of the pond. They had heard his plea and they understood it. They would find a way to get him out, even if he was watched and had no passport and could not travel in any of the normal ways. That's how powerful they were. He should stay where he was; they would come to him. Meanwhile, he should avoid surveillance. Stay away from germs. Stay alive.

He walked for several miles, along the border of Pardisan Park. The lights were still on at some of the rides and amusements. Twinkling, inviting, forgiving. A few families were still out walking. Even the tall needle of the communications tower in Nasr Park, which Karim ordinarily regarded as an insult to the Tehran skyline, looked harmless on this fall evening. He was not alone. They were coming to get him.

He found a taxi and told the driver to take him home to Yoosef Abad. The driver got lost coming off the Kordestan Expressway, so Karim had to direct him block by block to Yazdani Street. He stopped a block from his apartment, to be careful. As he walked home, still feeling that sense of elation, he cautioned himself that he must be especially careful now. The dangerous part was just beginning. He repeated to himself a Persian proverb. *Nafasat az jayeh garm darmiyad.* You are breathing from a warm spot. In other words, don't get over-optimistic. He would feel the cold in his bones again soon enough. He would wait. They would come. He turned the key of his apartment door and sat on his couch for a time, with the light off.

24

WASHINGTON

For those who understood the looming confrontation with Iran, Washington felt like an echo of March 2003, the month America invaded Iraq. This was a city where nobody wanted to be the last to know, so people in and out of government were suddenly possessed with the certainty that the United States was going to attack the Islamic

Republic. It was a matter of winks and nods, of inferences and messages between the lines. Questions about a possible U.S. strike against Iranian nuclear facilities began to surface at the White House, Pentagon, and State Department briefings. The spokesmen declined to answer, but then, they would, wouldn't they? Journalists began badgering government officials to come clean about the secret planning, and when they were rebuffed, the reporters implied that the officials were engaging in a cover-up. Think tanks began producing instant studies, with the help of terrier-like retired military officers, examining what targets the United States would hit in Iran if it chose to attack.

The question wasn't whether the United States was going to strike Iran, but when. The major news organizations began asking the Pentagon about arrangements for covering the conflict. Several newspapers even asked if it would be possible to embed reporters with U.S. forces—this for a military operation that wasn't declared, wasn't discussed, hadn't been agreed even by the principals. Yet already, in the floating island of the nation's capital, it had assumed the status of fact. Washington was talking itself into war.

Harry's alibi for the London trip had been the flu, so when he arrived at Persia House early on the morning of his return, people asked if he was feeling better. He wheezed on cue. In his absence, someone had put a bull's-eye on the chest of the poster of the Imam Hussein that graced the entryway. Harry laughed, but he took it down. He looked for Marcia Hill, but she was on the phone when he got in. At eight-thirty, he summoned the division's senior staff to his windowless office for the morning meeting. Even his team seemed to have been affected by the war fever.

Marcia Hill opened the meeting with a summary of new developments since last week. Before she began, she gave Harry a little wink. It was spooky: What did she know? She had a woman's intuition about people—when they were lying, when they were dissatisfied, when they were ready to bolt. That's what had made her a superstar, back in the day. After thirty years, she could read Harry better than his own wife. Whatever it was that she intuited, Harry she knew she would keep her mouth shut.

"We better talk about the Persia House surge," said Marcia. She turned to the group. "I briefed Harry on it while he was home sick. But I should give everyone else a fill."

"Go ahead," said Harry. So that was what she had wanted to tell him when he was in London. They were flooding the Iran zone, and she was covering for him. He loved her for the effortless, unbidden duplicity.

"On orders from the director over the weekend, we are sending additional officers into Dubai,

Doha, Istanbul, and Yerevan. They will be on temporary assignment to our division. We'll have more bodies in a few weeks, but no tasking as to what they should do. Any suggestions, Harry?"

"Have them write cables to each other. Stay out of the way. Who are the surgers, anyway? Do we know yet?"

"Half of them are contractors. The rest are retirees. Sounds like a joke, I know. But that's all we have. The White House wanted bodies. People on the Hill were complaining that we weren't doing enough about the Iran target. So we are surging. I surge, you surge, we surge. I think the Senate committee chairman put out a press release last night."

Harry shook his head. There was no point in pretending to his colleagues that he thought this was a good idea.

"What can I say? These people are nuts, honestly. But you all know that already, right?" Harry looked around the room. "I mean, you people understand that this is crazy. You don't just throw bodies at a target like Iran."

Heads nodded. They understood that their boss didn't want to be rushed. But there was excitement in their eyes, too. They liked the fact that their little division was at the center of the agency's universe.

"We'll manage the surge . . . slowly," said Harry. "Don't be in a hurry to get people out there. And when they do come online, make sure they don't bother the people who are actually doing the work. Okay? What's next?"

"You're not going to like this," said Marcia.

"Try me. Humor me."

"New tasking for tactical collection. Came over from the Pentagon last night."

"Shit. Does that mean what I think it does?"

"I'm afraid so. We are supposed to coordinate with Centcom, through our liaison officer in Tampa."

"What do they want?"

"Target acquisition. Target surveillance. Reporting on military movements and logistics— by the Rev Guard and the regular military, both. Weather reporting from the Iraqi and Turkish borders."

"Shit, shit, shit. They're going to do it, aren't they?"

"Who knows? But they're definitely getting ready."

"Well, give them what they're asking for. I'm sure Centcom isn't any happier about it than we are."

"Roger that," spoke up Martin Vitter, the operations chief. "I spoke to Tampa this morning. They were doing the rope-a-dope last night, hoping it would go away. But now they're moving a third carrier task force into the Gulf. And they are flying B-2s in from the States to Al-Udeed in Qatar."

"Is this supposed to scare the Iranians? Because

it's definitely going to scare the shit out of our friends. What else you got, Marcia?"

"We need operational approval to recontact BQBARK-2 when he arrives in Geneva."

"Remind me. Who is BQBARK-2?"

"He's in the Iranian foreign ministry. He was spotted by BQBARK-1 when they were both in Paris. He broke off contact when he was recalled home. Now he's being sent to their UN mission in Geneva on a six-month TDY. We want to renew contact. Pitch him again."

"Does he know any secrets?"

"Probably not. But it's another scalp."

"Okay. It's a waste of time, but so what? Use one of those 'surge' retirees to pitch him. Don't burn anyone who we might want to use later. Anything else?"

"Well . . ." she looked at Harry, not sure he wanted to go in this direction. "There's the restricted handling case. The 'Dr. Ali' case. I assume you're running that."

"Yup. Close hold. RH, plus. Sorry, gang."

Harry didn't want to say any more, but looking at the eager faces around the room, he knew that he had to. They were all cleared for the special-access program. If he didn't say anything, they would go away confused.

"I can tell you the basics: We're working with a liaison service that has access in-country that we don't. We are trying to establish physical contact.

As soon as we do, we will set up a normal operational protocol. If we don't make contact, well, we'll just keep looking in the email in-box. Right?"

The heads bobbed up and down. They didn't understand what the boss had said, but they knew he was on the case, which would have to do. Still, they looked anxious, as if they were waiting for something more that would put it all right. Harry gave them a big smile.

"Lighten up, gang. You know what Warren Buffett said when they asked him what his strategy was?"

"Who's Warren Buffett?" asked Vitter, the gung-ho ops chief. People around the table groaned.

"Only the richest man in the world. He said his strategy was to answer the phone. The best deals are the ones you don't plan for. So let's not get frazzled."

Marcia stayed behind after the others had filed out. She lit a cigarette, which was against the rules. Blue trails of smoke curled around her head.

"What's going on, Harry? Cut the crap. I know you too well. Where were you over the weekend?"

"Between us?"

"Of course. After all these years, who else would I tell? My cat?"

"I was in London. I'm working on some stuff with SIS. They have capabilities and authorities that we don't. We have a name and address for Dr.

Ali. We need to talk to him in a hurry. Obviously. Otherwise these crazy fuckers downtown are going to get him killed."

"Does the admiral know what you're up to?"

"Sort of. Enough to give me a fig leaf."

"Well, don't get caught. That's all I can say. In the meantime, how can I help?"

"Cover for me, the way you did today. I have to do some more traveling. And try to keep Fox and his friends from doing anything crazy. And keep your mouth shut."

"And if the balloon goes up?"

"Which balloon are you talking about? War with Iran?"

"No. I'm talking about you, Harry. What should I do if you get caught, doing whatever it is that you're not doing?"

"Lie."

She smiled and took a last puff on the cigarette.

"You got it," she said.

Harry called Arthur Fox. His secretary said he was on the seventh floor with the director. So Harry called the admiral's private line and asked if he could come up. The admiral said of course, he had been meaning to call Harry to ask him to join the meeting. He sounded embarrassed.

The view from the director's suite was a bland vista of trees, parking lots, the dome of the bubble-shaped auditorium where the agency gathered for what were usually tedious ceremonies. Long ago, when the CIA had reigned supreme, this must have seemed to Allen Dulles and his coterie the very height of modern elegance—this "campus" on the Potomac. Now, it was a monument to mediocrity. Even a middling state university had more panache among its faculty members than did the agency in its espionage corps.

The director was playing with one of his ship models when Harry entered the room. It was a battleship, long and fat in the hull. Evidently he had been waiting for Harry to show up. Fox was sitting on the couch with his back to the window. He was in shirtsleeves, wearing his green-striped Ivy Club tie as a secret signal to any Princeton man he might encounter. He had a sour look on his face, as if he had just eaten something that didn't agree with him.

"Harry Pappas, back from the dead," said Fox. "Sorry about your cold. We missed you."

"I'm sure you did, Arthur. But somehow I'll bet you managed on your own."

"Easy, shipmates. One big happy family here," said the director. "We were just talking about where we are going. Now that the White House has given us new Codeword policy guidance on Iran."

"And what might that be?" asked Harry. "If I'm cleared for it."

"You missed that too," said Fox. "Another NSC principals meeting yesterday. People asked after you. 'Get well soon.' That sort of thing."

Harry ignored Fox. He was like an unpleasant dog. The louder he barked, the more you wanted to take out a gun and shoot him.

"They want to go public," said the director. "Disclose the new evidence about the nuclear program in a big prime-time press conference in a week, maybe two. Then declare the embargo on Iran. Naval first, then air."

"Just like the Cuban missile crisis," said Harry.

"Precisely," said Fox.

"They don't want to take it to the United Nations?" asked Harry.

"No. Bad memories. Nobody wants another Colin Powell show."

Harry shook his head. He knew they had been heading in this direction, but the rush worried him.

"How much detail does the White House plan to reveal about the bomb program?"

Fox answered for the director, to whom the question had been addressed.

"We'll roll out everything we've got. Appleman's orders."

"But what we've *got* is ambiguous. And it will get our guy killed."

"Can't be helped. Casualty of war."

Harry turned to the director. He was playing with another ship model, a submarine this time. It looked like a big gray knackwurst. "Do you agree, Admiral?"

The admiral nodded. He looked uncomfortable. "Afraid so, Harry. This is crunch time. The Iranians have to know we mean business."

"What if the Iranians resist the embargo? Because they will. Some crazy asshole in the Revolutionary Guard will decide that he can win a one-way ticket to paradise if he takes out one of our ships in the Gulf. What do we do then?"

"We attack, of course," said Fox.

"I get it," said Harry. "You *want* them to attack. So you'll have a pretext."

"Let's just say the White House won't be unhappy."

"Oh shit," said Harry. "This is a big mistake. Everything tells me you're reading this wrong, Admiral." The director was silent. What his feelings might be, Harry wasn't sure, but he suspected they were similar to his own.

"You know what?" broke in Fox. "It doesn't really matter what you think, Harry. It's too late. This is a decision. What we are talking about now is implementation. And what you should think about is tactical intelligence. To support our brave soldiers and airmen who may soon be in battle."

"How long do we have?" asked Harry.

"Until the press conference? A week, two at most."

"That's insane," said Harry. "What's the rush? Why be in a hurry to make a mistake?"

"Because the president is determined to be firm. This problem isn't going away. Leadership is about making the tough decisions. But that's not your game, is it, Harry? You people always want more time. But we've run out."

"Why, for God's sake? Nobody knows anything about our new intelligence. Why don't we take the time to understand what it means?"

"That's not exactly true, Harry, that nobody knows. The Israelis have found out. The prime minister called the president over the weekend. He said that if the United States doesn't take action, others will."

"Shit! How did the Israelis find out?" Harry was glowering at Fox.

"Don't be so naïve, Harry. This is Washington. Nothing stays secret for very long."

Fox had such a smug look on his face that Harry suspected he must have been the leaker himself.

"Admiral?" asked Harry. But the director was brushing lint off the crisp blue serge of his navy uniform. He didn't want to hear about it.

They talked for another forty-five minutes about the new orders that had been issued by the Special Interagency Group that was now managing Iran policy out of the NSC. Harry asked how the director wanted to use the additional officers that were being surged into the Iran Operations

Division, but the director didn't have a clue. He just wanted to cover himself in the event someone asked later if there had been enough people to do the job. Fox didn't have any suggestions, either. So Harry said he would draw up an ops plan, muttering that it might have made sense to have the ops plan first, and then add the bodies.

The heart of the discussion was about tactical intelligence to support the planned naval and air embargo, and future follow-on military operations. The White House wanted to mobilize every asset the agency had in the Iranian military or Rev Guard corps. Unfortunately, that wasn't much, so the discussion didn't take very long. When they finished going over the requirements and tasking, Harry asked if he could see the boss alone for a moment. Fox protested, but the director for once showed a little backbone and asked the Counter-Proliferation chief to leave the room.

The two men sat down beside each other on the couch. It was an oddly intimate setting, without the usual buffers of distance and other people.

"You've got to delay this," said Harry. "We need more time. We're rushing into this for no reason. We're going to get my guy killed, but I can live with that if I have to. The fact is, we're going to get a lot more people killed, unnecessarily."

"I know," said the director quietly. "How much time do you need?"

"A month," said Harry. "Two months would be even better."

"Forget it. You'll never get that. You heard Fox. These people are ready to go."

"Three weeks," said Harry. He was thinking to himself how fast Adrian's team could get into the country, find Karim Molavi, and get him to someplace safe where they could talk to him.

"Two weeks is the best I can do, Harry. I know for a fact that the president himself isn't quite as hell-for-leather as Arthur and his pals. But this is in motion. I think he will take the full two weeks if I tell him we need that time to work our sources."

"Then I'll take two weeks, if that's the best I can get."

"What are you going to do? I need to tell the president something."

Harry turned away and looked out the window, to those rustling trees. They were beginning to lose their leaves in the early chill of October. Out by the parking lot, a cluster of Japanese maples had already turned fire-red. Harry wondered if he should tell the director what he was doing with Adrian Winkler. It would open too many doors, pose too many questions for which there weren't good answers. It was one of those situations where the right thing to say, paradoxically, was absolutely nothing. Harry had started down a road by himself, and he had no choice but to continue along it, to the end.

"Tell the president I'm working my ass off to get him what he needs. I'm doing everything I can to make contact with our Iranian agent in the nuclear program and get more information out of him."

"Right, but how are you going to do that?" The director spoke softly, as if his words might break something fragile.

"I don't know. Just tell the president I am trying to get him the information he needs to make a wise decision. And not to pull any triggers until I get back to him."

"And if you run out of time?"

Harry didn't answer. He wanted to say that if he ran out of time, he would plead for more, or lie to delay action another few weeks. But the truth was, he didn't know what he would do.

25

TEHRAN

An attractive foreign woman with an Hermès scarf tied loosely around her blond hair approached the reception desk at the Aziz Apartment Hotel on Esfandiar Street in North Tehran. She was muttering to herself in German, but when she reached the desk clerk she switched to a slightly accented English. Her suite on the seventh floor was acceptable, she told the clerk. It was very nice, very clean. The porters had carried the luggage up to the room, thank you very much, all four Louis Vuitton bags, plus the oversize makeup kit. But there was a problem. She would be needing two keys please, because she would have a visitor, coming and going, yes, and he would need his own key. She tilted her head, ever so slightly, and smiled at the clerk. She didn't have to explain any further, did she?

The woman was very beautiful—with bronzed skin and that silky blond hair that kept slipping out from beneath the luxurious scarf that was her attempt at a hijab. She talked loudly, so that others in the small lobby could hear, and when the desk clerk handed her a second key card, she smiled conspiratorially. She unfolded a ten-euro bill and left it on the desk, then strolled back to the elevator.

None of the Iranians who watched the woman, including the several who reported to the intelligence ministry, would have been in the slightest doubt as to what they had just seen. This German woman was the mistress of someone powerful; she was the sort of well-mannered courtesan who escorted international businessmen, even in a city such as Tehran. By Islamic lights, she was certainly immoral, but then, so were most Western women. Her status was confirmed a few hours later, when she received a visit from a gentleman caller—a wealthy Iranian businessman who resided most of the time in London and Frankfurt. The microphones in the woman's bedroom picked up the sounds of lovemaking—quite amorous and, by the sound of it, more than a little rough.

Jackie stayed in her room for several hours, reading a book. The gentleman, who never actually removed his clothes, sat in a chair. When it was dark, she led the Iranian man upstairs to the rooftop restaurant of the Aziz Apartment Hotel. The lights of North Tehran twinkled in every direction, and the night air was scented with the perfume of the garden's array of flowering plants. They ordered a lavish dinner, and as they waited for the courses to arrive, they busied themselves with cellular telephone calls, his and hers, as travelers will do.

Jackie's first call was to the number of a young man from Yemen who had entered the country that same day. His real name was Marwan, but she called him "Saleh." She spoke in her German-accented English, and only for long enough to confirm an appointment the next morning. Then she took another phone from her purse and called a hairdresser in the penthouse of the Simorgh Hotel, the newest and glitziest in town, and made an appointment to have her hair done.

When the food arrived, she flirted with the Iranian gentleman in her mix of German and English. Before she left the rooftop at the end of the evening, she and her friend walked over to an array of shrubs that marked the edge of the terrace. As she gazed out at the million points of light that was Tehran, she leaned toward one of the wooden boxes in which the shrubbery was planted. No one could have seen her remove a thin object from her purse and stick it into the soil of the planter's box, so deep that only the very top remained above the dirt. She walked away, leaving her relay antenna invisibly in place.

Marwan's flight from Doha was delayed by a sandstorm. And when the Qatar Airways jet finally arrived at Imam Khomeini Airport, Marwan couldn't find a taxi at first. The airport was so far from the center of town that the drivers didn't like to pick up passengers they couldn't cheat by doubling or tripling the fare. In his cheap suit and his garish tie, Marwan looked like an Arab hustler—a man who would cheat the cabdriver before falling prey to his tricks. But eventually a taxi pulled up in front of Marwan and the driver agreed to take him to the New Naderi Hotel, just off Jomhuri-ye Islami Street.

The hotel was a big ramshackle place in the middle of the downtown business district. A few blocks north were the main offices of the big Iranian banks—Melli, Sepah, Tejarat. Marwan had booked a cheap single room in his work name, Moustafa Saleh, and a cheap room was what he got, facing out on a courtyard that was little more than a ventilation shaft. The Iranians didn't much like Arabs, least of all the Yemenis who came to Tehran prospecting for quick ways to make money.

Marwan emptied the contents of his flimsy suitcase into the drawers of the wooden dresser. He opened the window to get some fresh air. Even if there had been surveillance in his room, nobody would have seen him attach a small rod to the exterior wall, hidden against the frame of the window. The second node of the communications relay net was up.

The Yemeni traveler took his dinner at a small restaurant on Sa'di Street. He had his cell phone with him, the one that had been configured so artfully in London; it transmitted to the high-gain antenna, and from there, to the satellite in space. Marwan took a brief call during dinner from a woman. Then he placed a call to a third cell phone, configured like the other two. That one didn't answer, but Marwan didn't leave a message. He knew that his Pakistani brother was coming.

Hakim's arrival in Tehran had been delayed by the ordinary realities of Iranian life. He had come into the country from Pakistan, crossing at the border post at Mirjaveh on the eastern frontier. He had boarded a bus operated by Cooperative Bus Company No. 8, which traveled the main highway of southeastern Iran, the A02. It wound through Zahedan and Kerman and Yazd—sour little cities frequented by smugglers and traders. The bus was supposed to connect in Yazd with another that would take him southwest to Shiraz.

But this was Baluchistan. The bus had a flat tire a few hours into the trip, and it took many hours to fix it. They limped into Kerman eight hours late. Hakim found a cheap guesthouse where he could spend the night and set off the next morning for Yazd. He missed one Shiraz bus, but found another and finally arrived in the city where he was registered as a purchasing agent for a construction project. He took the first transportation to Tehran he could find, the Sayro Safar private bus. The trip was almost a thousand kilometers—all night and most of the next day before the bus finally rolled into the Southern station, below Besat Park. From there he took a group taxi a few miles north to the dust and debris of the old Tehran bazaar and checked into the Hotel Shams. He was dirty and smelly, which gave his cover a gritty reality.

Hakim found a *qibla* in his room, pointing the direction toward Mecca; there was just enough space for him to put down a prayer rug. He walked to the window. It was broken, letting in the noise and smells of the bazaar. He found a gap in the molding around the window, and into it he placed the thin antenna of his relay transmitter. His cell phone rang as he was trying to catch a little sleep. It was Marwan, checking to make sure that he had arrived and confirming the meeting the next day.

Jackie left the Aziz hotel the next morning at nine. Her Iranian gentleman caller had departed at seven-thirty, dropping a lavish tip in the doorman's hand as he departed. Jackie made a grand exit, wearing black leather pants under her manteau, and carrying a flamboyant Fendi purse. She had reserved a hotel car and ordered the driver to take her down Vali Asr Avenue to the Simorgh Hotel. The hairdresser was on the top floor of the hotel. She made her way across the lobby toward the elevator, the leather of her pants squeaking from the friction of her thighs as she walked. From the other side of the lobby, an Arab man dressed in a business suit approached the elevator, entering it just after she did.

Marwan stood in the back of the elevator car, next to Jackie. She took from her purse something that looked like a small rock, of the dusty limestone color that was typical of the region. She held it against her side. In the same moment, Marwan reached out his hand, took it from her, and put it in the pocket of his coat. He got off one floor before she did, and then rode the elevator back down to the lobby. He walked out into the morning sun, carrying in his pocket the transmitter that had been prepared for Dr. Karim Molavi.

Marwan took a taxi north, up Vali Asr Avenue to Mellat Park, one of the biggest and most beautiful in Tehran. He had several hours to look for the right drop. He strolled toward the little lake at the eastern end but it was too crowded there, so he wandered deeper into the woods and gardens in the center of the park. He sat on a bench for a while, watching the flow of people and making sure that he wasn't being followed. The right hiding place would be off one of the main pathways, but not so far that someone would look conspicuous going in or out.

He walked toward the southern edge of the park, along Niyayesh Expressway, where there were fewer strollers. He passed the stadium where the Engelab team played its matches, and continued on until he found a path that led up to a pond named for the martyrs in the Iraq-Iran war. He walked up the path until he saw a small stand of exotic trees, off to the left; he walked toward the trees, counting fifty paces until he reached them. He looked at the terrain, the lack of people nearby, the way the site was obscured from the main path.

This was the right place. He took the simulated rock from his pocket and laid it behind a Japanese maple. It looked like a normal bit of local stone until you picked it up in your hand. He took a piece of yellow chalk from his pocket and drew a thin diagonal line across the tree trunk. The marking was hard to see unless you were looking for it. He walked back to the pathway, counting the paces again to make sure he had it right. This time it came out to fifty-two paces, but that was close enough. He walked back toward the park entrance on Niyayesh, counting the number of benches on his right side—fourteen.

Marwan took an index card from his pocket. On it he had already written the words: *We are working on vacation plans. We will bring the tickets to you.* That was the same message that had been sent in the last communication to Karim Molavi. Below that message, he wrote in neat block letters the directions to the site, and the instructions: *Go to Mellat Park tonight. Take the Martyrs' Pond entrance off Niyayesh Expressway. Walk north, passing fourteen benches on your left. Then turn left and walk fifty paces to a maple tree marked with yellow chalk. Behind the tree is a rock that is unlike any other. Inside the rock is a device. Remove the device and discard the rock. Press 1 and you will reach us.*

He folded the index card in half, so that it would fit easily in a man's palm.

They had the target's work and home address. Both were dangerous, but they had decided that the home address was safer. The office in Jamaran would be under constant surveillance. Anyone loitering there would be suspect, no matter how good their cover. This was the trickiest part of the operation. If they did it right, everything else would be easy. If they did it wrong, they would expose themselves and their agent, too.

Marwan had lunch in a cheap restaurant off Jahad Square, near where the mighty Esteghlal played its soccer games. He was killing time until his meeting with Hakim at 4:00 p.m. He had a coffee, and then another coffee, and then it was time to go. They had agreed to meet in Farabaksh Square in the Yoosef Abad district, a few blocks south of where they had identified Karim Molavi's apartment.

Hakim was there on time. He was dressed like a South Asian laborer, in coveralls and a sweat-stained cap. Migrant laborers were imported by the thousands from Pakistan and Afghanistan to do the jobs Tehranis felt were beneath them—cleaning streets and sewers, performing the donkey work of construction. They were a common sight around Tehran—especially at the end of the day when they waited for their rides back to the cheap guest-houses and labor camps where they lived.

Marwan stood next to Hakim in a clump of pedestrians, waiting for a break in traffic to cross the square. A policeman in green was on the far corner, writing a traffic ticket. Marwan brushed Hakim, and in the moment of contact, passed the folded index card with the directions to the drop site. The exchange would have been invisible even if you had been observing the two men. Marwan was clean now; all the danger had passed to the young Pakistani.

Hakim trudged up Shahriar Street six blocks

until he got to Yazdani Street. His back was stooped slightly, as if from a life of manual labor, and his legs were bowed. He walked with his head down, submissively—a humble Pakistani in the court of the Persians. The few people out on the street didn't even deign to look at him. He might as well have been a stray dog.

Hakim turned left on Yazdani Street until he got to No. 29. That was the address of Karim Molavi's villa, where he shared an apartment with another tenant who had the upper floor. Hakim's instructions were to sit on the curb and wait. If anyone asked him what he was doing, he should say *"mashin, mashin,"* the Persian word for car, as if he were waiting to be picked up, and then babble in Urdu. But nobody would speak to him if he looked harmless and submissive enough. That was the nice thing about prejudice: it made assumptions; it thought it knew the answers.

Hakim sat down on the curb and hunched his body so that his shoulders were almost touching his knees. He had studied a grainy reconnaissance photograph of Molavi just before they left London. The ops plan assumed that Molavi would return home between five and six in the afternoon. Hakim waited. In a paper bag he carried a book, the *Shahnameh* by Abolqasem Ferdowsi. The book was open to the page the American, Mr. Fellows, had specified, and a few lines were marked with a yellow highlighter:

He said, "Is it good or ill these signs portend?
When will my earthly life come to an end?
Who will come after me? Say who will own
This royal diadem, and belt, and throne.
Reveal this mystery, and do not lie—
Tell me this secret or prepare to die."

That was Hakim's recognition code. A bit of Persian poetry Karim Molavi had sent out of the ether, many weeks ago. If the target didn't recognize the poetry, then the mission was to be aborted.

The October sun was low in the sky, almost gone. Soon it would be dark, and it would be dangerous for Hakim to remain on the curb. People would ask questions about a foreign laborer after dark. He looked at his watch. It was nearly six. The ops plan said to wait until six-fifteen and then leave. The minutes ticked by too slowly. Hakim glanced up at every footstep along the sidewalk now, as men and women returned home from work. The few people who looked at him did so with an air of disgust, and one person muttered *"Boro gom sho!"*—Get lost!—but didn't do anything about it.

At six-ten, Hakim saw a well-built man in a black suit approaching the villa. He was still wearing his sunglasses, even in the dim light of dusk, so it was hard to see his face. He was walking quickly, as if he wanted to get home. As he neared Hakim, he turned onto the concrete walkway that led to the villa at No. 29. Hakim stood and walked toward him.

"Dr. Molavi, I have some poetry I would like you to read," he whispered in perfect English. "Perhaps you will remember it."

Hakim's demeanor had changed in an instant. He now stood tall, with his back arched; all the submissive gestures of the subcontinent had disappeared. His accent was so precisely English, it might have been Professor Henry Higgins speaking.

"A bit of poetry, sir," whispered Hakim, showing the cover of the Ferdowsi book.

A startled Molavi had taken several steps back toward his home when Hakim spoke his first words. Now he removed his sunglasses and looked the Pakistani in the eye, uncertain what was happening, but wondering, thinking.

"Come here, boy," said the Iranian, who by now was close to the safety of his doorstep.

Hakim stepped forward, into the shadows, and handed Molavi the book, open to the marked page. Molavi read the passage and shook his head. He muttered a phrase in Persian. *"Gheyre ghabel e fahm."* It is incomprehensible.

Hakim moved closer, and in a quick motion, brushed the folded index card against Molavi's hand. The Iranian, despite his fear, took it.

The Pakistani immediately returned to his posture of humility. In a broken mix of Farsi, Urdu, and

English, he apologized that he had the wrong house and backed away toward the street. The index card was in Molavi's pocket now, and in another moment, the Iranian was inside his apartment.

26

TEHRAN

Karim Molavi sat in an easy chair in his apartment, trying to calm himself. The impossible thing had happened. They had come to him. The tips of his fingers were still tingling from where he had touched the foreigner's hand. He put the buds of his iPod into his ears and selected some Indian sitar music, hoping that it would calm him, but he couldn't concentrate.

He looked again at the index card, and the words at the top. *We are working on vacation plans. We will bring the tickets to you.* They had promised that they would come, and now they were here. He read the instructions about where to find the "device," and saw that they hadn't specified a precise hour to collect it. "Tonight," the message said. Molavi decided that he would go right away, before the ministry had time to think or wonder, before any of the neighbors could tell the *basij* about the dirty foreigner on the street after dark, before his own panic began to set in.

He found a leftover lamb kebab in the refrigerator. He put it in the microwave and wrapped it in a piece of bread, but he was too nervous to eat. Reflexively, he took one of the photo albums down from the shelf and looked at a picture of his father as a young man. His father's eyes were fierce and fearless. Never let them see that you are afraid, his father had told him. Fear is your ally. Embrace it. Do not be afraid of fear, or they will see it.

Molavi found his street atlas of Tehran. He studied the page for Mellat Park until he thought he knew where the location was. He pondered the safest way to get there, and blocked out the route in his mind. The index card was sitting on the table, next to his chair. It was glowing, radioactive, neon white. He took the card into the bathroom and burned it in the sink, and then flushed the ashes down the toilet.

The young man looked at his face in the mirror. The swirl of black hair. The almost-pious beard. The eyes wide with fear and yearning. What was he afraid of? This was his moment. He had dropped his little stone in the water months ago, and the waves had rippled back to carry him away to his "vacation." His hands were shaking. He extended the palms outward and held them steady. He went to the closet and put on a jacket against the night chill. He buttoned his coat and headed for the door and then, in an afterthought, returned to the pantry and found a small flashlight, which he put in his pocket.

Molavi walked out of his villa. It was a clear

night, with only a small crescent moon. Even amid the smog and the lights of Tehran, you could see a few stars. The quickest route north to the park was the Kordestan Expressway, but he decided against that. He walked to the Moffateh subway station, nearly a mile away, and took the train north to the last stop at Mirdamad. He didn't bother to look for surveillance. They were either following him or they weren't. He walked a few blocks and then took a taxi to Piroozi Square, just west of Mellat Park. Then he walked, slowly and deliberately, along the southern edge of the park until he reached the pathway that led up to the Martyrs' Pond. Something like calm had settled over him. He was a young nuclear physicist, lost in thought as he took his evening stroll in the woods. Who could say that it was anything else?

Molavi turned into the pathway. A young couple was coming out, giggling. The girl was tugging at her manteau, pulling it down so that it covered her bottom. This was where young Iranians went when they couldn't afford a place to be together. The police patrolled the park for that reason. But surely they wouldn't pay attention to a solitary man out for a stroll. He walked north, counting the number of benches on his left as he headed up the path. Another swooning couple was cresting the hill. They eyed him warily. Perhaps they thought he was an undercover policeman.

He had a moment of panic when he got to bench number 14 and didn't see any stand of trees off to the left. Had he miscounted? He walked one more bench, and just over the rise of the hill he saw what might be the grove. It was hard to tell in the nearly moonless night. He turned toward the trees and walked the prescribed fifty paces, trying to make them American steps.

When he reached the trees, he searched for the maple with the chalk mark. In the dark, it was hard to see. He reached for his flashlight but then thought better of it. He examined the trees one by one, his nose almost up against the bark. He heard sounds from the pathway and froze until the footsteps had died away. His heart was beating too fast now; his fear was taking control. He had examined all the trees without finding the mark.

He bit down hard against his lip, to check the fear. He started looking again, and as he examined a tree toward the back of the grove, he at last saw a yellow line, lower on the trunk than where he had first been looking. He grasped the tree as if it were a lifeline and moved to the other side. Crouching now, he felt for a rock that was not a rock. He picked up one, and then a second, and then he touched one that wasn't stone but plastic. He put it quickly in his pocket. As he stood up, he felt a kind of vertigo. Now he was truly a spy, an enemy of the state. What he had in his pocket was a death sentence.

He made himself take a step, and then another, until he was back on the main pathway. More young lovers were coming down from the lake, and a policeman was following them. Molavi tried to control his fear, and make each twitch and shiver a jolt of strength. The policeman was approaching him. He was a beady-eyed young man with a thick beard, the kind who liked surprising young lovers in the woods. Molavi stopped. His palms were moistening. The policeman was speaking to him. What was he saying? *"Movazeb bashin!"* Be careful! The park would be closing soon. Only one more hour, please.

Molavi looked at the policeman dumbly; then he nodded. *"Hajj agha, nochakeram."* I understand, officer. Thank you. He turned and walked back the other way, toward the exit. If this policeman was scolding him that it was late, that must mean nobody else was watching him.

Molavi thought about where to make the call. His apartment was a bad idea; they might have planted a bug there months ago. His office was out of the question. A restaurant or café was impossible. The best place might be right here, in the outdoors. He walked past the Engelab stadium; a few people were milling about, but on the other side, in the formal gardens of the park, it was nearly empty. He found a bench that was secluded, hidden away in the shadows. He sat down and took the plastic rock from his pocket. He twisted it one way, then another, looking for a seam, and then it came open. Inside was a phone. He saw the keyboard and pressed the number "1." He put the phone to his ear and waited for someone to answer.

Jackie was sitting in the garden restaurant on the rooftop of her hotel when her special phone rang. She was eating alone tonight. The waiters were off helping another table. She put the phone to her ear and spoke the words carefully, in German, a language she knew Karim Molavi would understand.

"We have come to take you on your vacation," she said. "Listen to me carefully, and do exactly what I say."

"Yes," said Molavi. His hand was shaking as he held the phone.

"Leave work early tomorrow afternoon. Tell them that you are feeling sick. Then go to the Eastern Terminal Bus Station. Go carefully, you understand? Take the bus to Sari, on the Caspian coast. The trip will take about five hours. Don't tell anyone at work where you're going."

"Yes, all right," said Molavi. He was surprised that it was a woman's voice giving the order, and speaking in German. But that was the mystery of these Americans. They could assume any form.

"When you get to Sari, book a room in the Asram Hotel in Golha Square. The next morning, go to breakfast in the restaurant. An Arab man will approach you and ask if you are Dr. Ali. He knows what you look like. Ask him for his name, and he will say that he is Mr. Saleh. When he leaves the restaurant, follow him. Do you understand?"

"Yes," said Molavi.

"Repeat it, so that I knew you have it right."

"Bus to Sari. Asram Hotel. Mr. Saleh."

"You will be safe soon, my friend."

Karim Molavi was going to ask where they would go after that, but the phone had gone dead. He quickly put it back in his pocket. He dropped the plastic rock in a pond by the edge of the park. It floated for a moment and then sank, mercifully. As he walked toward the lights of Vali Asr Avenue, he felt as if something were fizzing in his stomach.

The next day, Molavi went to the nameless white building in Jamaran where he worked. He carried his black leather briefcase in his hand, as always, but today he had filled it with two extra pairs of undershorts, a toothbrush, and a stick of deodorant. As he entered the door and passed beneath the first of several surveillance cameras, he nodded to the receptionist and the security man. This might be the last time he ever saw them.

He walked slowly, almost shuffling, in the manner of someone who was coming down with a bad cold. As he passed through the lobby, he coughed loudly—a percussive sound almost like a

311

sneeze. *"Afiyat bashe,"* said the receptionist. Bless you! She asked if he was okay. *"Zaif,"* he answered. *"Larz daram."* Weak and shivery.

The receptionist looked at him sweetly, as if she wanted to mother him. Poor boy, she said. He was still a boy here to the older workers—the bright young physicist with the sweep of dark black hair, who kept to himself.

Molavi stopped at the office of the director, Dr. Bazargan, coughing again as he entered the room. He apologized for not shaking the director's hand, but he didn't want to pass along any germs. The director nodded sympathetically. He pretended to be busy, but he had little to do. He was a custodian more than a real boss. Dr. Bazargan asked how his research was going, and Molavi said it was going fine. In truth, as the director well knew, he was spending most of his time reading journals these days. They hadn't given him anything new to do in a month. Molavi coughed again and the director said perhaps he should go home until he was feeling better.

Maybe he would go home later, said Molavi. *"Sarma khordam,"* the young man said, shaking his head at the world's misfortune, and his own. I've caught a cold.

He sat at his desk for more than an hour, reading. First the newspapers, then the science magazines from America. He coughed occasionally, for effect. He turned the pages, past the bright advertisements, reading of the latest discoveries in the laboratories of America. How could it be that this giant cash machine of a country worried or cared about a little, deceitful nation such as Iran? Perhaps the Americans could explain it to him. He closed his eyes and thought of being on an airplane, flying away from Iran to somewhere else. To Germany, perhaps. He thought of the German girl who had befriended him at the University of Heidelberg. "Trudi." Her breasts were very big. He wished that he had touched them, when she asked. She was even more alluring now that he knew she was a Jew.

He opened his eyes. The morning was almost gone. He coughed again, a spasm that made his throat hurt. What else could he do to cover his tracks? He called his cousin Hossein, the former senior officer in the Revolutionary Guard. He proposed that they have dinner next week. Why not? His cousin agreed and named a day. His voice sounded far off, as if he had already smoked his first pipe of opium for the day.

"Bashe?" asked Molavi. Are you okay? That was a nice touch. Whoever was listening to the phone call would think that he had been planning ahead, to take care of his unhappy and ill-used cousin from the Pasdaran.

Jackie's Iranian friend arrived early that morning at the Aziz Apartment Hotel to collect her.

She came downstairs to greet him, draping her arms around him in a way that made the desk clerk and bellman uncomfortable. She would be leaving her room for a few days, she told the desk clerk in her singsong German-accented English. Her friend was taking her to Isfahan, the beautiful town in central Iran that was his ancestral home. She would leave some of her luggage at the Aziz Hotel, to collect when she returned. She took a wad of hundred-dollar bills from her big purse and peeled off two thousand dollars to pay for the room charges so far, which totaled less than half that amount, and to hold the room for when she returned.

The desk clerk said he couldn't possibly accept so much money, but then he did, quite happily. The bellman loaded two of her Louis Vuitton bags into the trunk of her Iranian friend's Mercedes, and they left two bags for storage. They got into the beautiful new car; the Iranian opened the sunroof, and as they drove off, the wind blew off her scarf, exposing for a moment that silky thread of blond hair.

Molavi went across the street to a *kebabi* for lunch, and brought the food back to his desk. He looked so forlorn now that even the security guard at the door, a burly man whose face had been badly scarred in the Iraq-Iran war, told him that he should go home and rest. Perhaps later, murmured Molavi.

They would be relieved tomorrow when he didn't come to work. He was taking care of himself, they would say, and keeping his germs at home. If they called his home and got no answer, they would think he had gone to the doctor, or even the hospital. And then it would be Friday and the Muslim weekend. It would be a week before anyone really missed him.

He sat at his desk until it was nearly three. He buttoned his coat up tight around his neck as if he were suffering from chills, and then picked up his briefcase and headed out the door. He stopped by Dr. Bazargan's office but the director was out, so he told the secretary that he was feeling ill and going home. The secretary suggested that he should see a doctor. Molavi said he would do that tomorrow if he didn't feel better. He shuffled down the hall to the receptionist, who gave him one more piteous look as he gingerly walked out the door.

A policeman stopped Jackie's Mercedes as they were spinning along the Resalat Highway. He was an upright young man with a bushy beard, who squinted at them with a busybody's suspicious eyes. He didn't like the looks of this European woman driving in a fancy car with an Iranian man. The driver asked what was wrong, and when the policeman said they weren't wearing seat belts, Jackie almost laughed. But it wasn't funny. The cop was asking to see the driver's

315

papers for the car, and then he was saying that something wasn't in order and that he would need to call his superiors on the radio for advice.

The Iranian was nimble. He asked the officer if he could speak to him privately. He got out of the driver's seat and walked to the back of the car, half hidden from the road. He talked with the policeman respectfully, humbly, and then said something that made the cop laugh. Then they were shaking hands, and Jackie knew that a bribe had passed from one man to the other.

"What did you tell him?" asked Jackie.

"I told him that you were a German whore, and that I only had a few hours with you. I asked him as a man to have pity on me. I told him I had borrowed the car to impress you."

"And he believed you?"

"Of course he did," said the Iranian. "I told him what he already believed. I made it a question of shame. If he detained me, I would lose face—not to mention my sexual pleasure. No Iranian will humiliate another."

Jackie shook her head.

"Bollocks," she said. "You were lucky. Don't get stopped again."

27

SARI, IRAN

Karim Molavi wobbled down the steps of the
white building in Jamaran and took the first taxi
from the queue across the street. He wanted to look
feeble and unwell, but inside he was elated. His
escape had begun. He told the driver to take him to
Yazdeni Street in Yoosef Abad. His instructions
had been to go from work to the bus station, but he
had decided that was unwise. They would ask the
cab driver later, when he didn't show up at work
next week, where he had taken Dr. Molavi. The
pieces of the story had to fit right.

When he got to his apartment, he changed out
of his black business suit into a pair of slacks and
a warm shirt and jacket, and added a cap that
would partially cover his face. He exchanged his
leather slip-ons for some rubber-soled shoes, in
case he would need to do some hiking. How did
one escape from Iran? Over mountains or
deserts? He had no idea. He added another pair of
underwear and two pairs of socks to his kit, and
put it all in a simple canvas bag, leaving the briefcase behind. He checked his wallet to make sure
he had all his identification cards. The special
phone was in his pocket. He was afraid to touch
it. He wished he had his passport, but they had
already taken that. His rescuers would have to

improvise. He headed for the door and then stopped.

What else could he do, to make it look as if he had expected to come back? He put some food in the microwave, and he turned on the television set in his bedroom, with the volume low enough that it wouldn't disturb the neighbors. What more? He wrote himself a little list of things to do—pick up the laundry, go to the dentist, buy a new shower curtain. He left it on his desk. Nobody thinks about buying a new shower curtain if they are planning to flee the country.

Molavi left his apartment by the back door and took an alleyway to the next street, heading north. That was the opposite direction from the one he usually traveled. He walked a few blocks to Farhang Square and waited for a taxi. A rusted orange Paykan, normally a group taxi, rumbled toward him. He called out his destination—the Eastern bus terminal. The driver shouted back, *"Dar baste?"* which meant "Closed-door?" It was an offer to drive the passenger alone if he would pay the single tariff. Molavi nodded yes. The fewer people who saw him on this trip, the better.

Molavi sat in front, next to the driver. There was a Koran on the dashboard, and a blue-colored ornament dangling from the rearview mirror, to guard against the evil eye. The driver wasn't in a mood to talk, fortunately. The Paykan rolled east, spewing exhaust. The afternoon traffic was heavy, the air so thick with smog that it caught in Molavi's throat.

Now he was coughing for real. When they reached the Damavand Highway, the road opened up a bit and the air got fresher. Molavi looked at his watch. It was nearly four. He had no idea how often the buses left for Sari, but he wanted to find one quickly and disappear into the seat.

The Eastern terminal was at the far edge of the city. Molavi arrived a little after four and bought a seat on a bus that was scheduled to depart at four-thirty. There were police in the bus station, but nobody paid him any attention. He had an odd feeling of invisibility; people saw him, certainly, but they did not begin to understand who he was. He bought a magazine and a sandwich for the road, along with a bottle of mineral water, and waited to board. This bus didn't have a separate men's and women's section, unlike the ones in the city. But women sat with women; men with men. Molavi took a lone seat near the back and hoped nobody would join him.

He settled into the seat. It was a new Volvo bus, a "super," as the Iranians called it. The seat was comfortable. With a loud honk of the horn, the bus rolled out of the terminal. Nobody had claimed the seat next to him. Molavi took a bite of his sandwich. For the first time in twenty-four hours, he began to relax.

The trip was so achingly beautiful that it made Molavi wonder for a moment if he really was ready to leave Iran. For the first few miles east, the road skirted forest parkland, rich and green. Soon they picked up the A01, the main route to the northeast, and the bus began climbing the steep slopes of the Alborz Mountains. The sun was low in the sky, and the majestic Mount Damavand was bathed in a golden wash of refracted light. They wound through the mountains for several more hours, the snow at the peaks faintly illuminated in the pale moonlight, so that the landscape looked as if it had been painted in shadow colors. He nibbled at his sandwich and sipped occasionally from his water bottle. He dozed off for an hour, and when he awoke the bus was descending from the mountains toward the commercial towns along the Caspian Sea. The bus stopped in Amol, and then Babol, and a half hour after that it rolled into the ancient town of Sari.

Molavi looked out the window. The town looked familiar. He had come here as a boy with his parents, before his mother became ill and it was impossible for her to travel. The bus passed the old part of town, graced by a white clock tower that gleamed in the floodlights. Did he remember this place, or was it the idea of this place that he was remembering? The bus stopped at the Sari main terminal, near the Tajan River. A few other passengers stumbled off, weary from the trip.

It was past 9:00 p.m., and the station was nearly empty. It had the desolate feel of a small bus terminal anywhere; it was a place people left to go to bigger cities, not a place they came back to. Molavi asked the station manager for directions to Golha Square and the Hotel Asram. It was just a few hundred meters south from the station, said the manager, an easy walk. Molavi walked along the bank of the river, thinking to himself: I don't want to die here. I want to live.

The hotel was modern and ugly, two words that often went together in Iran. The concrete exterior was lit in red and green, which made the façade even less attractive. The desk clerk gave him a room on one of the upper floors, with its own bathroom and a view of the old city and its whitewashed tower. Molavi wasn't ready to sleep, and the hotel made him uncomfortable. He found a café near the old city, close by a graceful fountain, and ordered himself a glass of fresh pomegranate juice. It was at once sweet and tart on his tongue. He went back to the hotel, washed his undershorts and socks in the bathroom sink, and hung them by the open window to dry. It was an act of faith that he would survive, washing his undergarments. He slept naked, the fabric of the cheap cotton sheets rough against his arms and legs.

Jackie and her Iranian agent took the fast road north from Tehran to Chalus on the Caspian coast. They passed through Karaj and then climbed the spectacular highway through the mountains to the sea. In Chalus, Jackie and her friend stopped at the Hotel Malek and dined at the stylish hotel restaurant. The atmosphere was more relaxed here than in Tehran, and Jackie loosened her head scarf, as had many of the Iranian women seated nearby. In the ladies' room, an Iranian woman said in perfect English, "I love your purse," and asked where she had bought it. It turned out she had a flat in Paris.

The two travelers were conspicuous enough that a dozen people could have testified who they were—a rich Iranian traveling with his mistress along the Caspian Sea coastal road, bound for the east.

When they returned to the Mercedes after dinner, an additional passenger was waiting in the shadows. He was a Pakistani man, dressed neatly in a black suit and tie. He looked like he might be a personal servant to the Iranian man—a valet, or perhaps an office manager. He was carrying an elongated travel bag, of the sort tennis players carry. He placed it in the trunk of the Mercedes.

The three drove east along the coast road, stopping for the night in Babol, just west of Sari. The Iranian man and his German woman friend took adjoining rooms at the Marjan Hotel. The Pakistani continued east a few more kilometers.

Molavi rose with the cry of the dawn prayers the next morning. He walked to his window and looked out on the city. It was uglier by day. The

buses and cars were starting up, making a fero-
cious rumble as they moved through Golha Square
toward the river bridge. They are out there, he told
himself. It seemed impossible that they would
come for him in this haphazard provincial capital,
but he had bet his life on that unlikely rendezvous.
He showered and dressed himself, and packed his
meager belongings into his travel bag. He sat on
the bed for a few minutes, to anchor himself in
time. He was at the lip of the volcano now.
Eventually he rose, and took the elevator downstairs to breakfast in the hotel's café-restaurant.

He wanted to eat, and heaped his plate from the
buffet table with meats and cheeses and a hard-
boiled egg. But when he sat down, his appetite
failed him. He scanned the room, looking for the
Arab businessman, the "Mr. Saleh." Several men
seemed like possible candidates, but they were all
concentrating on their breakfasts. None of them
made eye contact. One got up from his table, a
well-built man in a double-breasted suit, and for a
moment Molavi thought this might be his deliv-
erer, but the man quickly turned and left the room.
A second gentleman left a few minutes later.
Molavi had finished his breakfast now, and was
drinking his second cup of coffee. Maybe something had gone wrong, and they wouldn't be
coming. What would he do then? That was the one
thing he hadn't imagined. The possibilities had
been flight, or death, but never just sitting in a café

in a remote provincial city and then picking up and going back home.

Molavi was staring forlornly out the window, stroking his prickly black beard, when the first of the men walked back into the dining room. Rather than returning to his old table, he continued walking in Molavi's direction. The dining room was nearly empty. He stopped a few paces from the Iranian.

"Are you Dr. Ali?" he asked quietly. His manner was easy and friendly.

"Yes, I am," said Molavi. He felt a kind of electrical charge moving its way up his body. His mind went blank for a moment, and then he remembered that he was supposed to offer a response.

"And what is your name?" asked the Iranian, in a voice barely above a whisper. He tried not to look around him, to see if anyone was watching, but he couldn't quite manage it.

"I am Mr. Saleh," said the Arab. He stuck out his hand and smiled, as if they were old friends and business partners. "Perhaps we could take a walk and see the city."

"Yes," said Molavi. "I think that is a good idea."

The two men strode down Taleghani Street toward the road that led to the coast, which was fifteen miles north. Karim Molavi began to ask "Mr. Saleh" who he really was, but the other man cut him off.

"We should not talk now, my friend. You will be safe. That is enough. We will talk later."

Molavi nodded. They walked on in silence. The city was coming to life. The bazaar in the old city with filling with traders. Men were entering the local *hammam* to have their morning steam bath.

When they neared Shohada Square, Mr. Saleh turned right, down a side street crowded with parked cars. Mr. Saleh walked a dozen yards and stopped in front of a new Iranian Samand, with power windows and air-conditioning. He took a key from his pocket, clicked open the doors, and nodded for Molavi to get in the driver's side. Molavi stood motionless. He wasn't sure what he was supposed to do.

"You have an Iranian driver's license?" asked Mr. Saleh.

Molavi nodded.

"Then drive, my friend." He handed him the keys.

Molavi shook his head in wonderment. *"Kheyli zahmat keshidin,"* he said. You've gone to a lot of trouble. He drove slowly at first but he picked up speed and confidence as they left the town. They drove north, through orange groves and rice fields.

"How did you make all these things happen?" he asked Mr. Saleh when there were no other cars on the road and no sound but the hum of the wheels against the pavement.

"It is magic, my friend," said the Arab with a

wink. "That is what we do. We create illusions. You are living in one now. Relax, my brother. Enjoy your freedom."

It took Molavi and his Arab guardian nearly an hour to reach the coast. The shore road was busy with the cars of Tehranis who had flocked to the coast to get a last bit of fall sunshine. Holiday apartment buildings and villas were crowded along both sides of the road, filling every inch of space near the water.

They drove east through Farahabad and Gohar Baran. There were no police and, judging by the cars racing past, no speed limits. The seaside construction became a little less dense as they moved toward the Turkmenistan border to the east. Mr. Saleh was peering intently at the landscape now, looking for something.

"Turn left," he said to Molavi, pointing toward a small paved road. There was a little flag at the intersection, decorated with the colors of the Esteghlal soccer club.

Molavi drove slowly down the road. He saw a house on the right—a dilapidated old beach villa that looked as if it hadn't been renovated since the shah's time. It appeared to be deserted.

"Stop," said Mr. Saleh. He got out of the car and walked slowly to the house. On the way he grasped something from inside his coat and took it in his hand, pointing it straight ahead. It was a gun. He walked to the windows of the house and peered inside, one window after the other, until he was sure the house was empty. He returned to the front of the house and opened a garage door.

"Park the car," he said to Molavi. "Then come inside."

Two hours later, a Mercedes sedan carrying three passengers moved down the same coastal road. It proceeded past the little banner for Esteghlal, but stopped at the next turn. Two figures emerged from the car, a South Asian man and a European woman. The woman was dressed in a black chador. Underneath she was dressed in black as well—black spandex that covered her arms and legs like a second skin. Her blond hair was tied in a tight bun beneath her veil. The man was dressed in simple peasant garb. The only modern touch was the big bag slung over his shoulders.

The Iranian gentleman continued east in the Mercedes. His two passengers made their way on foot through the low brush along the seaside. In twenty minutes, they had reached the empty beach house where Molavi and his guide had taken refuge.

The woman in the chador made a sound that was like a warbling birdcall. She waited ten seconds, then made the same sound again, louder. From inside the house came back a similar warble, quickly, three times, answered by a long, low whistle from the woman. The door of the house opened, and Jackie and Hakim swept inside. He laid down his heavy bag and unzipped it. Inside were three automatic weapons.

Molavi watched this pantomime wide-eyed. When the woman entered the room, she removed her chador and approached him in her tight black suit.

"Dr. Ali, I presume," she said. "You don't mind shaking hands with a woman, I hope."

"Not at all," said Molavi. His face was alight. "I could give you a kiss, madam."

Jackie smiled. "Not yet, I think. Let's get you out of here first."

Molavi looked at the others, waiting for someone to say something, but nobody did, so he spoke up himself.

"And where are we going, please?"

"My dear Doctor, we are going to take a little boat ride. A fishing boat, I should think. The kind that does its fishing after dark. So for now, I suggest that we all get some rest and a little food, if our hosts have been able to arrange that."

She walked to the kitchen and found cans of tuna fish, a jar of mayonnaise, some crackers packed tightly in cellophane. On the floor was a case of mineral water. In a cabinet was an unopened jar of Nescafé. It was impossible to know whether these supplies had been left thirty years ago, or within the past week. But that was the magic.

28

LONDON

October is the month when Washington tricks itself into thinking that summer's promise isn't quite spent. The trees are shedding their leaves in the biological certainty that winter is coming. But humans are not so sure, on a bright day when the sky turns royal blue and the air blows in from another season. This Indian summer is a time to embrace Washington, but for Harry Pappas, it was urgently the moment to leave. He had been getting updates from London, and now the news was coming in a rush as the members of the Increment team deployed in Iran. Adrian had promised to tell Harry when it was time to go, and now the summons had come, not in an encrypted back-channel message, but in a call on Harry's office phone.

"It's time, old boy," said the SIS chief of staff. And that was it. He rung off.

Harry Pappas went looking for his deputy, Marcia Hill. He walked through the Persia House reception area, past the garish poster of the martyred Imam, to Marcia's cubicle. She was buffing her nails with an emery board, the thin nicotine-stained fingers incongruously capped with perfect lacquered tips. Another woman would have stopped when the boss arrived, but she continued.

"I'm off for a few days," Harry said. "Maybe a

week. Hard to be sure. Don't fuck everything up while I'm gone."

"I'll try to remember that." She looked at her nails and blew away the dust. "And where are you going? If I may ask."

"London, first, but after that, I'm not sure."

"And what am I supposed to tell your . . . how should I put this . . . your 'colleagues'?"

"Hell, I don't know. Tell them I'm on an operational assignment. Tell them I'm meeting an agent who will only talk to me. Tell them whatever will work."

"Should I say it's Dr. Ali?"

"No. If they think they know, fine, who cares. But I don't want any chatter in the system, anywhere. This could get complicated."

"How?"

"Just take my word, Marcia. This one has more creases and folds in it than a paper airplane."

Marcia touched his arm with one of her brown, buffed fingers. It was something she almost never did.

"Are you sure this is the right time to be leaving town, Harry? I mean, there are some people across the river who are ready to start a war with Iran in a week. You're supposed to stop that kind of nonsense. You are the head of the Iran Operations Division, or at least you were, last time I checked. So we, sort of, need you."

Harry took her hand.

"Don't go soft on me, woman. The admiral knows I'm not abandoning ship. So do you. The fact that these crazy bastards are beating the war drums is why I have to go. I can't explain it to you, but I probably don't have to."

"No." Marcia shook her head. She knew what he was doing, and she knew why he couldn't talk about it. She loved Harry, and she worried about him. He was carrying too much baggage. At some point, he was going to stumble and hurt himself.

"Call for help if you need it," she said. "Promise me that, Harry. Don't let yourself get turned upside down. You're good, but you're not Superman."

On his way out of the building, Harry went up to the seventh floor to say goodbye to the director. He wanted to keep faith with his boss, without making him complicit in what he was doing. The admiral was in his office, reading cables from a red-striped binder. He was wearing the dress blues today, rather than the summer whites of a few months ago. These admirals sure liked their uniforms. In another life, Harry would get a job running a dry cleaning shop near a naval base.

"I'm off again for a few days," said Harry, sticking his head in the door. "Marcia will run the division while I'm gone."

"Is this it?" asked the director, looking up from his cables. "Have you found your man?"

"Maybe. We'll see."

"Can I tell the White House?"

"I'd rather you didn't. It's off the books. It could blow up. I don't want anyone to get caught in the fallout, including you."

The admiral extended his hand. He wasn't an emotional man, but he felt something in this encounter that wasn't official, but personal.

"Bless you, Harry. Travel safe. Good luck."

"Yes, sir." Harry gave a little salute. He saw that the director's eyes were moist. Even in this building, where the bureaucrats always seemed to be gaining the upper hand, you couldn't entirely suppress the reality that this business was about life and death.

Adrian Winkler met Harry at Heathrow the next morning. He looked even more than usual like a rascal—a man who has his hand in the cookie jar and is so sure of himself that he doesn't care if you catch him at it. He was wearing a fine cashmere blazer, double-breasted with brass buttons bearing the crest of his London club, and gray flannel slacks that fell over his shoes, just so. Harry, tired from a mostly sleepless night on the plane, could only smile at his friend's dandy appearance.

"Hello, old son," said Adrian. "How are they hanging?"

"Stop sounding so cheerful. It hurts my head." Harry took another look at his sleek British friend. "You look like you won the lottery."

"We *both* won the lottery, Harry. My team is on the way out of Iran. Our team, I should say. And they have our boy."

"Thanks be to Allah. Where are we going to meet them?"

"Well, well, well. That's the question, isn't it? And I have an answer, most certainly do. But first we have a little bit of business to do, on our way into Vauxhall Cross."

"I'm kind of tired, Adrian. Can I get some sleep?"

"'Fraid not, old boy. This is an appointment we don't want to miss. Not really a choice, actually. We all have to pay the piper, you see."

"What the hell are you talking about, Adrian? I don't have any piper, and I hope you don't."

But the SIS chief of staff wouldn't answer. He patted Harry on the back and escorted him to his Rover sedan, parked in the garage alongside Terminal 3.

Harry fell asleep in the car, so he didn't know the destination until they had arrived at the townhouse on Mount Street. It was only then that he understood that the particular piper they were coming to pay was the Lebanese businessman Kamal Atwan.

A servant opened the door and led them upstairs, past the Renoir and the Monet and into the businessman's magnificent library. Atwan was sitting

333

in a chair looking at a Bloomberg terminal and occasionally punching numbers on his keyboard. He looked up when he saw his two visitors, and then back at the screen.

"A moment, please," said the Lebanese. "This is an opportunity I really should not miss." He picked up the phone to call a trading floor somewhere, to confirm that his buy order had been executed. When the business was done, he rose to greet them.

"It's easy to be smart when other people insist on being stupid," said Atwan. "If people persist in mispricing assets, well then, you take advantage of that, don't you?"

"Most definitely," said Adrian Winkler. "I hope you saved a little piece of the deal for me and Harry."

The British intelligence officer laughed, and so did Atwan. Harry wanted to believe that Adrian had been joking.

Atwan ushered them to the couches at the far end of the library and rang for a servant to bring coffee. The Lebanese was wearing his black velvet slippers, monogrammed with his initials, a velvet smoking jacket, and an ascot. Harry had never seen anyone dressed in an outfit like that, except in old movies.

"Mr. Fellows and I are about to go on a trip," said Adrian. "We thought we should stop by and see you first."

"Well, that's very kind of you, my dear. I must say. And where are you going?"

"Somewhere on the Caspian coast," said Adrian. "I was thinking of Turkmenistan. They say it's quite nice this time of year."

Harry shot his British partner a dirty look. What was he doing telling this Lebanese businessman their operational plan? And why was he telling Atwan before he had even briefed Harry? Adrian didn't even glance at him.

"Ashgabat is especially nice," said Atwan. "And quiet. One can work there without fear of being disturbed. If one knows the local customs. And the headman, of course. I was rather good to the old *baschi*, and the new one realizes he is in my debt."

"So you'll tell him we're coming?"

"Of course. I'll have someone call with the tail number of your plane. As we say in the East, you are most welcome."

"Thank you, Kamal Bey. I am most particularly grateful. And so is Mr. Fellows, though he is only now learning of our destination."

"Don't mind me, boys," said Harry. "I'm just here to clean up the mess."

Atwan laughed. "Oh, very good, yes. Clean up the mess. But Mr. Winkler assured me there won't be a mess, will there? No! Of course not."

The coffee arrived, along with some pain au chocolate and muffins and jam. Harry hadn't eaten much on the plane, and he devoured what was before him. The coffee roused him, so that he began to focus more clearly. He had the odd sense, sitting in Atwan's library, that he and Adrian were subcontractors, and that the real chief of this mission was the Arab gentleman seated across from them and dressed in the manner of Fred Astaire.

"Well now," said Adrian, "we do have a bit more business before we go."

"Ah yes. There is always more business in your business. And what are we talking about in particular?"

"We will be meeting in Turkmenistan with a young Iranian scientist. This individual is a nuclear physicist who works for Tohid Electric—"

Harry broke in before Adrian could finish his sentence.

"Whoa!" Harry put up his hand. "Hold on a minute. Can I talk to you for a moment, Adrian. Privately."

Adrian looked at Atwan and shrugged. "We have no secrets here. We're among friends."

"Maybe you don't have any secrets, chum, but I do. So humor me. Let's find a private place to talk. Now."

Harry rose and walked across the floor of the library, carpeted with an immense Persian rug from Ardebil. He waited for Adrian, who eventually followed after a hushed apology to Atwan.

"What the fuck are you doing?" said Harry

when they were together in an anteroom outside the library. "This is my guy. This is my operation. I don't have a clue who your Arab friend is, other than the fact that you seem to have your hand in his pocket. And I damn sure hadn't planned on sharing the details of our operation to exfiltrate my guy."

"But you already have, dear boy."

"Fuck you, Adrian. And stop the 'dear boy' crap. Level with me or I'm walking out of here right now and never coming back."

"Calm down. Take a deep breath, and listen to me. Kamal is working with us on some things that are more sensitive than you understand. He is not some Arab lightweight. He is the key to something very much larger than you realize. And he is utterly trustworthy. I assure you. He has far greater reason to stop the Iranians from making a nuclear weapon than does your government or mine. Or even the Israelis, for that matter. So please, relax and come back into the library with me. It will all become clear."

Harry moved to leave, but Adrian stopped him.

"And please don't make any more silly threats. This is not *your* operation; I thought we were clear about that. Your 'guy' is in the hands of my 'guys' at this very moment. There's nothing you can do about that now. You made your decision some time ago. It's really quite out of your control now, I'm afraid."

· · ·

Harry returned to the library knowing that he was caught in a box that was largely of his own design. He had set this process in motion, and he couldn't really complain now that it was continuing along its course, at its own pace and carving its own direction. He had given up control to another service and its network of people and priorities, because he had believed that was the only way to accomplish his larger aim. Now he had to see that decision through to its end.

When they regained their seats on the couches, Harry was the first to speak.

"Sorry, Mr. Atwan. It's been a long night, and I haven't had much sleep. I just needed to get some things clear with my partner Adrian. I was the one who originally made contact with the Iranian who works for Tohid, so this is personal for me. I don't like anyone shopping my kids without my permission. But Adrian tells me that you are one hundred percent reliable, and I trust Adrian. So I trust you. And there we are."

Harry reached out his hand to Kamal Atwan. They had greeted each other earlier, when Harry first arrived. But this time the Lebanese held the American's palm in his own for a good twenty seconds. Atwan's fingers were finely drawn but powerful, like those of a pianist.

"Trust does not speak in words, Mr. Fellows," said Atwan, finally letting the American's hand go.

"So let us think this through, eh, gents?" said Adrian, starting up again. "As I said before, our Iranian friend works for Tohid Electrical. And that, in turn, is a company to which Mr. Atwan has been supplying equipment for some years. Which provides certain opportunities, and also certain difficulties."

Harry nodded, but he needed to understand this better before he made any more mistakes. He turned to Atwan.

"What kind of equipment have you been selling Tohid?" he asked.

"Very high-end. A half dozen different items, I should think. Adrian has the list. We've sold them flash X-ray systems. I'm quite sure of that. We've sold them many different kinds of measuring equipment. Hydrodynamics is the name of that area of research, I think. Shock waves and all that. Very expensive."

"I'm sure," said Harry with a wave of his hand. He didn't understand money or care much about it.

"My dear, really, you have no idea. Hundreds of millions of dollars change hands in these deals. In the case of one item the Iranians particularly wanted, the price tag was half a billion dollars. How do you put a price on such an item? It is a matter of life and death, sir. So I—we—charge them what this most unusual market will bear. And we are generous with our friends and business partners. Always."

This line of discussion was grotesque to Harry. It is inevitable in a business that involves the systematic bribery of others that there will be a residue of corruption that sticks. But Kamal Atwan's operation seemed to have taken this to an entirely new level. Harry wondered not whether his friend Adrian Winkler was part of the business plan—that was already obvious—but whether the chain of partners in the firm extended upward, to Sir David Plumb, and perhaps others, higher still. He honestly did not want to know the big picture, so he focused on the details.

"How do you ship the equipment? Not from Britain, I assume."

"Of course not, my dear. It comes from a hundred different places. It is smuggled and sold and resold. We have witting cutouts, unwitting cutouts. We use every bit of artifice you can imagine, and then we add another layer or two. Our advantage is that we know what the Iranians want, and we know how to insert ourselves into the supply chain in a way that will, eventually, intersect their purchasing network. It's not for everyone, this sort of business, oh no. We know the sort of people whom the Iranians are likely to trust. We know who to pay, and how much. So the business gets done, you see."

"And the equipment you sell, how well does it work?"

At this, a smile came over Atwan's face, and then he began to chuckle aloud, and soon Adrian was laughing, too.

"How well does it work? That is very good, Mr. Fellows. It works, at first, exactly as it should. As the purchaser expects. But then, a month or a year later, it begins ever so slightly to deviate from the proper performance. But how can the purchaser tell? If a watch tells you it is eleven-fifteen, how are you to know that it is really eleven-sixteen, if you don't have a second watch? And then it's eleven-seventeen, and eleven-thirty, and so on. A year into a project, our miscalibrated equipment will have deflected you a bit from where you should be. And five years on, it will have deflected you a good long way. In ten years, you would be totally lost, I should think."

"So you've been sending this defective equipment to Tohid. And to other Iranian companies, I assume."

"Oh yes, we have quite a number of buyers. But you are quite wrong to describe the equipment as defective, Mr. Fellows. It operates precisely as designed. It's just that the design was a bit mischievous."

"Okay, let me add this up," said Harry. "An Iranian scientist sends us information saying that his lab has tested a neutron generator of the kind that could be used to trigger a nuclear weapon."

"Yes, very good. Very useful for you. A bit prob-

341

lematic for me. Potentially bad for business, but never mind that."

"Bad for business? How?"

"Never mind, my dear. Just a joke. Really."

Atwan laughed; Adrian laughed. Harry continued with his questions, not understanding Atwan's comment, but not paying very much attention to it, either.

"Okay. So according to my Iranian scientist at Tohid, the neutron trigger didn't work the way it was supposed to. The test failed. But if his lab was using some of your, let's say 'reconfigured' equipment, then it's possible the test never will work out right. Because all the measurements are screwed up."

"Not 'possible,' my dear, but 'likely,' I should say."

"So instead of setting off alarm bells, the report from this Iranian agent should actually be reassuring. Is that right?"

"Oh yes," said Atwan. "Very reassuring. Unless the Iranians for some reason came to doubt the accuracy of their measuring equipment, they would stumble on inconclusively for years and years, trying and failing and never understanding why. And buying more equipment, of course, to hedge their bets."

Atwan smiled with the air of a businessman contemplating a cash flow that would continue for decades.

"Feel better now, Mr. Fellows?" said Adrian. "A little less hot under the collar? Perhaps even happy that the firm of Atwan and Winkler has been managing your interests?"

Harry contemplated the complexity of the operation Atwan had described. The CIA had begun a gambit like this, according to Jack Hoffman, but had given it up a few years later when its supplier network was blown. He was happy to know that someone else had taken up the skein of deception—and that this someone had been the British Secret Intelligence Service and its business partner. But some questions were nagging in Harry's mind, and he struggled to put them in words for his colleagues.

"What if there's a second watch?" Harry asked eventually.

"Sorry, I don't follow that at all," said Adrian.

"What if the Iranians have a second watch that tells them the first watch is wrong. That it isn't eleven-fifteen, as the first watch said, but some other time."

"Ah! Clever man," said Atwan.

The Lebanese financier was quicker than Adrian, who expressed puzzlement again. "Sorry, still not getting your drift here, Harry."

"What if the Iranians have a second set of instruments that they acquired somewhere else? A second way of measuring how fast neutrons move in a bomb casing, say, or how quickly explosives push the fissionable material into the core. If they have a second way of monitoring things, then they'll know that one of the measurements is off."

"Why would they have two sets of instruments?" asked Adrian. "That wouldn't make sense."

"Because maybe they have two separate tracks, or four. Who knows? But they'd do it for redundancy. For insurance. For self-protection against devious bastards like us who they must know are trying to play games with them."

"But my dear Mr. Fellows," broke in Atwan, "what if *both* watches are wrong? Or all four, if that is the case. The watches may be telling different times, but all those times may be inaccurate."

"Is that possible? I mean, have you shipped so much spooky gear into Iran that you could be supplying multiple programs?"

"I would not like to brag," said Atwan modestly, adjusting the fluff of his ascot.

"I think that means yes," said Adrian Winkler.

Atwan called for lunch to be brought into the library. The chef had managed to poach an entire salmon, and graced it with new potatoes, fresh parsley, and fat, sweet English peas. A butler opened a bottle of 1978 Corton, sold at auction for the Hospices de Beaune with the unlikely name "Docteur Peste." It set off the salmon so well that the two tastes might have been married in the kitchen. Harry barely touched the wine. He was still trying to think his way through the transactions in Iran—and how they would run Dr. Karim Molavi when they finally had a chance to debrief him, face-to-face. Harry had begun to trust Atwan's judgment over the course of the morning, or at least respect the depth of his deviousness. And he wanted his opinion. So he asked.

"What should Adrian and I do with our Iranian scientist when we finally meet him?"

"You flatter me, my dear, to pose such a question."

"I don't flatter you. I need you. What do you think?"

"Well, sir, let me think." He paused, and then began again. "I would have three questions for him, I think. The first, about his home base; the second, about his neighborhood; and the third, shall we say, cosmic."

Atwan took a drink of the Corton, the tiniest sip. He didn't touch alcohol, normally, but with this very old and good wine he was making an exception. Harry and Adrian waited for him to clear his palate and his mind. Harry had taken a small pad from his pocket so that he could make notes.

"So I will begin at home, yes?" said Atwan. "My first question for this fellow would be about his own laboratory at Tohid. Do his colleagues suspect that anything is wrong with their instruments and readings? Have any of them said anything—anything whatsoever—to suggest that they see a reason for their lack of success? A reason other than the normal scientific process of trial and error, that is. If so, you must know that. If they have discovered this ruse, then you and Mr. Winkler must quickly plan another. Or reinforce it. Do you follow me, my dear Mr. Fellows?"

"I think so," said Harry. "We need to find out if Tohid knows we are playing games with them. And then plan accordingly. What's the second question—the neighborhood one?"

"Yes, my dear. The second question is whether your young gentleman knows about any other programs that are similar to his own research at Tohid. You surmise that such additional programs might exist in principle, but you must know that they exist in fact. Cities, addresses, people. Otherwise you cannot target this deception accurately, I am afraid. And then you will be lost."

"Okay," said Harry. "We need him to identify other weaponization programs. Redundant ones, which the Iranians created so that if the Tohid track fails, other tracks would be ready. Is that it?"

"Yes, yes."

"So what's the cosmic question?" asked Harry.

"The cosmic question, sir, is whether your Iranian man is smart enough and brave enough to go back in and steer this process in the direction that you want, once you have interviewed him.

346

And whether you, Mr. Fellows, are smart enough and brave enough to understand what he is telling you. Otherwise, it would be better really to let it all run, just as we have set it up, and not let this Iranian chap get in the way and make mistakes. It's awkward."

"For whom?"

"For business, my dear."

Harry Pappas and Adrian Winkler took off that afternoon from Mildenhall air base in Cambridgeshire, in a small business jet bound for Turkmenistan. The jet was registered to GasPort Ltd., a nominee company whose owner was a shell company in the Netherlands Antilles. The plane was unmarked, other than the tail number that had been furnished that day to the ruler of the country, in a private and personal call from a Lebanese businessman in London who had done him many favors, and would do him many more.

29
ASHGABAT, TURKMENISTAN

The fishing trawler reached the Caspian coast just before midnight. Jackie and her team were waiting on a sandbar that jutted out from the shore, east of Gohar Baran. The moon was a quarter full, casting a pale light on the murky saline waters of the Caspian. Karim Molavi was nervous: he studied every distant light across the water; he started at every automobile that passed on the coastal road. He fiddled in his pockets and removed his Iranian cell phone, and his "special" phone, and his Palm Pilot electronic address book. He asked if he should leave them behind, and Jackie answered, "God, no."

"I have no passport," whispered Karim. He was embarrassed. He had not wanted to mention it, for fear that it would create a last-minute problem.

Jackie laughed. She thought he was making a joke. "You won't need one on this trip," she said.

The members of the team were all dressed in black camouflage against the night, shadow figures along the shore. Jackie had a black wet suit for her Iranian passenger. Molavi tugged it on awkwardly, then donned the black balaclava handed to him by Marwan, whom he still knew as "Mr. Saleh." Marwan and Hakim had automatic rifles slung over their shoulders. Jackie had put down her gun and was squatting on the sand, positioning a small radio beacon.

The fishing boat had extinguished its running lights. They heard the slow chug of the old boat's motor before they saw the craft. The captain was a Turkman, wrapped in a heavy cape. He had been plying these waters for thirty years, ferrying cargoes to and from Iran since the days of the old Soviet republic. He had paid off the authorities on both sides of the border for so long that he was almost legitimate; all they asked was that he stay in the shadows and not get caught. With the Turkman was a British intelligence officer from Ashgabat station, dressed in a navy peacoat and shivering in the night air.

The four waded toward the trawler, Jackie leading the way, her gun hoisted high over her head. Molavi followed, and then Hakim and Marwan, facing to shore with their guns on automatic fire.

Jackie called out the name "Jeremy." The British man in the pea jacket answered back with her name, "Jackie." That wasn't much of a recognition code, but it sufficed. He lowered a ladder, and the four clambered up, Molavi first. The *putt-putt* of the engine grew louder and soon they were away. When they cleared Iranian coastal waters, Jackie told Molavi he was safe. He shook his head, as if he still did not believe his deliverance was real.

The Iranian looked at the British woman, snug in her wet suit, the rubber fabric clinging to her breasts and hips.

"Is it always this easy?" Molavi asked.

"Yes," she answered, "if you do it right."

An Iranian patrol boat bobbed at anchor to the east, guarding the border point below the Turkmen coastal town of Hasan Kuli. The Turkman smuggler gave the Iranian vessel a wide birth.

Molavi was exhausted, and he lay down under a heavy blanket. The others talked in low voices, drinking coffee from a thermos that Jeremy, the British intelligence officer, had brought along. Occasionally one of them would make a joke and the others, in the decompression after the mission, would join in the laughter.

As dawn broke, the boat made for a fishing village about ten kilometers north of Hasan Kuli. It was a barren spot, the town bleached as white as the Caspian sand. A jeep was waiting for them; it drove them several miles inland, where a helicopter was cranking its rotor. The markings on the side identified it as belonging to GasPort Ltd. A crewman from the helicopter handed dry clothes to Molavi and led him to a shed near the landing site, where he could change and use the toilet. The rest of the team changed clothes in the open air. The black wet suits were stowed in a carryall, and replaced with street clothes that might have been worn by a group of adventure tourists on a Central Asian holiday.

When they boarded the helicopter, Molavi had trouble attaching the four-way straps of his safety harness, so Marwan and Hakim on either side clicked the buckles. Jackie handed him earplugs to dull the roar of the helicopter engine. When they were all buckled and plugged, the helicopter levitated from the ground in an easy upward float that felt like the suspension of gravity. When the chopper was several hundred feet up, it lowered its nose and banked east toward Ashgabat.

• • •

The helicopter flew over the desert plains of southwest Turkmenistan, passing near trading towns with unpronounceable names—Kizyl Atrek, Gumdag, Gyzylarbat. To the south were the Kopet Mountains, a sharp ridge of peaks that guarded the frontier between Turkmenistan and Iran. Through the helicopter window you could make out the dry riverbeds and goat trails of this rugged, empty land. Molavi tried to stay awake and see the sights, but he couldn't manage it. Escape was a kind of narcoleptic drug. He enjoyed the sleep of a condemned prisoner, released.

Harry Pappas and Adrian Winkler landed at the Ashgabat airport, the plane coming to rest in a distant corner away from the commercial terminal. A powder blue Mercedes was parked on the jetway, a local security man in plain clothes standing beside it. When the two men descended the gangway, the Turkman greeted them stiffly and led them to the car. He rode in front with the driver, the two Westerners in back. The car peeled off the tarmac, avoiding customs, passport control, and the Ashgabat VIP lounge.

It was early morning, and the city was just waking up. It was a capital that appeared to have been built overnight. The new section of town was all white marble palaces, ceremonial state buildings, and grand apartment blocks. It was like a toy city. The buildings were stately and well built—designed in a sort of Turkic neoclassical style that was all noble pillars and gold domes. It conveyed the sort of permanence that a nomadic people would want in their capital, when they realized that they were sitting on the world's fifth-largest gas reserves and could afford to build whatever they wanted.

The nation's previous leader, who had modestly called himself *Turkmenbaschi*, or "leader of the Turkmen," had named nearly every one of these grand edifices after himself. He had even crafted a golden statue of himself atop a massive pillar at the center of town. It was motorized so that at every daylight hour the *baschi*'s body was facing the sun.

"Is this place for real?" asked Harry. "It looks like a Turkish Disney World."

"Beats me, old boy. Never been here. Not likely to come back, either."

"It's beautiful, in an ugly sort of way."

"Shhh," said Adrian, nodding toward the security man in front. "Remember, we are guests in the house of the *baschi*."

The powder blue Mercedes drove them south through the capital. They passed eccentric buildings designed to please the former leader's iron whim: the state publishing company, whose façade was built to look like the open pages of a book; the Ministry of Health, a skyscraper formed to resemble the caduceus—the rod entwined by two snakes that is the symbol of the medical profession. Ahead of them a dozen miles distant stood the Kopet range, rising sharply out of the high plain. The buildings here offered an unobstructed view of the mountains. They passed the President Hotel, open only to guests of the *baschi*, and then the presidential palace itself. Another mile and they came to a gated villa. The guard spoke to the security man in the front seat and then raised the barrier. As they rolled toward the white marble villa, the front door opened. Every aspect of this trip seemed to have been ordered by an unseen hand.

"This is a safe house?" asked Harry, looking at the splendid villa. "You might as well put out a neon sign."

"It's a police state, Harry. Everything is safe. The GDP is a state secret, for God's sake. If they tell us it's secure, it's secure."

"Have you set up the audio?"

"My people have. We'll be running a tape the whole time you're in with him. It will upload to London via satellite, so we don't have to worry about keeping a record here."

"Did you rig any countersurveillance?"

"Sort of. No bubble, but some white noise. We'll be all right. These people aren't going to shop us to Tehran. They have too much at stake."

Harry shook his head doubtfully, but it was too late to question these details. He had the feeling, not for the first time, that Adrian was taking risks that would not make sense unless he knew something that Harry didn't.

Karim Molavi was waiting in a pleasant sitting room when Harry and Adrian arrived. He was drinking a cup of tea and reading a copy of the latest issue of *Scientific American*, which had been left on a coffee table with other scientific periodicals. He was alone in the room. Jackie and her crew had gone somewhere else in the villa, to sleep or eat or practice their marksmanship.

Adrian peered through a keyhole into the room where Molavi was sitting and opined that the Iranian appeared to be content. They had agreed that Harry would do the initial debriefing alone. Behind Molavi, through a large plate-glass window, were the mountain peaks that buffered him from his homeland.

Harry Pappas entered the room. He took his first look at the man who until this moment had only been an email address. Molavi was bigger and younger than he had expected. He had a dark, handsome face, with a dominant nose and thick black hair. He had the bearing of an intellectual; confident, reserved, composed. The mystery was why he had risked everything to reach out.

"My name is Harry," he began. "I work for the Central Intelligence Agency. I received the messages that you sent to us. I'm responsible for your case, in our government. It is an honor for me to meet you at last in person."

He extended his hand to Molavi, who shook it softly, almost like a caress.

"Thank you, sir," said Molavi. He spoke English in a soft and measured voice.

"Are you happy? Do you have everything you need?"

"Oh yes, sir. The people who came to rescue me were like a dream. I thought that only happened in movies. They were English, I think."

"Yes. The British are working with us. We moved heaven and earth to find you and get you out, once you contacted us."

"I do not know what to say, sir. You came to me from so far away, and picked me up as if you were a great bird and I was your chick."

"Well, you're here now, son. And we need to talk."

Harry hadn't planned to call him "son," but it slipped out, and it seemed right.

"Yes, sir. Of course."

"Are you ready? Would you like to eat something first?"

"Oh no, sir. They gave me breakfast. It was very good."

"Don't call me sir," said Harry, smiling. "I am here as your friend and adviser, not your boss. You can walk away anytime you are uncomfortable."

"I am quite comfortable, sir. And where would I go? Please, I am not stupid. I am ready for your questions."

Harry began with the basics, as intelligence officers always do. Full name, parents' names, addresses, close relations, workplaces and addresses, foreign travels. He ran it like a doctor's checkup; taking the inventory of a life, item by item. He wanted to assemble the collateral that could be checked against available records and databases—not simply to establish Molavi's bona fides, but to provide a context for understanding him and what he wanted.

Harry was of the old school, in that respect. He believed that the essence of handling an agent was understanding what he wanted out of the transaction, and then attempting to give it to him, or at least the appearance of it. Something in the way Molavi spoke about his family history caught Harry's attention, and it was here that he made his first foray.

"Tell me about your father," said Harry.

"What is there to tell? He was a great man who never achieved what he deserved. He despised the shah. He believed in the revolution. But when he saw what it became, he despised the revolution, too. Iran is full of people like my father, who were unlucky."

Harry studied the young man. "He was never honored for his service, I take it."

"No. They gave him a pension, and free medical care because he had been tortured by Savak. But he was a professor of literature. He believed in the imagination. What use did they have for him?"

"You honor him," said Harry softly.

"What? I'm sorry."

"You honor him, Karim. By who you are and what you do. Especially by having the courage to be here today."

The Iranian lowered his head. Harry could not tell whether there were tears in his eyes, but he suspected that it was so. Harry took one more step. In the manuals of tradecraft, what he was doing was known as establishing "rapport," but that instrumental term did not begin to encompass the art of establishing a clandestine relationship.

"I had a son who would be almost your age now," said Harry. His voice was now so soft that it could barely be heard. Molavi had to lean toward the older man.

"What happened to him?"

"He died. In Iraq. He was a good boy. I grieve for him every day."

"I am sorry, sir."

"I mention my son for a reason. If he were alive today, I would want him to be as brave as you are. I would want him to have the same conviction as you, that there are larger interests than what your government tells you to do. I wish that I had taught my son better that his country's leaders do not

357

define what is true and right. If I had done that, he might be alive today. That is why I know that your father would be proud of you. I can see it with a father's eyes."

"Thank you," said Molavi. He had listened very carefully, and he knew that the American spy was speaking to him from a deep chamber of the heart, which had many echoes.

Harry grasped the young man's shoulder and held it, the way he once had held Alex's.

"Now, come sit here next to me," said Harry, "and let's talk about your work in the nuclear program."

Adrian strolled down the marble hall of the villa. He knew he should be listening to Harry's debriefing, but Harry could do the work by himself. And he had another concern. He had seen Jackie turn into a room off the main corridor when he and Harry first arrived, and now he wanted to find her. His heart was racing. It was like the feeling he used to get when he wanted a cigarette and couldn't find one, back when he smoked. To call it desire was being polite. It was an addiction.

He stuck his head in one door. It was an exercise room. Hakim was lifting weights; Marwan was doing crunches on a rubber mat. One of Hakim's Bhangra CDs was playing, the percussive sound of the drum marking the beat against the high wail of the singer. They didn't notice Adrian. They were in their zone; warriors at rest. Adrian went farther down the hall and opened the door on a vacant library lined with empty shelves.

The last door on the corridor was open a crack. He peered in and saw Jackie reclining languidly on a couch. She had showered and changed, and was dressed in sweatpants and a blue cashmere sweater. Her hair was not quite dry, and long blond ringlets were circling her neck. She was listening to music on her iPod, so she didn't notice Adrian at first. As he tiptoed into the room she looked up at him and smiled.

"Lock the door," she said.

Adrian secured the lock and walked back toward the couch. She had risen. The sweatpants were hanging low, below her navel, drooping almost to her crotch. As she took a step toward him, her breasts moved under the blue sweater like a swell upon the water. She shook her hair and the droplets of water came off her in a fine mist.

"God, woman, you are a sight," he said.

"I was waiting for you, darling. I was afraid you would be too busy to see me."

"I am too busy to see you," he said, taking her in his arms and whispering in her ear. "But not too busy to fuck you."

He pulled at the loose terry cloth fabric of the sweatpants, which fell to the floor. Her flanks were as taut as those of the fine horse she had ridden around the Serpentine in Hyde Park. He cracked her across the bottom with his open palm. She felt the sting, and smiled so that you could see her perfect white teeth.

"You want it like that?"

"Like what?" Adrian's voice had a tremble of anticipation.

"Take off your trousers, my darling, and you'll find out. Don't disappoint Jackie, or she will be *very* angry."

Harry worked patiently through the morning with Molavi. He was building his dossier. He asked first for a list of the experiments and research tasks Molavi had conducted, and then a list of all other research projects he had heard about. As he logged each answer in a spiral notebook, Harry would ask whether that particular piece of research had been successful. Had the equipment worked properly? Was anyone suspicious? He recalled Kamal Atwan's list of questions and tried to touch all those bases.

When this inventory was done, Harry asked for a list of locations where nuclear weapons work was done in Iran—all the places Molavi had ever visited, and the additional places he might have heard about. That was the most important information Molavi possessed, and Harry wanted to get it out in their first hours, in case they had to break off the meeting for some reason. Molavi mentioned only six locations. Harry knew about five of them. The sixth was new. It was in Mashad, near the eastern border with Turkmenistan.

"Why was it there?" asked Harry.

"I don't know. Far from Israel, maybe?"

Harry said they would come back to Mashad later. He wanted to know when Karim had gone to work at Tohid, and what that laboratory had been doing in the years when the weaponization work had supposedly stopped in 2003.

"It never stopped, really. The program stopped, but the work continued. I did the same things after the official termination that I did before."

"Why did you send us your first message?"

"To wake you up, sir. You had gone to sleep."

"Sorry, that's not a good enough explanation."

"Because I was angry. The regime was destroying everyone I cared about. My father, my cousin, me. I had to do something. Otherwise, Mr. Harry, I would die."

"Okay, but still not good enough. Revenge may have been a reason, but you're not just about that. There was something else."

Molavi searched his mind. He had never fully analyzed his motives until now. He had acted on instinct and compulsion, rather than a rational plan. But what was it that had made him take the risks, without asking for anything in return?

"I was ashamed," answered the Iranian. "I could

not live with myself if I didn't do something. So I acted. That probably sounds crazy."

"No," said Harry. "It sounds like the truth."

It was lunchtime. **Harry's** stomach was growling, and he knew that Molavi could use a break before they cycled back over the details. Harry stepped outside into the hall and looked for Adrian in the anteroom, next to the room they were using for the debriefing. Jeremy, the young British officer who had accompanied the boat out of Iran, was sitting at a computer, his earphones on to monitor the conversation in the other room.

"Where's Adrian?" asked Harry.

"He stepped out. Busy with something else, I guess."

Harry could guess what that was, but he didn't intend to discuss it with the junior officer with the earphones dangling around his neck, and probably not with Adrian, either.

"We need some lunch," said Harry. "Hot, and good."

"It's all ready," said Jeremy.

"With some cold drinks. No booze, just Cokes. And some coffee. And some ice cream, if there is any."

They ate a lunch of steak and chips, with a dessert of Häagen-Dazs Chocolate Chocolate Chip that the duty officer had somehow found in

362

Ashgabat. Molavi relaxed as they ate. He talked about his school days in Germany. Harry asked if he wanted to take a walk before going back to work, but Molavi said no. He asked to use the toilet, and came out with his hair neatly combed. He was fastidious that way. Harry worried about only one thing. Molavi was decompressing so quickly that it would be difficult to get him to go back in, if they decided that was necessary.

Harry began again. What scientific instruments did Tohid use? Where were they obtained? How were they serviced? Did people come from overseas to work on the equipment, or were they Iranians? Had Molavi ever seen any of the maintenance records, and could he get access to them? Did the Iranians question their suppliers? Were they suspicious? Did they compare one company with another?

The young Iranian apologized. He didn't have many answers, and didn't think he could get much more information now, at least at Tohid. He was under suspicion. They had already begun limiting the flow of information to him, or at least he thought they had.

"The test results you sent us from the neutron generator," pressed Harry. "Where did you get those?"

"From the Central Laboratory. I go there to do some of my research. It is a closed site. We are accompanied in and out."

"How did you take the material out?"

"I sent it to myself, in the computer system, from one secret account to another. It's not so difficult if you know how. That is the advantage I had. None of the Pasdaran security people are clever enough to track the scientists. They have to trust us. They have no choice. Until they decide that they do not trust us."

"The neutron trigger experiments that were described in those test results, were they considered successes or failures?"

"Failures," answered the Iranian.

"And what was the response of your colleagues to those failures?"

"To try again. You know the expression, 'If at first you don't succeed . . .'"

"'Try, try again,'" said Harry, completing the old saw. "But they kept failing, isn't that right? The tests were failing before the lab report you sent, and they have continued to fail since then. Is that right?"

Molavi nodded. His erect posture had eased. He was slumping a little in the chair now.

"And were they suspicious, that the experiments kept failing?"

Molavi paused, as if he understood the importance of the ground they were touching now. "Yes. They began to worry."

"How do you know that?"

"Because that was one of the subjects they asked

about when they interrogated me. The interrogator talked about trains going in the wrong direction, and equipment being unreliable. He wouldn't say any more. They aren't sure, you see. But I know that he was worried about it."

Harry rose from his chair and walked to the window. He needed to think a moment. There was a dusting of early snow at the very top of the mountain range that stood so starkly before them. The impression was of a fringe of white hair, atop a creased and pitted face. How far away was Iran? Twenty miles, fifty miles? Harry walked back to his chair. Molavi was sitting attentively, waiting to begin again. He was a good boy. It was not easy for Harry to think that he might have to send him back across those mountains again.

"So, Dr. Molavi, here is my question," said Harry, leaning in toward the young man. His bulk was a shield, and also a prod. "Suppose that someone decided that the work in your laboratory was unreliable. Would they have an option—to go to another facility, let's say, to conduct similar experiments?"

"Oh yes. I think so. That was one of the principles of the program. 'Robust and redundant.' They said that in English, because there are not good words for those ideas in Farsi."

"And where would they do this redundant

research, if they decided that the first track at Tohid wasn't working right? Do you know?"

"In my area of neutron research? At Mashad, I believe. That was the parallel site."

"How do you know? Did you ever go there?"

"Oh yes, of course. I was sent there for two months, back before 2003, when the official program was still going. I had a second cousin there, from my mother's family. I lived with them. But then they decided that the main research would be at Tohid, and Mashad would just be a backup. But that's where they would go. They have equipment there. Everything. It's called Ardebil Research Establishment."

"And they have confidence in this facility in Mashad—that it has not been penetrated or manipulated by us?"

"Oh yes. Why not? It is very secret. There were only a few of us who went there. My best friend from high school is still there, I think."

"Your best friend?" Harry was trying to contain his enthusiasm, but he was not entirely successful. "Your best friend from high school works at the neutron research facility in Mashad? A person who would do you a favor, if you asked. Is that right?"

"Yes, certainly. His name is Reza. He doesn't like the big bosses very much, either. Nobody does."

"Sweet Jesus." Harry shook his head.

"Excuse me, sir?"

"Nothing," said Harry. "Let's take a break. I need to think."

He walked out of the room with a buzz he couldn't have explained. It was like a logic cloud coming together, all the disparate shapes fitting together into something that didn't have words yet, but felt like an idea; a plan, even. But to make it real, he would need help in a hurry from someone he did not fully trust.

30
ASHGABAT, TURKMENISTAN

Harry eventually found Adrian Winkler. He was out walking with Jackie in the garden on the other side of the villa. He was whispering something in her ear, and she was giving him a little paddle on the fanny. Adrian had a flushed look on his face. Harry hoped it was from sex, rather than from drinking. Jackie pulled back from her boss as Harry approached. She was in control of him. Every gesture and movement said that.

"How's it going, old boy? Is the young Iranian doctor all that we dreamed about? Worth the effort? Do tell."

"Don't give me the 'old boy' stuff, thank you very much," Harry barked. "We need to talk, right now. So tell Miss Moneypenny to get lost for a while. Eh what?"

Adrian shrugged. He looked back at Jackie and

gave her a wink, and walked inside with Harry. He really didn't give a shit. That was the measure of his debauchery, that he didn't care whether his friend Harry knew that he had been fucking his brains out with a woman who was nominally his subordinate.

"Don't say anything, Harry, because it would be tedious. And it would be irrelevant. We all have our weaknesses. You just haven't been creative enough to discover yours."

"Shut up, Adrian. And get your nose out of that woman's pussy for long enough to sober up. We have work to do. I think I just figured out what the game is here."

"Oh, jolly good. So pleased. I would hate to think that this was just a dirty little weekend in Ashgabat."

They walked into the villa and found the anteroom where Jeremy was sitting at his monitoring station. Molavi had gone back to his bedroom to take a nap, the young officer said. Harry asked Jeremy to leave the room, and then closed the door. He poured some coffee for Adrian and told him to drink it. The British officer took a few gulps, and then helped himself to a piece of a Toblerone candy bar that was sitting next to Jeremy's computer.

"Are you back among the living?" asked Harry.

"Yes, more or less. And don't pay too much attention to my extracurriculars, Harry. That's always been part of my operational style."

"No apology necessary," said Harry.

"That's lucky, because I'm not apologizing. What's up? Did you break the bank with our Iranian friend? Hope so."

"I got a lot of good stuff. So much, actually, that I have a question for you. Can you make a secure call to Kamal Atwan if we need to?"

"Sure. That shouldn't be a problem. What do you need to know?"

"I want to know if he has shipped any equipment to Mashad, for starters. How would we make the call? Can you use the communications suite at the embassy? Because I want this done in a SCIF, or someplace just as tight. For real."

"I'm sure Her Majesty's Government would oblige. But there's no need to use the embassy gear to contact Atwan."

"Why not?"

"Because he's right here in Ashgabat. He wanted to come along in case we needed anything. Turkmenistan is one of his accounts, shall we say. He keeps a villa here. He has so many strings tied around the leadership, he might as well be Edgar Bergen. Hope you don't mind."

"Christ! You are out of control, do you know that?"

"Possibly, Harry. But it's too late to do anything about that now. And besides, so far everything is working out dandy. So settle down, if you please. I will see if I can raise Brother Atwan. He's probably sticking hundred-dollar bills in the *baschi*'s trouser pockets right now."

Harry and Adrian traveled to Atwan's villa, a few doors down from the presidential palace. That seemed to Harry the most secure alternative, or to be more accurate, the least insecure. The house was furnished less elegantly than Atwan's place in Mayfair, but only slightly so. There were fine carpets on the floors and paintings on the walls, including what looked to Harry like a Degas watercolor of racehorses at the track. And there was a British staff in place as well—a butler, maids, a cook. They seemed to live here permanently and maintain the place in perfect Atwanian order—all the foods and wines and sundries that the chief preferred, always ready for his arrival, no matter how infrequent or unlikely that might be. Harry wondered how many of these well-appointed bolt-holes Atwan had secreted around the world.

"My dear Mr. Fellows, always such a pleasure." Atwan kissed Harry thrice on the cheek. "I hope you don't mind that I took the liberty of joining you here. I do like some adventure, you know."

"I'm actually glad to see you here, Kamal Bey. I prefer to travel a little more anonymously, normally. But under the circumstances it makes things easier. I need your help, in a hurry."

"How nice. I cannot think of a greater pleasure

than being useful to someone who really needs my help."

"Can we go somewhere private? I'm sure you trust your people. But in a country like this, the walls have ears."

"Quite so. I have a room that's used for my private business. It's swept every day when I am here. I brought one of my London technicians along for just that purpose. He made a check a few hours ago."

Atwan led Harry past a library, which from the look of it had nearly as many volumes as the one in London. Down a hallway was a door that led into a windowless room equipped with several computers, a Bloomberg terminal, and a flat-screen television tuned to Fashion TV. The models, stunning young girls from Siberia and Belarus and God knows where, were prancing down the runway, planting their high heels in a way that made their tiny torsos pivot as if they were on cocktail skewers.

"My favorite program," said Atwan, switching off the television. "When I see a woman I particularly like, I place an order. I have a friend at one of the modeling agencies, you see. And many of these dear girls are available, for a price. You wouldn't think so, but there it is. They are exotic caged animals, and they know it. Peacocks on promenade. When I find the right girl, available, you know, I will send her as a special gift to a friend. Or send him, where that is appropriate. The boys are not so expensive. I will ship them abroad all tied up in ribbons and bows. It's so much nicer than the usual sort of gift. The personal touch."

"Not my problem," said Harry, taking a seat in one of the black leather chairs in Atwan's little hideaway. "It's just business."

"I am so glad to hear you say that, my dear. That's a very enlightened attitude. Just business indeed, and how can we afford to make value judgments when it comes to business? Now, my dear, how can I help *you* do business? Please. I am at your service."

Harry looked around the room. The door was closed tight. The only people inside were him, Adrian, and Atwan. He hated to share secrets with people he didn't fully trust, but he had no choice.

"The Iranians have a secret weapons laboratory in Mashad. At least it was unknown to me until a few minutes ago. Its cover name is Ardebil Research Establishment. Have you ever heard of it?"

Atwan paused and thought a moment. "I don't think so. We have shipped to Jamaran, and Esfahan, and Parchin, and Natanz, and Shiraz. But never to Mashad."

"We know about those other places. But Mashad is new to you, too?"

"I can check, if you would like. I took the liberty of bringing my records with me. They are very portable."

The Lebanese businessman reached into his pocket and removed a computer flash drive monogrammed with his initials. He turned to the bank of computers and plugged the little drive into the USB port of one of the processors. He clicked open the drive, and in a few moments the screen displayed a spread sheet of business records.

"You're good," said Harry. "The normal billionaire arms dealer would have someone else do that for him."

"I couldn't afford to hire such a person, my dear. The only assets I truly possess are the secrets I keep. I cannot entrust those to anyone."

Atwan studied the screen, looking for Ardebil Research Establishment among dozens of Iranian company names to which his far-flung affiliates and hidden fronts had shipped equipment over the years. He found nothing in this first scan; then he went back and looked for any business concerns in Mashad that might have touched his net. Again he came up dry.

"What did you say they were doing at this facility in Mashad?"

"I didn't," said Harry. "But my guess is that it parallels the work at Tohid. So they would be doing the basics of weaponization. Work on a trigger, probably with a neutron emitter. Work on timing the firing. Work on miniaturization of the core. Materials science, maybe. The key thing is the neutron trigger."

"Well, let's look, shall we?" Atwan went to a different document on his flash drive, this one organized by products sold. He went to the subcategory for neutron generators and the related instruments for testing and simulation. Tohid had been a customer, all right. Many shipments through various cutouts, over many years. But there was nothing for a company called Ardebil or for any concern in Mashad.

"Dear me," said Atwan, "they seem to have gotten past us. I wonder how anyone could have sold them this sort of equipment without it coming to my attention. That disturbs me, more than you might imagine."

"Accidents do happen," said Adrian. "Even to you."

Atwan ignored his genial British friend, who was still a bit red-faced and giddy from his earlier activities. It was as if he could smell the sex on Adrian, and he didn't like it. Atwan was peculiar in that respect; he used debauchery freely enough to get what he wanted, but he was not a debauched man himself. That was his power—to use others without being used.

"Perhaps you could get us something to drink, Adrian. Some tea, perhaps. A whiskey if you prefer. I'll have a cup of tea. And a sweet biscuit, please. How about you, Mr. Fellows?"

Harry said that he would have tea and a biscuit, too. Adrian knew that he was being sent away, but he didn't seem to mind. He had taken the master's shilling, many millions of them. And he did as he was asked.

"This is just about our worst nightmare, isn't it?" said Harry, turning to Atwan once they were alone. "I mean, we're spinning them for all it's worth on one side of the house—so much so that they're getting suspicious that we're playing games. Meanwhile, there's another side of the house we didn't even know about. And over there, they've got a whole other program on ice. As soon as they get spooked about Track A, they'll go to Track B. And then we're fucked. Pardon my French."

"That is the problem, my dear Mr. Fellows. Quite right. But it has an answer. We are not without resources. Certainly, I am not without resources. The question is how to use them."

Harry rubbed his forehead, as if by that action he could bring forth a plan. What were the tools he had to use? How quickly did he have to play his next move? What could Atwan's network do quickly that might make the pieces of this puzzle fit together the right way? In the space of a few minutes, he had gone from resenting Atwan's presence to depending on him for advice and operational support.

"Let me ask you some questions, Kamal. Do you mind if I call you that? I promise that I won't steal anything from your cookie jar or order one of your fashion models for Christmas."

"Of course you can, my dear. And I am sorry that you will not accept a present or two, but I quite understand."

"So, for starters, I'm wondering how quickly you could penetrate the supply chain for the Mashad facility. So that you could get your gizmos in, and make the equipment there as unreliable as the other tools the Iranians are playing with."

"Months, I am afraid. If at all. The Iranians are not stupid. None of their suppliers are, either. They go to very great lengths to avoid precisely the tricks that we are using. They accompany all their shipments. They have twenty-four-hour guards at all their warehouses. They do not hire anyone in the chain whom they do not know, and even then they test them for loyalty. To build my network has taken the better part of thirty years. I am using now penetrations that I set down when I was starting out in the business. I can work through many governments, it is true. But I cannot conjure up companies and shipments out of thin air."

Harry nodded. That was the answer he had expected. That was the reason the CIA had gotten out of the sabotage business. It was too damned difficult, it took too long, and it cost too much. And it was vulnerable to any asshole scientist who had been recruited for the mission but got pissed off and decided to tell someone about it. But intelligence work was the art of the possible; you used the tools you had in hand. And Harry's hands were not empty. Sleeping in the nearby safe house was a human key that could unlock the door that Atwan thought was impassable.

"Kamal, I want you to do a little thought experiment with me, okay? I want you to imagine that you had access to the research lab at Mashad. Assume you could get in and out safely. Is there something you could put in play, into the neutron generator, or into the computers, that would achieve the desired result?"

"Meaning to poison the project?"

"To poison it, but without a trace. So that if the Iranians turned to that facility, assuming that it was clean, they would end up screwing themselves. But they wouldn't know it for years. Do you think that would be possible?"

"Oh yes. I mean, my dear sir, that is what we do. We need only a few minutes' access to the equipment to do our little business."

"Would you sabotage the neutron generator?"

"Oh no. They would build another. Or buy one. The oil companies use them now, you know, for seismic work. No, the better way would be to manipulate the computer that does the simulation of the imploding core and the operation of the neutron generator. That's how they test a bomb without actually testing it, you see?"

"How in the hell would you do that?"

"We have ways to delete bits of code, pieces of chip, slices of memory. We can do brain surgery without ever cutting open the skull. We just have to be nearby. But it is access that is the problem. So you are asking me, if I could fly, could I fly to Mashad? And I answer yes. But of course, I cannot fly."

"Maybe I can," said Harry. "Or maybe I can put wings on someone."

They talked into the evening. The tea and biscuits were replaced with whiskey, and to Harry's surprise, even Kamal Atwan had a drink.

And Harry told Atwan about Karim Molavi; he tried to say as little as possible about the boy's background, but the Lebanese had a way of filling in the gaps. He seemed almost to know the story as Harry was telling it.

It would work, Atwan said. There was a special tool his people used, when they had proximity to a computer but couldn't get inside. It used an electronic pulse to alter computer circuits. It needed a lot of power to do its work, but that could be arranged, too. Atwan hadn't brought this gear with him, but he knew where it was in London. He sent an encrypted email message to his senior technical assistant back home. He told him to gather the necessary components and then fly that night to Ashgabat on another of Atwan's ubiquitous GasPort Ltd. jets.

Harry asked if the sabotage could be done remotely, without Karim having to take the risk of inserting a flash drive or rewriting code.

"As you like," said Atwan. "We need to have someone inside with our device. It is better than rewriting code. Your boy will not have to plug that device into anything. But he must plug himself back into Iran. Do you think he will do that?"

Harry's brow furrowed. He didn't like to think about this part.

"He'll do it if I ask him. That's my problem. He will do whatever I say."

Once the London technical team was on the way, they could all relax a little. Harry had a plan—a complicated and risky one, but not an impossibility. He nursed his Scotch; he still had a lot of work to do, and not many hours left. He had already begun thinking through the details in his mind, and he'd had one side talk with Adrian, when Atwan was sending his emails to London and ordering up his private air force. But it was still very much a work in progress, and Atwan knew it.

"You will need help getting the Iranian boy back in," said the Lebanese.

"Adrian has his team. They are multitalented."

Harry shot the British officer a look, and he could see that Adrian winced. Harry felt sorry for him, suddenly. He was an addict; he wasn't in control of himself.

"They're very good on the ground," Harry continued. "Much better than anything anyone else has. And the kid trusts them. They got him across the border once, so they can do it again."

"Adrian's team will need local help from the Turkmen, I should think," said Atwan. "Mashad is in their neighborhood. I would be very pleased to assist."

"With your own people, or with the *baschi*? I don't want to widen this circle any more than we have to."

"My dear, in these matters, they are *all* my people. National boundaries are impermanent. Personal loyalties are not."

"What could you do?"

"To get to Mashad, you would be wise to cross the border from Saraghs, in the eastern portion of this mercifully unpopulated nation. I have friends who can make arrangements for transport."

"And crossing the frontier?"

"Well, guards are guards, aren't they? A border is not an impermeable wall, but a collection of very permeable individuals. That is my specialty, I think."

"I need all the help I can get, Mr. Atwan. I threw the sextant overboard a while ago. When we do the operational scrub tomorrow morning, you sit in with me and Adrian. We'll make the pieces fit."

Atwan sat back in his chair, but not magisterially. He looked uncomfortable for a moment, and Harry wasn't certain why. This was a man who seemed supremely at ease in just about any situation. But there was something that was nagging at his conscience, if that was the right word. Eventually he took a long pull on his whiskey and spoke up.

"Your Iranian friend, the young scientist, do you plan on getting him out again?"

"Yes," said Harry. "Absolutely. That's a requirement."

Atwan measured Harry, at the same time weighing a question of his own.

"But that will be quite difficult, won't it? It will be hard enough to get him back into Iran, but it can be done. It will be hard to get him access to Mashad, but it can be done. Yet surely, my friend, at some point the alarm bells will go off. A nuclear scientist goes missing. Foreign spies running about the country on secret missions. I am sorry, but at some point the music stops."

"They don't know Dr. Molavi is missing yet. They think he went home sick, and it's still the weekend. By the time they've gone looking for him, it will be too late. He will have done his dirty work in Mashad, and he'll be out."

"But the Iranian investigators are already suspicious of him. Didn't you tell me that? He has been called in for talks. People know about him."

Harry looked at Atwan curiously. He was sure he

hadn't discussed anything Molavi had said about interrogation during the debriefing that morning. Atwan could see the suspicion in his eyes, and he eased back in his tone.

"Never mind. But my point is, wouldn't it be more prudent to plan on the likelihood that this young man will be caught. That way, if it happens, you won't bring the whole operation crashing down on you if he falls."

"No," said Harry. There was a surprising passion in his voice. "I hate sending this boy in. We will do everything to get him out alive. He is not expendable. He has put his life in our hands—in my hands—and I am not going to let him down. I feel about him as if . . . as if it were a personal commitment. I will not compromise on that."

"I see," said Atwan. Nobody spoke for a while. It was late, and they needed to begin briefing Jackie and Jeremy and the team on what would begin to unfold the next day.

As Harry stood to leave, Atwan took his hand and pulled him toward him in something like a hug. It wasn't easy, for Harry was such a big man, and Atwan was small and refined. But he took Harry in his arms, and held him for a long while before he let him go.

"It is a pleasure to work with you, Mr. Pappas," said the Lebanese, using Harry's real name for the first time. "And I am very sorry about the loss of your son in Iraq."

When Harry returned to the safe house late that night, he asked Jeremy, the SIS duty officer, to call Jackie's room. He wanted to talk with her, but he didn't want to knock on her door and risk finding Adrian there, humping his warrior goddess on the antique Turkmen carpet. Jeremy reported that she was still awake, and alone.

Harry rapped on Jackie's door. He was worried about her. She was the team leader. The lives of three other people were about to be entrusted to her. Everything depended on her judgment and reliability. Could she stand up under pressure? Harry didn't know. But what he had seen of her sporting with Adrian made him nervous. He didn't understand her. He knocked a second time.

Jackie opened the door meekly, her head bowed and a black scarf covering not simply her hair but most of her face. She looked away modestly.

"Ha!" she said, suddenly pulling the scarf away and letting it drop to the floor. "Fooled you, didn't I?"

"Not even for a second," said Harry. "Can I come in? I want to talk."

"Sure. I wasn't asleep." She opened the door. "Be my guest."

With the scarf gone, she was dressed in a tight black turtleneck and jeans that hugged her bottom. On her feet were fluffy pink slippers.

"Nervous about tomorrow?" asked Harry.

383

"Naw. I take a pill for that. I was going over the ops plan." She nodded toward a heap of papers spread on her bed, under a reading light.

She stood motionless, as if unsure where they should sit, or what it was that Harry had really come for. She was trying to read him, just as he was trying to read her. Was he another lonely, hungry man, looking for a place to rest his head and stick his cock?

She tilted her head, appraising him. Her cheeks were aglow, even in the low light. She began walking toward the bed, as if that were the right place to talk. In the same moment, Harry moved toward the couch deep in shadow at the far end of the room. He took a seat there; she followed.

All the ambiguity of the woman, hard and soft, was captured in her room. An automatic rifle was leaning against the bedpost. She had disassembled and cleaned it earlier that evening, and the oil still glowed where she had rubbed it against the barrel and the stock. Her workout clothes were in a heap at the far side of room, where she had left them after a round of weight lifting with the boys in the gym earlier in the evening. Her Muslim pilgrim dress was laid out for tomorrow. Open on the bed-side table was the book she was evidently reading. *White Teeth*, by Zadie Smith.

Harry wasn't sure how to start the conversation, but she made it easy for him.

"You're worrying about me and Adrian, aren't

you? I can see that look in your eye. It's not come hither, but go thither."

"Yup," said Harry. "You got it."

"You're worried that it will compromise the mission, the boss shagging the team leader."

"I wouldn't have put it so crudely, but yeah, that's exactly what I'm worried about."

"Well, don't. I have it under control. I'm not a lovesick damsel. I'm not a dick wipe. This is what women do now. They have sex and don't worry about it."

Harry looked at her. She was leaning forward on her haunches, her bottom barely touching the couch. The passion was impressive, but not entirely reassuring. Harry shook his head. He was puzzled.

"I don't get you," he said. "I know why Adrian wants to sleep with you, but I don't see it from your end."

"Sex is power, Mr. Fellows. I like to be powerful."

"Call me Harry."

"Okay, Harry. I'll tell you a secret. Just you and me. How's that?" She winked.

"What's the secret?" Harry knew he was being pulled into her vortex, but he couldn't resist.

"I get off having power over men. Men like to be in control. And you know what, Harry? So do women."

"But life isn't a bedroom, Jackie. You'll have

other people's lives in your hands tomorrow. I need to know that I can trust you."

Jackie paused. She licked her lips like a cat, reflexively, till they were glistening. She wasn't trying to be sexy, but she couldn't help it.

"Have you ever had an affair, Harry?" she asked.

"None of your business."

"Sure it is. You're asking about my sex life. Why can't I ask about yours?"

She had a point.

"Yes," said Harry. "I've had an affair. Several, as a matter of fact. I'm not proud of it, but it's a fact."

"And what did you like about it? Having an affair, I mean."

"The sex."

"Precisely. And did it make you a worse intelligence officer? Did it harm your performance?"

"No. I never let that happen. I always ended it before it got sticky."

"Precisely, again. Okay, Harry. One more question. Do you think I'm stupider than you? I mean, do you think that I would get so involved in shagging a middle-aged man, a man who pops a pill to get a hard-on, that I would let it get in the way of my mission? Do you think I would let it affect my ability to protect my brothers Hakim and Marwan? Or my determination to bring that Iranian boy back safe?"

Harry was silent.

"Do you? Because if you do, you should fire my

pretty pink ass right now. Otherwise, let me do my job."

Harry studied her. She was a predator, crouching across from him, ready to spring, her cheeks red with the blood of indignation and force of will, her every muscle taut and ready. In truth, he could not imagine a person more prepared to go into a danger zone and come out alive.

He rose from the couch. He wanted to give her a hug but resisted the temptation and instead shook her hand.

"I trust you," he said. "Do your job. Bring them home. Get it done."

31
ASHGABAT, TURKMENISTAN

The sun came up bright over the Kopet Mountains the next morning, its rays glinting off every trace of water on the barren range. Adrian Winkler rose before dawn to coordinate the operational planning. He was sitting at the computer in his villa studying maps and overnight cables. He seemed to have recovered from his fall into paganism and was once again doing the job of an intelligence officer.

After an hour of discussion with Harry and Atwan, the insertion team agreed on the basics of a plan. They would travel east by helicopter to a point near the border post at Saraghs. Atwan's men had already been dispatched there to make the necessary contacts and payments. A gentleman from the Turkmen Ministry of Interior who had long been on Atwan's payroll was installed in the villa, working with a technician to forge Iranian visas and the permission card from the International Visitors Office. Molavi wouldn't need a passport. He would be hidden in the vehicle carrying the others.

It was Adrian who proposed the travel legend. Mashad was a holy city, and so the team would enter the city as pilgrims. Marwan and Hakim were both Muslims who spoke Arabic and a bit of Farsi. They would be believable flotsam in the stream that flowed into the sacred city. Jackie would have to go as one of their wives, wrapped in chador and veil and as silent and untouchable as a good Muslim would wish his wife to be. Jackie dyed her hair and eyebrows jet black. When she returned in costume, a black form shapeless and invisible, Adrian appraised her.

"Damned effective cover," he said with a trace of a smile.

They hadn't known where in Mashad to find the Ardebil Research Establishment. But information came in overnight from Vauxhall Cross that identified the location. It had been hiding in plain sight all these years. The facility was a few kilometers north of the city, on the road to a little town called Tus. Soon there was a small avalanche of digital information. Satellite photographs, maps of the adjoining area, GPS coordinates for finding the place, even a list of nearby hotels.

Now they needed an appropriate vehicle. Atwan's headman in Saraghs found an old Mitsubishi minivan that plied the border regularly, taking in pilgrims and bringing out smuggled carpets and precious metals. The driver had a secret compartment under the rear seat of the van, well used for smuggling people and contraband in previous trips. Karim Molavi would go in the secret compartment.

Atwan's man emailed a photograph of the van—dirty, dusty, its dashboard filled with Islamic bric-a-brac and its hood and hubcaps decorated with spangly gold ornaments that made it look like a one-vehicle circus parade. The driver, a reliably corrupt man who had done business with Atwan's local operatives for years, would take the three "pilgrims" and the stowaway across the border into Iran and along the main road for the short three-hour journey to Mashad. He would wait there, and then, when the work was done, bring them out again. Getting in was the easy part. They all understood that. The heart of the operation would be Karim Molavi's contact with his friend Reza.

The young Iranian scientist rose after the others; his eyes were bright and his face had lost the stress lines of the day before. It was the sweet, soft color of honey in a glass jar. He asked for a breakfast of meats and cheese and rye bread, like he used to eat in Heidelberg. The German food was a special taste of freedom.

Harry walked in as the breakfast dishes were being cleared. He needed to have his talk with Karim. It was on their fragile bond that the mission rested.

"I need your help," Harry began.

"Of course, sir. I promised you yesterday that I would help you."

"Yes, I know, but now it's the next day and it's more complicated. I have a plan. It's a very important one, not just for you and me, but I think maybe for the whole world. If you say no, I will understand."

"Whatever it is, I am ready," said Molavi.

Harry loved his unblinking bravery, but the Iranian didn't know what the stakes were yet. Harry didn't have time to sugarcoat the pill.

"It's dangerous. You would have to go back to Iran."

Karim looked away. That was the one thing he didn't want to do. He turned his gaze back toward Harry.

"If I go back they will kill me. I am—what do you say?—an 'enemy of the state' now. I was very happy to get out. It is a great deal that you ask."

"I know. I would not ask you unless it was important. The most important thing."

"It is about Mashad, isn't it?"

"You are too clever for my secrets. You're right. It is about Mashad. It's about sabotaging the backup equipment there, so there is nothing else left."

Karim continued to look at Harry. He was still a young man, so innocent of the world.

"What do you think I should do? I am uncertain. What is right?"

Harry averted his gaze. That was the worst question the Iranian could ask. The hardest. But he knew the answer. A lifetime of training told him there was one button to push with this young man. His stomach hurt when he thought about what he was going to do. His head hurt. It was never enough, just to do your job. You had to pull others along with you. You had to make them do things you knew in your head and your gut they shouldn't do. The words formed on his lips. It made it worse that he knew so intuitively how to manipulate this boy.

"What would your father tell you to do?" said Harry softly. "That is the way you should decide."

Karim started at the words. He put his hands to his face and bowed his head. When he looked at Harry again, there was a gleam of moisture in his eyes, which he wiped away.

"My father would tell me to go back. He would say I should do my duty. He was a brave man. Always."

Harry bit his lip. He was going to do it. He was going to make the boy walk the plank.

"Your father would be proud of you," said Harry. His voice trembled. "He would know that you are his son."

Harry excused himself. He said he had to go to the bathroom. He closed the door and sat down on the toilet seat and stayed there until his hands stopped shaking. He had done it again. The worst thing in the world, the thing for which there was no forgiveness, and he had done it again. They say the biggest mistakes we make in life are the ones we make with our eyes wide open—the ones where we know what we are doing, and decide to do it anyway. But if it was a mistake, he had no choice but to make it.

"How will we do it?" asked Karim. There was a sharpness in his eyes, but it was hard to say whether it was from fear or excitement.

"We can get you back in. That's the easy part. We have made the plans. But you have to do the hard work. If we get you to Mashad, do you think you could visit your friend Reza and get inside the laboratory where you used to work?"

Karim pondered a moment. He didn't want to answer too quickly and boldly, and then not be able to deliver.

"I think so," he said. "I have all my passes, even

the one I used before in Mashad. I brought them out. And the guards will remember me. And my friend Reza can meet me."

"Reza won't think that it's strange that you're coming to Mashad, and that you want to visit the laboratory?"

Karim shrugged. "Iranians think that everything is strange and nothing is strange. It would surprise him if I was in Mashad and didn't come to see him. And what will I do when I am there?"

"Nothing," said Harry. "You just carry this in your pocket." He handed him a device that looked like something between a small brick and a fat cell phone.

"What is it?" asked the Iranian.

Harry knew it would be easier for Karim if he didn't know what he was carrying. But he had told enough lies.

"It can change the way a computer operates," said Harry. "It has a powerful pulse that burns some of the chips and connections inside. It's like a 'taser,' if you know what that is. It has been calibrated very precisely to do its work. You need to be with your friend Reza when he logs in. You need to lay the jacket down so that the device is resting on the computer processor. That's the hard part. Then you need to stay there with him for an hour while this does its work. We'll have a power source outside to feed it. Do you think you can do that?"

"Probably. Reza is proud. He will want to show

me what he has been doing. If I tease him a bit and tell him that we are doing all the hard work at Tohid, he will have to show me. That is the weakness for every scientist, sir. We must show our colleagues how smart we are."

Karim had Reza's phone number in his Palm Pilot, and they debated whether to call him in advance. Harry thought that would be too risky, but Jeremy from the Ashgabat station said the SIS knew how to use a GSM relay inside Iran to make it appear that a call was coming from there. So they decided to phone Reza. No sense in risking their lives for a clandestine rendezvous in Mashad with a person who was away from the city.

Karim sat with Harry and Adrian in the makeshift operations room at the villa. Atwan was out of sight; Harry had insisted on that; he thought it would spook the young Iranian to see the rococo Arab financier, in addition to compromising his security. But the technicians had done their work. Karim dialed the number on his Iranian cell phone. They waited while the phone rang, once, twice, ten times. A recorded voice in Farsi and English asked the caller to leave a message.

Harry shook his head: No message.

"Wait five minutes and try again. Maybe he was away from his phone."

Karim tried a second time, and again there was no answer. The air went out of the room.

"Wait thirty minutes," said Harry. They tried to busy themselves, looking at maps of Mashad and pondering where they would stay the night if they had to. Karim had the phone cradled in his hand. Eventually Harry looked at his watch and nodded. Last try.

Reza answered on the third ring. He had recognized Karim's number. He was delighted to hear from his old friend. You could hear the noisy enthusiasm through the little earpiece of Karim's phone. Karim said that he was coming to visit his relatives in Mashad, the cousin whose family he had lived with back when he worked at Ardebil Research Establishment. He would be in Mashad the next day. Could he come see Reza at the laboratory?

"Rast migi?" answered Reza. Are you serious?

Yes, Karim said. He was already en route. He would arrive the next day in the early afternoon. He proposed that they meet at Ardebil at two.

"Man hastam!" said Reza. I'm there! It was too boring in Mashad. All the old friends had gone. Just bring your pass, he advised Karim. He would tell the guards.

Adrian talked with his team that night. They would be leaving at first light the next day. It was agreed that Hakim would go to the site with the power source that would drive the chip-burning taser. He had to be within five hundred yards, but judging from the overhead reconnaissance, that shouldn't be hard. The outer perimeter was only three hundred yards from the compound. They talked about how to handle young Dr. Karim. And they talked a good while about his Iranian friend Reza, a conversation that was difficult for every member of the team, but necessary.

Harry joined them as the planning meeting was ending. He had been having one last run-through with Karim. Now he wanted to see each face in Adrian's team, each piece of the Increment. Adrian asked Harry if he had anything he wanted to say.

"Don't get caught," said Harry. "This is one operation where we cannot afford a flap. The things you would say if you are captured and inter-rogated, and the use the Iranians would make of them in a show trial, honestly, it's the kind of thing that starts wars. So don't get caught."

"Meaning what?" asked Adrian. He had willed himself not to think about this part and Harry had just burst the balloon of denial.

"I mean that if people try to stop you, serious people with guns, then shoot it out. Don't leave anyone behind. You either get out safely, or you don't get out. Nobody gets captured, no matter what. Understood?"

There was silence in the room. Adrian was looking away. Hakim and Marwan didn't move a muscle, either of them. There was a keen look in their eyes, like hawks that had sighted their prey and could not see anything else.

It fell to Jackie to respond. Harry had been right, in the end. She was the strong one. With her darkened hair and complexion, she seemed almost to have changed form. Adrian was still looking away.

"I don't think there will be a problem, sir," said Jackie. "We know how to do this. We'll get back. This is what we do."

MASHAD, IRAN

The helicopter trip from Ashgabat took just over an hour. The craft followed the main highway east and then banked south over ragged farmland ruined by decades of Soviet monocrop agriculture. Adrian and Harry had come along, each for a different reason wanting to be waiting at the other side of the border when the team came out. Both men sat in harness in the chopper, wraparound sunglasses shielding their eyes from the sun and wind. Nobody said much on the trip. Their focus was inward. Karim was dressed in dirty coveralls that cloaked the black suit he would wear to the laboratory. Jackie, Hakim, and Marwan were dressed in the modest pilgrim garb they would wear into Mashad. Weapons and other gear were packed into two bags.

The Mitsubishi minivan was waiting in a garage

on the Turkmenistan side of Saraghs. The driver stood beside the van wearing a round Turkmen hat that stood atop his head like a brightly colored porkpie. He had a wispy beard and high cheek-bones—a Mongol face of the steppes. He had been paid some money already by Atwan's man, enough so that he was attentive as a house dog. Hakim and Marwan approached him, miming the splayed feet and bad backs of men who had lived in the sun. Jackie followed submissively behind them, shrouded in black. All three had a protean ability to change shape and deportment. They could become whatever they had to be.

The driver spoke a little Arabic. Hakim spoke a little Turkish and Marwan a little Farsi, so they managed to say enough that they understood each other. Karim Molavi, the special cargo, was the last to arrive. He had been talking outside with Harry, having a few last words before the journey. He was dressed in a floppy cotton hat and his rough coveralls. The driver hadn't been given any explanation for who this mystery passenger was, and he didn't ask. Dressed as he was, Karim might have been a foreign worker smuggling himself to the West to look for work.

The driver raised the backseat, revealing the compartment where Karim would ride during the three-hour trip. He handed him a large bottle of mineral water and gave him a rough pat on the back, and then sent him into the well. Karim hunched into a fetal position. He was big enough that it was a tight fit in the narrow van, but he eventually arranged his limbs in the least uncomfortable position, and the driver lowered the seat on top of him.

The driver checked the documents of his other three travelers. He scanned the photos and stamps, and checked the visa page twice. He nodded and gave a half wink, as if to say, Good work, and smiled a nearly toothless grin. The most reassuring thing about him was that he was so obviously corrupt, and the certainty that Atwan paid better than anyone else.

The Mitsubishi rumbled through the Turkmen sector of Saraghs toward the border that bisected this ancient Silk Road town. They were nearly an hour at the frontier. The Turkmen side was easy enough; those skids had been thoroughly greased. When they had passed over to the Iranian side, the driver led his three visible passengers into the passport control office, where they stood in line with several dozen other travelers, all smelling of tobacco and the road. It wasn't Ramadan or Moharram, so the number of pilgrims was fewer than it might have been, which only meant the border police could work even slower. The driver handed over their passports and explained in his broken Farsi that they were pilgrims—a Lucknow Shiite from Pakistan and his bride, and a Shiite from the Zaydi sect in Yemen. The Iranian passport man barely looked at them. The two men looked dumb and dirty, and the woman didn't exist. The rubber stamp came down and they were through.

The driver moved on to the customs check. He gave the customs man his registration document with the usual ten dollars folded inside, but another man was working the post as well today, and he wanted his cut. So after some grumbling, the driver procured more money from his valise, and eventually they were on the road again.

They crossed the border into Iran proper just before 10:00 a.m. The highway rolled south through a gritty urban landscape and then into patchwork farmland. But you could see in an instant that Iran was a real country, with road signs and police and even a little airport on the Iranian side of Saraghs for the twice-weekly flight to Tehran. Gradually the highway rose from the desert floor to the uplands of Gonbari and Mozdurem. Passenger cars zipped past the wheezing Mitsubishi. Iranians were in a hurry to get where they were going, even at this eastern edge of the country. There was a high hum from the middle seat. Jackie was singing to herself and, she imagined, to Karim bundled underneath.

Mashad was an urban sprawl in the eastern desert. It was bigger than visitors expected, and more modern, with several generations of ring roads encircling the old city and the Holy Shrine of Imam Reza. The city's growth had been a perverse consequence of Iran's modern history; its population had nearly doubled during the Iraq-Iran war because it was the farthest city from the war zone, and it had never shrunk back to its old size. It was noisy and sulfurous, a jumble of people and traffic. That disorder was another bit of cover for the group in the Mitsubishi.

They took the eastern bypass and headed north until they reached a clover-leaf interchange called Ghaem Square. The driver had a rest stop near there; a petrol station run by Turkmen immigrants where he habitually pulled in for fuel and repairs. He steered the minivan into the garage and closed the door so that the vehicle was hidden from view. Hakim and his putative wife climbed out of the middle seat. The Turkmen driver opened the rear-seat bench and pulled a very sore Karim from his iron box. The Iranian's legs were so cramped that he wobbled at first, barely able to stand.

The driver left them alone to make their last preparations. It was now just past one. Karim planned to meet his friend Reza in an hour. The team would collect him two hours after that, at four.

Jackie handed Karim the super-taser that would burn out the synapses and memory links of the processor in the neutron laboratory at Ardebil. She had kept it under the billowing black folds of her chador. She went over the plan one more time: he must enter the facility with the device, be present when his friend was logging on to the system, and remain there with him for an hour, if possible. He should lay down his jacket so that the device physically touched the computer processor in the laboratory.

Marwan would be outside the facility, driving the chip-burning taser with a battery-powered unit that was now hidden in a dirty canvas bag hoisted over his shoulders. Hakim and Jackie would check in as husband and wife at a pilgrim hotel that would be their escape place. She handed Karim the address. The Tus Hotel on Shirazi Street. After they got the room, she and Hakim would return with the driver in the Mitsubishi van and wait at a park just south of the ring road, near Ardebil Research Establishment, until Karim emerged around four.

"Bring your friend Reza out with you," said Jackie. "Ask him to have dinner. That will make him think everything is normal."

"Okay, sure," said Karim. It sounded like an order. "What will you do?"

She was always smiling with confidence, but for just an instant she had an odd look on her face.

"We'll disappear. When dinner is over, we'll meet and get on our way."

The young Iranian nodded. This was not his

world. He was playing this role because Harry the American had asked him to, and had invoked the sacred memory of his father. The pebble he had dropped into the pond had created a wave that was now far larger than he was. He took off his coveralls and handed them to Hakim. His black suit was a bit rumpled, but clean. He combed his hair carefully in a mirror Jackie held up for him. He wished that he was wearing his father's gold cuff links, for luck.

Karim Molavi was an Iranian again, just like anyone else in these crowded streets. He called his cousin to say that he was in town, but there was no answer at the house so he left a message. Then he called Reza to say he was on his way. The young scientist sounded happy. He proposed that they have dinner together later, and talk about the old days. Reza said he had a girlfriend, at last. Maybe they could meet her after dinner. Karim was pleased. Perhaps this would all be easier than he thought. In and out, and away to a new life.

33

MASHAD, IRAN

The Green Express train from Tehran to Mashad took twelve hours. A solitary traveler had reserved one of the four-bunk compartments in first class. He lay on his bed, fully clothed, as the train sped overnight across the mountains that gird northeastern Iran. Open beside him was an Arabic translation of *The World Is Flat*, by Thomas Friedman, with notations in the margin. The man slept fitfully, awaking from time to time to relight his opium pipe and then drift back into a hazy region of consciousness that was not quite sleep. Outside his door, a guard kept watch through the night. The conductors on the train were frightened of the guard, and even more of the man inside the compartment.

Al-Majnoun, the Crazy One, had a rendezvous in Mashad. He had made the mistake of allowing danger to accumulate—of permitting a threat to continue, unimpeded, until it became so dangerous that it could destroy the enterprise itself. That was the difficulty of moving subtly and alone, as was his practice. Sometimes events moved so quickly that you could not keep up with them. You became so swaddled in secrets that you could not move a muscle. That could not happen in this case. If he failed here, even his own fearsome powers of violence would not protect him.

The train arrived in Mashad in early morning. The Crazy One descended from the carriage, carrying a Tumi briefcase that contained two lightweight automatic pistols, of different makes and vintages. He was dressed in a black suit, over a black merino wool sweater. He wore a cloth cap and sunglasses that partially hid his face, but in the glint of the morning, the scars were red and visible. It was a face that seemed to have been constructed with a putty knife; with little bits of flesh not quite adhering to the template of bone. It needed more skin or less. There had been another recent surgery, and so little tissue left to work with.

The bodyguard made to follow, closely at first, but Al-Majnoun waved him away. He walked with a stoop, and a stutter of the legs that was not quite a limp. He was agile, for all that. The legs moved in quick little steps, the body pitching forward at a slight angle, the briefcase tight against his side. He left the station and headed out onto Azadi Street, where he found a taxi. He placed a call to a contact in Tehran, and then another call, and then he wrote down an address in a tiny notebook little bigger than a deck of cards, which he kept in the pocket of his coat.

He told the driver to take him to the Iran Hotel on Andarzgu Street, close by the Shrine of Imam Reza. A colleague he had dispatched urgently from Tehran the day before was waiting for him there. The bodyguard followed in a second taxi.

Mehdi Esfahani sat at his table in the hotel restaurant, stroking the prickly hairs of his goatee. He wondered if the time had come to shave it off, to go without any sort of facial hair, as some of the bolder young officers at the Etelaat were doing. The waiter brought his eggs, sunny-side up. He

405

closed his eyes. Perhaps with no mustache and a new haircut, he would look like George Clooney.

Through the window he could see the green dome of the Great Mosque of Gohar Shad, in the sacred precincts of the old city. He had received a call from Al-Majnoun the day before back in Tehran, instructing him to travel by air to Mashad.

"The hour has come," Al-Majnoun had said. The great conspiracy was ripening and about to burst visibly to light. The interrogator should take a room overnight at the Iran hotel and wait for him at breakfast. He should tell no one at the Etelaat, and he should come armed.

The interrogator had booked the hotel room and the flight by himself. But he was uncomfortable. Al-Majnoun frightened him. He had done as the Lebanese operative had demanded, from the moment a few months before when they had first glimpsed a hint of this penetration of the inner secrets of the project. And he had not briefed his superiors on his work, as Al-Majnoun insisted. The Lebanese operative was the secret arm of the Leader himself; they wrote poetry for each other, so it was whispered. They were in the last inner chamber of the black box that was the ruling mechanism of Iran. To refuse his orders would be a deadly mistake.

But still, Mehdi was a careful man. He never left everything in one basket. So he had kept a log of his activities. And before he left for Mashad the previous day, he had sent a note to his top boss, the Revolutionary Guard officer responsible for security of the entire nuclear program, saying that he was going on an operational mission to Mashad, and that if he did not return for some reason, someone from the Etelaat-e Sepah should enter his office and remove a dossier that explained a secret and most sensitive investigation he had been conducting at the personal request of the Leader's special adviser. Al-Majnoun would expect as much, surely. No man goes on an operation where he has been instructed to bring a firearm without protecting himself.

Mehdi was waiting for the Crazy One, but he was startled nonetheless. The Lebanese crept up, approaching from behind so quickly that he escaped Mehdi's peripheral vision. The interrogator felt a hand on his shoulder, and then he turned suddenly to see that ghastly, doughy face. Al-Majnoun sat down. The sunglasses concealed his eyes. But even so, he looked different than the last time Mehdi had seen him. If he hadn't known to expect him, he could not have been sure that he was the same man Mehdi had met before. But that was the way with Al-Majnoun. He was a *jinn*, a black ghost of the spirit world more than a normal man.

"The worst has happened," said Al-Majnoun in a hoarse whisper. "The foreign spies are in our midst. They have their hands at our throat. Today is the day that we will expose them, and cut them out."

Mehdi nodded. He had known from his first encounter with the Lebanese operative that he would someday find himself in a place like this with the target in his sites. Al-Majnoun would not fail. He had the scent in his nose, from the first. He would follow it across the planet, but he would track it down eventually. And Mehdi was his chosen partner. He wanted to call his boss at the Etelaat, more to make sure he got credit than to protect himself.

"Who is it, General? Is it one of the men from Tohid or another establishment? Is it the scientist who studied in Germany?"

"You will see in a few hours, my brother," said Al-Majnoun. He spoke in his Arabic-accented Farsi, so sharp and guttural, so lacking in cultivation, so edged with poison. "In a few hours, you will be a hero. And I will vanish again."

Mehdi took his fingers to his goatee and twirled the little hairs at the bottom until they were as taut as a fine filament of wire.

34

The Ardebil Research Establishment was hidden away in an empty industrial park near the Azad Engineering University, just above the northern ring road. It had a wall and a security gate, but there was little else to suggest that it was special. Perhaps that was why it had escaped detection from the Americans and Israelis for so long—and even from Kamal Atwan. So often it is the special signatures of secrecy that give the game away. The best disguise sometimes is no disguise at all.

Reza was waiting at the gate. He kissed his friend, and then embraced him, and then kissed him again. Reza's beard was fuller and his stomach bigger than the last time Karim had seen him, but otherwise he appeared the same. He had the same mischievous look of intelligence, especially. He was a chess player, a puzzle solver, a compulsive player of electronic games. No wonder they kept him on ice out here. He was the reserve player— the sixth man on the team, held in waiting on this faraway bench for when one of the starters fouled out.

They were in the guardhouse now. Reza asked Karim for his special-access pass. Karim handed it up to the guard, who typed the number into the system.

"The pass has expired," said the guard.

"It's old," said Karim, trying to laugh. "Of course it has. Here's the one I use in Tehran."

The guard studied Karim. The young man pulled his black jacket tighter. He might as well have been standing naked. The guard stepped closer and peered at him. Then he smiled, the skeptical eastern smile of a Mashadi.

"Didn't you used to work here?"

Karim nodded. "Yes, but that was before. Now I work in Tehran, at Tohid. I'm here visiting my cousin. I thought I would come see my old friend Reza."

"You remember the old friends in Mashad? Usually you fancy Tehranis forget we even exist." The guard had a chip on his shoulder, but now he was smiling at this departed scientist who hadn't put on airs, and wanted to see the old lab.

"Salam, salam. Rooz bekheyr. Khosh amadi." Hello, hello. Good afternoon to you. You are most welcome.

The guard was opening the electronic door, and then he stopped and turned back to Karim.

"I am sorry, Brother Doctor. Do you have a camera or anything that can make a recording?"

Karim paused. What was the right answer?

"No," he said.

"Are you sure, sir?" The guard was friendly but vigilant.

Karim felt the device heavy in his pocket. He

410

centered himself on the one requirement, to avoid detection of the secret tool.

"I have a cell phone, with a camera. Do you need that?"

"Yes, please."

Karim handed him a phone. It was the Nokia he had bought in Tehran, with a new 3-mega-pixel camera.

"Thank you, sir," said the guard, handing Karim a ticket for his phone.

"Come on," said Reza. "I have to show you the new wing of the lab."

Marwan approached from the north. The taxi dropped him at a *kebabi* a half mile from the ring road. He bought a sandwich and a bottle of lemon soda and walked to the park that was near the Azad Engineering University campus. They had studied the park on a satellite map back in Ashgabat and, measuring the distance, had decided that it was just inside the transmission perimeter. Marwan found a tree in the park and sat down beneath it. He reached in his dirty canvas bag for the black box that would drive the device in Karim's coat pocket. The Americans could have done it overhead, with a focused energy beam from a satellite. But this wasn't an American operation. Marwan switched on the equipment and aimed it in the optimal direction. Then he took the sandwich in his hands and began to eat.

The Crazy One ate his lunch alone at a small restaurant near Ghaem Square. He had told Mehdi to wait for him at the Iran Hotel in the center of town. He would call when it was time.

The restaurant was Lebanese, or so the menu claimed. He ordered a tabbouleh salad with no onions, hoping that it would be easy on his stomach. But it was too spicy when it came, and he pushed it away and ate bread only, with a glass of peach nectar. He tried reading *The World Is Flat* again, but he put it away when a man at a nearby table saw it open and wanted to talk about it. He was a professor at Azad Engineering University nearby. He taught computer science. He thought Thomas Friedman was the best writer in the world.

Al-Majnoun didn't answer the man. The computer scientist looked once into the Lebanese man's face and then looked away, frightened, and returned to his seat a few tables away. Al-Majnoun did not like talking to strangers, ever, but especially not today. He was waiting for the time when he could finish his work and be done.

The Ardebil laboratory was quiet in midafternoon. Some of the researchers had left for lunch. Others were at their desks playing computer games. As in government labs around the world, people were passing the time waiting to go home. Reza escorted Karim down the corridor to the neutron research area where they had once worked together. The door was locked electronically, and marked with signs in Farsi warning against entry by unauthorized visitors. A security officer sat at a metal desk just outside. He was reading the football scores in the local newspaper, but when he saw Reza and Karim he snapped to attention.

The guard was glowering. His mustache was twitching from side to side. Didn't Reza know that no visitors to this part of the lab were allowed? Karim studied his face. He thought he recognized him from the old days.

"Ali?" he asked. "Is that you? Don't you remember me? The boy from Tehran who kept blowing the fuses?"

The guard stopped twitching and stroked his beard. "Dr. Karim?" he ventured. "You have come back?"

"Just for a day. I'm here to see Reza and my family, and then I go home."

The guard ventured a smile. *"Haale shoma chetoreh?"* And how are you?

"Khubam—shoma chetori?" Karim returned the greeting, and they wished each other good health.

"Can he come in?" asked Reza.

"Of course. We know him. He has to sign the book." He pushed a book toward Karim, who signed his name and his pass number.

They walked into the forbidden space, past the little office Karim had once used. The exterior wall had once been just past his cubicle, but now it had been extended. There was a door, but it wasn't locked or guarded. This was the new wing Reza had been talking about.

"Come on, Karim." His friend tugged at his arm. "You've got to see this."

Inside the new wing, on a table in the center of the room, was the precious neutron generator. The metal was still shiny, and it looked as if it had just recently been uncrated. It was a small cylindrical object, no longer than a foot. At one end was a thick metal casing, with a hole where the explosive trigger was inserted. In the middle was the electro-magnetic generator that turned the energy of the explosive into an electronic charge that could ionize the deuterium packed inside and accelerate it toward the tritium target. For all the complicated machinery, it was a simple physical process: the deuterium-tritium reaction produced a surge of neutrons—which could then bombard the plutonium core of the bomb and initiate the fission reaction. The result was a fearsome weapon, with the energy of the sun condensed into a few hundred kilograms.

"Not bad!" allowed Karim. "It's like the one we have in Tehran. Only it looks newer."

"And better, my brother. Soon we will be doing the work. You will see. You big boys in Tehran get the glory, but your work never turns out right. So now it is time for the Mashad team to teach you a little physics."

"Where did you get it? I thought we had the only one at Tohid."

"Shhh!" Reza put his finger to his lips. "We assembled it inside. That's the thing. We bought the pieces abroad and put them together. Nobody had done that before, my brother. And I helped. Your friend Reza, who wasn't smart enough to get a fellowship to Germany. What do you think now?"

This was the Reza that Karim remembered. Cocky and competitive. The young man who had to show you that no matter what you had done with your computer, he could do it better on his. The two of them had wasted many evenings writing graphics programs on the big simulators to pass the time—daring each other to import pornographic images from the Internet and send them anonymously to the bearded ones who rode herd on the scientists.

"You are dreaming, Reza. There's no way it works better than our machine in Tehran. We may have a few bugs in the engine, but you haven't even turned on the motor."

"Wrong, wrong, wrong. You are becoming Plan B, my brother. We are the new Plan A. Wait and see. You will be lucky if you can get your old job in Mashad back, when they close everything down in Tehran."

Karim scoffed. "How? With computers that don't work? With software you don't understand?

I remember you, Reza. You are the king of the error message. I'll bet you don't even know how to run the simulation for the neutron generator. This is all for show."

"You are a dog," said Reza. He walked to the console where the main operator sat. The chair had barely been used. The leather in the seat was still shiny; the computer console was bright and unmarked. The neutron generator looked as if it had just been unwrapped. They were keeping it dry and ready, in reserve for when it was needed. The real work was done on the big computer that simulated the interaction of the neutron trigger with the fissile material in the core. The ability to run these simulations was the long pole in the tent.

Reza took his seat and turned on the big processor, which hummed to life. The screen went from black to white and an interface gradually appeared.

"I'm hot," said Karim. "Mind if I take off my coat?"

Reza didn't even hear him. He was absorbed in the hum of his new super-toy. Karim laid the black jacket down on the case of the processor. A log-in display had appeared on the screen.

"Don't look while I type," said Reza, with a wink.

Karim turned his back while his friend typed in his username and password. The jacket and its silent electronic device were only a few feet away from his nimble hands. The screen dissolved again, and they were in the most secret electronic space in the Islamic Republic of Iran.

"Watch me now," said Reza. "We did some simulations of the generator last week. We're working to get higher yield. Goodbye, Tel Aviv! Watch this, Karim. We are going to make you fancy boys in Tehran look very stupid when we get the tests right and you can't."

Karim smiled appreciatively as Reza went through the simulation.

"Better than I expected. But it's obvious you don't have the real stuff. You're still subcritical. This will fizzle, brother, I promise you. You don't have the full package."

"You are so arrogant, Karim. The blood of the Imam Hussein would not make you shed a tear. So I will show you what the real men of science can do."

He punched some more keys, and the system hummed away as it moved through a new and more complex simulation. For every trick Reza knew, Karim asked about another one that he didn't. Eventually Reza even gave way at the terminal so Karim could show him some features of the equipment Reza hadn't understood. Karim looked at his watch. More than fifty minutes had passed since they began working the machines and bantering. The few other workers in the lab had drifted away, happy enough to let the whiz kids play their games.

Karim proposed one more test, to see if Reza really had the right stuff. It was a protocol for "boosting" the deuterium-tritium mixture to get more neutrons and a vastly larger explosion. In truth, it was one of the things that had failed repeatedly in Tehran. Reza attempted the maneuver, but now he really was out of his league, and Karim couldn't get the machine to perform the requested sequence either.

"It's the machine's fault. Just like in Tehran. Something doesn't work."

"No, Karim. The machine is never wrong, at least the homegrown Mashad machine of Brother Reza, the genius of the world. I know it's your fault. You know it's your fault. Why don't you admit it?"

Karim took a last glance at his watch and reached for his jacket.

"I love you, brother," he said. "And someday you will come help us with the real machines, the big machines, up in Jamaran. But right now, I am tired. I have all the miles between Mashad and Tehran in my bones. What do you say we go out and get a meal?"

Reza lowered his voice. "And later maybe some home brew. I have a new source. This stuff tastes like Russian vodka. I am not kidding you, Karim. The best. I live up in the hills, all alone. Nobody around. No one will see us. The *basij* wouldn't dare come looking even if we were holding an orgy."

"Quiet," said Karim. His friend's boasting made him nervous.

They traversed the long gallery of the new wing and then passed back through the locked door. Karim signed out on the guard's pad. Old Ali gave him a grateful kiss goodbye on both cheeks for just remembering his name. At the main gate, Karim picked up his Nokia. He shook that guard's hand, too, to thank him. He said he would be back soon.

The sun was low in the sky now. Reza asked Karim where he wanted to eat. There was a new restaurant on Khayyam Boulevard called the Silk Road. It was very tasty, and not just the food. Pretty girls from the Engineering University liked to hang out in the coffee bar. Reza beckoned for his friend. These Tehranis were too arrogant; they breathed all that smog every day and it made them dizzy. They thought they knew all the answers.

35

MASHAD, IRAN

The two Iranian scientists walked together out of the Ardebil compound. A soft late-afternoon breeze was blowing in from the farmlands, bearing the fragrance of saffron and the other exotic spices for which the region was known. Students were leaving the university campus across the way; cascades of them, the boys and girls walking in separate clusters. The women were so slim and fine;

you could see their shapes as the breeze blew their cloaks tight against their hips and bust. "Mashad girls rock," said Reza in English.

Karim looked up and down the street until he saw a dirty Mitsubishi bearing the glittery trappings of a shared taxi. It was moving slowly toward them and then stopped, about fifty yards away. He tried not to stare at the van; he was so close to being done, he needed only to keep moving. He put his arm around Reza's shoulder, not so much from affection as to bind himself to the other man a little while longer until his job was finished.

Reza's car was in the parking lot next to the Ardebil compound. It was a new Peugeot—not one of the Iranian knockoffs, but a real French Peugeot. That must be a token of official affection. They had tried giving Karim cars over the years, and vacation apartments on the Caspian, and special coupons to import consumer electronics products, but he had always refused. That had been part of why they trusted him at Tohid, because he appeared to be a scientist only, a man who had joined the program not for the perquisites, but for the intellectual challenge of the work.

Reza drove south toward the Silk Road restaurant where he had booked a table. It was in the Homa Hotel near the center of town. The late-afternoon traffic was heavy, but it was going the other way, toward the suburbs. Karim didn't speak much.

Reza popped a cassette into the music system. The percussive sound of R. Kelly filled the car; Reza turned up the bass and began nodding his head, in the way he thought a rapper would. Every time the singer said the word "motherfucker," Reza would repeat it loudly, because it sounded cool.

The little Mitsubishi van from Saraghs carrying its three pilgrims followed behind, the car stopping and starting in the traffic and the driver cursing in Turkmen at the Persian assassins at the wheels of the other vehicles. They were heading to the city center too, it seemed, doubtless to the pilgrim shrines of the *haram-e-motahhar.*

A third vehicle had been waiting as well outside the Ardebil Research Establishment. It was a black Paykan, hired for the day from the Iran Hotel. The driver of the car would have been recognizable to passengers who had traveled on the overnight Green Express from Tehran. He had kept watch through the night outside one of the first-class cabins, never moving once.

In the back of the Paykan sat Al-Majnoun and Mehdi Esfahani. Both men were carrying weapons. Mehdi, a man who was uncomfortable with silence, would occasionally start up a conversation, but the other man would leave it hanging in the air. His face was dead still, scanning the guardhouse of the Ardebil Research Establishment in the middle distance.

When he saw the two Iranian scientists emerge from the gatehouse, Al-Majnoun told the driver to start the car and follow at a safe distance. Mehdi peered toward the window and then pulled back.

"The Molavi boy!" proclaimed Esfahani in the stern voice of a prosecutor. "I was certain of it, always. The traitor. The dog. *Coondeh*!" The last word, spoken with special scorn, was a slang term for homosexual. "Who is the other one with him?"

Al-Majnoun did not answer. He removed one of the two automatic pistols from his black Tumi briefcase and attached a silencer to the barrel. He tucked the gun inside the belt of his trousers and then folded himself into the recess of the backseat while the driver followed his prey toward Khayyam Street and the Homa Hotel.

Karim and Reza ate a light dinner at the Silk Road. Reza wanted to pile on course after course, to show off, but his friend said he wasn't very hungry. Reza winked and whispered that what Karim needed was some of the home brew, the very best, like they used to have when they were young and crazy. He wouldn't take no for an answer, and Karim realized that he wouldn't mind something to dull the ache in his legs before the long ride back across the border, so he said yes, just one drink at Reza's villa in the hills, and then he would go. He had the telephone number of a taxi that would pick him up from Reza's place afterward, he said, so his friend could drink all he liked.

As they were leaving the restaurant, a dark form darted from the alley nearby. He was a compact, muscular man, dressed like one of the laborers who came across the Pakistan border like so many stray goats. As he neared Reza, he lurched toward him with his arm outstretched and bumped him on the upper arm. Reza cried out in pain. He reached for his wallet to make sure that he hadn't been robbed and then cursed the man, who had disappeared around the corner.

"*Akh*! That hurt. It stings, too, like he stuck me with something. The bastard. This country won't be safe for decent Persian people anymore. What did he do?" He was rubbing his shoulder where he had been bumped.

Karim was frozen in place. He had seen the man's face, just after he pushed into Reza, and he had recognized it. It was the face of the Pakistani operative Hakim, who had helped bring him out of Iran.

"Should I call the police?" asked Reza, still rubbing the bruise on his arm. "What do you think?"

Karim hadn't moved. He sensed what was happening, but he would not allow the true picture of it to take shape in his mind.

"No police," said Karim. "Let's go to your place. You'll be okay."

"I need a drink, bro, and maybe a ho," babbled

Reza in English, trying to sound like a rapper again. But already his voice was weaker.

Reza drove his Peugeot north again, toward the suburbs above the university. His driving was erratic. He would speed up and slow down at the wrong times, like an old lady, and other cars were honking at him. After twenty minutes, Reza apologized that he was feeling a little faint, and Karim drove the rest of the way to Reza's home. It was a villa in the hills above the city, with a bit of land around it; a reward to Reza for his service to the program. Reza directed Karim into a darkened driveway. He leaned against his friend's shoulder as they walked up the path and toward the house. The lights of the old city were twinkling in the distance, the green dome of the mosque appeared as a distant emerald.

"You need to lie down," said Karim. He could feel his friend's body going limp as the paralysis set in. There were tears in Karim's eyes as he laid Reza down on the couch. He brushed them away. His friend's breathing was becoming shallower and he was beginning to whimper like a dog that wants attention. How could this be happening?

Karim knew he should call a doctor. There was still time, perhaps. Reza groaned. Spittle was coming out of his mouth. Karim touched his hand. It had gone cold.

"There, there," said Karim. "You'll be all right."

Tears were pouring from his eyes now. What had he done? How had he set this in motion? Karim thought of the American, Mr. Harry. Who was this man who had acted like his friend? He leaned over Reza, covering him like a blanket with his body. He felt his breathing, each rise and fall slower, and the sound more raspy. And then the breathing stopped. Still Karim lay there atop him, trying to prevent the life spirit from slipping away from his friend into the Mashad night.

There was a sharp rap at the door. When Karim didn't answer, the door blew open with sudden force and two dark forms surged into the apartment. Karim clutched the body of his friend tighter.

"Get up, Karim, please," said Jackie. She was trying to soften her voice, but there was an edge of tension. "We've got to go. Now."

Marwan stood by the door, holding his automatic rifle tightly at his side.

"You killed him!" wailed Karim. "I trusted you. He was my friend. What did he do?"

"I will explain it later. We have to go now. The car is downstairs. Come on." She pulled at him, but Karim was a large man. She called for Marwan to come help.

"Stop! Do not force me. Let me sit here a moment." Karim's head was cradled in his hands. Jackie stroked his back. Marwan pointed to his watch, but Jackie shook her head. They had to let the young Iranian find a center, or they would lose him.

Another car had pulled into the driveway, lights out and coasting the last fifty yards. Hakim, keeping watch by the Mitsubishi van, saw it coming but he was too late. Through an open window of the black Paykan, a man in a black cloth cap fired once, hitting Hakim in the shoulder. Hakim spun, but before he could get off a shot of his own, a second shot hit him full in the head, producing a pulpy sound like a pumpkin splitting. The other man in the car, the Iranian intelligence officer with the carefully groomed goatee, let out a gasp. Despite his line of work, he had never seen one man kill another.

Al-Majnoun walked toward the vehicle. Two more shots and the rear tires of the Mitsubishi were gone. The Turkmen driver was cowering on the front floor under the steering wheel. Al-Majnoun put his gun to the driver's head and pulled the trigger, and then returned to the Paykan. Mehdi Esfahani was in the backseat, holding his gun in his hand but having no idea what to do with it.

"Get out," rasped Al-Majnoun. "Follow me." He took a second pistol from his black briefcase and stuffed it into his coat pocket.

The two men scuttled up the walkway toward Reza's house. Al-Majnoun's body was pitched forward as he searched for the rear entrance. He moved with the certainty of someone who knew the layout of the apartment. He found the rear door and gently forced it open. He put a mask over his face, pulling it down over the striated flesh. He was not a man, but another life-form.

Al-Majnoun dove into the house, rolling a gas grenade toward the living room where Karim was still recovering, head in hands. The room exploded with automatic fire, but Jackie and Marwan were shooting randomly; they couldn't see their target. As skilled as they were, they had been taken by surprise. They were already choking from the gas, and in another moment they could no longer fire their weapons accurately, or even focus their eyes.

Al-Majnoun waited until they were incapacitated and then crept toward the living room. Jackie's body was flaccid. She tried to move her gun, but couldn't. Marwan also appeared to be motionless, but when Al-Majnoun moved toward him, he summoned a spasm of muscle memory and let off a spray of fire. One of the bullets caught Al-Majnoun in the leg. It drew a clean shot from Al-Majnoun's automatic pistol, like the sound of a piece of plastic being ripped. The bullet hit Marwan in the chest; a second followed to the head. Al-Majnoun moved toward Karim Molavi's inert body; he tugged at the clothing of the lifeless figure and listened for his heartbeat, to make sure he was still alive.

Mehdi had lurked outside, but now Al-Majnoun called for him to enter the house. The interrogator tried to look composed, brandishing his pistol before him as if he knew how to use it. The gas from the grenade had dispersed now. Al-Majnoun pulled the gun away from Jackie's hand and slapped her across the face.

"Wake up, British lady," he said in English. He slapped her again.

Karim's world had gone all foggy. He tried feebly to rouse himself, to aid the woman he still regarded as his protector. Al-Majnoun pushed him back on the bed.

"Stay there," said the Lebanese. "You are my prisoner." He called Mehdi into the room. The Iranian approached slowly, looking at the carnage in the little room, two people dead, two helpless captives.

Al-Majnoun had taken his second pistol from his pocket. The Lebanese killer's face was throbbing and twitching, as if all the scars had come alive like so many worms. The look in his eye testified that he really was the Crazy One, that he needed one more act of mayhem before his play was done. Mehdi could see that the man was not in his right mind; not in any mind.

"Don't kill the boy," he said. "We need his evidence. We need to interrogate him."

Al-Majnoun turned toward Mehdi. The smile on his face was that of a jack-o'-lantern, illuminated from inside by a flickering candle. He raised his pistol toward Mehdi Esfahani. There was a look of absolute terror in the eye of the Iranian intelligence officer, and perhaps a glimmer of realization now, too late, that the game had been something entirely different from what he had believed.

"Al-Majnoun, what are you doing?" he screamed. "Al-Majnoun, please!"

Before Esfahani could speak another word, the assassin squeezed the trigger.

"You misunderstood," said the Crazy One, pronouncing the postmortem on his victim. The body had crumpled to the floor in one motion, like a suit that has fallen off its hanger.

Al-Majnoun wiped clean his first pistol, the one he had used to kill Hakim and the Turkmen driver outside, and Marwan here on the floor of the apartment. He put that gun into Mehdi's soft hand, and wrapped the finger around the trigger. The second pistol, which he had used to kill Mehdi himself, he put into the hand of Marwan. He picked up the gas canister and put it in his pocket. He surveyed the room to make sure the tableau would read to the Iranian investigators the way he intended.

Jackie squirmed on the floor, looking for a sharp object she could use to cut her wrist or impale her heart. That was the only thought she had left. She could not be taken prisoner. She had received that order of silence, and she was determined to obey it as a last command. But Al-Majnoun saw her, and slapped her again. In a sudden motion, he jerked her hands behind her and fastened them with a wire clasp. Then he continued with his inventory of the room. Karim sat on the couch, still staring at the body of his friend Reza.

"What are you going to do with us?" said Jackie quietly. All she had left were words, to barter or provoke; or at least, to comprehend.

"Let you go," said Al-Majnoun.

"I don't understand."

"Of course you don't. You're not supposed to."

Jackie looked at the Lebanese man. The face looked like a composite of old surveillance photographs; it was an Identi-Kit drawing in which the pieces didn't fit. She had been trained for everything but this. She wanted to understand the part that was real; the center line in this erratic and unpredictable skid of events.

"How do we leave?" she asked.

"There is a black car downstairs. My driver is waiting for you. He will take you to the border. Not at Saraghs where you entered. They will be looking for you there. But at Kalat, to the north. It is only a hundred kilometers from here. Do you have communication?"

"Yes," said Jackie.

"Use it. When you are in the car, call your people. Tell them where you are coming out. Have them wait on the other side. It is not an official border crossing, but the smugglers know it. My driver will take you to the other side. He has a gun. If they try to stop him at the border, he will shoot. Unless you are unlucky, you will survive."

"Who are you?" asked Jackie. "That man called you 'Al-Majnoun.'"

The assassin winced. The man with no face did not want to have any identity.

"The man lied. I have no name, because I do not exist. I could have killed you and this boy, but I gave you life. Now it is time for you to go."

He cut her hands loose and pushed her and Karim Molavi out the door of the villa, toward the waiting car. She and the young man had no choice but to do as they had been instructed. If they waited here, they would surely die. If they went in the car as this madman proposed, they might live. They went down to the Mitsubishi. Jackie was sickened by the sight of Hakim. The pool of blood around his body had begun to congeal. Insects had already found the wound on his head and were feeding on the blood and tissue.

Inside the van, the poor driver had bled across the little kilim pillow he used as a seat rest, the pool of blood seeping into the back of the van. Jackie began retrieving any items that might identify her and the other two as British agents, but Al-Majnoun pulled her away. When she resisted, he pointed his gun not at her, but at Karim, and she relented.

"I am saving you," said the Lebanese. "I want you to escape."

"Why?" asked Jackie.

Al-Majnoun did not answer.

The two got in the backseat of the Paykan. Al-Majnoun said a few words to his driver, to make clear that the delivery of these two to the border was now his only mission. Then he closed the door. The car turned sharply in the driveway and sped away, headlights extinguished.

Al-Majnoun took one more tour of the bloody array at the villa and then made a call on his phone. A car arrived ten minutes later. Al-Majnoun slumped exhausted into the backseat. He reached into his black bag and removed his pipe; he kneaded a ball of opium carefully into the pipe and fired it with his butane lighter, drawing the smoke into the lungs and the blood and the head. The car sped away in the night, and Al-Majnoun floated away to a place where he truly had no name, and no mission.

36

KALAT, IRAN

The black sedan rumbled north, up a long mountain valley toward Kalat. The moon was now full, bathing the landscape in an ivory half-light. The switchbacks and rocky hills all danced with shadows of the clouds, cast by the moonbeams.

Karim was asleep, finally. Jackie was trying to stay awake. She had combed her darkened hair, and put on the chador to veil her face. She was shaking underneath the black garment, fluttering like a moth stuck on a pin. There were a few cars out on the road, but no cops. Eventually someone in the neighborhood would call the Mashad police, and they would be summoned. There had been too much noise at the house. Then, as the police began to realize what all these bodies meant, a desperate hunt would begin. But maybe by then they would be across the border.

After they had been driving a half hour, Jackie took her GSM phone and called the operations room in London. The call was routed to Adrian at Saraghs, who was awakened from a dead sleep.

"We're coming out," said Jackie. Her voice was in a dead register of exhaustion. "Not the way we came in, but another way. It's called Kalat. It's due north from Mashad, up in the mountains. It's not a border crossing, but we're going to crash it. Wait on the other side."

"Darling," he said. He wasn't supposed to talk that way, but he could not help himself.

"Shut up. Did you get the exfil point?"

"Kalat," he repeated. "What time?"

"I don't know. Probably just after dawn." Her voice was heavy with fatigue and sorrow.

"Are you all right?"

"No. I have lost two people."

"Dead?"

"Yes."

Adrian groaned. "I'm sorry."

"The boy is alive. He's with me."

"Did it work? The thing?"

"I don't know yet. I can't tell. It all turned to shit."

"Are you okay?"

"What the fuck is going on, Adrian? Who is Al-Majnoun?"

Adrian didn't understand the question and asked her to repeat it. She said a few words and then stopped. She had been talking too long. The phone connection wasn't secure. There wasn't time for Adrian to explain now, even if he knew the truth. She repeated the name of the place where she would be coming out and ended the call.

The road rose toward Kalat. The town was topped with cliffs that were a natural fortress. The forces of the Persian warrior Nader Shah were said to have retreated here into the rocks to escape the hordes of the Turkmen conqueror Tamerlane. The driver had slowed. He was looking for his bearings.

A rosy gleam behind the eastern hills signaled the coming dawn. Jackie woke Karim. As his eyes opened and he came to consciousness, a look of deep sadness showed on his face.

"What happened to us?" he asked. "Why were all

those people killed? Who was that man? Why are we still alive?" He was too sleepy not to say what he felt.

"I don't know," she answered. "I just want to get you out of this place. That is the only way that any of this will make any sense. So please trust me a little longer, even though I don't deserve it."

They passed through the little town center. There was a police station. The lights inside were on. Why were they up so early? The driver muttered a curse in Farsi. It was the first word he had spoken during the trip. The border was ahead, up a narrow road through the high hills. The driver proceeded past the rock-ribbed houses that lined the road, the residents coming awake. From a mosque toward the north end of town, they could hear the tinny amplified call to the *Fajr* prayer at dawn.

The driver peered at the road ahead and then jammed on the brakes. There was a roadblock on the main route, a hundred yards distant. The figures of the policemen were indistinct in the dim light, but the barrier across the road was large. The driver cursed again. He backed up thirty yards to a turning, and took the fork to the left. It was narrow road, half dirt and half asphalt, and the Paykan shimmied and fishtailed on the rough surface. He was moving toward the high ground that would lead to the smugglers' routes that were drawn in his mind.

Jackie looked off to her right. They were even

with the roadblock now. She hoped the police at their barrier might not care about the car on the side road. She thought that perhaps they had passed safely, but in the next moment she heard a siren and saw that a police cruiser had set off from the barrier, and then a second one.

"Go, you fucker," Jackie screamed at the driver. But he didn't need encouragement. He gunned the car up the steepening slope, spinning out once as he rounded a bend but otherwise keeping the car under control. The two police cars were behind them now on the side road. They were both Mercedes sedans, bigger and faster than the Paykan. Every twenty seconds, the pursuers gained another ten yards.

The black Paykan spun around a high curve and neared the summit of the ridge line. The border must be ahead. Either that or the road would come to a dead end, and they were finished right there. But the driver seemed to know where he was going. He was talking to himself now, in a staccato chatter of Farsi. They crested the peak, with the Iranian car bolting over a bump and into the air, and coming down so hard on its springs that for a moment the chassis seemed to sag. The driver gunned the car faster still.

The road led down now, toward a ravine that was perhaps a half mile away. At the center was a dry riverbed that marked the frontier. There was a little bridge, blocked by a barrier, but off to the left and right were open tracks where a vehicle could pass across the riverbed and over to the other side. The police cruisers continued to gain ground. It was impossible to know which would intersect the Paykan first—the chase car or the approaching frontier.

There was a sharp noise behind them. Karim and Jackie turned with a start and saw the gun firing from the passenger side of the lead police cruiser. It was an arc of bullets, barely aimed, but with each burst they bracketed their fire closer to the target.

"Gun," Jackie shouted toward the front seat. The driver didn't understand. Jackie bounded forward across the seat bench and grabbed at the driver's throat.

"Give me the goddamned gun," she screamed. The driver pulled something from inside his coat and tossed it on the seat. It was a German automatic pistol. The gunfire from the police cruiser was continuing. A few rounds had hit the thin steel frame of the Paykan.

"Get down," shouted Jackie to her passenger. Karim drew tighter to her, as if to protect her.

"Get the fuck down," she said, pushing him to the floor. She opened the window and began firing the Walther pistol. She was a far better shot than the Iranians, and with her second round she hit the driver of the first car. The cruiser spun away, but the second was behind, and the police inside were firing automatic weapons from both wings.

• • •

Ahead was the riverbed and the border. A group was standing on the Turkmen side, their bodies shimmering in the rising light of morning. A helicopter stood waiting, its rotors rhythmically slicing the air. Two men stood at the head of the group, watching the approaching Paykan through binoculars.

The police cruiser kept spraying bullets, and it was the Paykan's tires that were most vulnerable. The right rear tire punctured first, and then shredded. The car continued to move forward on its rim, but when a second tire was hit, forward motion slowed to almost nothing. The driver swerved the Paykan off the road, into the dirt, hoping that he might limp somehow to the gulley that was only a hundred yards distant now and then crash into the riverbed. But the Mercedes was abreast now, firing volleys of bullets that ripped into the car. The driver was hit; he cursed but held on to the wheel. He tried to go faster, but the little car had no traction left in the dirt.

Jackie looked at the boy on the floor, and at her weapon. They were not going to make it. In a few more moments they would be taken, and that was impossible. Karim was curled against the floorboards, at once a man and a child. She took aim at his head and pulled the trigger. Then she turned the gun on herself.

• • •

From the other side of the border, the last few seconds were the hardest to watch. The automatic weapons fire from the Iranian police cruiser raked the Paykan from stem to stern, until the bullets found the gas tank and the car exploded in a blue plume. That was how they decided later that it must have been an actual police chase, and not an operation coordinated by the intelligence services. The intelligence services would never have blasted the car that way. They would have moved heaven and earth to keep those two passengers alive for questioning.

Adrian Winkler fell to his knees when he saw the bolt of flame, and let out a scream. Harry Pappas tried to find words, but he could not. This had happened to him once before, this sense of the life of a young man given to him for his protection, that he had not been able to save. The two men, in their grief, could not move. The young SIS officer named Jeremy from the Ashgabat station finally helped them to their feet and led them back to the helicopter. They had to get away before more Iranians arrived and things got more complicated.

37

LONDON

They flew back to London in a cabin of sorrow and failure. The deadness of loss was all they felt in the first hours. Kamal Atwan had already left Turkmenistan when their helicopter returned to Ashgabat—pressing business back in London, he said. But he had left a second plane at Adrian Winkler's disposal at the airport, fueled and ready to go. Jeremy from the Ashgabat station advised that they should leave the country now, before the flap ripened. He solemnly handed Adrian a cable that had just come in from Sir David Plumb in London. The gist of it seemed to be, "Get the fuck out of there, now."

Harry didn't argue for staying. He was trying to piece together the chain of events of the last several days, to the extent that he understood them, and he didn't much care where he was. He was feeding on a private rage—a loathing that included everyone and everything around him, but most especially himself.

The plane was a Gulfstream G-5, Atwan's personal jet for entertaining friends and clients. It was appointed like a flying salon, with a black leather interior and gaudy gold fixtures. The bathroom had a full-length window. The attendant was a well-endowed woman from the north of England who served drinks leaning in toward the passengers so that her bosom was in their face. Adrian seemed to know the plane. After they took off from Ashgabat, he went back into the aft cabin and had the attendant make up the bed. The sheets were black silk, and there was a mirror on the ceiling. He offered the bed to Harry, who refused, so Adrian closed the door and tucked himself in.

Harry sat in the deep leather of the armchair and closed his eyes. He didn't want to sleep, but to think. The story was there in his hands, but he couldn't read it. All he had were questions: How had four of his people died in Mashad? What had surprised the well-trained team from the Increment? Why had their original escape plan been abandoned? Where had Jackie gotten the black Paykan that had nearly reached the border? Who was driving the car? He had seen Jackie's face through his binoculars, but the driver was a stranger. And what had happened in those final moments before immolation? He had seen Jackie shoot at something on the rear floor before she put the gun to her own head. Who had been the target of that first shot? It must have been Karim. If so, did that mean he had been successful in his mission at the Ardebil Research Establishment, or that he had failed? And the Iranians: How long had they known that this operation was coming at them? Had the operation been compromised from the beginning? Harry hated to admit that possibility; it shamed him. But with so many dead bodies, he could not exclude it.

And what was Kamal Atwan's role? That was the part of this story Harry understood least. He had been the essential facilitator of every transaction in this process. He had acted with the assurance of a man running his own intelligence service, and he had delivered everything he had promised. But the end product had been a disaster. What had Harry missed? What could have helped him to foresee the disaster that had befallen his team when it took his agent, Karim Molavi, back into Iran? Had he killed the boy, through his own inattention?

Harry let Adrian sleep for two hours and then woke him up. He brought a cup of black coffee with him back to the aft cabin.

"We need to talk, brother," he said. "Wake up."

"I'm busted up, Harry," the British officer answered groggily. "I loved that woman. I took some pills. I need to sleep. Let's talk in London."

"Get up." Harry handed him the coffee. "I mean it. I need some answers before we land. This whole thing is going to blow, and I want to know what the fuck has been going on."

Adrian groaned and took the coffee. He knew that Harry wouldn't leave him alone until they talked. The American had a pliable exterior, but he didn't bend on things that mattered. The British officer wobbled back to the aft lavatory, decorated

442

in a plush red fabric. He brushed his teeth and splashed some water on his face. When he emerged, Harry made him finish the coffee and then gave him a second cup.

"Is this plane bugged?" began Harry. They were sitting next to each other in the aft compartment. The bed had been packed away.

"Fucked if I know," said Adrian. "Probably."

"Then talk in my ear, and I'll talk in yours. This is for us, not your business partner."

Adrian winced. "Ease up, Harry. I've got my whole career coming down on my head. If this comes out wrong, I'm destroyed."

"So what? My career is wrecked, too. Worse than that, maybe. Talk in my ear so no microphone can pick it up, and we'll do fine."

Adrian nodded. Harry leaned toward the other man's head and spoke in a whisper.

"Jackie called you to tell you she was coming out another way. Right? You told me she called."

"Correct," he whispered. "She said we should go to Kalat. She made me repeat it."

"What else did she say?"

Adrian paused and closed his eyes, then leaned back toward Harry and whispered again.

"She said she had lost the two boys. She said Karim was with her, alive, and they were coming out."

"What else? Did she explain? Did she say what

had gone down in Mashad? Why there was a change of plans?"

"Nothing. It was a short conversation. She was afraid it would be insecure. She wanted to get off the phone."

Harry pulled back. His eyes were flashing. He spoke loudly, almost in a shout.

"I don't believe you, Adrian. That can't have been all. Tell me the goddamned truth. What else?" He grabbed the other man by the collar and pulled his head toward him.

"Nothing," Adrian croaked.

Harry slapped him hard across the face.

"You are a lying piece of shit, Adrian. Tell me the truth. It was an operational call. It was routed through London. You think we can't intercept and decrypt that? You're out of your mind. I'm going to find out anyway. The only question is whether I'll have an ounce of respect left for you. Now tell me the truth, you stupid, selfish prick." He slapped him a second time.

Tears were streaming from Adrian's eyes. Not from the blows, but from a deeper anguish. He knew precisely what Jackie had said. Her accusing words would burn in his mind until the day he died. He put his head on Harry's shoulders. Harry could feel the wet of his tears through his shirt.

"Here's what she said. *'What the fuck is going on, Adrian?'* She wanted to know what had gotten screwed up, so that the ops plan had turned to shit.

444

She said she didn't know if they had succeeded or failed. She was frightened and angry. I could hear it in her voice, even over the satellite link. I called her 'darling' and she told me to fuck off. That's how upset she was."

"What did you say? When she asked why the operation was blown?"

"Nothing. I didn't know. I don't know."

Harry looked at him, not sure whether he believed Adrian or not. He let it sit.

"What else did she say? Come on. Goddammit! There has to be more."

Adrian's eyes filled with tears again. There was a plaintive look to his face now, not just penitent but frightened. He leaned in toward Harry and spoke in the smallest whisper.

"She asked me, *'Who is Al-Majnoun?'* Right after she asked what was going on, she wanted to know who this Al-Majnoun was."

Harry held him steady in his arms, their foreheads touching.

"What's the answer?"

Adrian shook his head. His eyes were red, from weeping and exhaustion.

"I don't know," whispered Adrian. "I had no idea what she was talking about. That's why I was so scared."

Harry let Adrian's head fall back limp. He thought that his shattered friend was telling the truth.

When they landed in London, Harry debated whether to confront Kamal Atwan immediately. Adrian was a spent force. He would get no help there. He decided against seeing Atwan now. The Lebanese businessman would expect it; he would be waiting in his elegant London mansion, with every detail arranged as neatly as the paintings on the walls. All the pieces of this puzzle that Harry could see had passed through the Lebanese businessman's hands, but unless Harry could distinguish their shapes and edges better, he would never be able to fit them together. Or worse, he would assemble them into the shape Atwan intended, without being able to see an alternative combination. So Harry would wait until he understood better. By then, perhaps, he would be a private citizen.

Harry paid a visit to Sir David Plumb during his London stopover. He didn't tell Adrian and called the chief's office directly to set up the appointment. But when he arrived at Vauxhall Cross, Adrian was waiting with Sir David in his office. They didn't break ranks, the Brits. It didn't matter much in terms of what Harry wanted to say.

The meeting didn't last long. What Harry wanted to know was what London would do now. Sir David explained the situation; he was quite cheery, all things considered. The Iran mission, despite its rough edges, had given the prime minister what he

446

needed. The Iranian nuclear program was well under control. The British had understood that all along, they had it by the head and the tail, but the Americans hadn't listened.

"But we don't know what happened in Mashad," said Harry. "There's quite a lot we don't know."

"Psah!" said Sir David, waving his hand. "The details will emerge. We know enough to brief the P.M. And the P.M. knows enough to take sensible action. We won't go down with the ship again. You must realize that. No more Iraqs! The special relationship isn't a suicide pact. Before the White House does anything crazy, the prime minister will take his own actions."

"What will the prime minister do?"

"Sorry, old boy, but you're not on that bicker list. In fact, the only real problem that No. 10 has with this plan is you, Harry. I'm afraid they don't trust you. But I told them not to worry."

"And why did you tell No. 10 that, Sir David?"

"Because we *own* you, Harry Pappas. You're our man now, and you'll do what we like."

WASHINGTON

The taxi driver at Dulles wanted to talk. He was Iranian, of course. They all were at Dulles. He wanted to rant about how terrible the mullahs were, and how America should go to war now that the regime was in trouble. Harry said he didn't know anything about Iran; he was just a businessman and wanted everybody to be friends.

Andrea was still at work when he got to the townhouse in Reston. He left his wife a note that he was back. He thought of taking a nap, but he was restless. He wanted to go into the office and read back into the cable traffic—and troll through the overhead imagery and the SIGINT, to see how much he could piece together from that record about what had happened in Iran.

Harry was about to leave for Langley when the bus dropped off his daughter Louise. She bounded into the house and leapt into his arms.

"You're home, you're home!" she said.

Louise wasn't usually so demonstrative. Harry was pleased. He wanted to be hugged.

"I *need* to talk to you, Daddy," she said dramatically. "I've made a big decision. I don't want to go to college."

Harry was flummoxed. Louise was a junior in high school. This was the year she needed to be thinking about getting ready for college, not about how to avoid it.

"College is important, Lulu. Unless you go to college, you won't get a good job. And you'll be poor, and you'll have to work at Wal-Mart or mow people's lawns or be a bum. You have to go to college."

"I'll go to college sometime, Daddy, but not now. That's what I meant. I don't want to go now. I want to do something else. The world is such a mess. I couldn't concentrate if I was in school, I would just think about all the people who are miserable. I want to work for Doctors Without Borders. They talked about it on *Scrubs*."

"But Lulu, you have to be a doctor to work for Doctors Without Borders. Or a nurse. Get your education. The world will still be a mess when you graduate, I promise."

"No, I want to go now. I need to. There's this cool organization I found out about called FXB that helps AIDS orphans in Africa. Maybe I can work for them. I can't just sit here and let it all *happen,* Daddy. I can't."

"Let's talk about it later, Lulu. I understand what you're saying, but I have to go to work now. I'll be proud of you whatever you do. You have a big heart. That's the most important thing."

She gave him another hug and walked him to the car. As Harry was driving down Route 7, it occurred to him that Louise was like her brother Alex. She was an idealist. She couldn't wait to make a difference. She was talking about saving orphans in Africa with the same passion that Alex had expressed about stopping the people who had destroyed the Twin Towers. Maybe that was the difference. A page had turned.

Harry got to headquarters in the late afternoon. The foreign liaison officers and the larcenous contractors were streaming out the door. Harry badged himself through the gate and walked the short distance down C Corridor to the Iran Operations Division. Someone at the gate must have forewarned Marcia, because she was waiting just inside the door, next to the Imam Hussein.

"We need to talk," she said. "Now."

"Not yet. Let me read into the traffic and run some traces. Then I have to see the director, tonight or tomorrow. Sometime."

"No, sir. You do your reading, but then see me. And don't go near the seventh floor until we've talked. You have a problem you don't even know about. It has three initials. F-B-I."

"Oh fuck. What do they want?"

"They aren't sure. They wanted to question me about your travel. I told them to piss off until they had a subpoena."

"Do they have anything?"

"Who knows? They're such assholes, anyway. So how can I help? What do you need, other than a glass of Scotch, which you'll have to get for yourself?"

"I need good intelligence about Iran. Especially now. Make sure I have all the Iran traffic over the past week. Then call all the liaison officers in town who know *anything* and tell them I need their best current stuff, immediately. Have them pulse their people back home, no matter how late it is. And tell NSA I need special onetime access to the raw

Iran SIGINT. Whatever has been translated. If anyone squawks, tell them I personally will make sure they get sent to a listening post in Okinawa."

"What else? You said traces."

"I want you to run every database you can for the name 'Al-Majnoun.' That means 'the Crazy One' in Arabic, so presumably he's an Arab. But he's in Iran. Or at least I think he is."

"I know what Al-Majnoun means, for God's sake," Marcia muttered, walking away. "Maybe I even know who he is. Not that you would care. But let me check my sick, alcohol-poisoned memory to make sure. Any other demeaning requests?"

"Call the National Reconnaissance Office. Tell them I want to TiVo Mashad, forty-eight hours ago."

Harry went into his office and closed the door. He logged on to his computer and began searching the cable log. He wanted to lay down for himself a picture of the cards that were visible in the intelligence reporting they already had. The U.S. intelligence community didn't know much about Iran, but it knew a little. And its liaison partners knew more: if there was commotion within the security establishment of any foreign nation, it usually left some electronic or physical markings that could be captured and analyzed.

The agency's own reporting was thin. How could it be otherwise? They had one good source in the

Iranian nuclear program, and now he was dead. Harry found one report that had come in two days ago from the station in Dubai. They were running an agent who was a member of the Ministry of Intelligence; he picked up talk from people who had access to real secrets.

The header on the cable was SHAKE-UP COMING IN TEHRAN? It reported Iranian corridor gossip that heads would be rolling soon in the Revolutionary Guard's intelligence because of a big screwup there. The station chief, wanting to show how smart he was, had played down the rumor as sibling rivalry, noting that MOI officers were always forecasting doom for the Rev Guard. But Harry had reason to take the report more seriously. He messaged Dubai to call a crash meeting with its source, to see if they could pull more.

Next Harry checked the foreign liaison file, which had gotten a little fatter in the past few minutes since Marcia sent out her whip. Multiple sources were reporting that there had been some unusual gatherings in Tehran the past few days. The Turks had a source who claimed that the head of the Ministry of Intelligence had been summoned to the Supreme Leader's compound by the national security adviser. A Mossad agent within the Syrian moukhabarat, who happened to be on a trip to Iran, reported that there was a panic within Rev Guard intelligence over the disappearance of one of their senior officers involved in security of the nuclear program. The Iranians feared that the officer had defected to Israel. No such luck, said the Mossad representative in Washington.

The most intriguing report had come in that day from a Russian intelligence officer planted in an IAEA inspection team that was visiting Iran for yet another discussion of inspection procedures. The Russian reported that over the past twenty-four hours, access to all Iranian nuclear facilities—declared and undeclared—had been shut down. Even Iranians with normal security clearances couldn't get into their usual workplaces, as of this morning. The IAEA team had made an urgent query to their contact on the Iranian president's staff. And that office was in a panic, too.

Harry felt a little of his gloom dissipate. Something bad had happened inside the Iranian nuclear program. They were trying to figure out how bad. Senior people were being summoned. Scientists' access was blocked. Even the Iranian president was nervous. A shit storm was rising in Tehran. That was promising.

Okay, so what did he know? What *had* to be true, no matter what had happened on the way to that deadly fireball across the riverbed at Kalat? He knew that even if the operation in Mashad had been a total washout, the Iranians would be scrambling. A scientist in their nuclear program was dead. By now, they would have identified Karim

Molavi's body in that burnt-out car. Probably they wouldn't be able to identify Jackie from what was left of her body, and the identities of the other two members of the Increment team were probably covered, too, unless the Brits had been sloppy. So the Iranians wouldn't have proof, but they were paranoid enough to guess at the truth. Their scientist had died trying to escape Iran with foreign intelligence agents. He had been recruited as a foreign spy. Everything he had touched was contaminated, and they couldn't be sure how far the stain spread. They had to suspect that the worst had happened: their nuclear program had been penetrated.

The Iranians would have to take action quickly. Harry knew he wouldn't see it outright, lit up in bold. They were too careful for that. But he would see shadows, as people moved to protect other parts of the nuclear program that had suddenly come under suspicion. He would hear echoes of voices, summoning people for interrogation, calling them back from posts overseas where they were vulnerable. That was what he would look for—the aftershocks.

Harry dug into the NSA file. The messages were queued in a way that made them hard to search, so he called in Tony Reddo, one of his smart kids, and asked him to set a filter that captured anything that involved a sudden recall of personnel or change in status within the past forty-eight hours. It didn't work at first, but Reddo made a phone call to a friend at NSA and played around with the search parameters until he had something for Harry to look at. And you could see it, when you put in the right keywords, just looking at the list of intercepts that came up. They were pulsing their system: Frankfurt, London, Dubai, Beirut. They had code breaks for only some of the traffic, but even where they couldn't read it in plain text, the traffic analysis suggested that key people—known members of Iran's secret establishment—were being pulled out of their normal positions and brought home.

On a hunch, Harry called the cybergeeks at the Counter-Terrorism Center and asked them to do a quick check of all passengers who had traveled to Tehran from Europe the past two days. Get the names and match them up with any known intelligence, security, or defense people. It came back in an hour, and it confirmed what the SIGINT had indicated—that a lot of very senior people were being called home in a hurry.

Marcia stuck her head in the door. Harry could smell the cigarette smoke on her clothes. She really wasn't supposed to do that, but it wasn't a night in which he wanted to enforce the rules.

"It's getting late," she said. "You should eat something."

"I'm not hungry. Go away."

"Tough shit, Harry. I brought you something

anyway from the cafeteria. It's not very appetizing, but that's life." She handed a tray through the door and dropped it on Harry's desk. It was a bowl of pea soup and a cheeseburger. Harry ate it all, gratefully.

What about Ashgabat? The Iranians had to be mobilizing there. They would have found the Mitsubishi van that had crashed the border, and the dead Turkman driver. They wouldn't learn much, but they would realize that Molavi had been smuggled into the country from Turkmenistan before the botched attempt to exfiltrate him. That would scare Tehran all the more. They would pull whatever chains they had in the Turkmen capital to figure out what had gone down.

Harry phoned the chief of the CIA's two-person station in Ashgabat, a woman named Anita Pell. It was already early morning there, but she sounded as if she had been awakened from a deep sleep. Poor Anita. He hadn't informed her that he had been in Turkmenistan, and he didn't do so now. What would he tell her? He had gone there as an operative of a foreign power, Great Britain.

Harry asked Anita Pell to call her liaison officer in the Turkmen security service, right now, and request any information they had about unusual Iranian activities the last few days.

"And wake him *up?*" Anita Pell sounded shocked. Yes, Harry said, wake him up now, and go see him as soon as he'll receive you. Send anything you get, as soon as you get it.

Harry felt sorry for her. She had been the only officer to bid for Ashgabat when it came open last year. Her husband had run off with his secretary eight months before, so she said yes. Turkmenistan had been a nice, easy nap until this moment, when all the shit in the world had come down on her head.

Two hours later, Harry had his Ashgabat file. The chief of the Turkmen security received Anita Pell himself—that was a first. He reported highly unusual activity at the Iranian embassy. The lights had been on all night the past two nights; the Turkmen guards posted outside said people had been coming and going constantly, and that the Iranians were burning documents inside the compound. What's more, the Iranian consulate on the Turkmen side of the Saraghs border crossing had been working nonstop, too, and several dozen Iranian security officials with diplomatic passports had come across the border two days ago, questioning their contacts on the Turkmen side.

"The Turkmen want to know if they can help," Anita explained on the secure phone. "The chief was very agitated. He said something big went down on the border a couple days ago. He seemed surprised that I didn't know anything."

"What's there to know?" Harry answered sweetly.

"Don't humiliate me, Harry. I don't deserve that. What's going on?"

"Stay tuned. It will all become clear. Either that or it won't. But however it plays out, you're going to need some help. I'll send you one of my kids tomorrow."

Anita Pell protested that she didn't require any assistance, thank you very much, but she sounded relieved, nonetheless, that she would be getting some.

Harry wanted to be on the ground in Mashad. That was impossible, obviously. The CIA had precious few sources in Tehran, let alone eastern Iran. But thanks to technical coverage, he was able to get pretty close. His advantage was that he knew what to look for. He had the coordinates of the Ardebil Research Establishment, and it was easy enough for the cartographers to do a quick fix on where it was, just above the northern ring road. The imagery was there—the satellites made their passes over Iran every day like clockwork, so that there was near-constant coverage, and every digital transmission lived forever in the magic archive. You could play back reality as if it were on tape.

The National Reconnaissance Office maintained an ops center at Langley for agency officers who wanted to look at the world on rewind. Marcia had phoned the technicians a few hours before and made a special request. They were grumpy and hard to deal with, but so was Marcia. She gave the techs Harry's search parameters. When they were ready, she called Harry and toddled off with him to a distant room in the new wing, out by the Brown and Yellow parking lots.

"Don't be a jerk with these people, Harry," Marcia said as they made the long walk to the NRO ops center. "They are doing you a favor. People still do that. Even here."

"I *am* a jerk," said Harry. "Do you have a problem with that?"

Harry had the NRO techs dial back to the time Karim was supposed to have left the research center in Mashad, about four in the afternoon. The daylight cameras were still working, so the resolution was good. It took a few minutes, but Harry finally identified the Mitsubishi waiting outside. In the imagery of the Ardebil employees departing the lab, Harry saw what he thought was Karim, leaving with someone who had to be his friend Reza.

It was all there in digital memory, like a playback of life. Harry watched Reza's Peugeot head south to the restaurant; he saw the Mitsubishi tagging behind, too. He sped the images ahead while Karim and Reza were in the restaurant, and then resumed the visual narrative when Reza's Peugeot was driving north again, once more followed by the Mitsubishi van.

The two cars headed toward the hills above the city, slowly winding through traffic and taking the main road toward Tus, until Reza's Peugeot turned into the drive of what must be his home, followed thirty seconds later by the Mitsubishi van. Karim led Reza up to the front door of his villa, and then inside. A bit later, a lithe figure that had to be Jackie went into the house with a second operative, leaving behind the third man, it looked like Hakim, to keep watch outside.

And then it all went haywire: a black sedan pulled into the drive; you didn't see it at first, because it wasn't showing any headlights. The first sign was the bright spark of a weapon being fired, and then the dreadful sight of Hakim falling, shooting as he went down. Night had fallen now, and the infrared images were harder to read, but you could see enough to understand what had happened. The shooter got out of the black sedan and swiftly executed the poor Turkmen smuggler who had been unlucky enough to be hired for this pilgrim journey. Then the shooter stutter-stepped to the villa, followed by a second man.

Who were they? What had brought them to this place? Had the Iranians been following Karim all along, with Harry too blind to see their footprints?

The two mystery men entered the villa by a different entrance from the one the others had used. A half minute later, there was a flash of light from the building, as if something had exploded inside, and later more sparks of light, as if from gunshots. Harry kept muttering to himself as he watched the play unfold. It was horrifying to witness these events after the fact without being able to affect them, or to understand fully what was happening.

Eventually two figures emerged from the villa. One looked to be Jackie, dressed in her chador, and the other was surely Karim. Had Jackie shot her way out? What had happened to the other people inside? And then a third man emerged, following them—but no, he was leading them toward his black sedan.

It was the shooter, the gimpy man who had killed Hakim and executed the Turkmen driver. He prodded Jackie and Karim toward the sedan and waved them inside. He spoke a word to the driver, and then the black sedan was gone—beginning its journey to the border at Kalat, Harry knew. And the lone man, the shooter, was left there with what had to be four dead bodies.

"Who the *fuck* is that guy?" muttered Harry. He was speaking to himself. And in truth, he thought he knew the answer. But it was Marcia Hill who answered.

"That's Al-Majnoun," said Marcia. "The Crazy One."

Marcia didn't want to talk about it in front of the NRO techs. She was strange that way. After a career at the CIA, she didn't really trust anyone, least of all other members of the U.S. intelligence community. So she waited until they were safely back in Persia House before she said any more. She padded to her cubicle and returned with a file folder and a pack of cigarettes.

"Give me one," he said.

"But you don't smoke, Harry."

"I just started. Now tell me about Al-Majnoun."

Marcia took a photograph out of the folder. It was a grainy shot of a man whose face looked like it had been drawn with a haphazard Etch A Sketch.

"*This* is Al-Majnoun," she said. "I know it's a crappy picture, but it's the best one we have of him, version 2.0, or 3.0, or whatever this is."

She removed a second photograph from the folder. It showed a younger man, someone who, from the image in the photograph, appeared to be entirely different from the dark and disfigured man in the first shot.

"This is Al-Majnoun, version 1.0. Or at least that's what some of my Israeli friends think. These are their photographs. His name back then in Lebanon was Kamal Hussein Sadr. He was one of the first people the Iranians pulled into what became Hezbollah. He was a wholly owned subsidiary of Iranian intelligence, from the start. They used him as an enforcer. When they didn't trust one of their own people, he took care of it."

"Why don't we know about him?"

"Because he was killed, supposedly. In 1985, by

the Israelis. They were patting themselves on the back for months. Car bomb, body blown to bits in Baalbek so they couldn't ID him afterward. But seriously dead, everyone thought. So everyone forgot about him. Except for a few skeptical SOBs at Mossad. And me."

"What happened to him?"

"He went to Iran. In 1985, after the Israeli hit that almost got him. Personal invitation of Khomeini. So it was said, if anyone bothered to listen to the chatter, which no one did because the Israelis had killed him and the Israelis never make mistakes. But he was there. He knew he would need a new face if he was going to stay undead. So the surgeon's healing arts were applied. They put so much new skin on this guy, they probably gave him a new dick, too."

"Get a life, Marcia."

"Bit late for that. Anyway, when you run the traces—meaning Marcia's private traces, because honestly, honey, the main registry is useless—what you find is that Mr. Majnoun kept doing special jobs. Super Wet Work. When a dissident faction surfaced in the Rev Guard in the early nineties and people got revolverized, guess who pulled the trigger? When Rafsanjani had a problem with the Ministry of Intelligence and a few people got knocked off, who got the call?"

"The Crazy One."

"But of course. He was the cleanup guy. Nobody

owned him, you see, except the Leader's office. And check this out."

She took a third photograph from her file. It showed a tidy little man with a neat beard standing in front of an airplane. In the shadows behind him was a man in sunglasses, with the Identi-Kit face.

"This is the president getting off a plane in Damascus. Secret trip, never announced. The Israelis got the picture. The official Mossad line was that the messed-up-looking guy in the shades was just some fixer who was traveling with the president. But my pals down in the boiler room in Tel Aviv knew better. This is Al-Majnoun. The Leader's personal enforcer. The man who doesn't exist. And, I am sorry to say, the man who took down your operation."

"You are one crazy old bitch." Harry leaned across the table and kissed her.

"Thank you," she said.

"But you're wrong about one thing. I don't think Al-Majnoun ran this Mashad operation for the Leader of Iran. He did it for someone else."

Harry had a last, agonizing piece of the puzzle, and he didn't understand it until after midnight, when he was about ready to go home. The remaining mystery was the identity of the second man who had entered the villa with Al-Majnoun but had never left. He appeared to be the shooter's accomplice, but who was he? Was he also part of a secret cell, operating under the protection of the Leader? Or did he represent other parts of the Iranian secret world?

An answer surfaced in urgent liaison reports that arrived from two friendly services that had been apprised of Langley's hunger for fresh rumint about anything involving Iranian intelligence.

The first was from the little spy service of Azerbaijan, which had a surprisingly good network, thanks to the large Azeri community in Iran. The cable from Baku reported that senior officers of the Revolutionary Guard's intelligence service had been spotted the day before at the funeral of one of their colleagues—a certain Mehdi Esfahani, who was said to have been a senior investigator with responsibility for security at some of the covert facilities of the Iranian nuclear program. There had been a long reception afterward, at the family's home. The talk was that Esfahani had died in Mashad—the body had been flown back home in great secrecy, and that it had been riddled with bullet holes. The family had been told he died a hero's death, and a special martyr's pension had been approved.

The second overnight report was from French intelligence. It, too, had a few long-standing sources within Iranian intelligence. The head of the French service, a contact of Harry's since they had been in Beirut together years ago, made a point of calling himself, even though it was just past seven in the morning in Paris. He said he was transmitting a flash cable that might be of interest to his old friend *Har-ry Pap-pas*. And indeed it was.

The French reported that commanders of the Revolutionary Guard's intelligence, the Etelaat-e Sepah, had been briefed the previous day on a top-secret operation. The chief had explained to his elite cadres that thanks to the service's dedicated efforts, especially the heroic action of martyr Mehdi Esfahani, the Guard had foiled a plot by Western agencies to steal Iran's nuclear secrets. A traitor who worked at the facility known as Tohid Electrical Company had been killed; so had his accomplice, who worked in Mashad at the facility known as Ardebil Research Establishment. The organizer of this operation was the Little Satan, Great Britain, whose operatives had been killed while trying to organize the escape of the Iranian traitors. Behind Britain stood the Great Satan, whose perfidy and incompetence had once more been exposed. The Guard was taking appropriate action to discover any other participants in this conspiracy. Fortunately, thanks to their prompt action, the integrity of the Iranian nuclear program as a whole was certain.

There it was. Everything Harry Pappas could have wanted, packaged with a neat ribbon by an Iranian intelligence service that was as eager as Harry's own agency to cover its backside when it had made a very big mistake. What pleased Harry most was that the Iranians really didn't seem to understand just how serious their problem was.

It was past 2:00 a.m. when Harry finally drove his Jeep Cherokee out of the parking lot and went home to sleep for a few hours before he went to see the director.

39

WASHINGTON

The admiral was at the White House for the morning briefing and yet another "deep dive" with the president about terrorism, so he didn't get back to Langley until nine-thirty. Harry had asked the security guard on the seventh floor, whose son went to the school in Fairfax where Andrea taught, to call him as soon as the boss returned. That allowed Harry to stick his head in the admiral's door moments after the boss had set down his big briefcase and straightened his blue zip-up navy jacket on the hanger, and before the strokers and time-wasters who were assembled in the anteroom could begin their daily assault. The secretary made a pro forma attempt to stop Harry, but the door was open and she liked him better than the others, anyway.

"Got a minute, sir?" asked Harry.

"Where the hell have you been? A lot of people are looking for you."

"That's kind of a long story, sir. It's going to take a few minutes. May I close the door?"

Harry didn't wait for an answer. He pushed the door firmly shut, just in time to block the way of the general counsel, who had been apprised that the FBI's new poster boy was on the seventh floor.

"You are in deep water, shipmate. Do you know that the Bureau was over here this week? They want to open a criminal investigation on you."

"For what? If I'm allowed to ask."

"Espionage, treason. Hell, I don't know. They seem to think that you have been operating as an agent of a foreign power, whose capital is London. On some Iranian caper. Is that true?"

"Yes, sir, more or less. I told you I was going to contact the Brits. They had the assets in Iran and we didn't. Remember? We talked about it."

The admiral shrugged. He was wearing a white shirt that had his gold stars on a neat board attached to the epaulettes. They looked like little shoulder pads.

"I don't know what I remember. I'll have to talk to the general counsel. But you, Harry, you had better get a lawyer. The FBI is serious. The deputy director spent an hour with me. They have some tipster in London who is shitting all over you. Names, dates, photographs. Someone has set you up, my friend."

"Yes, sir. I know. You don't know the half of it,

actually. But as you say, that's my problem. I'll sort it out."

The admiral looked relieved. He absentmindedly took another of his endless supply of ship models from the front of his desk. This time it was an Aegis-class guided missile cruiser. The admiral turned it over so that he could look at the underside of the hull, as if checking for barnacles.

"Good. Well, I wish legal problems were your only difficulty, but they're not. The White House is ready to pop on Iran. I have been holding them off the past two weeks, as I promised you I would—I do remember that—but they have run out of patience. I got an earful from Stewart Appleman this morning. They are ready to go public, with everything. Damn the consequences."

"And what will the White House do then?" asked Harry.

"An embargo of Iran, sea and air. If the Iranians resist, they'll bomb. They're going to announce the embargo in three days. Bombing is just a matter of time, I reckon."

"But they don't need to bomb anything. The Iranian program is falling apart. They don't know which end is up. They're shitting bricks in Tehran. That's what I came here to tell you. We should just let them self-destruct. An American attack is the only thing that will save them. You know that."

"Sorry, not my department. I don't do policy."

"But you're the CIA director."

"So? That doesn't count for much, if you hadn't noticed. But why are you so sure the Iranian program is falling apart? Did you get that from your agent Dr. Ali?"

"He's dead. That's part of what I came to tell you. He died a hero, truly. And he did something so sweet before he died that the Iranians shouldn't be able to run a glow-in-the-dark watch for a while, let alone build a nuclear weapon."

The director put down the Aegis ship model.

"Uh, perhaps you had better explain, Harry." He buzzed his secretary and told her that he wasn't to be disturbed until he said otherwise, and when she asked if that even meant the general counsel, who was practically beating down the door, he said that it meant especially the general counsel.

So Harry told the story of what he had been doing over the past several weeks, leaving out only the parts that would get him into irreparable legal jeopardy, and the parts involving Kamal Atwan, which he intended to handle on his own. He described his operational planning with Adrian Winkler at SIS to get Dr. Ali out of Iran for debriefing. He explained how the team from the Increment was recruited and sent in to exfiltrate Dr. Ali so that Harry could meet him in Turkmenistan. He explained bits and pieces of the sabotage operation—telling the director enough so he could understand that Dr. Ali's messages really had been a confirmation not that the Iranian program was succeeding, but that it was failing. And why.

And finally, Harry described what had happened a few days before in Mashad. The CIA's agent—the brave young scientist whose real name was Karim Molavi—had agreed to go back into the heart of the Iranian nuclear beast to sabotage a secret outpost that was Iran's ace in the hole. He had died on his way out, along with all the members of the British team. But as near as Harry could tell, Molavi had succeeded in his mission. Iran's only clean hardware had now been contaminated, too. They wouldn't know what, if anything, to trust.

Whatever the Iranians did now in their nuclear program, they would make mistakes. Their most senior intelligence officials had been humiliated. It would take them years to recover. The chatter in Tehran showed that they were trying desperately to explain and cover up what had happened. All the United States government needed to do now was put a few more details on the record, and the disaster would be complete.

The admiral was wide-eyed as he listened to Harry's account. He didn't appreciate all the nuances. He was a boat driver, not a spy. But he liked what he heard, and by the time Harry was finished, he was actually smiling. And then he was frowning again.

"This won't convince the White House to stop," said the director. "They will just say that it's more proof the Iranians are a threat. They had a secret weapons program, and a backup, too."

"But it's ruined now. It's shot. We don't have to bomb anything."

"Harry, my friend, some people like to bomb. It makes them feel like they have a strategy, when they send the military in."

Harry paused. He picked up one of the models on the director's desk. It was a Navy F/A-18 bomber, one of the planes that would be used to attack targets in Iran, if it came to that.

"Well, sir, I'm not playing."

"What do you mean, Harry? You have to play. You're an American. You work for an agency that is an arm of the president."

"Nope. I'm off the team. I want to retire. As soon as possible. That's the other thing I came to tell you."

"What about the FBI?"

"They'll go away eventually. The FBI likes to make trouble for the agency, but even they will realize that this case is a loser. Someone is pulling their chain, so they're pulling mine. But that will stop."

The director squinted at him. "Who's pulling the chain?"

"I think it's a certain Arab gentleman. You don't want to know the details, sir. Believe me. Let me worry about it. It's safer that way."

The director nodded, but he was still unconvinced. "So what do you get, Harry? Do you just crawl in a hole when this is done?"

"I want to retire," Harry repeated. "I've had it. I'm busted. I lost my son, and then I lost this boy. I still have time for my daughter, if I'm not stupid. I don't want to do this work anymore. That's my only condition, actually. I want to retire, as soon as the paperwork clears. I don't want to keep my clearances. I don't want any of it. It's over."

The director shook his head. "You Greeks are weird. You know that? All the drama, and then, poof, there it goes. Good seamen though. That counts for something."

Harry Pappas left the director's office and went back to the dingy first floor and Persia House. The Imam Hussein had never looked so lachrymose; his eyes were weeping blood. Harry summoned Marcia Hill and explained what he had told the director. And he told her that he would be leaving again.

"And where will you be, Harry darling, if I may ask?"

"I'll be away. I have to take another little trip. After that, I'll really be away."

"How really is really?"

"Live at the summer house all year round. That kind of really."

Marcia wagged a nicotine-stained finger at him.

"You're quitting, aren't you? You miserable bastard. How dare you quit before me. That is unforgivable. After all we've been through, I at least deserve to be the one to say 'fuck you' first. And now I have to stay around and clean up after you. Typical."

She walked back to her cubicle muttering to herself, leaving Harry alone with the dewy-eyed martyr.

After he left the office at midday to head once more for the airport, Harry placed a call to London, to Sir David Plumb, direct. He reached him at his club. Harry said that the British had another twenty-four hours to do whatever they were planning. After that it would be too late.

40

LONDON

The next day at noon, the British prime minister delivered an unscheduled address from his office at No. 10 Downing Street. The British television networks were given only thirty minutes' warning to get their cameras in place. The U.S. Embassy in Grosvenor Square was informed of the address five minutes before the prime minister began to speak. The embassy was told only that it would concern Iran. By the time a frantic call was placed from the White House, it was too late. The prime minister had begun speaking.

474

The British leader said he was taking the unusual step of revealing a secret intelligence operation. Over the past several months, the British Secret Intelligence Service had obtained new details of Iran's covert nuclear weapons program. They had discovered that the Iranians were experimenting with some of the technologies needed to produce a bomb, but that their research was impeded by serious technical problems the Iranians had not anticipated.

Britain had received secret help from a brave Iranian scientist who worked inside one of the front companies used by the regime to shield its nuclear research, the prime minister continued. During the past several weeks, British intelligence agents had helped that scientist escape from Iran to a third country, where he was debriefed extensively. The scientist described weapons research at a previously unknown covert facility in Mashad. The scientist had bravely agreed to reenter Iran with the team of British intelligence officers who brought him out, so that he could gather more information. He was killed, along with the three members of the British covert team. They were all heroes, the prime minister said. Because of their courageous actions, Iran's effort to develop nuclear weapons had been dealt a mortal blow.

The prime minister said that at that hour, Britain's ambassador to the United Nations was turning over a detailed dossier of evidence about

Iran's nuclear program to the International Atomic Energy Agency and the United Nations Security Council so that these organizations could take appropriate action. He said that Britain would oppose any effort by any nation—he repeated the words "any nation" for emphasis—to impose an embargo against Iran or take other military action. The Iranian nuclear program had been exposed by Britain's intelligence operations, he said. The proper course now was vigilant monitoring and nonmilitary sanctions to make sure the program was not reconstituted.

The prime minister concluded by saying that he would be consulting soon with the president of the United States to work out a joint position at the United Nations. But he was certain—quite certain—that the United States would cooperate with the policy he had just announced.

Harry Pappas arrived at Heathrow a few hours before the prime minister's speech. He had one more chore, and he was rather looking forward it. He didn't like symmetry, normally. Most loops in life don't get closed, and for good reason: they aren't really loops but loose strands that only appear to connect. But in this case, there was something that should come full circle, and then stop.

Harry treated himself to a London hotel room when he arrived. He slept through the morning with the television on, just in case, and he was awakened by the sound of the prime minister's voice. When the speech was over, he dozed for another few hours. He wanted to be fresh for his meeting. He was about to play a game in which he held many good cards, and knew some of what was in the other man's hand. But a satisfactory outcome would depend nearly as much on his demeanor as on the substance of what he had to say.

Harry arrived at Kamal Atwan's residence on Mount Street in the late afternoon. It was a brisk November day; loose bits of trash billowed along the streets and alleyways, and low, rain-laden clouds scudded by overhead. The butler said stiffly that Mr. Atwan wasn't home, but Harry suspected he would say that to any unannounced visitor. So he repeated his name, Harry Pappas, and said to tell the master of the house that he was visiting from Washington and needed to speak to Mr. Atwan urgently, right now, about a matter of great importance. The butler retreated upstairs and descended a minute later to say that Mr. Atwan had returned home and would see his guest immediately.

The art that lined the walls didn't make quite the same impression on Harry this time. It was so much loot, gathered from the treasure troves of other people less clever or larcenous than the proprietor of Mount Street. Who even knew if it was real? The luminous Monet painting of the water lilies that dominated the entrance hall: How could you know if it was a masterpiece, a brilliant fake, or something in between—an authentic object that had been detached from its original owner and converted to this man's personal use? "Provenance" was the word art dealers used to describe the ticklish problems presented by such a collection. How did you know where anything came from, and what of its putative history was real and what imagined? That was in fact Kamal Atwan's business—blurring those lines of provenance so that people weren't sure whether what they had was true or false.

Atwan was standing at the top of the stairs. He was wearing a new double-breasted smoking jacket, with rich black velvet lapels and a fine paisley print in the body of the garment. His long silver-gray hair was meticulously combed. He looked like an Edwardian dandy, a man out of time.

"How good of you to call, my dear," he said, taking Harry's hand as he reached the top step. "Did you hear the prime minister's speech? Very bold, don't you think? Preempts any other sort of action, I would say."

"Good speech," said Harry. "War with Iran is a bad idea."

"Your American friends will be angry, I think."

"They'll get over it," said Harry.

• • •

Atwan led Harry by the hand into the library and sat him down by a gas fire. On a table between two comfortable chairs was another fat novel by Anthony Trollope, this one titled *He Knew He Was Right*.

"I have been waiting for your visit, my dear Harry. I have been worrying about you."

"I'm sure you have, Kamal Bey, worried to death, and for good reason, too. Do you know that someone has been spreading nasty stories about me to the Federal Bureau of Investigation? Can you imagine that? That someone was suggesting I had been doing secret work for the British government. Treasonous work, some people could say, under a false name."

"How dreadful," said Atwan, throwing up his hands in apparent horror. He was a good actor, you had to give him that.

"Yes, but that's all taken care of. I went to see my boss yesterday in Washington. My real boss, the CIA director. He'd been fully informed of what I was doing, obviously, but we talked it through anyway. Not a problem, all over. My lawyer will work out the details with the FBI. But thanks for your concern."

"Oh *good*. I am so glad."

There was a hint of actual mirth in Atwan's voice. He was a sporting man; he knew that he couldn't win every rubber.

479

"I actually came to give *you* a bit of advice, Kamal. A warning, really."

"Oh, how thoughtful. And what might that be, my dear?"

"Well, sir, I'll be frank, even though we're not in a secure location, and you never know who might be listening. I believe there is an acquaintance of yours who is in a bit of difficulty in Iran. A Lebanese fellow originally, like yourself. His name, or at least the one he was born with, is Kamal Hussein Sadr. He travels under various labels these days, but the one people seem to use most frequently is Al-Majnoun. Does that ring any bells?"

Atwan tried to laugh. It came out dry, more like a croak.

"But my dear Mr. Pappas, this gentleman Sadr, or Majnoun if you like, he died more than twenty years ago. The Israelis killed him, if I'm not mistaken."

"Yeah, right. Well, somehow he's come back to life. And the problem is that the Iranians are onto him. They suspect he had a hand in our little caper in Mashad. They don't know all the details yet, so they're going to arrest and interrogate him, and find out. Unless someone moves pretty damn quick."

Atwan coughed. He was trying to conceal something, but the tension was evident. "Why should this possibly concern me?"

"Well, the problem is, the Iranians are going to find a little device that was smuggled into a nuclear laboratory. A sophisticated device that could melt parts of computer chips and change code. Supplied by a certain Lebanese businessman who resides in London. We've picked up a lot of chatter through our technical collection, as you can imagine, and they seem to know more about you than I would have suspected."

"So what are you saying?"

"What I am saying, *sir*, is that unless you do something pretty goddamn fast, a big pile of shit is going to land on your head."

"What a vulgar expression. That is unworthy of you, my dear Mr. Pappas."

"Perhaps, but an accurate one. But hey, what do I know? I'm just an American. I don't understand how really sophisticated people like you operate. Just a word to the wise, that's all. The facts are that Al-Majnoun was working for you, and that you were working with us—and the Iranians are just naturally going to figure it all out. They'll realize he killed our guys, and their guys, and they're going to be pissed off. I would hate to see your business ruined, after all the good work you've done."

Atwan rose and walked to the mantel. Over the fireplace was a pastel by Edgar Degas showing a group of ballerinas preparing for class. Pappas wondered if it was real. The Lebanese businessman stared at the picture for a few moments, composing himself, and then returned to his chair.

"And what do you propose, Mr. Pappas?"

There it was, inevitably: the solicitation of a bid. Atwan was a dealmaker, first and last, and now he was looking to make a bargain.

"I don't propose anything. Except that you better move quickly to get your man Al-Majnoun out of Iran. To London, probably, where you can keep an eye on him. I think you better do that before he takes you down, and a lot of other people with him. That's not a threat, obviously. I'm not in the threat business. Just a suggestion. Otherwise, I would have to say that, as we Americans so vulgarly like to put it, you are fucked."

Atwan looked away, to mask his expression. He was a man in absolute control, always. He was thinking about his options, evidently, weighing what he had to lose, depending on what options he chose. They say there are chess players who can calculate many dozens of moves ahead that flow from the exchange of one piece on the board. Atwan had that facility. He had worked as hard as possible to take risk out of the world's riskiest business. He turned back toward his guest.

"You're being quite aggressive, I see," he said stiffly. "Well then, message received."

Atwan rose from his chair, still lost in his own private calculations. He didn't take Harry's hand this time, just led the way out of the library and back down the stairs. The show was over. That was the virtue of crude speech. It broke through the false layer of politeness that covered the facts, and got down to the bare reality of things. Atwan walked slowly, one step at a time. You might have thought he would be eager to get Harry out of his house, but he was taking his time, weighing another bid.

He stopped at the bottom of the stairs in the entrance hall. It was raining outside now. You could hear the beating of the raindrops against Atwan's leaden windows. He took Harry's hand again.

"It is not a nice evening out, I think. Beastly, as the British would say. Why don't you stay a bit longer, Harry, until the clouds have passed."

Atwan led Harry into a sitting room off the main entrance hall and closed the double doors. Harry took a seat while Atwan went to the intercom. He rang his chief of staff, waited a moment, then said a few words in Arabic.

"I would like a drink tonight," said Atwan. "I rarely drink, you know, but tonight I think that I should make an exception, with you, my dear. Is that all right?"

"Of course," said Harry. "I'll have a whiskey."

Atwan went to a mirrored bar, set in an alcove of the room, and poured two glasses of whiskey, neat. He paused, and then poured a third.

"Another guest coming?" asked Harry.

"Yes, I think so. A little party. A reunion, you could say. Why not?"

Atwan brought the whiskey to Harry and sat down on the couch next to him. The host took a sip and then a large gulp that nearly drained the glass. There was a knock at the double door. Harry expected that they would be joined by Adrian Winkler, the partner in this bizarre enterprise, but he was mistaken.

The double door swung open, and a man in a black suit entered the room. He walked with a quick, erratic step, almost a scampering. His head was down as he entered the room, and black sunglasses covered his eyes, but when he reached Harry, he stood up straight and removed the shades. It was the oddest human face Harry had ever seen. The eyes were tight at the corners and tilted up slightly, as an Asian man's might be. The nose was bulbous, as if a new infusion of flesh had been added. The lips were almost feminine, pumped with fat and gel so that they appeared as little pontoons. The face seemed almost to be in motion, the different pieces going in different directions. Scars were visible along the edges, and there was a bit of puffiness, as if the man had just had another operation to recombine and rearrange.

Atwan walked over to this most peculiar gentleman. He was smiling now, as if he were a farmer exhibiting his prize pig. He patted Al-Majnoun gently on the back, and then steered him toward Harry.

"My dear Harry, let me introduce Kamal Hussein Sadr. Al-Majnoun. The Crazy One. You know the name of course, but perhaps not the face." He laughed to himself, as if this were a private joke.

Harry took Al-Majnoun's hand in his. The tips of the fingers were like an emery board, from so many efforts over the years to remove identifiable traces of what had once been the man's finger-prints. When they had shaken hands, Atwan nodded for Al-Majnoun to take a seat in a corner of the room.

"So you're not fucked," Harry said.

"Quite so."

"And my warning wasn't necessary. The man is already out of Iran, obviously."

"Oh yes. In the flesh. All the many layers of it. You did not think I would be so stupid as to let the Iranians have my man. After nearly thirty years? That would have been quite unwise. No, he was on his way out of the country as soon as he had done his work."

"His work." Harry let that phrase fill the room, and repeated it. "His work. Which included killing three British intelligence officers, I think. Not to mention a brave Iranian agent."

"Two, my dear. Only two, unless you count that silly Turkmen driver. The others were not my fault. I made a promise to you that I would try to get your Iranian boy out of the country, and I endeavored to keep my word, truly. And I knew that our friend Adrian was bewitched with the girl, so I tried to save her, too. But not everything is possible, my dear, even when we do our best. You should know that, better than anyone. You have suffered a great loss, but it is wrong that you should blame yourself."

Harry winced at the reference to his son. And he resented that Kamal Atwan presumed to give him personal advice in the presence of a hired killer. But he stayed silent. That was Harry's weapon, that he could keep the pieces together inside, even when they hurt so much that he wanted to kill with his naked hands the man standing across from him.

"It's over," said Harry.

"And why should that be, my dear? In our sort of world, it's never over. How can it be? The world is too ambiguous a place for endings."

"The Iranians think it's over."

"No they don't. My dear Harry, I don't think you've grasped the essence of the matter. The Iranians have no idea what is going on. Listen to your famous NSA chatter, and you'll see. This man, the scar-faced man in black, was said to be an intimate friend of the Leader. Do you think the mullahs can allow themselves to imagine that he was working all the while—all the while!—for a foreign conspiracy? Of course not. It would bring the whole tower down. The Leader himself would be suspect. Who could accept such a thought, or even tolerate it? It would destroy the regime, my dear, root and branch."

"Not a bad idea," said Harry.

"Oh come now, don't be a romantic. You sound like those neoconservatives. Poof! Let us transform the evildoers, at a stroke. That is not the way the world works. It progresses from one shade of gray to another."

"Bullshit," said Harry.

"You want to provoke me, my dear, but you will not succeed. The truth is that we have drawn the Iranians, who so much want to see only black and white, into my gray world where nothing is quite the way they want it to be. And in the gray, it is very hard to find your way."

"They'll know someone has been diddling their nuclear program. That's for sure."

"Well, yes. The prime minister has highlighted the role of that poor young man, Dr. Molavi. But they won't know how far his deception went. Some will say all the problems at Tohid were his fault, and they will overlook the bias in the equipment we have been selling them. Others will suspect the equipment, too, but they won't know how to prove it. And then there is the other facility, at Mashad. Will they suspect that, or not? There's really no way for them to know."

"The Iranians certainly will know when they find the device Karim was carrying."

"Ah yes. The device."

Atwan called out something in Arabic to Al-Majnoun, who rose from his chair in the corner and tiptoed across the room. When he reached Atwan, he put his hand in his black jacket and removed a rectangular object and gave it to his patron.

"Do you mean *this* device, Mr. Pappas? Recovering this was a major reason I decided to involve my friend Majnoun in the first place. That and to cover over any other tracks that might be left by, you will forgive the term, your *tradecraft*. My faithful Majnoun took it from the Iranian boy's coat and planted a piece of plastic. I have learned that when it comes to details, it really is best not to leave anything to chance. Or to the secret services of the United States and Britain, which is roughly the same thing. So in answer to your question, no, I do not think that the Iranians will 'have a clue,' as you like to say."

"So what will the Iranians do? They're certainly not going to give up."

"They will keep trying. The UN will have new sanctions, and the IAEA will have new inspections. But the Iranians will come back. They will make new plans. Buy new equipment. And I will be there to sell it to them. Or, I would like to think, *we* will be there to sell it to them. I have come to admire you, Harry. Despite your Americanisms, you would make a quite suitable associate. Adrian, while he has many virtues, has gone a bit soft around the edges. But I sense you are made of stronger stuff."

"No fucking way," said Harry.

"Such an unattractive way of speaking. But it is part of your style, so I suppose I have to accept it in a prospective business partner."

"I am not your partner. I'm not anyone's partner. I'm out."

"Nobody is ever 'out,' my dear Harry. That is another of your illusions."

"Sorry, Kamal, but I'm a black-and-white guy. I don't do gray. I'm 'in' or 'out,' and in this case, I'm out."

Atwan shook his head. "You Americans really should stay at home, where these quaint monochromatic notions of yours have some meaning. I really do not think you understand our part of the world, my dear. There are no endings. Which side of the coin is heads or tails? What time is it? Where is the train going? Who can say, my friend? Who can say? Will Iran get the bomb? Not today, but there are so many tomorrows. And suppose that somehow they succeed and build the little nuclear monster. They will never know if it will work. Never."

Harry had stopped appreciating the subtlety of it all. He felt something like revulsion.

"Why did you do it, Kamal? Why did you set this murderer Al-Majnoun in motion? You killed a young man I made a promise to. You killed brave

British officers. You're the crazy one. What is wrong with you?"

"I was protecting my investment, my dear. It is not enough to be on one side of a transaction. To be really safe, you must be on both sides. That was why I had Al-Majnoun watching from the first moment you put your little man Molavi in play. To protect, to control. If I had not done so, someone else far more dangerous might have taken my place."

"Bullshit. You're an arms dealer. You just wanted to keep selling more crap to Iran, and making more money."

Atwan shrugged. He gathered the velvet lapels of his smoking jacket so that they were aligned. If Harry didn't appreciate what he was trying to do, well, so much the worse.

"I am in the ambiguity business, Mr. Pappas. I stand for uncertainty. I stand for the artifice of business, which is the essential reality in our part of the world. I seek to foster the ambiguity that allows each side to continue along its way, without ever coming to a point that we could call the end of the road. Endings are dangerous."

"You are out of your fucking mind, Kamal. And your friend Mr. Potato Head should spend the rest of his life in a dark cell picking at his scabs."

Harry didn't bother to shake hands, make an appropriate phrase, say goodbye. He turned and walked toward the door, but Kamal Atwan called after him.

"Before I let you go, my dear, I must ask you one final question. It matters rather a lot to my future business dealings. How did you know that Mr. Sadr here, the Crazy One, was working for me? That was a rather well-guarded secret. Are your technical tools really that good? That would worry me."

Harry laughed. It felt like the first good laugh he'd had in a very long time.

"What could possibly be funny about that question, my dear?"

"Nothing, except that it shows you're a sucker."

"I beg your pardon?"

"The truth is that I didn't know about Al-Majnoun. I guessed. Until you told me that he was your man, I didn't know for sure. Lucky I was wearing a microphone to transmit the conversation out to my lame-ass CIA colleagues, in case anyone ever needs it. And you know something? With all due respect, you talk too much."

And now, Harry did leave. Out the double doors of the sitting room, past the Renoir and the Monet, past the butler hovering at the door and into the London evening. It was pissing rain outside. Harry walked several blocks to Piccadilly, where he found a coffee bar. It was filling up with young people coming off their jobs, many of them not much older than his daughter Lulu.

Harry took out his cell phone and placed a call to an old friend at MI5, the British internal security service, whom he had met many years before in Washington. They talked for nearly a half hour, with the other man taking notes, stopping Harry occasionally for details, but finally they had it all straight.

Then Harry called Adrian Winkler. The SIS chief of staff still sounded soggy, little affect in his voice even when he tried to be cheery, and Harry understood that his British friend really had loved Jackie with her crop and riding boots and extraordinary courage. That made him feel sorrier still for Adrian, but it didn't change what he had to do.

"Your friend Atwan is going down," said Harry.

"What do you mean 'going down,' old boy? That man is the best asset we've got."

"Exactly what I said. He's going down. It turns out that Al-Majnoun was his man. The guy who killed your team from the Increment was working for your pal. That's what Jackie was trying to tell you. He's with him now. Kamal, your pal, is harboring a terrorist. No other way to slice it. And he's going down."

The phone went dead for a moment. You could sense the panic on the other end, and also the anger.

"Say it again, Harry. I want to make sure I heard it right."

"Al-Majnoun is here. He's at Atwan's townhouse

on Mount Street. You need to call MI5 and Special Branch right now—this instant."

"Tall order, Harry."

"Not so tall. They already know. They're on their way to make the arrests. That's why I called you, brother. You'll go down, too, if you don't get on the phone to 5 and Scotland Yard right now."

"I see," said Adrian. The air went out of his lungs for a moment, but he recovered.

"You think you can stop this, Harry, but you can't. Who do you think keeps Atwan in business? Do you think it's me? What a joke. I just take some of the loose goodies that fall off the back of Atwan's truck. He survives here because he has friends, way up, who think he is valuable to the country. For 'reasons of state,' old boy. Morality doesn't enter into it. Nothing you or I can do about it."

"Yes there is. I've already done it. It's over."

"It's never over, Harry."

Harry ended the call and put the phone back in his pocket. He ordered a coffee, but after taking a sip, he realized he didn't really want it. It had stopped raining now. He stepped out onto the sidewalk and walked along the gray blocks of concrete, the blinking neon lights of Piccadilly Circus marking his way.

ACKNOWLEDGMENTS

The real Iran will intrigue us for decades, but this novel is about an imaginary country. It is a work of fiction, and none of the characters, companies, or institutions described in this book are real. People who look for real intelligence operations in this invented story will only deceive themselves.

In sketching this imaginary Iran, I received help from a number of people and sources. Azar Nafisi of Johns Hopkins University kindly discussed Iranian literature and gave me fine new translations of the classic *Shahnameh* by Abolqasem Ferdowsi and *My Uncle Napoleon* by Iraj Pezeshkzad. My friend Karim Sadjadpour of the Carnegie Endowment for Peace read the manuscript and gave me many good suggestions. Dr. John R. Harvey, a physicist with the National Nuclear Security Administration, helped guide me through the unclassified open literature on neutron generators and other aspects of weapons technology. Other friends and sources who will go unnamed here shared insights about the puzzle of Iran.

In sketching my fictional portrait of Iran, I recalled the sights and sounds of my own two-week visit there for the *Washington Post* in 2006. I also drew on several excellent books: Christopher de Ballaigue's *In the Rose Garden of the Martyrs* offered a brilliant personality sketch of the regime.

Azadeh Moaveni's *Lipstick Jihad* was a source for some contemporary Iranian slang and Persian poetry, as well as a woman's view of the Islamic Republic. The Lonely Planet guidebook to Iran was a great source of local lore. And I would have been lost without my Ketab-e Avval "Tehran Directory."

I offer special thanks once again to Garrett Epps, my closest friend since we met as freshmen in college, who was the first reader of this, as of all my previous books. His friendship bolsters me every day. My friend Jonathan Schiller again offered me a novelist's hideaway at his law firm, Boies, Schiller & Flexner. This book is dedicated to him and Dr. Richard Waldhorn, two dear family friends.

I am grateful to others who read and commented on early drafts: my wife, Dr. Eve Ignatius; my literary agents, Raphael Sagalyn and Bridget Wagner; my agent at Creative Artists Agency, the incomparable Robert Bookman. I am lucky indeed to be back at W. W. Norton, and I thank Starling Lawrence for his fine editing, as well as Jeannie Luciano, Rachel Salzman, and many other friends at Norton.

Finally, for the tolerance that allowed me to continue with my day job as a columnist while I worked on this novel, I thank Fred Hiatt, the editorial editor of the *Washington Post*; Alan Shearer, who runs the Washington Post Writers' Group; and most especially my boss and friend, Donald Graham.

Center Point Publishing
600 Brooks Road ● PO Box 1
Thorndike ME 04986-0001 USA

(207) 568-3717

US & Canada:
1 800 929-9108
www.centerpointlargeprint.com